The Arlington Orders

The Arlington Orders

Elliot Mason

The Arlington Orders

Printed in the United States of America
ISBN 978-1-967279-28-9 (sc)
ISBN 978-1-967279-30-2 (e)
ISBN 978-1-967279-29-6 (hc)

2025.04.29

This book is printed on acid-free paper.

Because of the dynamic nature of the Internet, any web addresses or links contained in this book may have changed since publication and may no longer be valid. The views expressed in this work are solely those of the author and do not necessarily reflect the views of the publisher, and the publisher hereby disclaims any responsibility for them.

Blue Ink Media Solutions
1111B S Governors Ave
STE 7582 Dover,
DE 19904

www.blueinkmediasolutions.com

Fact

In March of 1864, a plot against the government of the Confederate States of America was uncovered. Its implications sent shock waves throughout the South. A short time after what became known as the Dahlgren affair, the decision was made to evacuate the Confederate capital of Richmond, Virginia.

Preparations were commenced, including plans for a covert operation to move all the gold and silver reserves, the remaining wealth of the Southern government, to a secret location.

However, during its implementation, the Confederate treasury disappeared without a trace. If found, it would represent the richest and most significant discovery in American history.

I believe we live two lives, the life we learn with and the
life we live with after that.

—Glenn Close
from the motion picture The Natural

Prologue

May 20, Present Day, Roanoke, Virginia

Each time he turned his head, his breath fogged the glass in a sort of circular pattern before slowly dissipating as it cooled. He had been in his car for nearly two hours, gradually stiffening from being in a seated position for such an extended amount of time. It was a little after 9:30 p.m., and the battle to remain patient was increasing in difficulty ever since his target had returned home. Pouring himself a third cup of coffee from his dented thermos, he slowly sipped the strong brew, relying on the caffeine infusion to keep himself at the ready. The small gulps were only interrupted by intermittent glances at the modest house he was casing.

His attention was broken once again as the hot liquid dribbled from his lips and onto his beard. *It doesn't matter,* he thought as he wiped away the moisture. Like everything else in his life, the bristly patch would not last. He hated being in this situation. It was something he was hoping to avoid. However, it was inevitable. Someone somewhere would eventually stumble upon the secret and, in all likelihood, not even know it. Yet if this information were to be discovered, they might inadvertently make it public, allowing others to make the connection. Then all control would be lost. That was why he now found himself sitting in a parked car on this sleepy little street. The person he was tracking was only doing his job, diligently digging into the past, never realizing that in doing so, he was placing himself in the crosshairs.

As the time approached, the observer exhaled in one long release. He realized there were other avenues to handle this problem, and normally, that would be his recommendation. But not tonight. They might have been able to monitor this person and ultimately take care of the final task, but they would not be able to confirm what was needed to be known or whether that final action was necessary. It would be tantamount to using a nuclear bomb to take out an anthill. This required a more professional and thoughtful approach.

Through the large window at the front of the house, he could see his target turn out the kitchen lights and then follow his dim silhouette as it headed toward the back room. Inside the home, Professor Terry Sipe had just placed small round bowls on the floor for his hungry felines before entering his study. It was a tiny enclosure that felt even more confined due to the stacks of books lining the walls and the mountains of paper covering every square inch of his small desk. Yet this nondescript room served as the center for all his research. It was his most private space.

For over thirty-five years, the elderly man with the stringy white hair and almost painfully thin frame had been teaching Civil War history at Hollins College in Roanoke, Virginia. Although he was not well-known, the professor had several published works. However, they were rarely seen outside academic circles, and even those were not widely reviewed, as his scholarly writings failed to receive the notoriety of professors at some of the more well-known universities. Professor Sipe's classes were well attended but did not generate the excitement of instructors covering the more glamorous parts of Civil War history. While most of his colleagues were wrapped up in the exploits of Robert E. Lee, Ulysses S. Grant, and Stonewall Jackson, his focus was on facets rarely mentioned in the textbooks.

Instead, the elderly professor's concentration dealt mainly with the internal functions of government during the conflict, particularly that of the Southern administration. If you were looking for dramatic retellings of First Bull Run, Antietam, or Gettysburg, Sipe's class was not for you. Rather, his academic indulgences included organizational preferences of the Southern aristocratic class, trade agreements between the Confederacy and foreign powers, and Southern manufacturing plans to support the war effort. The learned professor had well-researched books on all these topics. Some were even referenced in Civil War magazines, although they were usually only seen in some small quotations or other abbreviated forms. However, it was one of these short seemingly insignificant articles that the professor had published on the internet that had attracted the attention of the man now camped in front of his home.

To most, even the academics, it would appear mundane. Only the most tedious of researchers would find it slightly interesting, but hardly noteworthy. The topic concerned last-minute requisitions that President Jefferson Davis made in the final months prior to the fall of the Confederate capital of Richmond, Virginia. Horses, carts, guns, ammunition, footwear, gunpowder, and all the other items one would expect to see during wartime were represented. Yet there was one item that stuck out to the professor's observer, a very large order for wood crate boxes. In the piece, it was not highlighted, just listed in a very matter-of-fact manner. At least from appearances, the professor had not connected the dots. A realization had not been reached. But it was all out there for the whole world to see. The only thing left to do was correctly process the information, and then access would be granted to the greatest find in American history.

The observer closed his eyes. His pulse quickened. He could see the consequences as he imagined the pursuit of his dream being trampled by those chasing a treasure newly revealed, clamoring after what was rightfully his, what he had earned. He could not let it happen. The professor's delving into the past had to be stopped before any other discoveries could be attained. For next time, such information would not languish on some obscure website but on much more heavily traversed highways of information.

"What were you up to, Mr. Davis?" the old professor asked himself as he pored over various documents spanning the final doomed days of the Confederacy. "Ah... you knew there was no other way to move that kind of cargo without the Yankees getting ahold of it." Professor Sipe moved his frail fingers down the paper, only occasionally lifting them to press back his glasses, which gradually slid off the bridge of his nose. "Oh, you sly dog, so that's what you had in mind. Rhett... Scarlett," he said, looking at his orange tabby cats, who had now joined him in the study. "I think our friend Mr. Davis had some special plans for these crates. It makes sense... it was all there. But I had no idea there was so much of it. My original estimates were way off according to these numbers. They wouldn't match anything in any of the historical accounts I've seen. But still… there's something off."

The professor eyed the original requisition orders again, copying them down on an index card, as was his habit. He attempted to find an indication, any evidence whatsoever, that could explain the discrepancy. He cross-referenced the accounts with the unusual order for woodboxes, placing the information alongside his previous research on the card. But it still didn't fit. Was the South wealthier than what was originally believed? Had their fortune increased by some last-minute acquired riches? Yet most perplexing was, Why were so many of the boxes slated to be placed on ships that ran Union routes? It was completely illogical, based on their final destination. They would have wanted to keep such valuables as far out of Northern hands as possible.

Then, as if his heart had temporarily stopped beating, the elderly academic froze. He crunched the numbers again and again. It matched perfectly. He continued to look for another explanation, trying in vain to process his find. But even though it was before him, his brain was having difficulty comprehending what his eyes were providing it.

"This can't be right. It would be hidden… but why would they…" Slowly he brought his hand up toward his face and cupped his mouth. "Oh my dear god."

"Surprising, isn't it, Professor?" a voice stated from behind.

The old man jerked around to see a darkened figure in the doorway.

"I had no idea of the amount either. I think we're the only ones who know its true value," said the cloaked individual.

"Who are you? What are you doing in my house? What do you want?"

"I'm interested in your work, Professor. I wanted to know how far you've progressed, and now that question has been answered."

"I don't know who you think you are barging into my house," the old man said defiantly while trying to make out the man's features. "You must leave immediately! I keep office hours at the college if you wish to speak to me."

"I'm sorry, Professor, but this is far too important for that."

The nervous old man stepped back. "I don't understand. What do you want?"

"I want it never to get out."

The professor glanced down at his index card as the understanding hit him. "Wait… I'm not sure about anything. I haven't told anyone."

"But you know its value, and now you can confirm its existence. It's mine. I have invested too much, and I'll not allow you to interfere."

The professor was now pinned against the wall as he glimpsed the large knife the figure had unsheathed. "How could I possibly interfere? I'm an old man."

"Your age is unimportant. It's your knowledge that's dangerous. I already have to share this. I will not add another."

"Please"

"I'm sorry." He had no desire to cause the old man pain. It was a quick slash from left to right, one powerful thrust to the chest, and it was done. He then grabbed the index card off the desk.

As he exited the study, he turned to see the old man's cats rubbing themselves against his slumped body, one last sign of affection for their caretaker.

The secret will be safe with them.

Chapter 1

February 27, 1864, Arlington, Virginia

Dear God, it's miserable tonight, he thought as he buttoned up his wool overcoat. It had been raining lightly earlier in the day, but tonight it had become a deluge, coming down in sheets, soaking his heavy clothing to the bone.

Colonel Ulric Dahlgren was in Arlington, Virginia, reporting to the new Union headquarters, awaiting orders he was told had come from the top of the chain of command. Dahlgren was used to issuing orders to his regiment; waiting for them in the middle of a torrential downpour was something in which he was not accustomed. Yet he was dedicated to his craft and always professional in his approach. If performing his duty required him to wait in the rain, no matter how unpleasant, then that's what he would do.

Dahlgren was a trusted servant of the Union Army, and his attention to detail had caught the top brass's eye. He had come from a prestigious lineage of military service. His father, a respected admiral in the Union Navy, handed down a sense of discipline that became ingrained in his impressionable young son. Ulric had taken well to his military responsibilities, and by the age of twenty-one, he was already a respected leader.

Dahlgren was the model of what was expected out of a Union officer. His spit-and-polish reputation and ability to follow orders without question were the imperative traits needed for this operation. Thus, two weeks earlier, he had received a dispatch that he was to be part of an important undertaking. No details were given, just a very explicit meeting location and an order that was simply but confusingly signed, "Your Commander."

Now he found himself in Arlington in this terrible weather, waiting to see what would be his charge. He was told to remain at the base of the property to await further instructions. As he looked up the hill, he caught glimpses of the elegant mansion as it lit up in quick flickering images each time lightning flashed in the distance. It shone in tones of gray and white with every discharge over the river it bordered. Each crisp blade that cut the sky was followed by a thunderous roar he could feel in his chest and then reverberate throughout his body. Water poured over him, causing his boots to become completely encased in the mud that cascaded down in a steady torrent from the pathway leading to the mansion. He continued to gaze upon the surreal image, reflecting on the recent horrific times the nation had endured. The weather itself seemed to add an ominous sensation, mirroring the mood of the country. It came with a realization of the incalculable loss Americans had experienced since the beginning of this conflict. There was also an overwhelming feeling of irony when he thought about what had taken place in that beautiful residence just three years earlier.

The House at Arlington was a cross between classical Greek and Southern charm. Built in 1802, it was designed by the famous English architect George Hadfield, who had cemented his legacy in the American landscape with his previous work on the State Capitol building. He designed it in the traditional Greek style that was so popular in his day.

Dahlgren gazed in admiration of its grandeur. Its distinctive columns flowing down the front of its main entrance suggested the strength, wisdom, and integrity of its former occupants. The triangular shape of the facade, which was the foundation of all classical Greek structures, gave it a distinctive look that hearkened to a time when architecture suggested the power of the culture it represented. Its strategic positioning included breathtaking views of the Potomac and the ever-evolving Capitol dome, which, like the foundations of the nation's future, had yet to be completed. The House at Arlington was so much a part of the American fabric that the land it rested on was originally slated to be part of the nation's capital before being annexed by Virginia.

After the attack on Fort Sumter in April of 1861, and just prior to the onset of the major battles, its owner had been approached concerning the impending confrontation between the North and South. Recognizing his tactical brilliance, and based on overwhelming recommendations, President Lincoln summoned him from his elegant home, offering the command of the Union's most important Army to this veteran and West Point graduate. Shocked, he considered the president's offer, displaying the dignity that had become his reputation, yet declined to give an answer.

Virginia was his home, and his love for his state was beyond measure. He could not imagine any other place like it on earth. Its fertile fields, rolling hills, and majestic forest were part of his soul, and like many Americans, he considered himself first and foremost a citizen of his state, before his allegiance to the Union. He admired Lincoln, but what he was being asked to do was incomprehensible. He was being offered the reins to one of the mightiest armies on earth, to lead in a war against his home state, which had decided to break its ties with the Union.

That night, the distinguished gentleman with the silver locks and beard incessantly paced the marble floors of his home. His anguish wore on him, worrying his wife, as she recognized this mental torture. He loved his country and disapproved of secession and slavery. Yet leading an army against the land of Washington and Jefferson was unimaginable. The gentleman did not sleep that evening. As he stared out the windows of his home in the direction of the nation's capital, where the fractures in the Union first appeared, his pain was that of a parent being asked to choose which of his children should live and which should die. Grief-stricken that the nation could not resolve its differences, the decision lying before him would soon turn into an agony-laden evening spent with the horrific predicament of selecting sides.

As dusk melted into night and then relented to the glow of dawn, he had come to his decision. The exhausted gentleman sat down and penned a letter resigning his commission in the Union Army. Robert E. Lee would not take up arms against his home. Instead, he would offer his services to the Confederacy. In a very short time following his resignation, he would be leading the Army of Northern Virginia.

Now, three years later, Dahlgren could not help but think of the irony. This former residence of one of the nation's most respected citizens had turned into a symbol of one of its greatest betrayals. The graceful property was confiscated by the federal government in retribution for Lee's treasonous act. Its reassigned use was that of a command center for Union forces, teeming with officers scheming for new ways to delve out destruction on their Confederate adversaries.

In a final insult to Lee's legacy, a plan to inter Union war dead in its peaceful fields was implemented. By 1864, thousands of Northern soldiers would be buried at Arlington, forever consecrating it as hallowed ground for the Union, while cursing the memory of the Lee family in the process. Since that time, little had changed. The impending war when the Southern gentleman made his decision was still raging in early 1864. As the weeks turned to months and months turned to years with little end in sight, confidence in the North's prospects had been shaken. A nervous government, becoming weary of the carnage as well as its citizens' willingness to continue the fight, began to believe that if something was not done soon, they would lose this war of attrition.

That was why Dahlgren was here. He was not sure what his assignment would be, but he was told that if he carried out his mission successfully, it could end the war.

So he continued to wait, staring longingly at the mansion at the top of the hill, wishing he were in the confines of its warm and dry interior. He did not understand the reasoning for keeping him away from the residence. However, he had strict orders that he was not to enter it. Instead, his instructions would be brought directly to him.

A little after 10:00 p.m., he saw a man on horseback making his way down the muddy trail. As the proximity of the rider drew closer, the image of a young private mounted on top of the beast came into view. He could not have been much more than eighteen years old and did not seem to be handling the weather well as he approached the colonel shivering and struggling to get his bearings. Dahlgren looked up wearily yet was glad to finally see his orders being brought to him, so he could get out of the relentless storm.

The young private gingerly dismounted his horse and gave a respectful salute. "Colonel Dahlgren, sir, I have your orders," he said, his breath clearly visible in the chilly night air. The private pulled out two papers but did not immediately hand them over. When the colonel reached out his hand, the private reluctantly pulled back. "I'm sorry, sir, but my orders are that I'm to read you the instructions and you are to memorize them as written."

Perplexed, Dahlgren responded, "Am I not here to receive those orders?"

"Yes, sir, but I am under strict orders to only read them to you. You may write them down later in your own hand if you wish."

Pausing for a moment, Dahlgren responded, "Proceed, Private."

The young soldier began to slowly dictate the instructions. Dahlgren listened intently, making sure he committed every detail to memory. Then, as the private continued, he heard an order that stunned him, as if he had been struck by a bullet.

"I beg your pardon?" A shocked Dahlgren looked up. "Could you please repeat that?"

The private, papers trembling in his hands, repeated the order. Dahlgren felt the blood rush out of his face and his legs become weak. He stared at the young soldier, looking for some reason, some interpretation that would provide him another way of deciphering the order, yet no reprieve came.

The young man finished the task and nervously awaited a response.

"Is that all, Private?"

"No, sir, there's something else. You are to speak of this to no one."

"I understand," he answered with a slight nod.

Dahlgren felt a terrible weight, believing he carried a mass beyond his capability to bear.

Nonetheless, he mounted his horse, saluted the private, and slowly made his way down the hill. The burden was his.

Chapter 2

March 2, 1864, Richmond, Virginia

The warm glow emanating from the fireplace did little to calm his nerves. He paced back and forth, frightened yet, at the same time, fuming. This had crossed the line. This violated all ethics of war.

Confederate president Jefferson Davis never trusted the Yankees. However, this incident confounded even him. *How could they plot such a cowardly deed?*

As horrific as this war had been, there existed certain codes, rules that gentlemen on both sides had quietly understood not to violate. Civilian heads of state would not be targeted under any circumstances. Now, in one fell swoop, that agreement had been obliterated. President Davis continued to agonize, searching for a solution in which they could continue the struggle against their Northern adversary. Ever since the summer of 1863, he knew he might be confronted with this decision. However, what was discovered on this dead Union colonel earlier that evening had accelerated the urgency. The capital would have to be moved. The people that made up the government, the intelligence, the battle plans, and of course, the wealth all had to be evacuated.

In exasperation, he ceased pacing, slowly sat down at his desk, and placed his head in his hands, his bony fingers extending up the sides of his face. All the power that represented the South's last hope for independence rested with him. What he decided would determine their fate. *What's the best course of action? How should we respond?*

He knew he could not transport so much cargo on main roads with so many Union troops lurking nearby. This would have to be a clandestine operation that ensured what remained of the South's power would reach its destination, escaping detection. Confederate hopes depended on it. If confiscated, all would be lost.

A message needed to be delivered into the proper hands, codified so only those who were meant to understand could grasp its meaning. The cargo's value was too immense to take any chances, and only the most competent and trusted of individuals must be recruited for success. Taking out a piece of parchment, he paused momentarily. Quietly dipping his pen into the ink, he thought about the history of this region and how he could apply it to this most important undertaking. He drafted his words carefully, recognizing the significance of each syllable. The task continued into the early morning hours. Ignoring the stress and exhaustion, he pushed on until he finally completed the project.

That morning, he sent a dispatch to his most trusted servant, General Robert E. Lee. This effort would demand nothing less. He needed his resources and guidance. The message was concise and simple.

Dear sir,

I require your wisdom in a most important decision that is crucial to our survival as a nation. Information must be delivered that is vital to our cause. I would be in your debt if you could provide me your most gifted courier. I will leave you to make that assessment. Expediency is a necessity.

—Jefferson Davis

Chapter 3

March 4, 1864, Arlington, Virginia, Union Headquarters

His horse pounded the pathway leading to the mansion, kicking up chunks of dirt and bits of rock on the way. The soldier's mount was dripping with perspiration and foaming at its bit. The steed had been ridden nearly to exhaustion by the time its rider dismounted. Walking toward the front door and past the ancient-style columns, the weary warrior saluted the two guards standing post at the door, appearing every bit as grimy and disheveled as his horse.

He entered the large elegant foyer, where immaculate officers continuously crisscrossed in front of him. None of them took notice of the young man. Instead, they were buried in dispatches and orders, their heads rarely turning up to take in their surroundings.

The soldier turned 180 degrees until he spotted the crisp white door where he was to deliver his report. Taking a deep breath, he took three steps before a bespectacled man sporting a dark suit and a gray beard that looked to be fashioned after a billy goat began marching toward him.

"What is it?" he asked the soldier.

"I must see him, sir."

"You can inform me. I will deliver the message."

The soldier grimaced and looked down. "Begging your pardon, sir… I can't do that. I must see him personally."

"Young man," the older civilian said sternly, "I'm his closest and most trusted adviser. I'm fully capable of delivering your message."

"You must forgive me, sir, but I'm under strict orders to give him the information personally."

"Private, do you know who I am?" he annoyedly responded. "I assure you that my position outranks and supersedes that of whoever gave you that order. Who is it that gave you such a charge?"

"Your boss… sir," the nervous private replied.

The elder gentleman looked silently at the fatigued young man, taking a few moments to gauge his authenticity. He began to sense this was not a normal situation. "Is it so grave?" the gentleman asked in a softened manner.

The soldier bowed his head and looked at his mud-caked boots that were in stark contrast to the gleaming marble floors. "I'm afraid so, sir."

The gentleman sighed. "Very well… but for God's sake, go clean up. Your appearance will only alarm him further."

The soldier complied, making his way to the pantry. Scooping water from a pail located at the back of the room, he rinsed off his face and groomed his hair the best he could. The coolness helped revive him to where he could at least present the information in a collected manner. Slowly he began his trek toward the office to complete his mission. His footsteps echoed in the cavernous dwelling, almost giving him the sense of a condemned man marching to a drumbeat as he approached the gallows. Closing his eyes once he reached his destination, he delicately tapped on the door.

"Enter," a voice said.

The soldier slowly pushed open the portal. There in the middle of the room was the gangly figure, the gentleman who was to be the recipient of the message. He was sitting at a small round table. His angular form looked to be struggling to fit into the confined space he was seated. His shoulders were slumped, and his white shirt and black pants hung off his frame, displaying the weight loss the previous three years had taken from him. His coarse hair was no longer a deep brown but now interspersed with streaks of gray. A large stove-pipe hat sat on top of a pile of papers in front of him. It was strange to see him without it on. It always made him appear larger-than-life. It was a dramatic difference to this mere mortal.

"What is it, young man?" he asked in his high-pitched voice crackling with stress.

"It's about Colonel Dahlgren, sir… his efforts were unsuccessful."

The man did not turn around; instead, he slowly removed his glasses and placed them next to his hat. "Where is he?"

"I'm afraid he's dead, sir… killed just outside Richmond. They discovered his location and ambushed him."

The man's shoulders slouched further as his head nearly disappeared beneath them. "Good god… did he have a chance to destroy them?"

The soldier paused, knowing he was about to compound the bad news. "By the reports we have received, it appears not. We believe the enemy is aware of them."

The commander turned his head slightly, displaying his sharp profile. His deep-set eyes and prominent nose, which were backlit by the lamp, gave off a morose aura. "That may have been our last chance," he said softly. "Now it will only serve to heighten their rage and increase their desire for vengeance. God help us."

The private had never seen him like this. It was unnerving. His commander had always been a source of inspiration. Never had he witnessed him in utter despair.

"Private"

"Yes, sir."

"You are never to speak of this to anyone… ever. Do you understand? This goes to your grave."

"Yes, sir."

The soldier saluted, turned, and walked toward the door. As he reached for the knob, he paused and glanced back at his commander. A deep sense of sympathy came over him as he looked upon his leader sitting motionless at the table. Yet at the same time, he desired reassurance.

"Sir… I beg your pardon. But what do we do now?"

"We pray, Private, we pray."

Chapter 4

March 22, 1864, Richmond, Virginia

The steps cracked as the soldiers descended the staircase leading to the large room underneath the barn. It was dark and musty, and the heavy air held the stench of decaying hay, tobacco leaves, and dirt.

The younger of the two gently removed the kerosene lantern mounted on the wall and lit the wick. Its golden light gradually illuminated their surroundings as he lifted it to shoulder height to examine the cargo they were assigned to protect.

There, set in neat rows, were the wooden encasements that held the South's last hope. The soldier handed the lantern to his comrade and walked over to them, dutifully checking each for signs of tampering. Nothing could be left to chance. If this were to fall into the wrong hands, the Confederacy would no longer be able to fight the war. The cause would be lost.

Rumors were abundant that the valuable cargo was to be moved. However, Union troops were scouring the area, making it a risky venture. The Yankees had heard reports of the South's wealth; thus, any large caravan would be targeted. For now, however, it was hidden from prying eyes. Yet with news spreading of the latest Union attempts, it was obvious that keeping the cache from danger was going to be increasingly difficult, if not impossible, if it remained here.

The soldiers finished their sweep of the area and then took their positions of vigilance. It was hard for them to believe their nation's chances had dwindled to what lay behind them. Independence seemed a certainty such a short time ago. Now the survival of that goal was teetering on the brink. They would perform their duty, but their charge seemed trivial to the challenge that lay ahead.

Chapter 5

November 12, 1864, Virginia

I t was good to be able to light a fire. November nights in Virginia could be quite cold, but he had refrained from igniting one as Union troops could be heard in the distance. The Yankees were rarely quiet, but even though they were careless, they would have no problem spotting a fire in the pitch-black night of the Virginia forest. So he waited patiently for them to pass before indulging in that luxury.

Though he was not informed as such, William Hatton believed this would be his final mission. The urgency expressed in President Davis's eyes led him to such a conclusion. He was honored that General Lee thought so highly of his abilities to pick him for this most urgent of tasks. But upon his arrival at the president's headquarters, the desperation could be sensed. He was directed to head into the Deep South of Georgia to deliver instructions to an officer in the Confederate Navy. Though that was nearly the extent of his knowledge. Still, he did have his suspicions to what this mission was in reference.

Hatton cozied up to the fire, rubbing his hands together in an effort to stay warm. He took out a small flask the president was kind enough to provide him, even filling it with some of his finest brandy. The veteran courier was committed to the cause, but his loyalty stemmed more from sectionalism than politics. He was educated and loved his country before the conflict arose. He did not hate the enemy. The vitriol that was a constant in others' proclamations never touched his tongue.

The disintegration of the Union was something that hurt him deeply. While his countrymen often saw it as a weight lifted from their backs, Hatton viewed it as a golden opportunity squandered, never to be realized.

Staring at the flickering fire, he removed the leather-bound book from his coat pocket. He had been keeping a journal. In essence, it had become an ongoing dialogue between his heart and mind. The emotions of his latest were swelling inside him. It was time to write.

Journal Entry, November 12, 1864, William Hatton Courier, Army of Northern Virginia

We are losing. The nation is dying. We have fought and perished for a cause that may have been noble in thought but foolish in its undertaking. It could have been avoided. We could have found common ground. Why is that such a shameful concept? We like to think of ourselves as uncompromising. What lies we have told. That has always been our true gift. Our whole nation was built upon our ability to do the very thing that we loath to say.

We are as guilty as anyone. Slavery was not sustainable. It had to perish eventually. Those of us who partook in the practice knew that it was not long for this world. We built our existence on the backs of slaves but, in the process, obliterated our own independence. A society cannot exist with one definition of itself. We thought we were protecting our way of life, but our efforts only served to destroy us.

We should have worked to change their minds, not punish them for weaknesses we all possess. How could it have come to this? It was our responsibility to make personal freedom and liberty our mandate. Instead, we were lost behind the saving of an outdated institution.

Slavery was not our blessing, but our curse. Our attention was always situated on the symptom and not the disease. This war was about preserving an idea our forefathers had set forth, not to fight for one part of our culture. This is about the right to individual liberty and to keep a distant government from determining our lives. This was never about protecting one part of our Southern heritage. The shame is ours that so many of our young men who had never played any part in its perpetuation have died.

We did not learn from history. Every society has institutions and ways of life that change. No culture has ever maintained one system of economic growth throughout its existence. Yet in our efforts to preserve what we understood would eventually end, we lost sight of what was truly important. We ignored the significance of what our forefathers taught us. We lost our identity that separated us from the rest of the nations of the earth.

It is too late now. We have passed the point of reconciliation. I have one last duty to perform, and then my war comes to an end. I must deliver my message and complete the president's bidding. I pray that someday they will understand what our true loss was in this conflict. This is not what I wished to happen, but it is necessary. Unfortunately, we must commit the reprisal of the sin that was committed against us. We need to keep a segment of our original identity alive. There is not much hope that the true meaning will be preserved.

May the tunnels that lead to the black sands of time revitalize our nation, and may our heavenly Father forgive our transgressions.

Chapter 6

December 4, 1864, thirty miles northeast of Savannah, Georgia

Although reliable news came slowly, the recent information was disturbing. Since Gettysburg a year earlier, Lee's forces had been in tatters, and it seemed as if Southern efforts had been pushed back and defeated at every turn. What started out so encouraging in '61 and '62 with victory after victory had now become a war of attrition, one they were fated to lose. Southern resolve to defend their homeland was still strong, but this new tactic they were facing looked indefensible. William Tecumseh Sherman had turned the world of war on its ear and flaunted the lack of respect for previous chivalrous conduct in the faces of each state he marched through. The South could not resist this onslaught much longer. It was going to lose the war.

"We need to have six men to dispatch to check on possible enemy movements!" yelled Colonel Tanner.

Colonel John Tanner was a sturdy, broad-chested man who commanded respect from his subordinates. A decorated veteran, he had seen several military engagements ranging from First Bull Run to Fredericksburg and the Siege at Vicksburg and managed to survive them all. He was one who insisted on discipline but displayed a genuine caring for his soldiers, earning him great loyalty.

"Williams, O'Brien, Sandstrom, Connor, Jeffcoat, and Wagner, you will make up the dispatch. Everyone else, let's set up camp here and we'll move out tomorrow morning."

Young Josiah Willet was relieved. While he wanted to prove himself dedicated to the cause, he was wise enough to understand it would most likely be in vain. He might eventually have to fight, but it would not be today.

The evening was cool, but not frigid, given they were just entering winter. Southern winters were often mild, and this one had been fairly pleasant. It was far better than the humid months of summer, where not only were you battling dangerous armies but also debilitating heat and relentless mosquitoes that attacked morning, noon, and night. The soldiers had set up camp, making sure defensive preparations were complete. Soon the warmth of fires offered a soothing break from the dreariness of their day as the smell of cooked pork and hard tack was sent wafting through the camp.

Josiah was drifting, his thoughts dancing around like the sparks coming off the fire and then dissipating into the air. "Do you think we'll ever see 'em?"

"I don't know. Maybe," Ben murmured.

"I hope they don't have as many as we've been hearing."

"Me too," Ben said as he poked a stick into the fire in an effort to distract himself.

Ben Kates was from Atlanta and had been getting reports in more detail than most of the more rural inhabitants making up the majority of his regiment. He looked different from them as well. He worked at his father's printing shop, and while pulling on a printing press was difficult work, the look of a city boy was far different from someone who toiled in the fields their entire life. He had bulging biceps and a barrel chest, while most of the farm boys like Josiah had a sinewy appearance, wirelike and taut.

"I have a feeling things are going to change tomorrow," Ben said hesitantly.

"Why's that?"

"Something's going to happen. They've been talking about our group splitting up and being used for other duties."

"Duties?" Josiah's hair stood up on the back of his neck. "I thought we were supposed to chase after Sherman's boys."

"Shit, that's a lost cause. He has sixty thousand men. What have we got, maybe six thousand? We can no more stop him than a fly can stop a cannonball."

Josiah felt a sudden rush of nerves as sweat started to bead and drip down his neck. On the surface, not having to face Sherman's army might have seemed like a blessing. Yet there was comfort in staying with your unit, and the idea of splitting from them was very disconcerting.

"What are these new groups supposed to do?" Josiah stammered.

"Don't know. No one seems to know. The only thing I can tell you is, whatever these groups are supposed to do, it ain't coming from Tanner."

"Who's it coming from?"

"Hadn't heard, and if anyone has, they ain't saying." Ben hesitated for a second. He looked over at Josiah and could see his concerned boyish face glowing orange in the light of the fire.

"I do know one thing, though," Ben stated.

"What's that?"

"The orders came from Richmond."

Josiah could feel a lump building in his throat and his heart pounding hard against the walls of his chest. He knew instantly what that meant. Richmond was the capital of the Confederacy. Southern generals and officers were mostly left to their discretion on military strategy. In most circumstances, orders were given by brigade commanders. The highest up he had ever heard his unit referred to in receiving orders that affected them directly came from General Beauregard, and that was just to send a few of their best marksmen to act as support forces in one of their engagements.

Receiving an order from Richmond meant something unusual and quite important. This was an item coming directly from the leaders of the government, possibly President Jefferson Davis himself. Whatever it was, it had to be of the highest importance. There would be no reason for an order to come from the capital, bypassing high-ranking commanders, to be given, unfiltered, to a small unit colonel like Tanner.

Josiah felt a sense of dread as he entered his tent to turn in for the night. His body was tense, and it seemed he would not be able to keep the strain at bay. As he lay down on the hard earth and tried to quell the thoughts racing through his mind, he could not help but think of his mother and sister back home. Even though he was not privy to what those orders were, he had the uneasy feeling that somehow, they would affect his life and might result in his death.

Chapter 7

Colonel Tanner poked his head through the tent. It could not have been much past 5:00 a.m., as the sun had yet to rise.

"Willet, Kates, I need you to report in fifteen."

Josiah Willet and Ben Kates slowly pushed away their blankets and put on their uniforms. It was cold outside, and a heavy mist hung over the grassy rise, giving everything a very wet and ominous feel. Both took a deep breath, acknowledged each other with a glance, and started walking toward Tanner's tent. They knew what awaited them, as they had been informed the night before that some in their unit were being sent on a special operation.

"How did I know that it was going to be us?" Josiah rhetorically stated. When they arrived, twenty-five other men were there, waiting patiently.

"Any of you know what this is about?" said a weathered soldier. No one gave an answer; most just shrugged in confusion.

Tanner then appeared from his tent. "Gentlemen, I've received orders that you're to meet up with a new regiment seven miles north of here at this location," he said, pointing to a map he had laid out on a table. "Once you arrive at this point, you'll meet up with a Colonel Piel. He'll give you further instructions at that time."

"Sir, what's this about? Why are we leaving our unit?" asked a young private.

"Son, I wish I knew. I can't really afford to lose any more men, but I don't have a choice. All I know is that you're supposed to report today. You have twenty minutes to prepare and head out."

The men begrudgingly returned to their tents and gathered their gear. They knew it would not be an easy assignment. Something was happening, and it seemed like this was much more a move of desperation than military expediency.

At the northern end of the camp, the men collected. They were a motley group looking disheveled in appearance and bewildered in expression. Colonel Tanner joined them to make sure everyone was accounted for and to see them off.

Josiah noticed the look of concern on his face, making him feel even more anxious. *What are we heading into?* he thought as he saluted his commanding officer, turned toward the trail, and proceeded down the desolate path. The dirt road seemed endless. The terrain it traversed was unimportant and nondescript. There was nothing that would offer any advantage from a strategic standpoint. It just kept going and going, with little to give any clue why they were headed this direction.

There wasn't much talking between the soldiers. Many were still in a semi-comatose state, as if sleepwalking. Occasionally, some would attempt friendly banter, but the fear of what lay ahead and pure exhaustion kept that to a minimum.

Josiah kept scanning, looking for any sign to give him some understanding. It never materialized.

They were only a little over two miles from their destination. No troop movements were evident, no cavalry, and not a single soul crossed their path. Then they heard it.

"That's gunfire," said the soldier directly behind Josiah. "We need to move faster."

The company started running as the sound of blazing guns became louder and louder. It almost sounded as if it were moving toward them. It was certainly closer than where their destination was supposed to be. It was only moments before a tree line came into view, with white smoke visible above its branchy crest. Fighting was just ahead.

Josiah's heart raced as he and his fellow soldiers charged at the smoke. Now, not only were the mechanisms of battle audible, but also the screaming that accompanied warfare. The voices came in all forms; some were shouting out orders, some were calls for help, and others others bellowing in agony. Those chilling cries of the wounded came down like an avalanche.

As they moved off the trail in the direction of the trees, the conflict came into clearer view. A group of blue-coated men were firing down onto a huddled group of Confederates desperately looking for cover. Choking smoke engulfed the entire area as guns discharged their deadly projectiles.

Ben and Josiah broke from their group and sprinted toward the Confederates who were looking for protection behind a rock. As they ran, Josiah heard Ben screech in pain. He turned to see him curled up on the ground, clutching his leg. A bullet had ripped through his calf, creating a bloody mess.

Josiah fell to his knees to aid him. Ben writhed on the ground, oblivious to the whizzing bullets flying over their heads. He was not going to be able to get out of there on his own. Josiah reached underneath him and, with what strength he could muster, pulled him to his feet.

Bullets struck the ground all around them, kicking up dirt in short, small bursts, but Josiah managed not to suffer the same fate. He placed Ben's arm around his shoulder and dragged him as fast as he could to the closest cover. Spotting a thicket of shrubbery and trees, he laid Ben down behind an oak and then eyed the field, looking for anyone from his regiment to assist him.

"I'm going to get help!" Josiah yelled.

As he looked up, he could see more Confederates being pushed back. He ran to their position and managed to gain cover behind another grove of trees and bushes. He then loaded his gun and discharged it in the direction of the advancing Union troops, not sure if he hit anything. Nervously he fumbled with his Springfield rifle, struggling to jam the powder and miniball into the barrel. He turned, aimed, and fired again. His heart immediately sunk into his stomach. He saw a Union soldier go down in a heap. His emotions were a convoluted mix. He did not feel joy or fear or anger. Instead, a sudden sadness took hold, followed by intense nausea. He had just killed another human being, someone's son, husband, or father. Josiah keeled over and vomited, as bullets cascaded off the trees he had taken refuge behind. He thought he should reload, but it was becoming obvious it would do little to repel this overwhelming force.

He could no longer stay in that place. He had to move. The Union forces were advancing, and there was no way their beleaguered regiment could hold their position. He instinctively began to sprint back to the path, but before he moved more than a few yards, he tripped and fell hard, his rifle leaving his grasp and flying several feet in front of him. Reaching desperately for his weapon, he felt something holding him back. It had his leg in a vise. He jerked to get loose while looking to see what was impeding his movement.

"I need you," he heard a ragged voice say.

He could see nothing. The bushes were high, obstructing his view. He reached over and pulled the foliage aside. A horrible sight invaded his vision. An older Confederate soldier was lying in a pool of blood. He had been struck in the abdomen by a miniball, which had torn a gaping hole through his midsection, his hand placed over the wound in a futile attempt to stop the bleeding. His face was caked with a mixture of dirt and sweat. A single tear streamed down his face. Josiah knew at once that the wound was a mortal one.

"You can't let them have it," the wounded soldier said, reaching out with his right hand, holding a folded piece of paper. "No one can see this. Please, you have to take it."

Josiah took it from him, not knowing what to say.

"I failed, we can't win," the soldier said, placing his other hand over his wound.

"What would you like me to do? Whom should I give it to?"

"No one. The duty was mine. Just keep it hidden. It's the only thing I can do now. Please, promise me you'll keep it hidden."

Josiah nodded.

The man took a deep breath and barely muttered, "The instructions are simple. It has value." He then turned his head, gasped, and passed away.

Not having time to contemplate what had just happened, Josiah got up, grabbed his rifle, and ran to the trail. No one from his regiment was in sight. He made his way down the path for what seemed like an eternity but could not locate his comrades. Hours passed as he was completely separated from anything of familiarity. Knowing the search for his company would be fruitless, he turned his attention to finding a place to rest for the night. He was a man without a place. He belonged to no one.

As the light receded, it dawned on him that he had not looked at the item the dying soldier had given him. Sitting down, he slowly pulled the bloodstained paper from his pocket, nervously anticipating what it would reveal. As he unfolded it, he wondered what made this paper so worthy of preservation that a dying man would make it his last act of concern.

Josiah could barely read. His education was very limited, having been pulled out of school when he was eight years old to work on the family farm. As he stared at the words and tried to sound them out, none of it made sense. *These instructions are not simple.*

Unfamiliar phrases such as "pillars of faith" and references to strange things such as "vara" greeted his eyes. Josiah recalled the last thing the man said, "It has value," but he could not see any in this meaningless collection of words.

Yet he possessed an intense sense of duty and loyalty, a code that had been fostered in him by his father. *Never break a promise,* his father's words echoed in his mind.

Josiah might not be the best soldier, but he was always a dutiful son. With that thought, he folded the paper and pulled out a photograph of his parents that was housed in a small tin frame. Realizing this was the best way to preserve the item, he inserted it in the frame behind the photograph, knowing it would be protected from the elements. He also figured if he lost his life, no one would think to check behind the picture, ensuring Josiah would keep his word.

The young man looked at the western sky. He stared at the heavens, meditating on his feelings, letting himself get lost in the purples and oranges of the sunset as it dipped farther beneath the horizon. A sense of peace came over him. Somehow, this had to be a sign. He had experienced battle and the terrible waste and carnage it produced. He never wanted to see it again. He could not explain it, but he knew that was it for him. His war was over.

Chapter 8

Present Day, Nashville, Tennessee

"**D**amn it," she muttered to herself after the keys slipped through her fingers and fell to the ground. Then a struggle ensued as she strained to control the full bag of groceries she was holding while attempting to retrieve them.

Once she grabbed ahold, she inserted the key into the lock, opened the door, and proceeded straight to the kitchen. The slight aggravation faded quickly. And why shouldn't it? Things had been improving in Madison Callum's life.

For months, she held on to the anger that was accompanied by a burgeoning insecurity. Yet heeding their marriage counselor's words, she had to make a choice. If she wanted to salvage their relationship, she must learn to forgive. Yes, his infidelity was painful, a dagger to the soul. But now she was convinced that even those deep wounds could heal. To cling to past transgressions, to constantly dangle that above her husband's head while at the same time claiming the desire to repair, would be hypocritical, to say the least.

So tonight would be a celebration. It was her way of announcing she had broken from the past. A surprise was in order.

She had taken the day off work to get ready for the evening, and what better way to signify her new outlook than preparing his favorite meal, prime rib, a fine cabernet, and crème brûlée for dessert. And of course, there would be a physical reconnection. She had even splurged on the perfect attire at Victoria's Secret for the sensual night ahead.

She looked at the clock; there was plenty of time. He wouldn't be home for hours. Her mind flashed forward, contemplating how she would greet him when he arrived. Should she just let him wander past the entryway to discover the candlelit table? Maybe greet him at the door, wearing nothing but her newly acquired lingerie? Or even better, how about a trail of petals leading up to their bedroom? Peering out the kitchen window, she spotted the beautiful bloom of rosebushes in the backyard. *That's it!*

Grabbing a pair of clippers, she headed for the sliding glass door. It was just when she reached for the handle that she heard it.

At first, it sounded like semi-muffled squealing, or maybe a television with the sound turned to barely audible levels. She froze as her feet felt like they were cemented to the ground. Madison could only manage to swivel her head, her eyes fixated on the stairs, which suddenly appeared as insurmountable barricades but, at the same time, beckoning her to ascend them. The first step caused excruciating pain. By the time she reached the base of the flight, she was already out of breath.

The sound increased in volume and seemed to rise to nearly deafening levels once she reached the top. It was a convoluted mix, alternating between giggles and ecstasy.

As she reached the bedroom, the floor began to roll in waves, like it had been liquefied. She placed her hand against the door, but her strength began to leave her as she barely managed enough power to push it open.

The image appeared blurred and indiscernible. It was brown and pink, black and white, flowing golden blond and sinewy dark. The smell was sweet and pungent, a mixture of perspiration and perfume. It was an aroma of exertion and intensity, but most of all, sex.

Madison couldn't remember running back down the stairs. She had no recollection of the woman's gasp of shock or her husband's voice as he called out to her. All her senses were heightened to such a degree that every stimuli had melded into a white noise in which one could not be extracted from the other. About her only memory was the sensation of wetness on her face and the feeling of betrayal.

Chapter 9

January 4, Present Day, Savannah, Georgia

"Get down! Get down!" the warning came just as a hail of bullets struck the rim of the trench.

"Where's it coming from?" Des asked.

"About a hundred and fifty yards over that ridge. We have..."

Once again, the soldier's voice was drowned out by the sound of automatic weapons and mortar fire, which was quickly followed by howls of agony.

"It's Dave. See if you can help him," the captain ordered.

Des ran toward the screams, tripping over a pile of munitions that had been knocked over by the vibrations of the shells and mortars striking in such close proximity. When he reached his friend, he found him in a seated position, his back pressed against the dirt embankment. His body had been twisted and torn by the force of the shrapnel and small rocks that had been hurled at supersonic speeds by the force of the explosion. It left his flesh hanging off his mangled frame, which resembled a bloody pretzel. The once-handsome face of Dave Grayson would not be recognizable, even to his wife and two young children.

"Come on, Dave… you're going to be okay. I'm right here," Des said in a futile effort to comfort him.

Once again, the distinctive whistle of an incoming shell could be heard, its decibels increasing as it approached their position. Des threw himself over Dave just as the ordnance made contact with the ground. The trench shook with incredible violence that was accentuated by the deafening explosion.

Slowly Des raised himself off his comrade, ready to offer more assistance, but he was already gone. Dave's face had turned to the right, his once-vibrant blue eyes now coldly staring into the abyss. His last thoughts were evident as Des saw the small photo of his family clutched between his blood-soaked fingers.

In a rage, Des grabbed his weapon and opened fire over the trench wall, his frustration fueled by his inability to save his friend. The unit was ordered to fall back, but he ignored them, continuing to fire, looking for absolution. It wasn't vengeance, but anger meshed with guilt. It was a cruel twist of fate. Only moments earlier, he had been where Dave was; it was he who should be lying dead in that dusty trench.

Then a calmness took over. The rage coursing through him mere moments ago gave way to the soldier. All the training, all the preparation, flowed from within. He was ready. The mind and body were synchronized, waiting for the opportunity to engage. It took only a few seconds before he saw a figure move out of the shadows. It was cautious, obviously timing his actions to avoid any retribution.

Des took careful aim, waiting for his enemy to make a fatal mistake. The figure was backlit by the sun, carefully biding his time. He was getting ready to make his dash, hoping he wouldn't be targeted.

Des's emotions raged again, certain the individual now in his sights was responsible for his friend's demise. His finger was placed gently on the trigger. His breathing slowed to ensure supreme accuracy, stillness at the ready.

The target popped up like he was sitting on a spring, lurching forward in an all-out sprint. Des didn't hear the shot or feel the kick of his rifle as it released its bullet. All he could hear was the body of his target flailing as it rolled down the steep rise. It was all slow motion, blurred and instinguishable. Des's limbs went numb. There was only consciousness and thought as he watched his enemy slide to a stop about ten yards from his position.

Although there was a body attached, he couldn't see it. He could not see the color of the tribal clothes or the redness pouring from the kill shot. All he could fixate on were the hands, the fragile hands. They were not ones of a hardened warrior, rough, dirty, and cracked; they were slender and appeared soft, even genteel.

His vision was then drawn to the face, the angelic little face. The lips were small, the nose only a tiny protrusion on his profile. Finally, there were the eyes, staring right at him as if to say, "Why have you taken me?" The boy couldn't have been more than twelve years old.

Desmond Cook jumped off the couch like he had been yanked by a rope attached to a semitruck. He placed his hands on his face, which instantly became drenched with perspiration. He was panting, and his stomach was twisted in knots of such severity that he could not hold back the nausea. He ran to the bathroom and vomited, releasing the nightmare along with the contents of his breakfast. He then turned to the sink and cupped lukewarm water into his mouth and onto his face.

It wasn't the first time Des had this nightmare, and in reality, it wasn't a nightmare. It was a flashback. It was the reliving of the most horrific moment of his life, and along with the always-visceral effects came the shame of survival.

This was what was left over. The trigger could be anything. A photograph, a conversation, or even a distinctive odor could flip the switch and he was back in that trench in Afghanistan. This time, it was a news report on television about the war on terror that did the trick. Things had improved, and this was the first flashback he had had in quite some time. But nonetheless, it was a devastating one.

He rubbed his eyes and took in a series of deep breaths to regain his composure. He could not show up his first day of volunteering looking like a drug addict searching for his next fix.

After emerging from the shower, he focused on being in the present. *Find the positives.* He was on the homestretch of his master's degree studies, and he was in his most beloved of cities. If he would revert to memories, this was the city that held the happiest of them. No place could soothe him like this refuge by the sea.

Savannah, Georgia, might be the most beautiful city in America. Yet when people thought of the words *planned community*, generally it conjured up images of cookie-cutter housing or senior retirement homes.

So there was a sense of irony when one learned a city as poetically graceful as Savannah started out as just that, a planned community.

Founded in 1733 by James Oglethorpe, it was designed as an agrarian society. In need of settlers, it became a bastion of tolerance, as religious groups from all over Europe were welcomed with open arms, creating a diverse and rich cultural tapestry that enhanced everything from architecture to cuisine.

While Atlanta had been the center of Georgia commerce for years, it actually did not hold the distinction of the state's largest city until the late 1800s, a title Savannah held until that time. Diverse and sophisticated, Savannah was a treasure trove of Southern history and had attracted academics and tourists alike. That's why Desmond Cook loved this town. It had become his home away from home. As a student at the University of Georgia, he would often come to the coastal enclave to vacation. There was certainly no place like it on earth.

When he was a youth, his father brought him here for the first time. An amateur Civil War historian, Theodore Cook enthusiastically came to Savannah with his young son Des in tow, teaching him about the Antebellum South, sharing its stories, architecture, and important standing in Southern culture. The young boy was mesmerized by the magical town.

Des had always had his eyes on Savannah and wanted to eventually make it his place of permanent residence. He was not quite there yet but was getting closer. He had been diverted on his journey to his ideal home through personal tragedy. His father passed away unexpectedly when he was sixteen, and with only his mother's income available to them, Des went to work at odd jobs to help support himself and his younger brother, Theodore Jr. When he graduated high school, the family's financial condition dictated where he would continue his education. Des settled for the local community college, not having the funds available to enroll at a university, even though academically he had proven his abilities worthy.

It was a difficult road. His performance in the classroom was admirable, but the need to continue to help support his family slowed his progress to a crawl. Many nights, Des would sit in his room feeling the despair of having the advancement toward his future delayed to an excruciatingly slow pace. He could see his hopes slipping away, yet still, he trudged forward.

It would take four years, but after he received his AA degree, his desire to continue his studies did not wane. Yet the money situation had not changed either. In fact, it was tighter than ever. He did not wish to burden his mother by asking her for the funds. He hated seeing her anguish over her inability to meet her children's needs. If he was going to reach his goals, it would be without causing any more heartache to his mother. So Des arrived at a decision; if he was going to be able to continue the quest, he would have to find another avenue. Reluctantly he enlisted in the Army, hoping he would be able to reserve enough funds to pay for his education. After six years of service, Des felt he had enough to follow his dream.

He enrolled at the University of Georgia and excitedly geared his studies to attain a history degree. While he was thrilled to be there, he did feel somewhat awkward. At twenty-nine years old, his advanced age seemed out of place with the young nineteen and twenty-year-old students who occupied his classrooms. He shared their interest in history, but beyond those limits, there was little else they had in common.

After three more years of intense study, Des emerged with his bachelor's degree. He felt vindicated in a way. So many people believed he should move on and look for other opportunities, but he persevered and, with the degree, was able to justify his dedication. However, he also felt empty, lost, and unsure of what would be his next venture.

Graduate school was a move made more out of a need to stall having to make a career decision than it was of actually making one. Plus, the money on his GI Bill had not been completely depleted, so continuing his educational journey made perfect sense. He was not quite sure what he would do once he marched down the aisle with another degree, but he took solace in not having to make that decision now.

In the fall, Des continued his historical studies, specializing in Civil War history. The War of Northern Aggression, as many Southerners still referred to it, was a popular subject in this part of the country. Although the way the South had been portrayed by professors had changed in the last twenty years. Gone was the romanticized version of the Old South, with a more realistic and accurate depiction taking its place. Des always believed this was important. While he loved the South, he recognized the sins of its past should not be overlooked and that by doing so, a true disservice would be committed upon its youth.

Des diligently continued through the first semester of graduate courses. Although he was intent on obtaining his degree, a sense of complacency was taking over. There was a stagnation in simply going to classes without any definitive goals. His internal compass was not pointing in any specific direction, and he was becoming depressed that he was so far behind the age range of his classmates. It seemed there were only three directions anyone with this degree was pointed to, and none of them interested him.

Teaching was admirable, and certainly, a professorship at a university would be desirable employment, yet his shy nature and the recognition of how incredibly difficult it was to attain those jobs were discouraging. The other possibilities, becoming an attorney or running for political office, were not appealing in the slightest. Chasing after clients and spending your days tied up in a courtroom, in his opinion, was akin to having your teeth drilled, while politics was every bit, if not more, distasteful. Des was looking for something enlightening, something that would reinvigorate him. That opportunity would present itself in an unexpected way.

Prior to the start of the spring semester, he found a unique prospect. While perusing the flyers on one of the bulletin boards dotting the University of Georgia campus, Des came across an ad that caught his eye.

The Savannah Historical Foundation needed volunteers for a preservation project. Over the previous three years, the foundation had been collecting government documents, photographs, contracts, letters, and other items from the local population, with the goal of digitizing the material, in effort to preserve history as well as create new information banks for researchers and historians. It needed individuals who would be willing to take on this tedious and time-consuming project.

Des's eyes lit up, and his mind raced with new, exciting possibilities on how he could incorporate this opportunity into his studies. More than anything, he felt a change of scenery would give him focus and help him find the direction he so desperately desired.

For the upcoming semester, he would be embarking on his master's thesis. Originally, he contemplated submitting an essay on how the Southern war strategy changed after the death of Stonewall Jackson. However, he was never very enthusiastic about the premise and was quite aware it could easily be adjusted to another topic if he could spend the next six months inspired by historic Savannah. So almost without hesitation, and certainly with no ideas in mind for his term paper, Des packed his bags and headed to the Georgia coast.

Chapter 10

Walkerton, Virginia

How he hated them. With every thought, with every action, with every fiber of his being, he hated them. He knew it was not real, he knew this was just a recreation of past events, yet the sight of those men clad in those blue uniforms filled him with a rage as tangible as the replica Civil War weapon he held in his hand.

With each step they marched forward, he reflected upon his ancestry. His father, who preached the evils of the federal government; the grandfather, who always maintained his staunch adherence to segregation; his great-grandfather, who marched with the Ku Klux Klan in a Washington, DC, parade; and his great-great-grandfather, who died on a Georgia field trying to hold back Sherman's March to the Sea, set his feelings about an oppressive government in a permanent state of abhorrence. It was as if his lineage had permanently marked his DNA, a natural force he could not deny.

The young man looked every bit the part. His baggy Confederate uniform hid a thin but toned body that possessed strength far beyond what his size revealed. Though he had not advanced further than a high school education, his voracity for authenticity and his attention to detail would cause the most sophisticated of historians to blush. He was extremely intelligent and patient enough to look for ideal opportunities when they presented themselves. At times, his anger did reveal itself, but only in controlled environments, which was why these Civil War reenactments were so therapeutic.

His real name was Trevor, a name he despised. Over his formative years, little had changed about the twenty-three-year-old young man.

As a kid, there was nothing to distinguish him. Skinny and of average height, his wispy blond hair and freckled face made him appear like the poster child for the average American youth.

In school, he was a decent student, but not spectacular. His B average, like the rest of his life, was solid but hardly outstanding. As he moved through his high school years, his looks barely differentiated from his elementary ones. They had certainly not moved in a direction to garner the attention of girls or gain him the popularity that so often accompanied the shallowness of that quality.

He had a small group of friends he commiserated with, yet only on a superficial level. He was the boy who was introduced and then as quickly forgotten once his presence was gone.

While he never displayed misery, he had never shown true happiness, nor did he give any indication of the obsessiveness that would later grip his life. In fact, there was never any hint he was capable of being dedicated to a purpose.

His first encounter with what would ultimately become his compulsion actually began with little fanfare. However, he would often reflect on his initial contact with the rich history of his ancestry.

"Come here, Trevor. I want to show you something," his grandfather said.

The young boy entered the study. It was a small room filled with shelves of books. So many they bowed at their center with the weight of their contents. Trevor's grandfather sat in the corner at his small cherrywood desk, with more books piled atop it in heaps.

On the walls were paintings of Civil War battle scenes. The boy was mesmerized by their colors, finding himself drawn into the events they portrayed. He could almost hear the gunfire and smell the black powder.

Trevor turned and placed his index finger on the binders, slowly reading their titles in a whisper, "*The Cause... The War of Northern Aggression... How the Union Betrayed the South.*"

His grandfather motioned for the young boy to stand beside him. "Do you know what this is?" he asked Trevor, pointing to a weatherworn book on his desk.

Trevor shook his head.

"This is your great-great-grandfather's Civil War journal… or what you may think of as a diary. His name was William Hatton. He was a very important man. He was a courier in the Confederate Army."

"What's a *courier?*" Trevor asked excitedly, hoping this was a special type of fighting man.

"A courier is a man who delivers messages from one group to another."

"So he wasn't a fighter?" he responded disappointedly.

"Don't look so let down. He was a very important man. He was the most trusted courier for General Robert E. Lee, the most famous general in the Confederacy."

"So what's it about?"

"It mainly tells of what his life was like during the war and his personal feelings about the *cause.*"

"The cause?"

"Yes, that's what we refer to as the reason the South fought the war."

"I thought the war was about slavery?"

His grandfather's face went from serenity to aggravation. "Don't believe all the crap they teach you in school," he responded sternly. "It wasn't about slavery. It was about our right to be free from control of the Yankees. It was about the right for the states to determine for themselves what they could and couldn't do. You don't like being forced to do something, do you?"

"No."

"Neither do I, and that's what the war was really about."

"What happened to him?" the young boy asked, pointing to the journal.

"He was killed by the Yankees while trying to deliver an important message. That son of a bitch Sherman… his troops shot him down."

"What was the message?"

"We don't know. We'll probably never know. But he was sent personally by President Jefferson Davis. So it had to be important."

Trevor placed his hand on the journal and ran it across its cracked leather cover. His eyes widened as though he had been jolted by the power of his family's heritage.

"I wanted to show this to you. When I'm gone, I want you to have this. It's very important to our family. You see, Trevor, we Southerners are different from the Yankees. We have a deep connection to our past that we cherish. The Civil War wasn't just something that happened, it's who we are, and one day, when you're old like me, you'll have the responsibility to pass it on to your children and grandchildren."

"Should I tell them he was a hero?"

"You should tell them the real reason… the real cause that he died for. If you do that, then you'll have fulfilled your responsibility. In telling them, in a way, you'll be completing his mission. That's the most important thing."

Trevor's grandfather passed on during his senior year in high school. However, his interest had waned since learning of his family's past. Upon inheriting the journal, he only skimmed through the pages with tepid attention. What he saw didn't induce much excitement. It mainly spoke of the terrible food rations and the daily drudgery of army life. No battles, no major encounters with the enemy, and no heroics were mentioned. Just endless days of relentless boredom and monotony in what became so commonplace in a soldier's life. So the journal remained largely unread and, eventually, tucked away.

After graduation, Trevor bumped around from job to job, making meager money. His prospects of success in anything seemed remote. No matter the endeavor, he felt lost, unattached to any people or events. His superficial relationship with his peers left him directionless, and he found little solace in the bitter theories of his father. Everything was distant and alien, and the depression that came with that isolation drove him farther into a hole.

It wasn't until a couple of years later, when he was watching late-night television, that his malaise would turn into obsession. While flipping through the stations, he came across a documentary on the fall of the Confederate capital of Richmond, Virginia, which was just a few miles from where he had been born and raised.

The program covered much of what he was already familiar with. The demise of Lee's forces, the inability to obtain the resources needed to continue the struggle, and the gut-wrenching decision to surrender at Appomattox Courthouse were all highlighted.

Yet there was one segment that caught his attention, the evacuation of the Confederate government from Richmond and all their resources, including the treasury. Trevor quickly moved himself from the couch potato position to one of upright alertness. *Could that have been his mission?*

He sprinted to his room and began to rifle through his closet, desperately searching for his family heirloom. *He was a part of that, I know it.* As he threw down item after item, his closet floor soon became a hill of clothing, old yearbooks, and sports paraphernalia. He discovered it in the corner of the upper shelf. Grabbing the journal like a man dying of thirst who had discovered a mountain spring, he leaped off his chair and sat down on the corner of his bed.

Eagerly, he began to read. Each syllable, every word, once dreary and dull, now came alive. The meaningless thoughts that previously failed to gain his interest had become riveting. Before, he saw his great-great-grandfather as stoic and single-minded. Now he began to see him in a new light, one that showcased an individual of great thoughtfulness and intellect.

Trevor pored over the pages. He read descriptions of battle-worn soldiers splattered with dirt and blood. He learned of the techniques his ancestor used to elude enemy troops while carrying his precious messages. He read of the sadness and despair of the loss of friends and the loneliness of being separated from his wife and children.

But what captivated the young man the most was his great-great-grandfather's political views. In them, he found an individual who could see beyond the superficial points of the cause. To William Hatton, slavery was nothing more than a clever argument to increase the federal government's power. It was the guise, the shiny object in the cloak of a humanitarian mission to distract the populace from the true intention. The Confederacy, as William Hatton saw it, made slavery a symbol, which, in turn, falsely became the overriding topic and the reason for their separation. In the process, the North not only fooled their masses but the South's as well.

Trevor's viewpoint began to change, and for the first time in his life, the mediocrity that had defined him was now giving in to a small fire, soon to become a raging inferno. His ancestor's thoughts, his feelings, were becoming inseparable from his own. He read and reread the journal over and over. With each review, he let the words slowly redefine who he was and what he was meant to be.

The obsession sparked new desires. The need to connect with his heritage could not be satisfied solely through the written word. He craved a more visceral way of uniting with the past.

He began to attend local meetings of the Sons of the Confederacy, where he found a group of kindred spirits. These were not just people who spent their time lost in nostalgia or mimicking stereotypical presentations of Southern culture but were actively trying to change perceptions about the cause. They were individuals who found not only shortcomings in traditional historical teachings but also parallels to problems America faced today. Though the times had changed, they experienced the same fears that William Hatton had written of so eloquently. To them, the cause still existed. The war was not over, but stalled.

Trevor was enthralled with this interpretation of history. It only heightened his desire to feel what generations of Southerners had felt before him. He started to absorb their frustrations and their rage. The emotions they produced acted as fuel, stoking his internal furnace. Soon he found himself touring throughout the South to participate in Civil War battle reenactments. Antietam, Bull Run, and Cold Harbor were just some of the war-scarred sites where he attempted to become one with the Southern soul.

Yet even with this total immersion, he was frustrated and empty. No matter the time and effort, there remained a gap he could not fill. It was a fissure dividing him from his own identity. It kept him lost in a self-imposed purgatory, with no way to access his own concept of who he was. It left him with a longing, an unquenchable yearning for self-realization. One that always seemed just out of his grasp.

Frustrated, he continued to study the journal. He read it so many times that nearly every word was committed to memory. Trevor knew, if he could find the purpose of the message his great-great-grandfather carried, he could find his own.

When it finally came, it was not so much a bolt of lightning as it was a state of higher consciousness, the equivalent of a historical nirvana. It revealed itself in an entry with traits of deep sensitivity and intelligence yet started with simplicity.

"We are losing. The nation is dying. We have fought for a cause that was noble in thought but foolish in its undertaking. Unfortunately, we must commit the reprisal of the sin that was committed against us."

Blood rushed into Trevor's face, his body began to tremble, and his eyes filled with tears. He now understood the extreme value of the secret his ancestor took to the grave. It was the South's power, her true wealth.

For the first time in his life, he understood who he was and his destiny. Trevor Hatton, for all intents and purposes, died at that precise instant. He no longer knew who Trevor was and fathomed he never really existed at all. With the death of that identity, this generation's William Hatton was born, and along with it, a new purpose.

But it was incomplete. The transformation could only come with a full release of any semblance of his prior self, one that would take the essence of who he once was and fully commit it to his new identity. He believed he had a path to this end, but it would only come with great sacrifice, a sacrifice he was uncertain he would ever get the opportunity to make.

The responsibility was his. The blood flowing through his body came with an indoctrination, one laced with profound loyalty and a deep sense of commitment.

Yet there were differences. Where each of his ancestors fought against the constant assault of the Yankees, who wished to destroy the socioeconomic and social fabric of what was their way of life, he was more pragmatic in his approach. For him, this was not about righting an old wrong; it was about correcting and reversing the erosion of individual rights. His was not an anger based on antiquated ideas of lost institutions, but on the belief the nation had strayed far away from the founders' visions of what the country was supposed to be. It had lost its concept of liberty and individual rights. The North's victory was not about the freedom of an oppressed people but the reinstitution of a tyrannical environment they fought so hard against in their struggle to free themselves from Britain.

It was incomprehensible to the new William that so many went about their days in such an unconscious state. How could they be so unaware of what was happening to their rights? The federal government was eroding the peoples' privacy, taking away freedom of speech, encroaching on freedom of thought, finding ways to impede on every aspect of their lives.

The Civil War was the impetus. Slavery was just the distraction, the fiery object that pulled peoples' attention away from the true issue, and still, politicians and historians continued to miss the mark. Slavery was a symptom, the festering boil that Unionist maintained their focus on rather than looking at the cherished document that was the basis of the Southern argument and that they all claimed to share as a sacred script. It was conveniently ignored and continually overlooked as the immorality of that ancient institution was the mark rather than the very set of laws that were created to protect individual sovereignty. This was about the Constitution. The Southern states acted upon their constitutional rights to secede. They understood this was just the beginning, the states' right to determine their own destiny and for their citizens to live in true freedom from an oppressive government was being threatened, pushed to the brink of extinction.

It was happening again. Slavery was gone, but now there was something more the government wanted. It desired complete control; the National Security Agency, the CIA, the FBI, and other government entities spying on their own people, monitoring phone calls, checking internet searches, peering at us through satellites and the endless array of cameras documenting every part of the citizenry's lives, was the final step in a process that began over a century and a half ago.

Terrifying as this seemed, the final act of this governmental odyssey was destined to play out. It was just a matter of time. It could not continue. A second reckoning was needed. The conflict that began in 1861 was not over. They would see the result, an act of change beyond comprehension. He just needed the location. He needed the final clues. He knew the legends.

Where were the rest of the instructions that he carried? He knew he had to find them. The stories passed down were valid. *What did he know? Where did it go? I must keep searching!*

He would keep his eyes open. He would use the government's tools to find what he needed. Somewhere, someone would come across the piece of the puzzle he needed.

It has value.

Chapter 11

Savannah, Georgia

There was something about this place that put him at ease. Every image, every color flooded his senses and brought peace. The homes had an ethereal quality; a mixture of colonial style with Southern plantation added an almost regal feature. Even the trees seemed to be designed to reach into the soul and smooth its rough edges.

One of Des's fondest memories was holding his father's hand as they walked through the beautiful tree-lined trails of Forsythe Park. The elegant arches their branches created over the pathway made the young boy feel as if he was at his coronation.

He had rented a small apartment not too far from the Savannah Historical Foundation. Even though he had a bicycle, he preferred to walk, letting the memories of those holidays he took with his father cascade upon him. As he made his trek down York Street toward the olive-colored building with the white trim, Des found it hard to contain his excitement. He truly felt this would give him some inspiration about what he wanted to pursue in his life.

He didn't know quite what to wear; after all, this was not an interview. He was a volunteer. He decided to try to pull off the typical college look, wearing khakis and a light-blue oxford shirt. He approached the building, brushing back his sandy-brown hair with his hand and then walked up the steps. Opening the door, he saw a pleasant-looking woman who appeared to be in her early sixties and smiled with disarming Southern charm.

"Hello, can I help you?" she said, peering over the top of her glasses.

"Yes, hello. I'm Desmond Cook. I'm here for the preservation project."

"Oh, yes, thank you for coming. We've been trying to get more volunteers. We have so much to do. Stuff has been coming in every week, and we're so far behind in trying to catalog everything."

"Well, that's why I'm here," Des said enthusiastically.

"Oh, very good," she said, lightly clapping her hands. "My name is Frances, but everybody calls me Fran."

"It's a pleasure to meet you. I'm excited to get to work."

"Well, let's get you started, then," she said, motioning for Des to follow. "This is our back room. Oh, are you good at using the computer?"

"I'm pretty good. I'm not an expert, but I think I do okay."

"Actually, we need someone who's good at the computer and scanner. I'm terrible. Not my generation, I guess," she said with a grin.

"I've scanned papers for my classes."

"That should suffice. You see, what the foundation is trying to do is preserve our history going back as far as about 1850. We've been collecting pictures, documents, letters… all sorts of things from various people. Some come from libraries, others from private donations, and so forth. The problem is, many of the things we get are so old or have changed hands so many times we don't know what we're looking at. Others, like this photo," she said, picking up a tattered old picture out of a cardboard box on the floor, "are deteriorating to such a point that we're afraid we're going to lose them. So the idea is to try to scan everything so they can be preserved and researched."

"It sounds like an important job."

"It is, Desmond. There's so much we've not gone through. We have boxes like this all over the place. There's more in the next room."

"Am I the only one working on this project?"

"Oh, heavens, no, honey. We have quite a few people coming in, but we still don't have enough. We hope to get more in the next week or so. We have ads out on the college campuses and on the internet. Do you want to give it a try?" she said, eagerly gesturing to the computer.

"Sure, I'll give it a go." Des took the photo from Frances's hand, walked over to the workstation, and carefully placed it on the scanner. Then he walked back to the computer and clicked on the program. "Let's see here. I think I need to click here and then check this to make sure everything is ready and… click here." The scanner hummed. Des smiled and looked back at Frances. "I think I got it."

"I think you do."

He spent the next hour scanning some old letters written during the Spanish American War. He did not read a lot of them, but most seemed to be to the quartermaster complaining about the lack of rations.

Des left in the evening and went to the local coffee shop to jot down some ideas for his master's thesis paper. He also stopped by a bookstore and picked up a crossword puzzle book to occupy his time when he ran out of patience with his studies. Des loved puzzles, and even though he was an excellent student, he often felt he would have been better served as an investigator trying to solve crimes rather than a historian. It was his inquisitive nature about mysteries that fascinated him.

Although he never admitted it to his classmates, and certainly not to any of his professors, he always loved the quirky side of history, the myths and legends. Those stories were often frowned upon by academia as not serious historical study or use of resources. They saw it as giving in to an Indiana Jones fantasy rather than actual research. Yet he enjoyed them, and while he would never use them as part of any academic submission, he certainly saw no harm in being entertained by them. So while his serious side would always be on display for his academic career, the mythology and mysteries of history would always make up his soul.

Chapter 12

Capitol View, Virginia

He sat in his room, night after night, and checked. Nothing was there. After returning from another reenactment, the young man who wished to be known as William stared at his computer, going through his specialty spying program, trying to find whether anyone had searched his key words. He glared in frustration at the lifeless screen. Once again, he had run the program and, once again, had drawn a blank.

He glanced up at the shelves above his computer. They were strewn with books covering every inch of Civil War history. Yet even though he reveled in examining the past, the books were useless, failing to provide what he desired.

Maybe I missed something. He closed his eyes, trying to recall the details. Taking another sip of tea, he took a deep breath. *Maybe not tonight, but it's out there.*

There was not much to go on, only what had been passed down through family stories.

In March of 1864, General Lee received an urgent telegram. The government of the Confederacy had to be moved. In a shocking development, a Union colonel was killed a few miles outside the Confederate capital of Richmond. Not realizing the importance of this individual, the body was not immediately buried. A young boy rummaging through the pockets of the Northern officer came across a set of documents and delivered them to his teacher, a captain in the Confederate Army. These papers would change the course of the war.

The documents included orders revealing a plan to exterminate the president of the Confederacy and his entire staff and cabinet. Then they were to burn Richmond to the ground. It was an unbelievable breach of what was considered to be the most sacred of military etiquettes. Until that time, civilian heads of state were not to be targeted under any circumstances.

This change in Northern policy could have only come from the very highest echelons of the Union government. Without enough military force to protect the Confederate capital, drastic action needed to be taken. They needed to move.

Yet along with the people, there were other items of great importance, namely the Confederate treasury. Gold and silver from allies in Mexico and France were maintained in Richmond and needed to be transported and hidden. If Union troops were to take possession, the entire Confederacy would go bankrupt, no longer having the funds to continue the struggle.

Jefferson Davis had only a few people in mind who would have the resources and skill to pull this off successfully. They needed to be contacted, and that message needed to be kept secret. After speaking with a few of his advisers, he believed he found the ideal location. Fearing a written message falling into the wrong hands would expose them, Davis codified the information to be understood only by those for whom it was intended. He also needed their most reliable courier, William Hatton, to deliver the message.

That was where the story ended. To this day, no one knew what happened to the Confederate treasury. The legend was well-known, and there had been theories, most prevalent of which was that it was buried in Danville, Virginia. However, only circumstantial evidence had been produced, nothing verified.

Now, over a century and a half later, this generation's William Hatton was continuing the search. For years, he had researched documents and stories. He knew this wealth would fulfill his dreams, everything he had envisioned for a new independence, the way of life Americans were meant to lead. He could reverse the deterioration of his beloved country.

Most of what was public record only led to dead ends, but he had another resource, his ancestor's diary. Contained therein were clues the general public was not privy to, and as he got older, he believed it had presented him an avenue, a way for him to change the direction of the nation. It obsessed his thoughts.

The diary sparingly recounted his ancestor's duty. It referenced the assignment of an important mission for President Davis. The writing had almost a frantic feel. The capital was "about to be besieged," and he was charged with the task of helping in the evacuation of all items that could be useful to the enemy.

While it was fascinating reading, it provided little help in deciphering a location of where this wealth possibly resided. However, throughout his writings of the impending danger, there were two pieces of information that had William's mind racing.

> *I understand the importance of this journey, and like they do, I understand how the legacy of the father will hold their place.*

This statement always seemed peculiar. Like many in his family, his great-great-grandfather was a man of faith. While this seemed an apparent religious reference, it somehow did not fit. As he continued to turn the pages, William was struck by another passage.

> *I know what I have been ordered to do, and I know what this is for, but the details seem to be more than just about the transferring of monies. There was one verbal instruction I was given, and that was to make sure that my contact knew that he was "to protect this wealth from those who try to take it, and in their attempts, may they encounter a chasm of destruction." I'm not sure what that means, but I will deliver the message. I will perform my duty.*

Such an odd passage. Was this a metaphor? William had his beliefs. Most importantly, he had the devotion to find this treasure. It was his obsession, and he would have his prize.

Chapter 13

Savannah, Georgia, May 20

Des was savoring every part of life in Savannah. There was a sense of freedom in it. Every day it was like returning to the well of what made history such a wonder to study.

He had been volunteering four times a week for the past several months. His work consisted of scanning documents and old photographs, many of them well over a hundred and fifty years old, into the foundation's database in order to preserve them for posterity as well as create a rich treasure trove of information for researchers and historians. He had already made a small group of new friends, and unlike his previous experience, he did not encounter the alienation his separation of age brought him at the university. Many of the volunteers were over thirty years old or at least in their late twenties, and they had much more to talk about than just how plastered they got over the weekend.

Each day he made the journey to the foundation, he took in the beauty of the oak trees with their Spanish moss draping off their branches. The imagery was iconic to the South, and their spiritual effect was something he had only known as a young child. He was finding peace in Savannah and hoped it was permanent.

"Hey, Fran, how are you this morning? I got you some coffee," he said, handing her the hot drink as he entered.

"You're such a dear, Des. Thank you."

"Always my pleasure. Any new arrivals today?"

"There were a couple of new boxes brought in yesterday. I think mainly Civil War era. Madison and Josh are back there, already working on it."

"Okay, thanks."

Des always enjoyed working with Madison and Josh. They both shared his love of history. Josh was from the Atlanta area and had moved to Savannah with his wife and young son six years ago. He worked in a sporting goods shop and was the coach of his son's Little League team. Extremely active in the community, Josh was always encouraging others to get involved with local charitable entities.

Madison Callum was a thirty-two-year-old divorcée who came to Savannah a little over two and a half years ago after the failure of her marriage. She was originally from Tennessee, born and raised just outside Nashville. The only child of Raymond and Katherine Callum, she grew up in a lower-middle-class black neighborhood about three miles from the railway station where her father worked. Her mother was employed as a receptionist at a dental office and taught Sunday school at their Episcopal church. Both parents highly valued education and instilled that love of learning in the young Madison.

An extremely shy and sensitive youngster who usually preferred spending her days reading books under the dogwood tree in their backyard, Madison differed from the other kids in the neighborhood, who chose to play on the streets or visit the local swimming hole. Quiet, kind, and gentle, the young girl was introspective, but also insecure, which gave off an awkward vibe.

As she made her way through junior high and high school, that lack of confidence received no help from the superficial world of teenagers. Skinny, with thick glasses and braces her parents could barely afford, she was often the victim of cruel jokes and taunts by her classmates, only making her reinforce the shell she built around herself.

Her one outlet was her academic prowess. Committing herself to her studies, she fought through the pain of her social ineptitude, which eventually led her to becoming one of the most outstanding students at her school.

After graduation, she accepted an academic scholarship to attend the University of Tennessee—Chattanooga. Madison loved the environment, and it was there the gawky and introverted child went through a pronounced transformation. Gone were the glasses and braces, and her once unstyled, matted hair became a beautiful arrangement of curls that dangled gracefully onto her shoulders. The boy-like body, which had been an object of derision, was replaced by a slender yet distinctly feminine one that was both attractive and alluring. However, even with her physical metamorphosis, she had a shy naivete, creating vulnerabilities.

One thing that didn't change was her academic drive. An African American history major with a focus on the Harlem Renaissance period, she continued to excel in her studies, impressing fellow students and professors alike.

Yet despite the fact her educational pursuits allowed her to continue to succeed in arenas of which she was already familiar, for better or worse, it also introduced her to experiences in which she had little background. The dating world was one of those she was ill prepared to take on. In retrospect, Madison was primed to fail.

With her being away from home and finally attracting attention from the opposite sex, the stage was set for mistakes. Toward the end of her freshman year, she became enamored with a handsome psychology student, Marvin Tillman. They met while standing in line at the college bookstore, and after their first date, the two were inseparable. Marvin was four years older and had already entered graduate school, easily wowing the impressionable girl.

As the two grew closer, Madison put her own goals on hold, and even though she graduated at the top of her class, she decided to forego her plans to get advanced degrees and opted to marry Marvin just a few months removed from her commencement.

For the first few years, things appeared to be going smoothly. Madison worked as a hostess at a local restaurant and was later employed doing clerical work for a law firm. Marvin completed his studies, earning his PhD, and started building a successful psychology practice.

He was extremely driven and rapidly earned an income that allowed for luxuries Madison had never been able to indulge in previously. Marvin continued to expand his endeavors, combining his practice with other psychologists, authoring books, doing consulting work, and even providing a weekly column to a few regional newspapers. It seemed his ambition had no end. But unfortunately, that same ambition applied to women.

After catching him in several affairs, Madison, being insecure, was desperate to try to patch up their marriage. She tried counseling, changing her habits, changing her looks and investigated everything she could to spice up things in the bedroom. Her emotions were in shambles, fluctuating between resentment and self-blame. As much as she tried, though, she could not stop her marriage's death spiral. The final straw came when she discovered Marvin in their bed with the shapely neighbor from across the street.

The divorce was bitter, hurtful, and messy. But she did walk away with enough money to get her own apartment and return to school. She picked up right where she had left off and received her doctorate in history with honors.

Yet school drained a great deal of the money she was awarded in the divorce settlement. There were few opportunities where she lived, so she began looking in other places. Searching the internet, she came across a posting for a part-time faculty position at Savannah State University. She applied and, within six weeks, was offered two classes. It was hardly enough to live on, but at least she had been able to get her foot in the door.

She immersed herself in her teaching. Sharpening her skills, she became an excellent lecturer and received high marks on her end-of-the-semester reviews. She volunteered for research projects and was receptive of critiques by her fellow instructors. It was her hope the valuable experience she attained would lead to a full-time position. It didn't happen.

As she applied for job after job, the rejections began piling up. It wasn't just losing out on full-time positions that was so disheartening, but whom she was losing them to. Young graduates in their mid-twenties with little or no teaching experience on their résumés were being awarded assignments, while Madison was left in limbo, wondering how many part-time classes she would be able to scrape together. There were times she believed she had a position locked up, only to see it slip through her fingers in the interview process. Humiliation began to build while her confidence started to wane.

Ashamed to go back home a failure, she found additional work, taking a hostess gig at a seafood restaurant. She continued to teach her two classes, but her failure to obtain a full-time position haunted her. Having no support structure only exacerbated her frustration.

Since her rapid relocation to Savannah, most of her social life consisted of acquaintances rather than friends. Her fellow professors were much older and played the role of colleagues instead of people she would feel comfortable confiding in. Most of her evenings were spent accompanied by macaroni-and-cheese dinners and a glass of wine in front of her small television. Her days were even less eventful. Going on her morning run, reading the paper with a cup of coffee, and then waiting to leave for the college or restaurant was what made up the bulk of her daily schedule.

Before the spring semester, her luck took a turn for the worse. She was informed that due to recent cutbacks, one of her two classes was being canceled. It was another shot to her already-faltering self-confidence, not to mention her pocketbook.

With few other prospects, she fell into despair. She called her mother in hopes of a sympathetic ear, but the response she received was completely unexpected. The advice was curt and simple: "Stop feeling sorry for yourself and find a purpose." At first, it stuck like a knife. Yet after a few days of sulking, Madison decided to look for other opportunities.

In the morning paper, she came across an ad for volunteers to work on a restoration project at the Savannah Historical Foundation. With the words of her mother still ringing in her ears, she decided to take control. That day, she marched to the foundation offices and put in her name.

She had only been at the foundation for three weeks when a young man came walking in with a cautious gait. He was white, about six feet tall, with sandy-brown hair and a strong, distinctive chin. He was trim, but not bony. His mouth and cheeks displayed warmth, especially when he smiled, and his hazel-colored eyes conveyed tenderness while, at the same time, appearing to be hiding a deep sorrow.

Yet what really caught her attention was his sharp intellect and passion for history. He took pure joy in immersing himself in the past with an intensity that could only be matched by her own.

Des and Madison soon became friends and, at times, were even flirtatious. However, their insecurities and stations in life kept it at just that. Both had their reasons, and it was those reasons that only allowed things to go so far.

But as the weeks went by, her fondness for him grew. She had not allowed herself such indulgences since the failure of her marriage. And while she did not show those feelings, it nonetheless was comforting for her to know that she was still capable of them.

At the very least, she had found a true friend. Not a colleague or an acquaintance, but a kindred spirit. But there was a sadness she sensed in him, a part he seemed to protect. Madison would never pry, but it bothered her that he shared so little of his past, always reluctant to give too much of himself away. It was that mysteriousness that intrigued her and always kept her wanting to know more. It was her hope such an opportunity would present itself.

Chapter 14

Newport News, Virginia

Their slight gleam was part of the attraction. He had collected them for years, a hobby that brought the past to the present. It made him long for a simpler time, when things were not so complicated by technology and instantaneousness.

His job was one of tremendous responsibility, a position that most of society held in high esteem. It wasn't enough. He wanted more. Something was missing, but unlike so many who wandered in a daze, looking for the meaning of life, his desire was not so convoluted.

He wanted his chance at greatness. He needed an opportunity to prove he was more than just a professional dispenser of judgment. More than just a functionary of the court. He desired to be placed alongside the legendary names in history, the ones who had etched their identities into the fabric of world consciousness.

He had not found it yet. He knew the avenue and had taken steps in the right direction, but he was stalled, waiting for another. It was frustrating knowing his progress was dependent on one so young and inexperienced. *How did I end up in the position?*

If anyone knew his life goal was completely reliant on a kid, they would laugh. He was always in command. He always had the final say. But not now.

In times of quiet desperation, he would look for inspiration. In this room, he would find the meaning behind his drive.

No one will get in my way. I've proven that.

This thought was reinforced as he picked up the Civil War knife. It was one of the most prized in his collection. The legend spoke of it being carried by a young Confederate who had supposedly used it to kill a Union commander. As he gripped the hilt, he felt its power. He felt the raw emotion that must have driven its previous owner.

May that same passion keep infecting me.

Chapter 15

Savannah, Georgia

"Hey, guys, I heard we got some new stuff in," Des said as he started to open one of the boxes on the floor.

"Yeah, we've been going through it. Josh found a photo of someone who looks like you," Madison said, smiling.

"Oh, really? I can't wait to see this," he replied, rolling his eyes.

Josh handed it over. It was a Civil War photo of a young soldier who had scruffy hair that looked like it had never been brushed and two of his front teeth missing. Other than a small resemblance in the eyes, Des saw nothing of himself in this young man.

"Really, this looks like me?"

"Oh, yeah, you can see he has the same face shape as you," Josh said.

"Oh, come on, he looks nothing like me. His face looks like he made his living as a boxer and he lost every fight," Des said, grinning.

"Josh, let me see that again," Madison asked, reaching her hand out. "Well, I don't know. I can see some resemblance. Hmm, well, maybe not. No, you're right, Des, he's much better-looking than you," she said playfully, winking at him.

"Thanks for the vote of confidence," Des answered sarcastically. "So what are most of these of?"

"The majority of them are pictures of Civil War soldiers. They need IDs. You're usually pretty good at that. There are quite a few documents in here as well. Why don't you take the soldiers and I'll work on the documents?" Madison suggested.

"Hey, I'm going to finish this one up and then I have to get going," Josh said, checking his watch.

"Why are you leaving the party so early?" asked Des.

"Anniversary tonight. My wife would kill me if I was late for our dinner reservations."

"For God's sake, get going, then. I'll finish this up," Madison said, practically shoving Josh out the door. "I would kill you too. Go home and have a nice, romantic evening."

"Okay… thanks," he said, exiting the room.

"I guess it's just you and me. The two lonely souls without a social life," she said, smiling at Des as she started to sort through the box for more items.

"How are the job prospects at the university? Any news?"

Madison sighed. "No, unfortunately not too much to report. I'll be lucky if I get a couple of classes this semester. How about you? What's going on? Have you figured out what you're going to do your thesis paper on?"

"I have some ideas, but nothing in stone. I better figure it out soon, or I won't have enough time."

Des continued to scan pictures while Madison worked on documents, making small talk that touched on the edge of flirting. It was tedious work, but both of them found it a mental respite from the stress of their daily lives.

Des was finding the new batch of pictures to be more challenging than previous ones. Most of them were early daguerreotype photos of soldiers, and because they were made of tin, they were oftentimes more difficult to scan. Many of them were oxidized, and without proper preservation, they would be damaged beyond recognition. Madison was also having every bit of a difficult time as she continued to meticulously handle the fragile documents and scan them into the database.

"Oh, wow, this is going to be tough one to scan," he said as he pulled another photo out of the box. "I don't see too many of them framed like this anymore."

It was quite common during the war for soldiers to carry pictures of their families and loved ones. Many of them were kept in small frames that protected them from the elements. However, over the years, a great deal of them had been removed from their holders. Even though Des could appreciate the uniqueness of finding one still in its frame, it also made it more difficult to scan, as the frame prevented the picture from being placed flush against the glass of the scanner.

Des went into the tool drawer and pulled out the special tweezers made for performing this very operation. The picture showed a man and woman who appeared to be in their mid-forties. Most likely, they were married, and this was either carried by the husband or son of the couple. Des momentarily stared at the photo, attempting to get a sense of what these people must have been like. No matter how many of these pictures he had seen, he was always touched by the humanity of the those affected during that horrible conflict.

He then examined the frame, looking for the best way to extract the picture without damaging it or the encasement. Running his his fingers around the edge, he looked for a gap, and as he placed his index finger on the bottom of the frame, the break in the contour of its structure became evident. *That's where it must have been inserted.*

He turned the frame over and delicately inserted the tweezers into the opening until he could feel them grip the edge of the photograph. Gently pulling, it was not an easy task. It was tightly wedged but gradually began to release its hold. He continued to slide it upward when suddenly something fell onto the table at the moment the photo was freed from its casing.

What the hell is that?

Placing the picture on the table, he studied what had fallen. It appeared to be a folded piece of parchment, brownish in color, with some type of staining near its edges. Turning it over, he took a deep breath and slowly began unfolding it. With every position he placed it in, he could hear it crinkling, causing him to wince in the process. He repeated the action until only one fold remained. Des bit down on his upper lip, as if it were helping. He then undid the last fold.

What appeared before him was a set of confusing sentences faded to the point of being nearly indecipherable. Brownish stains covered the top, impairing his ability to read some of the writing.

He murmured the first sentence at the top of the page, "The instructions are simple." What followed made little sense.

"Hey, Madison, could you come over here for a second?"

"What's up?"

"This paper fell out of the back of this frame. Your eyes are better than mine. Can you make any of this out?"

Madison leaned over Des's shoulder, peering down at the brown paper. "The instructions are simple," she said, puzzled. Then she looked more closely, slowly reading the lines that followed.

> *Burned in the first revolution, the mark is represented in the pillars of our faith in the home of the beginning of the second.*

> *It lies shallow at the pinnacle of the single Roman Vestige, a half of Vara.*

> *The bows that lay at its entrance suggest lineage of leadership.*

"What is this?" she asked.

"I don't know. Like I said, it just fell out of the back of that frame. It says they're instructions, but to what, I have no idea," Des said, staring at the paper.

"Is it poetry?"

"Maybe, but I've never seen any poetry like this, and that wouldn't explain why it says the 'instructions are simple.'"

Madison continued to study the first line. "These stains don't look like dirt, and they're definitely not mildew."

"Rust?"

"Possibly, but I don't see much rust on this frame," she said, studying the tin holder. "It kind of looks like dried blood. That stain is covering some of the writing at the top. Do you see?"

Des nodded. "Could you grab the magnifying glass for me?" he asked, gesturing toward a drawer. Madison returned, handing it to Des. He held it over the top of the paper, adjusting the height to give him the best perspective. The top line started to come into better focus, and he could see there was definitely some writing obstructed by the stain. But it was still difficult to make out. The ink had faded to brown, nearly matching the color of the paper and the stain. In the mid 1800s, iron gall ink was the medium used for writing. Over the years, as the iron in the ink oxidized, it would turn the color of rust, sometimes making old documents very difficult to read and especially difficult if they were stained with matching colors of other substances.

He continued focusing his full attention on the top line when he noticed a blemish near the letter *i* of the word *simple* and another by the *e*. "What is that?" The more he looked, the more clarity came. Then it hit him, as if someone had struck him a physical blow. "Oh my god! You gotta be kidding me!"

"What? What is it?"

"It can't be," he said, examining it once again. He thought it might be his imagination, but it was definitely real.

"Tell me, what is it?" she asked excitedly.

"It doesn't say 'The instructions are simple,' it says 'The instructions are Semple's.'"

"I don't understand. Why is that important?" She knew Des had found something, but this change in the word was not significant to her, being that her expertise was in times over sixty years later. "What is Semple's?" she questioned, almost begging for an answer.

"It's not a what, it's a who. I can't believe this. He was put in charge, but there was never any trace of it."

"Trace of what, Des? What the hell are you talking about? Tell me!"

Des's eyes were dancing wild in his head as he continued to look up and down the weathered document. Smiling, he turned to Madison. "During the Civil War, as you know, the Confederate capital was in Richmond, Virginia. But in the spring of 1864, they were forced to move it. But they had one big problem. The entire treasury had to be moved as well. All their wealth... their gold... all their silver reserves had to be evacuated so it wouldn't fall into Union hands." Des moved over to his computer. "It's easy to move people, but moving that much material was nearly impossible. Jefferson Davis knew he needed to find a way to move the gold and silver a long distance without being seen. According to all the historical records, he entrusted the job to a Navy officer. His name was James Semple. They moved it out of Richmond to transfer it to Semple. He was then supposed to transport all of it to a hidden location in Canada or Europe."

"So what happened to it?" asked Madison, with thrill written all over her face.

"Well, that's just it, no one knows. It just disappeared. Some say it was dispersed. Some say that Semple spent it. There are some legends saying it was buried in Danville, Virginia, but there is only circumstantial evidence of that, and that legend only concerns the silver and not the gold. Many believe it's still hidden somewhere, but there has never been any credible evidence to point the way. The treasury would be worth multimillions today just in its metallic value alone, not to mention its historical value. People have been looking for it for over a hundred and fifty years, but no new clues have ever materialized."

"Until now," she said, smiling.

"Well, I don't want to get ahead of ourselves. I'm not sure what this is, and we don't know what this means. A guy like Semple would have received hundreds of orders over the course of the war. We can't assume this has to do with the missing treasure. Plus, there's no date on this message. It could have been sent at any time, but it's intriguing, I'll give you that."

Des leaned over his keyboard and started to type in searches. First, he typed in" James Semple." Information he already knew came up: an officer in the Confederate Navy, confidant of Jefferson Davis, date of birth and death, and other general information one would expect to find in any history book. Next, he entered the words "Lost treasure of the Confederacy." The first search results focused on the quantity of silver. It was from cotton sales to Mexico, amounting to nine thousand silver coins, and would have been impossible to transport quietly. Most theories, according to the website, had the silver buried in Danville, just as Des had mentioned earlier. However, there was no accounting for the gold.

"What about what these other lines say?" Madison asked, pointing to the paper.

"I don't know how they relate to Semple. I'll try to get some info." He rapidly typed in, "Semple and first revolution," "Semple and faith," "Semple and revolution," and finally, "Semple and Roman," but nothing of value appeared on the screen. The pair continued their search for the next several hours, completely ignoring their jobs. Yet their efforts provided no additional facts, legends, or associated events.

"I want to figure this out, but I don't want to do it here," he said, suspiciously looking at his surroundings. "Can you meet me for coffee at about eight?"

Madison nodded. "Yeah, the Foxy Loxy?"

"I'll see you there," Des said, carefully slipping the paper into a manila folder and putting it inside his coat. They calmly walked toward the exit. "Good night, Fran. We'll see you in a couple of days."

"Good night, you two."

As they headed down the foundation steps, they glanced at each other. It was just a moment, but it spoke volumes. Both of them had a sense they had discovered something unusual, and although they had no proof this document had any value whatsoever, the historian in them both felt that even if it was just for a moment, they were about to share in something significant. The excitement of not knowing was maybe the best part. That was when all was possible.

Chapter 16

The Foxy Loxy is a local Savannah coffee shop and restaurant that's more upscale and has a unique, independent, noncorporate feel that differs from the national ones that had sprouted up all across the country. Its patrons reflected sophisticated qualities. Along with its java, food, and assorted drinks, it also featured wonderful artists displaying their works in a gallery that changed each month. Both Des and Madison enjoyed its atmosphere and found it much more toward their intellectual liking than the local tourist hangouts.

Des had stopped by his apartment to change before trekking down to their meeting spot. On the short journey, he kept going over the sentences in his mind. *How are any of these items related?* He drew a blank. Nothing added up. He continued to mull it over when an epiphany struck him just as he entered the restaurant. He scanned the warm decor until he saw Madison's curly hair. She was sitting at a table in the back of the room, her face buried in her smartphone.

"Hi! Any luck?" he asked as he pulled the chair out.

"No, nothing, but I guess I really don't know what I'm doing."

"You know, I think we're going about this the wrong way. We've been trying to see if there are any connections between Semple and some key words in those underlying sentences. But we keep forgetting the first line, 'The instructions are Semple's.' Obviously, these were meant to be delivered to him and he never received them. He was military. These are instructions,… orders. We have to start looking at these independently and try to figure out what they each mean."

"Well, let's look at the first instruction, then."

Des took the folder out of his jacket. At that moment, a waitress approached their table. He looked up nervously at first, withholding pulling out the contents. Noticing Des's reaction, Madison quietly chuckled to herself.

"Can I get you something, sir?"

"Sure, coffee and um… do you want dessert? You like apple pie?"

"That sounds good." Madison smiled.

"Two coffees and two apple pies, please." Des continued to eye the waitress until she left the table.

"I think the coast is clear," Madison said with another giggle.

Des smiled back and laughed. "Point taken."

"So you were saying you think we need to look at each instruction individually?"

"Yes. Like I said, these were military men. They were used to following orders exactly as given. Jefferson Davis knew this. He understood whatever orders he gave, they would be followed to the letter."

"Okay, let's read the first one."

Des took the paper out and placed it in front of them. "All right, let's see here. 'Burned in the first revolution, the mark is represented in the pillars of our faith in the home of the beginning of the second.'" Des gestured to the paper. "Well, there's something that jumps out at me right away. Here it says, 'Burned in the first revolution.' That's obviously a reference to the American Revolution. Then it says, 'In the home of the beginning of second.' Many in the South referred to the Civil War as the Second Revolution."

Madison looked at the sentence again and started to repeat the line to herself. "'The home of the beginning of the second…' 'Home of the beginning…' I see what you're saying. If they're talking about the 'home of the beginning,' they must be talking about where the Civil War started, Fort Sumter!"

Then there was a pause before they looked at each other. "South Carolina," they said, nearly in unison.

"This other part, I don't understand. *The mark is represented in the pillars of our faith,*" he said, confused.

"Well, let's break it down. What things are associated with faith?"

"The Bible, God, a minister."

"Yeah, but I'm not sure those are things we should consider."

"Why's that?"

"They're too portable or they're not permanent structures. The word *pillars* suggests something concrete, a physical point of reference."

"You're right," Des said, running his hands through his hair, trying to think of the next path they should take. "Wait a minute, a physical structure... a church!"

"That would make sense. Churches were a central part of the Southern life during that time." Then she sighed. "One problem, though, there were probably a hundred churches or houses of worship all over South Carolina back then. Every small town had one, if not more. It could be any of them."

"Yes, that's a problem." Des pondered other possibilities. "Wait," he said, nearly knocking over his coffee. "I think we're looking at this too figuratively. *Pillars* is not something that was meant to be taken in the abstract. It's part of the physical structure of the church itself. I can't imagine there were too many churches back then that had pillars. Most churches of the time would have been wooden house-like structures, or even schoolhouses. Can you check on your phone?"

Madison eagerly grabbed her phone and started typing away. She used the specific key words for her search, "Church burned, South Carolina, Revolution." Immediately coming up were matches for one specific house of worship, Old Sheldon Church. She clicked on the link. Her mouth gaped open.

"What is it?" Des asked.

Madison turned her phone around, showing him the display. There in her hand was a picture of Old Sheldon Church. It was a burned-out relic, but what did remain was a set of classical Greek-style pillars. "I guess we're going to South Carolina."

Chapter 17

Capitol View, Virginia

The young man who called himself William walked into his house and marched into the kitchen to make tea. Not one for wasted motion, he believed every action should have intent. In order for an individual to attain what they desired, it required total application of thought and movement.

For years, he had been searching, looking for information to fill the gap in his knowledge. He had ravenously researched, reading every book, examining every piece of material available on the missing wealth of the Confederacy. But the result was always the same, a dead end.

Last week, he had driven to Washington, DC, and visited the Library of Congress. He found nothing to enlighten him. Every bit of information he came across was previously known. The efforts of President Davis to move the nine thousand pieces of silver, his contacts in Georgia who were to move the gold out of Savannah, and the stories of James Semple's denial of hiding the treasure were all well recorded.

All he could do was attempt to find people who had discovered new details that would allow him to continue the search. Yet rather than feel despair, he felt hope. The amazing world of the internet provided something no library could, access to people. He recognized that someone in that universe would provide him the information he desired, and most likely, it would be completely inadvertent.

So once again, William went through the ritual. Turning on the computer, he logged into his program designed to search the searches. With each implementation, he checked on what people were accessing. Although he had his key words, it was still an arduous task. The software his accomplice provided was not a scalpel but a broadsword, picking up every minute detail, requiring him to sift through a proverbial melting pot of information. This time, there were the college students in Texas searching the key words "lost treasure" and "Confederate," the random search in Washington state for "James Semple," and even one in his home state of Virginia who looked up "Danville treasure." Nothing was useful. Another wasted night.

He needed new key words; otherwise, these fruitless searches would continue. William went back to the only resource unique to him, his great-great-grandfather's journal. Maybe there was something he overlooked, some piece of information, some reference that would crystalize his search.

Turning the tattered pages, William studied every word, every line. *There has to be more.* Yet, all he saw were mundane references to routine parts of every Civil War soldier's life. Speaking with comrades around a campfire, complaints about the rations, and the never-ending rhetoric about the hated Yankees.

Hold on! He never considered it before. He had always passed over it as unimportant, not representative of anything. It happened on the night his ancestor received orders from Jefferson Davis. He spoke of overhearing a conversation between the president and one of his subordinates. *Where is that passage?*

Turning the pages in an almost-rabid obsession, he frantically looked for the verses. Here was his great-great-grandfather receiving his orders from Lee to report to Richmond. Another mentioning the night he made camp on the way to his destination and the nervousness he felt as he heard Union soldiers in the distance. *That passage is close!*

Here it is! William excitedly read the paragraph. It was as if he had been transported to the very night William Hatton sat outside Jefferson Davis's office. He found what he needed.

> *The president was very upset tonight. I sat outside his office and could hear him yelling. He kept going on about the failure of the Army to keep the Yankees on the other side of the Potomac. He mentioned about sending someone, which*

turned out to be myself, to deliver the final message. I felt uncomfortable that I could hear his conversation but still waited outside, for those were my orders.

The president soon dismissed the gentleman and wished him good fortune. The gentlemen then stated that he will look for a sign that the gods will smile on them and that may the tunnels that lead us to the black sands of time revitalize the nation. I remember hoping for the same good fortune in my new assignment.

He had found it. *This is the clue!* He had previously overlooked it as the meaningless banter between two Southern gentlemen in the downward spiral of a lost cause. Now he could fortify his search.

Chapter 18

South Carolina

The drive from Savannah to Old Sheldon Church in Yemassee, South Carolina, was a relatively short one. Only about fifty miles north of Savannah, the journey could be made in a little over an hour on a straight shot down the highway. The main route, Interstate 95, is one of the oldest highways in the nation and one of the most scenic. Through Georgia, the traveler is met with marshlands and the Atlantic coastline as the road hugs the shore for much of the journey. With the moist air and wet spring times, foliage is green and vibrant most of the year.

Des and Madison took the day off their obligations and made the journey north. Ironically, they had no idea what they were searching for, but this trip was more about adventure, about living in the moment. As they continued their drive, Des started to get a feeling he hadn't experienced before. Even though he did not know how true purpose would present itself, somehow, this piece of tattered paper had given him a sense of direction. It was a little bewildering, but nonetheless, he reveled in the feeling.

"I feel kind of silly," Madison said as she peered outside, looking at the greenery as it passed her window.

"Yeah, I do, too, but I'm not sure why." He could see Madison deep in thought as she took in the sights. Her curly black hair swayed with the breeze coming through the slightly open window, her brown eyes fixated on the view, but not really focusing on anything.

"I'm trying to figure out why this is so important to me. I mean, I love history and all, but for whatever reason, this just seems ridiculous, like I'm playing some childhood game," Madison said as she felt an uncomfortable silence start to creep into the moment.

"I understand completely. For some reason, I really need to do this too. I mean, we study history, yet it's one of those fields that can become stagnant. Most of the time, we're just looking for new interpretations of old information that hundreds of historians have already discussed. Yet with all those books we've studied, somebody at some time had to be the first. I was always jealous that I could never be the first. I guess that's why I'm so intent on doing this."

"You make it sound like some type of calling," she said, smiling.

"You know," he said with a grin, "in a way, it kind of is. Ever since high school, I knew I wanted to continue my education, but I could never figure out what I was going to do with it. It's always frustrating, because I don't know the next chapter." Des's expression then changed. "I feel like I've wasted so much time. Maybe this little excursion we're taking is my way of not treading water."

Madison gazed at Des with an empathetic look. "I had all these goals in mind too. Then I met someone, thought I was in love, and did something really stupid… got married. That didn't work out at all. I put my entire life on hold, and by the time I realized what a mistake it was, I had passed on so many opportunities. I should have been a full-time professor by now. Instead, I'm trolling around, looking for scraps, and even though I know I'm not that old, I feel like I'm at a disadvantage because so many of the applicants for jobs I go up against have accomplished so much by the time they're twenty-five."

Des understood her feelings. He, too, experienced that same sense of loss. They both knew the curse of self-awareness.

"I think this is the exit," he said, looking at his directions.

"Well, this must be the place for us to find all the answers." Madison's expression was one of hope for affirmation more than of excitement. Deep down, she knew it would not accomplish that goal, but it would be a comfort knowing she was not passing up another opportunity.

Chapter 19

Yemassee, South Carolina

As they pulled off the interstate and made the turn down Old Sheldon Road, glimpses of the church came into view. The majestic aged structure reflected an orange-reddish glow as it bathed in the late-afternoon sunlight.

Old Sheldon Church was built in the Greek Classic Revival style, which was popular in the mid-1700s. Completed in 1753, it was originally named Prince William Parish Church. Funded and organized by William Bull, whose remains were interned at the center of structure, it was an integral part of Christian life in this part of the country during colonial and postcolonial times.

Like many historical sites in the South, it is surrounded in as much legend as fact. Most of its mythology stemmed from its current condition, a shell, with only the brick pillars and arches that maintain the original structure still standing. The church did have one renovation after 1779, when the British burned it to the ground in efforts to destroy its use as an arms depot during the American Revolution. Southerners later insisted its second destruction was owed to William Sherman's forces, as they set fire to it in his vengeful March to the Sea near the end of the Civil War. However, new evidence suggested that Union forces had little to do with it, as its current condition was most likely the result of being raided by local civilians who needed construction materials for their own homes. Today it serves as a haunting yet elegant reminder of early American architecture and was the backdrop for curious tourist and picturesque weddings.

They turned off Old Sheldon Road and drove into the parking lot adjacent to the structure. It was cool outside, and no other tourists were in sight. It was beautiful and, at the same time, eerie. Adding to its mysteriousness were the scattered graves surrounding the church. Some of its tombstones were tilted or sinking, giving it the aura of a haunted house.

"Wow, this is amazing!" exclaimed Madison as she exited the car.

"Yes, it is."

Madison approached the front of the church and examined the posted bronze tablet giving the landmark's biography. It had been placed there by various historical and community groups in 1937, and while it gave a short detailed history of the structure, it made sure the most prominent statement listed was that it was "burned by the Federal Army."

Even though they were excited to begin their search, their historical-minded makeups took over as they began to wander through the arches, running their hands down the rough bricks of the columns.

"We're definitely in the right place. The description fits that first clue perfectly," Des said.

"Yeah, that plaque kind of confirms it. That second clue, though, is not so clear. I don't understand what it means by 'Roman vestige.' Can you read me the second line again?"

Des carefully removed the paper from the folder. "'It lies shallow at the pinnacle of the single Roman vestige, a half of vara.' Do you see anything here, like a Roman symbol maybe?"

"I'm looking, but there's nothing on any of these bricks that I can see. No marks at all."

"Maybe it's on one of the gravestones."

"I'll go look," Madison said as she started to head toward the cemetery.

"I'll keep trying over here."

Des wandered in and out of the ruins, examining its walls, looking for any sign of a Roman marking. There were carvings in the bricks, none of which remotely related to Rome, and certainly much more recent, as many visitors had inscribed their names into their soft red surface. He continued looking when he noticed Madison's slender frame approaching. She had a confident walk that almost had an air of cockiness to it.

"Did you find anything?" he asked with hopefulness.

"Oh, yeah, I found something, all right."

"Really, where is it?"

"You're standing under it."

Des immediately looked up and scanned his field of view. "I don't see anything."

"I guarantee you it's there," said a brimming Madison.

Des kept searching for a plaque, a stone, anything. Nothing garnered his attention. Then it dawned on him, and he began to laugh. He was standing under the greatest example of Roman engineering, the arch. That was his vestige.

"Okay, we have it, but we have to figure out what that whole line means. It says, 'It lies shallow at the pinnacle of the of the single Roman vestige, a half of vara,'" Des reemphasized.

Once again, they perused the eighteenth-century structure, paying close attention to the arches, which made-up the eye-catching part of the ruins.

"That's it!" Des exclaimed. "Look, the front of the building has three arches, the sides have five each. Look at the back." He pointed to the rear of the structure. It contained one large-size arch that was completely different from the front and sides. "That has to be it."

Madison walked underneath it, staring up, almost in disbelief. "It says it lies underneath the pinnacle of the Roman vestige. It must mean the arch itself."

"What time is it?"

"It's about seven," Madison said, checking the time on her phone. "We probably have about fifteen to twenty minutes of light."

"I don't want to do this in daylight. This is a historical landmark. I don't think they would take too kindly to us digging right under the main structure."

"Well, what do you want to do?"

"Come back in about an hour, when it's dark."

Des and Madison sat on the ground against the wall that held up the back arch, staring at the ground, contemplating what they were about to undertake.

"There's one thing I don't understand. Who is *vara*?" Madison asked.

"That's about the only thing I did understand when we took the trip. Vara is not a name, it's a system of measurement that was used during colonial times. It's a little over two and a half feet."

"How did you know that?" Madison asked, impressed.

"At the university, I one time volunteered to go on an archeological dig in a colonial settlement. We had to learn old systems of measurement before we were allowed on the dig. Ironically, I did not find anything of interest. I never figured I would get any useful information out of it."

"So half of a vara would actually not be that deep. Wow, I always thought if there was something you wanted to hide that important, you would want it really well hidden, much deeper than one and a half feet."

"Well, whatever was hidden was probably not meant to be hard to access for those who were meant to find it. If Semple had to move the treasure quickly, he probably wouldn't want to spend his time digging all day, especially if Sherman's army was marching toward him."

"I just realized something. Do we have anything to dig with?"

"Well, you look like you have pretty strong hands," Des said, trying to feign a serious expression. Madison flashed him a sarcastic look. Des laughed. "When I realized that it said whatever it is we're looking for was shallow, at about half a vara, I kind of figured there might be some digging. I brought a small spade. It's in the trunk of my car."

As the sun sunk deeper into the horizon, both became very quiet, almost guarding their find. They knew they had to go in a few minutes, but there was a sense of vulnerability, that if somehow they did not protect the area, someone would pounce on the opportunity and take the precious item for themselves. They realized that was a ridiculous notion, yet this search was beginning to create a sense of uneasiness. They both had lost opportunities in their lives; they were going to be damned if anyone was going to take this one.

Chapter 20

Newport News, Virginia

"I told you not to call me unless it was urgent," he growled. "Encrypted text only! Why do you think I have the damn thing?"

"I'm paying you enough. You need to answer my calls," he retorted.

"I don't give a shit how much you're paying me," he scoffed. "I work on my own terms, and I set my own rules. If you don't like it, then you can go fuck yourself."

The Judge tightened his grip around the phone and bit down on his upper lip. No one talked to him like that, but he needed to choose his words carefully. This was not someone he could afford to lose. He breathed in deeply. "I'm sorry, it's just this whole goddamn thing has me off my game."

"Everything's under control. I told you I would take care of the problem. But you keep insisting there are things I don't know. I assure you, that's not the case. Remember, this is what I do."

The Judge clenched his free hand and pressed it firmly into his couch cushion, hoping its softness would muffle the blow, hiding his ever-growing frustration. "I can't afford any leaks."

"Yes, that's true, but it's your impatience that's going to blow this whole fucking thing up if you're not careful. You've already proven that."

"What should I do?"

He paused momentarily, running his hand through his coarse beard. "Just do like the old saying: keep your friends close and your enemies closer. You do know the difference, don't you?"

There was momentary silence. "Yes, I know the difference."

"Good, then text me when you need my services."

The Judge ended the call, got up, and walked out the sliding glass door onto his backyard patio. He rubbed the back of his neck and then pulled a thick Cuban stogie out of his shirt pocket and placed it between his dry lips. Chewing on the end of its pungent tip, he pulled it from his mouth and studied the label encircling its center, then momentarily watched the flickering glow at the end of his lighter while sucking in the thick smoke as he touched the flame to its end. It was a foolish mistake, lying to a man whose sole training had been centered on knowing when people were doing that very thing. Because truth be told, he wasn't sure he could tell the difference.

Chapter 21

Yemassee, South Carolina

Des and Madison returned to their car and left the parking lot to make sure they gave the appearance they were finished with their visit. They drove about half a mile down Old Sheldon Road. Finding a secluded street, Des pulled to the side of the road to await darkness.

"I sure hope whatever it is we're supposed to be looking for is there," Des said. "I'll feel like an idiot if it's not."

"Well, if we don't find anything, it was a lot of fun taking the trip up here. It sure beats the hell out of my typical day."

They waited another half hour, watching the narrow road leading to the church fade to black. As darkness enveloped them, the sounds of night started to emanate from the various creatures inhabiting the woods. Every pitch, every octave of noise became conglomerated into a musical mass.

"I guess it's time to make our way there," Des said as he opened his car door.

"We're going to walk?" Madison asked, slightly shocked.

"Yes, we're about to commit a crime. It probably would be best if we didn't drive into a quiet location with our headlights blazing."

"You have a point," Madison conceded.

As they proceeded down the road, a tad of moonlight helped them navigate their way. The sounds of nature swirling around them gave a sense of foreboding as they contemplated their upcoming task.

Des carried his spade in one hand and a flashlight in the other, which he used sparingly, fearing a bright light in so much darkness would draw attention. Madison felt herself gravitating over to Des, hoping his physical proximity would add some level of protection. As they drew within a couple hundred yards of the ruins, her hands began to tremble, a little from the excitement of discovery and a lot from the fear of getting caught.

Old Sheldon Church at night had a much-different feel than in the daytime. The ruins, majestic and beautiful in the sun, were ominous and menacing in the darkness. This, in addition to the fact that you had to pass through a cemetery to get to the structure itself, did not help in generating any warmth. Both of them slowed as the noise of the surrounding wilderness seemed to dissipate. The only sound was of their feet swishing through the grass. It was a sound of softness, which ended upon reaching the church, where that mild noise gave way to the harshness of their shoes stirring through the gravelly dirt within the ruin walls.

They quickly made their way over to the large arch making up the back part of the structure. Luckily, the day before, there was a light rain, softening the ground, which would make it easier to dig. Madison looked up, examining her position underneath the arch. The mark had to be directly underneath the pinnacle. She moved her head up and then down, repeating the motion several times before she felt certain she had located the spot.

"I think it's here," she said in a whisper while pointing to the ground.

Des got on his knees. Just before he pierced the soil with his spade, he looked at Madison with an expression signifying this was the point of no return. He then pushed the tool into the earth and pulled out a chunk of dirt. He looked around again, but all he could see was a wall of blackness extending into the distance. With every thrust of his spade, both of them could feel their paranoia increasing. He had excavated about twelve inches of earth but still having nothing to signify anything of importance. Though according to the clues, he still had a little ways to go.

Perspiration began beading on his forehead when they heard a rustle in the surrounding woods. Quickly they slid behind the wall. Des put his finger to his lips and tried to peer around the corner. Again, he heard a commotion, and this time he slid back so fast he smashed his skull against the bricks. It took nearly all his strength not to make any noise as the pain shot through the back of his head. Then Madison tried to take a glimpse. Having keener vision than her partner, she could make out an object moving in the distance, appearing to be two legs. Yet as she continued to observe, she could make out a torso, one that did not look human. Grabbing the flashlight from Des, she shone it in the direction of the object. As soon as the light found its mark, it scampered away. It was a deer.

Both breathing a sigh of relief, Des went back to his digging. Wanting to get out of there as quickly as possible, he hurried the pace, shoveling faster and faster until his spade hit something solid.

"I think there's something here," he said in excited whisper. "It's definitely not stone. It almost feels like wood. Hand me the flashlight."

He stuck the flashlight into the hole. Looking into the small crevice, he could see something, and it definitely was not a tree root. Increasing his efforts, he looked for the object's edges. He found one corner, and then another, and another, until he could see the outline of a small woodbox. Being careful not to damage it, Des moved the spade several inches to either side, allowing for enough room to extract the object.

"I can feel the bottom of it. It's not that big," he said, reaching into the hole.

"Can you pull it out?"

Des tried to grasp underneath it. "It's pretty jammed in there. I'm trying to get it to move a little... ah, I think I can get it." Des pulled more dirt out of the hole. "I think if I can get my other hand in there, I can get it," he said with the excitement of a kid who had just entered Disneyland for the first time.

He pulled and yanked until, finally, he felt it start to release. With one last heave, he freed it from the earth that had held it for over one hundred and fifty years. Madison gasped a sound of disbelief and relief all in one.

"Let me have the flashlight so we can see what's inside," she said.

"No, let's fill in the hole and get the hell out of here. We'll look at it when we get back to the car."

"You're right."

They began shoveling the dirt in a hurried frenzy, using their feet as well as their hands to rush the job. After it was sufficiently filled, Des jumped on top of the mound, firmly packing it back to its former state. They speedily walked out of the church grounds. As they exited, their pace became faster, caused by equal parts thrill and fear.

Their walk soon became a jog, which, in turn, became a sprint as they began to run in an all-out dash back to their vehicle. Suddenly, headlights appeared in the distance.

Des grabbed Madison's hand. "Come over here!" he yelled as he pulled her behind some bushes lining the road. "Keep your head down."

They stared at the growing bright beams as it rapidly came toward them. Almost on instinct, both of them held their breath, watching the lights grow brighter and brighter, blinding their view. The car whisked by them without any hesitation.

"I think we're being a bit paranoid," Madison said, panting.

"Maybe. I just didn't get a good feeling there."

They watched the red taillights of the car move away, shrinking into the distance. But as they tried to collect themselves, blue and red lights flashed on top of the vehicle. It then stopped, pointed a spotlight into the ruins, and turned into the church parking lot.

"I guess being paranoid has its advantages," said Madison as she exhaled.

They stayed in the bushes for another few minutes, waiting for the lights to disappear. They had obtained their goal. Now all that remained was finding out what they had actually found.

Chapter 22

Five miles south of Richmond, Virginia

William sat in front of his computer, excited he had new information to place into his queries. It seemed like forever that things had been stagnant. For months, he had been tracking searches from across the country, looking for any key words to set off the warning alarm that someone had discovered a new lead.

Miraculously, he saw something that he had previously overlooked. He had perused the journal, which had been a part of his family legacy for generations, and in its pages, once thought exhausted, was provided a new enlightenment.

> *"With that, the gentlemen stated that he will look for a sign that the gods will smile on them and that may the tunnels that lead us to the black sands of time revitalize the nation. I remember hoping for the same good fortune in my new assignment."*

Gods—he had never considered it before, but the gentleman mentioned *gods*, in the plural. *Why didn't I notice how out of place that was?* Yet what preceded it was even more vital. He said he would "look for a sign." Apart, these two references meant little. Together, they spoke volumes.

Early American life through the Civil War was heavily influenced by Greek culture. The inception of the nation, its political structure, architecture, and philosophy, had all borrowed from that ancient civilization. America hearkened to it as the ideal of an enlightened society.

Jefferson Davis was an intensely religious Christian man. He would have never referred to "gods" in the plural or as something to draw strength from in the abstract unless it meant something else. *Gods*, for the nineteenth-century American, could only be a reference to the mythology of ancient Greece. In addition, to mention that along with a reference of looking for a sign, it was obvious to William that information was being exchanged between these two men.

William feverishly brought up his search program on his computer and began typing in new additions for it to explore. "Greece," "Greek gods," "Greek signs," "Greek symbols" were entered into the program's lexicon. If any of these words were used in conjunction with his previous entries, he would find his new source, bringing him one step closer to his reward.

He sat back in his chair, smiling, satisfied with his abilities of discovery. He pressed the Enter key, initiating the investigation once more. *It may not happen right away, but they're out there. I will find my accomplice. They will lead me to the access required to reach it, a treasure that cannot be measured in mere monetary wealth.*

However, his enthusiasm was short-lived. He realized this new information had to be provided to his collaborator. It was always an arduous task. His partner's vision was limited. He had never grasped the significance of what lay at the end of this journey. He had become a necessary evil. His knowledge and expertise was needed, but mostly his financial backing.

William picked up the phone and begrudgingly dialed the number. The voice on the other end was thick, as if he needed to clear his throat.

"Yeah, what do you have for me?"

"I found something, a new set of reference words for the program to search."

"How long?"

"You know I don't have an answer for that, but I think these words will be effective. No one else would know about them unless they had come across information that could help us."

"Well, I hope this works. I'm losing patience with what you've come up with so far."

"You know this isn't easy. I'm using all my resources to make this happen," William said emphatically.

"Look, I know you're making every effort, but that in itself does not encourage me to keep on this."

"I think we're getting close. Just be patient. Let me try this."

"All right, I will, for now. Let me know if anything else comes up."

William needed and, at the same time, resented him. He didn't hate the man, yet he was frustrated he could not see what this search could lead to. The Judge did not see how it could be used for the required change.

Sitting at his desk, William reached out and touched the frame that held his ancestor's photograph. He was different from what most would imagine. Bespectacled and balding, with a long thick beard, he did not look the warrior but more like the owner of a general store. *Appearances can be deceiving. Oh, don't I know.* William realized he might be required to have the same cunning. Like his great-great-grandfather, intellect would be his weapon.

Whatever was necessary, the only thing that mattered was, the treasure would be used for its intended purpose. The American society the forefathers envisioned was in a deep state of decay. This would reverse it.

He would work to make him see the necessity for change. He would try to convince the Judge of this need. But if he couldn't, he would have to pick the most opportune moment and take it.

Chapter 23

Yemassee, South Carolina

Des and Madison emerged from the bushes and sprinted the last two hundred yards to their car. Throwing the doors open, they hurled themselves into the vehicle. Yet instead of going right to the object, they sat quietly and processed what they had just accomplished. Madison then looked over at Des. Slowly the serious look on his face began to dissipate as he felt her gaze. He was trying to keep the intensity of the moment, feeling its significance dictated such an expression. It was pointless—he could not hold it in. He started to laugh, and Madison followed suit.

"I can't believe we just did that," she said, looking back, checking to make sure the police were not in pursuit.

"I'm amazed, too, but more shocked that we actually found something."

"Let's see what we got here," she said, reaching over to turn on the interior light. It was still fairly dark inside as the weak light in the compact car did not provide much illumination.

Madison examined the wooden box. It was made of dark oak that was greatly warped and cracked from spending over a century and a half in the soil. She ran her fingers over it, wondering if they would come across some information escaping her vision.

As she moved her hand to the sides of the wooden container, she felt a metal latch on the front. It was rough to the touch, pitted with erosion. On the top of the box was a raised symbol with some sort writing she could not make out.

"Could you flash the light on here?" Madison asked, still running her fingers over the surface of the fascinating object.

As Des pointed the flashlight, he was immediately struck by the markings on its lid. It was a recognizable insignia that those who had studied military history would be familiar with, two cannons crossed over each other in the shape of an X. On top of them lay an anchor wrapped in its own rope. It was surrounded by a wreath of leaves and flowers. Directly below the anchor were capitalized letters CSN, and just underneath it, the inscription "Aide Toi Et Dieu T'aidera."

"Is that Latin?" asked Madison.

"French, it means 'Help yourself and God will help you.'"

"I assume that *CSN* stands for 'Confederate States Navy.'"

Des nodded. "It makes perfect sense. If this was meant for James Semple, he was a Navy officer."

"Are you ready to open this?"

"I think it's time."

Madison reached down and placed her fingers on the latch. As she started to pull it up, she could feel it bend, sounding like it would break. "This makes me nervous. It's so brittle it feels like it's going to snap off. I don't want to do it. Do you want to give it a try?" she asked, offering it to Des.

He took the box, placing it on his lap, and then pushed the seat back, giving him more room to operate while Madison held the flashlight.

He took a deep breath and started to pull on the latch. At first, it didn't budge, and then he felt the weak metal giving in to the pressure of his thumb and forefinger. He stopped for a second and lifted the box, seeing if there was anything he could do to make the task easier. "Oh, screw it! If it breaks, it breaks."

Des tugged on the latch again, hearing it creak as the pressure began to loosen its grip. He pulled a little harder, causing it to move slightly until, almost in one motion, it surrendered. Both of them let out a gasp as it lifted. Gradually opening the lid, Des peered inside.

It was lined with green felt looking similar to that of a pool table. At the bottom of the box was a piece of paper, which felt greasy to the touch. It was folded and sealed at the edge with stamped red wax.

"Unbelievable," Des said as he gently removed the paper from the box. "I think we need to go somewhere else to open this. Here is probably not the best place. I'm afraid if we try without the right tools, we'll damage it. We're only about forty-five minutes from home."

"Are you hungry?" Madison asked.

"Starving."

"I'll order in pizza. We can check it out at my place, if that's okay."

"Sounds like a plan." Des started his car, pulled off the isolated dirt road, and headed back to the main highway. His mind was racing with the possibilities of this new find. Already, it had surpassed his expectations, and they had yet to break the seal.

Chapter 24

Savannah, Georgia

They returned to Savannah a little bit before 10:00 p.m. The short trip seemed like it took an eternity. They hurried up the stairs to Madison's place on the second floor.

"You'll have to forgive the mess," she said as she put the key into the door.

"I'm sure it's fine. I guarantee you, it's better than my place. That's the real disaster."

She pushed the door open and turned on the light. "I'll order some pizza. Make yourself at home. Is pepperoni okay?"

"Perfect. Hey, where do you want to take a look at this thing?"

"The table over there would probably be the best place."

Des walked over to the small dining room table, which was adjacent to the equally small kitchen, and placed the wooden box at its center. The apartment was basic, with a nondescript master bedroom, another quaint room converted to an office, and a common area for eating, relaxing, and watching television. It was the type of apartment most single people got when they realized their lives were not eventful enough to justify anything more exciting.

"Do you want some wine?" Madison asked, fumbling through her refrigerator, trying to be a good host.

"That sounds great. Thanks."

She took out a couple of glasses and poured, feeling a little uneasy. Her expertise was not in the area they were about to traverse, and she was nervous Des would find her not up to the task.

"Here you go. I hope you like chardonnay. It's all I have."

"This is fine, thank you."

After serving Des, she called in their meal. It had been quite some time since she had anyone over, and certainly under much less thrilling circumstances.

"Okay, the pizza is on its way. Let's get started."

There was a moment of awkward silence as Des took a sip of wine and placed it onto the table. It was kind of funny; as nervous as Madison was feeling, he was also experiencing a sense of pressure, not wanting to disappoint her if he was not able to figure out what they had in their possession.

Des opened the box carefully, still creaking with age and exposure, then delicately extracted the piece of paper and held it up to the light. "I would like to know more about this red seal. Do you have a computer handy?"

"Sure," she said, heading back to her office and quickly returning with her laptop.

"What does that look like to you?"

Madison took the piece of paper, carefully studying it. As she turned it to different angles to catch the light, an image started to come into view. "It kind of looks like a man on a horse," she said. "You see?"

Des moved closer. "It does, and that *CSN* on the front of the box is definitely Confederate Navy, which gives me a direction to go in." Des typed in a search while Madison kept looking for any more details. "I think I got it. Look at this."

Madison moved over to see what Des had pulled up. "I think you're right. What is it?"

"It's the seal for the president of the Confederacy."

The official presidential seal of the Confederacy was used to mark any important documents coming from Jefferson Davis's desk. It consisted of an engraving of George Washington sitting atop his horse in full colonial military regalia. The image was surrounded by a wreath of leaves bound together by a red-white-and-blue ribbon. It was then enclosed in a ring of stars. In most representations appeared the words "Seal of the President of the Confederate States of America." However, it was not unusual to find them without wording and only the image. This was the one they had in their possession.

"So you're telling me this was sealed by Jefferson Davis?" Madison asked excitedly.

"That's exactly what I'm telling you."

"Oh my god!"

"Do you have a nail file? I want to try to open this without damaging the paper."

Madison reached into her purse to retrieve it. "I hope this is okay," she said, handing it to Des.

He took the file and placed it near the seal's edge at the bottom, but then changed his mind and moved it to the side, hesitating before attempting to pry it up. "I'm sweating. This is crazy," he said nervously.

"You're doing fine," Madison said, placing her hand on his shoulder.

Des smiled, acknowledging her reassurance, and then slowly moved the nail file underneath the wax seal. Little pieces of red shaving started to appear as Des delicately pushed it underneath the adhesive, working it in about three-fourths of the way. He then looked at Madison, took a deep breath, and quickly turned it. The seal broke loose from the wax paper with only a small chunk remaining attached to the other side.

Des smiled. "We got it."

He carefully started to unfold the paper. As the parchment gradually came into view, there was a moment of disbelief beginning to take ahold of both of them. They had come to a realization that they had discovered an amazing artifact, something no one else had laid eyes on in over one hundred and fifty years. All those professors, all those renowned historians, all those young PhDs—none of them had discovered anything so significant.

As he laid it out on the table, beautiful writing greeted their eyes. There in front of them was another group of sentences, a new set of clues. As before, they were cryptic in nature. The question was, Would they have the same fortune in making sense of them like they had earlier this evening? Would their expertise be enough to put the pieces together, or would the trail run cold?

As she moved her curly hair away from her face, Madison scanned the parchment. Des could not help but notice what an incredible ability she had to focus, and while a perplexed expression encompassed her brown face, there was a joy intermingled with the confusion, giving her a glow. She began to read the instructions aloud with a voice rejoicing in the very fact that these were the words it was given to speak.

> *It begins with the author who in death ignores the office and overlooks the dome.*

> *Stand at the base in the corner of his ordinance and look its opposite.*

> *Resting in the heart of his highest learning, it is fixed in the home of the rector.*

> *Above the sound of God's calling lies the key at its anchor.*

> *It will lead you to the symbol of Darius's defeat.*

These set of instructions were even more complex and mysterious than the previous ones. There seemed to be no starting point. The last set included physical references. This provided no such clues. They were a mere collection of words that, while not random, did not seem to offer a key that would allow them to deconstruct the message. The two young historians were in a state of shock and awe, only beginning to breathe again when the doorbell rang.

"Pizza is here," Madison said, smiling.

"Okay," Des responded, still mesmerized at what was in front of him. Even though he was famished, somehow the situation eased his hunger. This had become more than a simple search. Instead, it was quickly becoming a significant moment, and possibly a life-altering one.

Chapter 25

Newport News, Virginia

He never felt good after speaking with William. Instead, there was always a sense of frustration dealing with the disorganized young man. The value of what they were chasing was beyond anything discovered in the last century, but William's attention did not ever seem to focus on that reward. Instead, his calling had taken his eyes off the wealth.

William chose to see it as a path to another reality, one in which he would not elaborate. To him, however, his goals were not so convoluted. He wanted the prize for its monetary value and the prestige it would bring.

For years, he had heard the legends of the lost Confederate treasury and even attempted to locate clues on his own. Unfortunately, he had very little to go on, and like every other individual who attempted to locate it, he really never got close.

Though he still desired to find it on his own, after hanging up with the young man and learning of the recent information he had come across, he knew he still needed him. What William possessed was invaluable, and the riches they were searching for would be enough to last ten people twenty lifetimes. In finding it, he could attain his greatness and finally move beyond the limits of a profession that could no longer fulfill him—not that it ever did. So as annoying and exasperating as this situation was, he would continue to tolerate him. Once he got what he wanted, he would put his plan into place.

For the past twenty years, the middle-aged man had served as a federal judge. Handing out various sentences and decisions which had affected so many in such profound ways, he rarely considered the impact of his actions. His reputation was that of a hard-line law-and-order man who doled out punishments that even the unscrupulous US attorney prosecutors viewed as overly harsh. Ironically, the Judge's behavior in his private life could never meet the standards of the moral conduct he so often demanded of the defendants who appeared before him. Through numerous affairs, questionable financial dealings, and even illegal business arrangements with some of his former defendants, the Judge had built up quite a reservoir of wealth but always desired more.

It was a little over two years ago when a new possibility presented itself that had the potential to change his future forever. The Judge had been traveling throughout the South, reliving the past through reenactments of major Civil War engagements. He had always been fascinated with history, especially that time period. While he was at the university, he even flirted with the idea of becoming a professor but eventually decided a more prudent and certainly more lucrative profession would be that of an attorney. So law school became the choice.

However, his captivation with the past never ended, and many of the vacations he would take were based on this attraction. He rarely read the popular books marking the best sellers' list, always choosing more academic texts, ones usually found on the shelves of a professor's personal office.

Although he could recite with tremendous accuracy most facts attached to the pre- and post-Civil War South, his interests were more widespread. He had the luxury of not being part of the academic community, allowing him to stray from the mainstream discipline.

As much engrossed in the legends as he was the facts, growing up, he was spellbound by the grandiose stories. However, he realized those legends were oftentimes based on conjecture, modified versions of the truth, or just plain Southern pride, where tales of heroism were the focus and accuracy was not a concern. Still, even with those prevalent mythologies, the stories of the lost Confederate treasury were different. Yes, they were entertaining, but they were not simply based on legend but actual historical accounts. This kept him maintaining a heightened interest, one that was more than just a passing item discussed around the campfires during his historical excursions.

His initial impression of the young man did not leave him enthralled. It was during a reenactment of the Battle of Bristoe Station where he first made his acquaintance. The evening was cool but pleasant. Participants were gathered around the fire, trying to imitate life during the harrowing days of the war. Ironically, even though most of the focus was put on recreating the combat engagements, a more representative piece of the time could be found in these simple fireside chats. The majority of a soldier's life was usually spent doing humdrum, often boring activities, only being interrupted by the terror of battle on short, brief occasions, if ever at all.

The Judge did not take immediate notice of William. He was not distinctive in his look, dirty-blond hair, a trim build, with a pale complexion susceptible to sunburn, as the red tone on his forehead demonstrated. There was nothing physically to make him stand out, although with everyone wearing the same Confederate uniform, it was hard to set oneself apart. Yet what did distinguish him was the way he spoke. His tone, his language, even the way he patterned the spacing between his words was quite different from the others', and certainly unusual for someone his age.

At first, he did not approach him as William sat with members of his unit, sipping tea and discussing the day's events. In actuality, the Judge was listening more for entertainment value than anything else. The conversation twisted and turned from every topic, ranging from where to find replica Springfield rifles to the following day's schedule. Though eventually, it went to where most conversations at these types of events went, the validity of the South's cause.

While most today recognize slavery as an evil, not identifying with that part of Southern heritage, it did not mean the entire cause was thrown onto the trash heap of history. The lack of identification with that central issue did not preclude people from speaking about the constitutionality of the North's interpretation of states' rights and how the Union denied what was written by the forefathers. However, generally, when spoken of, they dealt with how past events could have been affected differently or how it might have changed the outcome of the war but was rarely, if ever, applied to current times.

Yet while others debated in the abstract, William's comments were much more pointed and made to be applicable to the present day. According to him, the cause still existed, only the technology and modernity of life had changed. As he continued to speak, his fervor made those around him uncomfortable, as the expression on their faces transformed from one of great interest to sarcastic tolerance.

William continued with his rant. "The federal government has always violated its own set of rules when it comes to getting what they want. The Dahlgren affair is a perfect example."

"I've heard of that, but no one has ever told me what it was," said a middle-aged reenactor sitting across from him.

"Colonel Dahlgren was a Union soldier who was sent on direct orders from the US government to go to Richmond and assassinate Jefferson Davis and burn Richmond to the ground. He was killed in an ambush before he ever got the chance. He was found with the orders on him."

"Why is that so significant? I mean, there've been reports that the South targeted Lincoln. I've even heard people talk about a possible connection between Davis and John Wilkes Booth."

"Well, until that time, there was an unwritten rule that civilian heads of state weren't to be targeted," William said, becoming visibly aggressive in his gestures. "Lincoln probably would have never been killed had it not been for that attempt on Davis. They broke the agreement, as they always have and always will. That was also the reason the capital had to be moved out of Richmond, along with all of the South's gold and silver."

"What happened to it?" asked the gentleman, noticing William's agitation growing and trying to get him to move away from the subject of government conspiracies.

"No one's quite sure, but I've been looking into it for some time. I've got some sources that no one else has."

While most of them rolled their eyes at the young man's statements, William was not deterred and continued. The Judge noticed the group's change of demeanor, as he could see the looks of disbelief in the young man's claims. However, he felt differently. Even though he believed

William was bordering on the absurd, there was a certainty in his voice that caught his attention. He spoke about the subject as if he had something more substantial to add, more than just theories.

The group predictably began to thin as William's intensity increased with each passing moment. The Judge sat quietly, observing from the sidelines, waiting for the last individual to abandon the conversation. After the final excuse was made on why they had to go, the Judge decided it was time to interject himself. He approached the visibly dejected young man.

"You know, I've heard stories about the treasure and of Dahlgren. You have some interesting information and obviously great knowledge of the subject," said the middle-aged man with the salt-and-pepper hair as he slid in by the fire. "I've studied the whole episode quite extensively and always felt the treasure was out there somewhere, but the trail has been cold for years. It would be wonderful if someone had new information."

William's eyes lit up. Someone shared his interest and actually wanted to discuss those historical events on an intellectual level. "I have some unique information that no one knows about," he said excitedly.

"Really? That's amazing. How, may I ask, did you come upon this information?"

"Well, let's just say it's a family heirloom," William said eagerly. He was encouraged by the man's enthusiasm but still guarded in what he revealed.

Recognizing the young man's caution, the Judge realized he needed to tread lightly. He understood, if he was too aggressive, he would not be able to extract the information this individual claimed to possess. In actuality, it would be easier than he thought. William was bright yet an isolated person hoping to identify with anyone. The Judge, being more mature, recognized the signs of a needy individual, having seen it many times in his courtroom, allowing him to manipulate the conversation.

"That's fantastic! Your family must have a rich history when it comes to the War to have such an unusual heirloom," the Judge remarked. "So you must have had family serving in an important capacity during that time."

He knew appealing to a family's history was the best way to trigger a sense of pride as well as spark a discussion. Southerners were fiercely proud of their heritage and always willing to discuss the distinguished service of one of their kin in the most important event in Southern history.

"Yes, my great-great-grandfather served as a courier for General Lee. He was always chosen to carry the most important messages because he was considered the best."

"I had family that fought in the War too, but no one with any important connections. So he knew General Lee personally?"

"Oh, yes, he was his favorite courier."

"Wow! I've never met anyone with family that had such close ties with Lee, and I've been coming to these things for years," the Judge said respectfully. "This is so fascinating to me."

He could see William's eyes widen as he enthusiastically continued on about his family history. He told the Judge about the important missions his ancestor was entrusted with and how many of his assignments were instrumental in some of the war's most important battles.

The Judge then began to turn the conversation back to the treasure, sensing William had begun to let his guard down. "So what happened to him? What did he do after the war?"

"He did not make it through. He was killed in Georgia," answered the young man.

"Georgia? That's a long way from Virginia. What was he doing down there?"

"He was on an important mission for Jefferson Davis."

"Davis?" he said excitedly. "I thought he was a courier for Lee."

"He was, but President Davis requested Lee's best courier for a special assignment right before the evacuation of Richmond."

The Judge immediately recognized the importance of this information. The Confederate government, before the evacuation, had to make arrangements to move the treasury but encountered difficulties. "If he was summoned by Davis to be a courier right before the fall of Richmond, that assignment had to be extremely important."

William looked at the Judge intently. "It was maybe the most important thing they had to do." He was testing the Judge's knowledge before he could trust him fully. He needed to know the Judge understood the significance of what his ancestor carried without him having to say it.

"His assignment wouldn't have anything to do with the moving of the Confederate treasury, would it?"

William grinned. He knew he found someone who understood, who was thinking on the same level, a sort of kindred spirit he could confide in. "Yes, I believe that was exactly what he was involved in. I have information that talks about him meeting someone in Georgia to deliver a set of instructions that he said 'has value.'"

"I know the treasury was supposed to be moved out of Savannah, but it never got there. I've always wanted to know where it ended up, and I'm willing to commit a substantial amount of my personal resources in order to find out," he said, looking at William to gauge his reaction.

It was music to William's ears. For years, he had wanted to make a true search but never had the means to do so. He had the diary, yet he needed the finances to pursue it. Like most treasure hunts, money for an effective operation would be required. Now, for the first time, he would have the funds.

For the next several hours, it was as if the world did not exist. All that was reality was the year 1864, the treasure, and the legends surrounding it. They talked in great detail, sharing their knowledge. The Judge's research, William's stories handed down from his father, and of course, the journal were all part of the conversation leading to a partnership. They would pool their resources. They would find it.

Chapter 26

Savannah, Georgia

When the pizza arrived, Des and Madison dived in as their appetites had reached ravenous level. At the same time, they were still trying to unlock the mystery of this new set of clues, but the excitement and stress of the day's events were beginning to take their toll.

"I still don't understand what they're trying to get at," she stated. "Who is this author, and what office are they referring to?"

"I'm not sure. I do know one thing, though. We still didn't utilize all the clues that sent us to South Carolina. We were able to get this box, but we're still missing something."

"Do you think this one clue has something to do with the first set, like maybe they're meant to be connected?"

"It's possible. I can't believe it was put there for no reason." Des placed his hand on the back of his neck, trying to massage out the knots. "What was that third clue again?"

Madison took out the tattered paper that had sent them to Old Sheldon Church.

The bows that lay at its entrance suggest the lineage of leadership.

"I can only assume they're talking about the entrance to the church," Des said while he paced the floor and took another sip of wine. "The bows have to be the arches."

"Well, there were three arches at the church, but what leaders?" Madison stared at the paper again. She poured herself some more wine and then walked from the table and sat down on her small couch.

"There were no more instructions to look for anything else at that church?" Des asked as he looked at her for assistance.

"Wait, the number of arches is important."

"Why is that?"

"That has to be it." She stood up and looked at the instructions once more.

"What have you figured out?"

"There was only one lineage of leadership at that time, the presidency. There were three arches, meaning the three presidents, and all three of them were Southerners."

"Jefferson!" Des exclaimed.

"Exactly! It all makes sense. He was also the only author of the first three, the author of the Declaration of Independence."

Des and Madison both smiled from ear to ear. They had cracked the first clue. It was a satisfaction beyond anything they had ever experienced. As children, they had both read *Treasure Island*, fantasizing about discovering a lost prize, and here they were, beginning a journey that had brought that fantasy to life. Yet it was becoming more than that. They were discovering lost history.

"I wish I could do that," Des said with a smile.

"Do what?"

"When I have wine, all I get is sleepy. You have wine, and you're as sharp as a knife."

"It's a gift. What can I say?" she said, glowing.

She brushed the hair out of her face with her hand, trying to hide the fact that she was blushing. She could not remember the last time she had this much fun. Des put his hand on her shoulder in a gesture of congratulations. He then looked back at the clues.

"'The author who in death ignores the office and overlooks the dome,'" he muttered under his breath. "That's fairly simple. Can you pull up a picture of Thomas Jefferson's tombstone for me?"

Madison clicked on the internet icon and began her Google search. Almost instantaneously, pictures of the obelisk-shaped tombstone appeared on her screen. She turned the computer toward Des so he could see.

"It's not there. Look, it's not there," he said excitedly.

Des turned the computer back to face Madison. She immediately recognized what Jefferson's epitaph had left out.

Here was buried Thomas Jefferson.
Author of the Declaration of American Independence,
Statute of Virginia for Religious Freedom, and
Father of the University of Virginia

"He doesn't mention the office of the president," she said in amazement. "'In death he ignores the office.' We're going to have to make another trip, aren't we?"

"I believe so. The next step states we have to 'stand at the base in the corner of his ordinance.' The only way we can do that is to physically be there."

"What do we do when we get there?"

"I have no idea. I guess we'll have to figure it out once we're at Jefferson's home."

Even though the thrill of discovery was still strong, Des was starting to feel the weight of the day's events. He was exhausted, his eyes burning as the fatigue settled in. The day had been full of emotion, and it had drained most of his energy. This, in addition to the two glasses of wine, had effectively finished him off. He sat down on the couch next to Madison and sighed. She, however, was still engrossed in the clues.

"You know, we should probably make a copy of those. Those old papers will not stand up to us handling them all the time. Eventually, they're going to fall apart," Des said, checking his watch.

"You look tired. Don't worry about it. I'll take care of it."

"Thanks. You know, there's one thing that's really odd about these clues. After the first instruction, the next few seem to have to do with finding a physical location. It talks about standing at a base or resting in a community,' and it even references a 'key lying at its anchor,' but the last instruction seems different. 'It will lead you to the symbol of Darius's defeat.' That's the first time an actual name is mentioned. Do you have any idea who Darius is?"

"It doesn't ring any bells. I can do some searching tonight to see what I can find out. When do you want to go to Virginia?"

"Well, I don't have any pressing engagements. How about tomorrow?" he asked, smiling.

"I was hoping you would say that."

"I can't believe this whole situation. I feel like I'm living in some surreal dream, like a kid on some kind of treasure hunt."

"It has definitely been interesting."

"You know, I'm like the least impulsive person, and here I am, traveling all over the place, willing to go anywhere on a moment's notice, chasing God knows what. I don't know why this has suddenly become so important to me. I could easily be accused of being obsessed."

Des looked at his watch again. It was nearly 1:00 a.m., and he was officially gassed. If he was going to be worth anything tomorrow, he was going to have to get some rest, and so was she.

"Well, I think it's time I get going. If we're going to make another trip, I've got some preparing to do." Des got up off the couch and grabbed his jacket.

As he walked to the door, he felt Madison grab his arm. When he turned to face her, she reached over and grabbed him, holding him in a long embrace. A little shocked, he put his right arm around her, returning the nurturing hug.

"What was that for?" he asked.

"I just wanted to thank you for including me in this. It means a lot to me. This has been the most fun I've had in I don't know how long. Just... thank you."

Des smiled. "I'll call you tomorrow morning before I leave to pick you up. We can grab some breakfast, my treat. Thank you for the pizza and wine. I'll see you tomorrow."

"Good night."

After Des had left, Madison was still too excited to sleep. She still felt like exploring. *Okay, let's see about this Darius character.* She returned to her laptop, took another gulp of wine, and started typing away.

Chapter 27

Capitol View, Virginia

William had just checked his computer for matches on the key words he had entered into his program. So far, his search had turned up little of interest and certainly nothing to impress his business partner.

The Judge was becoming increasingly impatient with the lack of results, and in turn, William was becoming concerned the Judge's enthusiasm for this project as well as the funds he was providing would dry up. He did not share the same goals but needed his resources. Without him, the likelihood of making the discovery was doubtful.

He ran the program again—still nothing. He pounded the desk with his fist in frustration and then threw the books lining his shelves across the room. "Goddamn it!" he screamed while pacing the floor.

Then, as if someone had shut off the power in his body, he stared at the posters arranged in neat rows on the walls of his room. The map of the Battle of Gettysburg, the photograph of General Lee on his horse, and the picture of Stonewall Jackson were some of the images adorning the dark-colored sides of his space. They had been there for years, serving as a source of inspiration. Yet now he felt like he was failing them, disgracing their legacy.

But there was one poster which provided the greatest reservoir of fury. It was a map of the battle that defined the motivation behind his actions. It was arrogance, pure, unmitigated arrogance. And to William, it was the prime example of Southern heroics and Union treachery. No matter how many times he had viewed the image, it never failed to enrage him. It was more than a wrong; it was a betrayal.

The event took place in a Virginia field in 1863. Confederate and Union forces had fought intensely for weeks, and the end result was a bloody stalemate. Entombed in trenches, neither side could dislodge the other. Yet even in these most brutal of conflicts, there was a code of conduct. Rules of engagement both sides held sacred. And they had been, until that day.

Desperate, the Union commander ordered a new tactic. They would dig. For the next several weeks, Union forces tunneled, forming a passageway nearly a half mile long. Their plan was not to give the enemy the dignity of face-to-face combat. Instead, they would place explosives underneath the Confederate lines and execute them.

But breaking the codes of honorable conduct came with a price, a steep one. Somehow, unexplained forces intervened to dole out justice.

Union troops successfully detonated the explosives. Then they rushed across the field and jumped into the massive hole it created in order to finish off the enemy. What they found was an empty cavity. The Confederates had evacuated before the explosion. Moments later, the Southern units returned to slaughter the helpless Union forces gathered at the bottom of their self-dug grave. It was like shooting fish in a barrel. They were decimated.

To William, the episode known as the Battle of the Crater was the definition of Union cowardice and the lack of principles held by the federal government. It represented all the reprehensible qualities the Union had obtained and were continuing to acquire.

It reminded him of his responsibility. He could not quit. He had to carry out the birthright left to him by his ancestor. He could not disgrace the memory of all those who sacrificed. He must find the treasure to change the direction of his beloved country.

Taking another deep breath, he calmly walked into his kitchen. *I have a responsibility. I have a responsibility. It must be completed. The black sands of time await me.*

Thoughts raged through his brain. Knowing he must stay focused and that any operation needed to be approached in a cool, collected manner, he worked on gaining complete control. He began to fix himself a cup of tea with military precision, and thus initiated his ritualistic process of relaxation. Measuring the tea leaves and making sure the water had reached its peak temperature before dowsing the mixture, he sipped slowly, savoring the aroma and taste. He closed his eyes and shut out the world, clearing his mind of clutter, slowly regaining its sharpness.

After finishing the drink, he walked slowly to the bathroom, inhaling deeply with each step. Turning on the shower, he undressed, folding each piece of clothing neatly and laying them on top of the hamper. He studied himself in the mirror, searching for any imperfections that would cause him to slow or be unprepared for his eventual task. Steam filled the room until the image was fogged over with the loose vapor swirling through the air. *I will focus. I will prepare.*

The water poured over his body as he shut his eyes, concentrating, searching his memory for any missed evidence. *Could I have overlooked something? Is there more that the diary could tell me?* He had implemented a new protocol. Now, time would have to be his aid.

As he laid his head on the pillow, a calm settled in, and he found a clarity he had only known on rare occasions. He closed his eyes and inhaled deeply, propelling the oncoming sleep. Tomorrow, there would be new opportunities. He could feel it.

The next morning, the ritualistic behavior that ended his night continued. Awakening and paying no heed to his surroundings, he marched back to the kitchen to make his brew. Letting the aroma fill his nostrils, he mentally prepared himself for the day. After reaching a level of heightened concentration, he returned to his room.

Turning on his computer, he waited for it to load so he could run his search. The light of the screen reflected off the young man's face as he calmly entered his password and launched the program. Codes and numbers flashed as it reached its tentacles into the internet void, looking for any connections to a relevant match. Again, nothing.

Dejectedly, William turned away when he heard the computer sound a high-pitched ping. As if on a swivel, he quickly turned, just in time to hear another, and another. He rushed back to the desk and clicked to see what it had found. Another click, and then one more, and there it was. His breath quickened and then suddenly stopped. He had something, a definite find. It was coming from Savannah, Georgia.

The chase had begun.

Chapter 28

Savannah, Georgia

The knock came at 7:00 a.m. Madison opened the door to see Des standing with a cup of coffee in each hand and a smile on his face.

"Good morning," he said, handing one to her.

"Hi! Thank you. That's sweet. Let me get my stuff."

"Okay, no rush." Des walked into the entryway. Even though he had been there just a few hours ago, it looked much different from the previous night.

"I was able to do some more searching last night after you left. I think I made a little headway on the Darius issue, but it still doesn't make a whole lot of sense," she said, her voice emanating from the back room.

"What did you come up with?"

"Well, Darius came up in several searches, but the only one that made semisense was about the former king of Persia. Once I got that info, I cross-referenced it with words like *defeat, symbol,* and *Confederate treasure* and got one relevant match. It seems our King Darius suffered a huge defeat against the Greeks during the Greco-Persian wars. At that time, Persia was the world's dominant power. The Greeks were so stunned by their victory they celebrated by building the Parthenon. That must be the symbol they were talking about."

"Yes, you're probably right. But it still doesn't give us a whole lot. As far as I know, there are no copies of Parthenon here. I mean, there's plenty of Greek-style architecture examples, but that's a long way from being the Parthenon."

"Yeah, you're right. Those examples are a far cry from the Parthenon. I tried cross-referencing the info with other words relating to the treasure but drew a blank. Maybe we'll find the answer at Jefferson's home."

"I hope so. It will be an awfully long drive for nothing if we don't."

"Okay, I think I've got everything I need," she said, grabbing her bag. "Oh, yeah, I also made new copies of the instructions. Here are the originals," Madison said, handing him a folder with the papers inside.

They headed down to Des's car and loaded her things into the back. The journey ahead was over five hundred miles before they would reach their destination of Charlottesville, Virginia, location of the famous Jefferson home, Monticello. Most of the drive would take place on Interstate 95, the same one they utilized for their trip to South Carolina a day earlier.

"I was thinking about some of the other instructions," Des said as they made the turn onto the highway. "But I have some concerns."

"Like what?"

"Well, the instructions were probably written around 1864. Obviously, things were much different than they are today. If these clues are supposed to lead us to actual physical structures, there's no guarantee they even exist anymore."

"Well, we know that Monticello exists."

"Yes, it does. But I assume we're going to have to go to his grave site for the next clue."

"But we know the grave is still there. We saw the pictures."

"Yes, but the tombstone itself isn't the original one. They replaced it a little over a hundred years ago with the one you see today. If there's something we need on that original tombstone, we won't have access to it. I'm concerned this may be a problem with a lot of the clues we come across."

Madison pondered this reality, feeling a sense of disappointment beginning to fill her.

Noticing a change in her demeanor, Des tried to shine a more positive light on the possibilities.

"However, there might be other ways to find what we need. For instance, the original Jefferson tombstone is on display at the Smithsonian.

If we need information, we can always go there," he said, trying to uplift her spirits.

He noticed a look of relief and a reinvigoration of confidence in Madison with those comments. She needed to take this journey. It was something fulfilling her on more than just an academic or intellectual level. This was about a reaffirmation of who she was and her capabilities to meet the potential she saw in herself. For such a long time, she had felt those around her had lost faith that she would reach her goals, and she had done little to prove otherwise. This was her chance at redemption.

Chapter 29

Newport News, Virginia

The phone rang early, startling him from a peaceful sleep. Moving slowly, he debated whether or not he was going to answer the call. Annoyed, he picked it up with a frustration fueled by the belief that nothing could be so important to bother him at such an early hour.

"Yes," the Judge said sternly.

"We got a hit."

"Do you realize what fucking time it is? This better not be another false lead."

"No, this is a solid one. It was based on one of the new key words I put into the search last night."

"What words?"

"I had hits on the words *Greek* and *symbols* combined with *Confederate* and *treasure*. Those terms are far too irrelevant to one another to be used in the same search. It's too much of a coincidence," William said confidently.

"Where did the search come from?"

"That's the other interesting bit of information. It came from Savannah."

The Judge got very quiet, recognizing the significance. Savannah was the location that James Semple was supposed to take the gold out of Confederate territory to relocate and hide from Union forces. However, he was never able to do so.

Theories had been abundant of why the gold never made it to its destination. Some believed Savannah was just being used as a decoy to divert Union troops away from its actual hiding location. Others contended the pressure of Sherman marching toward the seaport city made it impossible for them to evacuate the cargo from those docks; thus, it was moved somewhere else.

"I need you to give me the information on that search, their IP address, times, and locations. I'll get it to my people so we can find out who this individual is and what their progress is toward finding it."

In his years serving on the federal bench, the Judge had made many connections. He had dealt with almost every aspect of law enforcement, from the FBI and Customs Enforcement Agents to the US Attorneys' Office. He also knew that while these were supposed to be the entities working for the public good, some of the most corrupt individuals imaginable occupied those same halls. With the right connections and influence, all it took was a few favors here and a few greased palms there to be able to have them do your bidding. He made certain to maintain those relationships as he understood their unique set of skills would be useful eventually.

In this case, he was going to contact what he considered the bottom of the barrel in terms of moral behavior, and those were the people in the electronic monitoring programs of the FBI. These offices were filled with individuals who believed it to be within their rights to spy on their fellow citizens, using any means, anytime, anywhere on anyone. Hacking people's email accounts and listening in on phone calls without just cause was something they had done for years. Whether it had any legal justification or relevance was rarely taken into consideration, which made them perfect for this type of operation.

He had done some favors over the years for their investigators and the US Attorneys' Office by denying legitimate motions of defense counsel to throw out evidence due to illegal searches or a lack of issuance of a search warrant without probable cause. He did this in some of their most high-profile cases, thus guaranteeing convictions. Ignoring constitutional rights was common practice with these agencies and in his courtroom. Now it was time to call in some of those favors. Plus, he had one more fringe element he could bring in if necessary.

"Can you tell how far along they are in their search?" the Judge inquired.

"Unfortunately, no. The only thing I can tell is, they have some unique information because this was way too random a search to be thought of out of the blue. Something or someone is helping them."

"Well, there's no way I'm going to allow anyone else to have a share of this. I've invested too much money and time to allow that to happen. If need be, we have to make sure, whoever this person is, they cannot be allowed to make progress without my… our control of the situation. We have to find and prevent them from getting there before we do."

"Okay." The young man's voice shuddered. "But what if they have information we need? What if they know how to figure out things that we can't? What do we do?"

"Don't you worry about that," the Judge said sternly. "That's my job. I'll take care of it. I know the right people who can assist me."

William became very quiet. He knew what that meant. The Judge was a man who, once set on a goal, would do anything to attain it. He hated that he needed him. The Judge could not see the overall goal. He did not understand. His impatience would blow this whole thing if he could not be contained.

"I think we need to be careful. If we remove them too soon, we might lose information we need," William stated, trying to make the case for restraint.

"We're not going to lose anything. Just keep looking for more information on your end. You came up with some new leads. I'm sure there are other things you've overlooked."

William cringed. He knew there was more information he could provide the Judge. Though he had already given him a tremendous amount. Still, he was cautious. There were items he did not readily release to the magistrate. He was waiting to see if the Judge shared the vision, if he truly understood the nature of this treasure. Yet there was no indication of any comprehension. He was still focused on the wrong wealth. He wasn't ready.

"I'll continue to look for more," the young man said dejectedly.

"Good. I'll call you very soon to let you know where we need to go. Make sure you're ready, and keep your phone close."

The Judge hung up, feeling validated. He could hardly contain his excitement as he leaped out of bed. Searching his phone, he scrolled through his contact list to find the number.

"Hello! Remember that favor I needed?"

"Of course," a voice said on the other end of the line.

"Well, I have the information. How long will it take for you to process it?"

"Not that long. Maybe an hour."

The Judge carefully recited the information to his contact, making sure no details were missed. As he read the data, the adrenaline started to rush through his system, causing him to sweat profusely. He could feel his goal within reach. His life was about to change.

"Okay, so I'll wait to hear from you in about an hour or so. Thanks," the Judge said before hanging up the phone. An aura of confidence enveloped him. He knew this search had breached a new level.

But the other end of this business relationship did not feel the same ease. After the conversation ended, William ended the call gingerly. He was in a dilemma. It was obvious the Judge was not someone he could trust to share in his vision. He also understood that in his haste, the Judge might ruin the search altogether.

William would do what he was asked and obtain more information, though he would dispense it sparingly. Only he comprehended the prize they were searching for. He had to make sure his interest was protected at all times. And of this individual they were now hunting, he must protect them.

Chapter 30

Interstate 95, North Georgia

The breeze coming in through the car window brought the smell of the fresh greenery and flowers that were in full bloom from the springtime rains. Madison and Des took in the scenery as they made their way through the northern part of Georgia. It was truly a magnificent state. Pink blossoms, graceful fields, and elegant trees were scattered throughout the rolling landscape. A mix of colors swirling and bleeding into one another gave the image a dreamlike quality, reminiscent of any of the great nineteenth-century impressionist painters.

Their conversations mainly dealt with the issue at hand. However, that topic was soon exhausted. They could hypothesize all they wanted about the clues and what might be their hidden meanings, yet after a certain point, it became counterproductive. They would not know anymore until they reached Monticello. Rehashing the same ideas over and over while attempting to guess what the cryptic information meant was a little like diagnosing a patient without being told the symptoms.

"Des, can I ask you something?" she said.

"Of course."

"Why do you talk so little about yourself? We've been working together at the foundation for several months, yet I know almost nothing about you."

"There's not really much to tell."

"Oh, come on, that can't be true. Your life has to be a hell of a lot more interesting than mine."

"Believe me, it's not," Des said, squirming a little bit in his seat. "I find your life a lot more compelling."

"I don't see how. What would be the fascination?"

"Look how much you've accomplished. We're the same age, and you already have your doctorate, and you're teaching at a college. Here I am, still struggling to get my master's."

"You're avoiding the question," she said, smiling in an attempt to bring down his guard. "I know you went into the military right after junior college. What made you decide to do that? You don't really seem like the military type."

Des dropped Madison a look as if to say, "I don't look tough enough to you?"

Recognizing the glance, she immediately defended the question. "You know what I mean."

"I needed the money. My dad died when I was young, and my mom didn't make enough to send me to a university. So after I finished my AA degree, I enlisted."

"I'm sorry about your father. That must have been difficult."

"It was, but we managed," Des replied, feeling uneasy at the questioning. He had always found it taxing talking about himself. Whether it was being reminded of his trying past or the discomfort of knowing he had not accomplished what he envisioned so many years ago, it was an agonizing process.

"Were you stationed close?"

"At first, I was fairly close, Fort Benning, but I was deployed to Afghanistan for the better part of three years."

"That must have been so hard. I can't even imagine." Madison could tell the conversation had taken a very serious turn. She could see him lost in thought, like he was not in the car but at some distant location. However, this was the first time she felt she was really learning about him.

"There were things, both good and bad."

"Well, there has to be more to your service than that. You make it sound like it was just a typical part of life, like it was no big deal."

Des was becoming very uncomfortable. He knew she just wanted to learn more about him. They had spent so much time together. It was natural curiosity. The irony was, he wanted to open up. He desperately wanted to talk to someone about the horrors he had seen. They had been trapped inside him, pressing on his nerves for what seemed like an eternity.

It was the right hand. It always started with his right hand. A slight tremble in the fingers that, if left unchecked, would lead to an uncontrollable, violent, full-body shake before he was back in Afghanistan, back in that trench, hearing the deafening sounds of war.

Madison noticed his quivering hand, struggling to maintain its grip on the steering wheel. Her heart ached; she realized she had dug too deep. "I'm sorry. I shouldn't have brought it up. It must have been awful. I should know when to keep my big mouth shut."

"No, no, it's okay. You did nothing wrong," he answered, trying to ease her guilt.

"Well, if you ever need someone to talk to, I'm always here." *God, Madison, how cliché!*

He looked at her. She was smiling, a simple gesture offering great comfort. He knew if there was anyone he could talk to, it would be her. She seemed to be able to understand the pain; her empathy for others was developed by a hurt-filled childhood.

But how could he tell her? How could he explain to someone that he had killed a child? There was no way to convey the guilt or explain the toxicity it created, one that ate at his being daily.

"I'll be okay," he stated unconvincingly.

Madison reached over and gently touched his cheek. The softness of her fingers was soothing beyond description.

"Okay," she said as her finger slid slowly downward, caressing his skin. She smiled once more, but inside she was seething, angry at herself for being so foolish. *Why couldn't I have just left well enough alone?* Yet after contemplating the exchange, her viewpoint started to change.

Madison recognized she was treading on some very sensitive nerves, though now, she was not so regretful. She had always believed the pain experienced in life was every bit as important as the joy. Still, she wondered what awful things he must have seen.

"I must seem pretty dull to you," he said, looking over at his companion. "A guy my age, still looking for what he wants to do, with no social life to speak of… it looks pretty sad, I bet."

"Des, believe me, my life is hardly an adventure. I'm thirty-two years old, already been divorced, and working as a hostess in a restaurant because I keep losing out on full-time teaching positions to applicants who look like they're in the middle of puberty. It seems like it doesn't matter how much I've accomplished, what experience I have, or what recommendations I provide—I never seem to catch a break." She glanced at Des, trying to gauge his reaction, but she was unable to do so. "I'm sorry. I must sound like I'm whining. You must think I'm pretty pathetic, considering what you've had to endure."

"No, not at all. You've been through a lot. A divorce has to be excruciating enough without having to start over again. I've always admired people who have been brave enough to make that commitment to another person in the first place. I know there are no guarantees, so it's such a leap of faith. When I came home from my deployments, I saw my friends go home to their wives and children, and I always felt they had a special level of courage to serve while still being able to commit to their families. It was amazing to see."

She had never heard anyone describe her decisions in those terms, especially an individual with this sort of life experience. She could feel a trust growing, one based on mutual respect for the other's journey. It was something she recognized but had not felt for some time.

Des felt her gaze. However, his shyness kicked in, and the intimacy of the moment made him look for a way to change the direction of the conversation.

"I don't know about you, but I'm starving. How about that breakfast I promised you?"

"That sounds perfect."

Seeing a small billboard for a local diner, Des pulled the car off the highway at the next exit. "Biscuits and gravy would be the best right now."

Chapter 31

Newport News, Virginia

As he turned the pages, the feelings washed over him. It always worked but was still perplexing on why it left such a scar. It was eons ago and would be considered by most an insignificant speck of time in the span of his life. Yet even after all this time, it still drove him.

Maybe he was primed for that amount of pain due to his impressionable age when it occurred. His vulnerability was at its highest. But in the present, it did not matter what those conditions were; it was only relevant to what it would become. It was the fuel that powered the motivation. It was the stoker of the fire. From that point forward, his brilliance would be in the emotion rather than the rationale.

As the Judge fixated on the photograph in his senior yearbook, it all came flooding back. All the hurt, all the shame, and what would later become the maniacal drive could be traced back to that moment.

If he were to ask her now, she probably wouldn't even remember the instant she altered his life. Ironically, he recognized he was in her debt for committing the transgression. But the thought of offering her gratitude, even after the passage of so many years, still left him with a bitter taste in his mouth.

Then, he was the shy boy with the freckled round face and portly build. It was an appearance that continued to add a multitude of barriers in gaining his classmates' acceptance throughout his youth. In junior high, he was maligned, bullied, and worst of all, ignored. He was left out of parties and gatherings and then taunted with that very fact. In high school, things did not improve, as the emotional abuse only increased.

Daily, he was surrounded by thousands of kids but could not have been more isolated.

He had much to offer. His homely facade hid a deeply sensitive soul of superior intellect. Yet his own self-hatred viewed that asset as a curse, and he would often attempt to subjugate his intelligence in order to be seen as lacking depth, which was such a typical trait of the teenage social condition. It was to no avail. His appearance continued to override his efforts, never allowing him the slightest infiltration. He would be kept on the other side of the glass.

However, a glimmer of hope came when he met Denise. He actually knew of her all too well, as she came from the upper levels of the high school social hierarchy. She drew attention from all those who mattered. Beautiful, graceful, at ease in the social arena, and supremely confident in her abilities, Denise was everything he envisioned such status could attain. Yet he, being the antithesis of all that age valued, would never venture to believe she would engage with him.

It started out innocently enough. Struggling in science, Denise asked him for help. His strategic placement in the desk adjacent to hers gave him access to indulge his hopes. As the school year progressed, she requested his assistance with greater frequency, and on each of those days he guided her, his infatuation grew. It was a constant battle to keep himself in check, as he would have to try to refrain from staring at her gorgeous face, admiring her raven-black hair or losing himself in her blue eyes.

As the fall gave way to the spring, the challenge only increased with the greater amounts of skin she revealed in the warmer temperatures. It was almost too much. Her scent was intoxicating as it enveloped him when she leaned in for help. She would stand behind him, looking over his shoulder, sometimes grazing his back with her soft breast. As she spoke to him in her angelic voice, he could feel her breath dance on his cheek as their personal spaces seemed to combine. The fantasies were his constant companion.

He would try to bring himself back to reality, often believing this could only be a product of his imagination. She ran with the popular crowd. Her people wouldn't give him the time of day, much less accept him. How could she possibly take him seriously? *She wouldn't hurt me. She's too kind.*

His desires were soon overtaking the common sense of his experience, bolstered by what he saw as new conditions. Denise would speak to him and many times within visual range of her friends. In class, she would place her hand on his shoulder, touch his arm when she was making a point, or giggle at her own silliness. He even believed he caught one of her friends smiling at him in acknowledgment of his existence while passing in the hallway.

Maybe their viewpoints had changed. This new comfort level they had been demonstrating toward him seemed to prove the assumption. It was time to take it to the next level. And why not? She was not committed to anyone. It was time for him to conquer his fear and ask her to the prom. Then he would be in. This would be the moment that would elevate him to more than just passive acceptance but an active force within his high school social scene.

He chose the time. High school, if anything, was a series of predictable movements. Coordinating the event was simplistic. She would be at her locker just before the beginning of science class. It was most opportune.

Reflecting on it now, the Judge saw the whole episode in slow motion. He descended the stairs and peered around the corner. There she was, wrapping up a conversation with two of her girlfriends. He attempted to gather himself, inhaling deeply to try to calm his nerves. *Okay, you can do this.* He was just about to make the turn when he heard his name.

"Denise, what's with you two?" her friend asked.

"What do you mean what's with us?"

"Well, I see you talking to him. I hear you hang out in class. Are you two an item?"

"That fat geek? You gotta be kidding me. Do I look desperate?"

The pain of her words was so intense it felt like the life was instantly sucked from him. He couldn't face her and instead walked back up the stairs.

His next memory was of leaving the campus, attempting to hide the tears. He wouldn't return to school for the remainder of the week. When he finally came back, all had reverted. It was just an illusion. Denise had moved to the other side of the classroom. He was invisible once again.

For months he was consumed by depression as he spent his days locked in his room, with the shades pulled down and the lights turned out. He was hurt, embarrassed, and ashamed. But mostly, he was angry at himself for being so foolish.

However, as graduation approached, all those emotions relinquished to rage. No longer would he try to conform to their ideals. No longer would he hide his intelligence. No longer would he succumb to kindness or sincerity. Instead, he would immerse himself in the anger. He would allow it to purify and focus him. It would be his weapon, which would never again allow him to be at the mercy of another. He would not look for objectives; he would become one. The pursuit of a goal would always be the same, to prove his own greatness.

He dove into college with a voracity bordering on the obsessive. He treated his classes not as avenues to learn or a road map to a career but as a showcase of his dominance over his fellow students. He didn't study, he attacked, and whenever he felt his competitive edge begin to wane, he thought back to that moment of shame and would find himself reenergized with a ferocity few could conceive of, let alone match.

His desires never seemed to be quenched. The shy chubby boy from his high school figuratively and literally melted away. But the rage remained. Disguised as confidence, it pursued money, possessions, and women on a scale that would make the most prolific hedonist pale in comparison.

However, it was never enough. There was still a hole. In his own mind, he had not achieved greatness. It was an emptiness bringing him back to his lonely youth. Without attaining it, he would remain hollow.

Fury, though, had served him well. He would never release it, as it was his most prized possession. At his twenty-year high school reunion, the Judge returned a heralded and handsome success. There he encountered a much less accomplished Denise. She was still beautiful, but now her maturity led her to recognize the one that got away. She did not wish to make that mistake again.

She was flirtatious all evening, attempting to entice him. Even going as far as to invite him back to her place. It was tempting. She, the once-untouchable goddess, the source of his high school fantasies, was unabashedly offering herself to him.

I'm in. She has opened the door. I will have the last laugh. I can find the peace I've always wanted between her legs.

He couldn't do it. If he caved in to the prospect of spending the night in her bed, he would lose the very thing that drove and defined him. He respectfully declined, allowing the object of his hatred to remain intact.

In doing so, he would always have access to the replenisher. Whenever the need presented itself, he would pull out his yearbook and marinate in her image. The strategy which had served him so well would continue.

However, while his past pain gave him an edge, it didn't always give him control. Before, he would be damned if he allowed the circumstance he was currently enduring. But he had not had the opportunity to reach his elusive goal like what had been recently provided.

Still, this partnership he begrudgingly remained in made that maddening lack of control more pronounced. The Judge put down the yearbook and began to pace in a frantic rhythm.

They told him it would only be about an hour, and already it was nearly two. *What could be the holdup?* This matter was beginning to consume him. Every elapsed moment seemed to be another step he had fallen behind this entity that was wandering uncontrolled in the void, searching for what was rightfully his. The situation had gone from stressful to nearly intolerable, and what made it more maddening was his partner appeared aloof to the significance of what they were chasing.

He could not seem to calculate or quantify William's interest in this lost treasure. While at times he appeared excited about the wealth it would provide, his enthusiasm seemed to stem from some other inspiration. The young man wanted the treasure, but the monetary significance was inconsequential. It was a means to an end, and the Judge could not figure what that end was.

However, he spent little time focusing on that issue as his own difficulties dominated his attention. *What he does with his share is his business, and I have ways around it.*

He would work and rework the figures. It was estimated that the Confederate treasury had huge amounts of silver coins acquired from cotton sales to Mexico. However, as impressive as that amount of coinage would seem, the true treasure was the gold. The calculated wealth of the mesmerizing metal alone, ignoring its historical value, would be in the twenty- to thirty-million-dollar range. Combined with its provenance, this collection would be one of the most significant discoveries in modern history, attaining the founder a level of wealth and prestige beyond anyone's imagination.

Finishing his second cup of coffee, the Judge was returning to his kitchen when the morning silence was broken again by the loud ring of his phone.

"Yes, tell me you have good news." His expression changed from one of concern to thrill. They were able to track the individual who initiated the search. "Very good. So she's still in Savannah?"

The Judge tapped his fingers on the counter as he listened to his investigator. It was both a relief as well as an anxiety inducer. They had discovered the identity of the individual. They also were able to track her location by monitoring the use of her cell phone. It put him in the position of advantage he was hoping for.

"Excellent work. I'll need you to be on call with your team. I may need you to get more information on-site." He hung up the phone with a new energy and invigorated sense of purpose.

He took a moment to gather himself, preparing to notify his business partner, something he wished he could avoid altogether. *It won't always be this way. It's coming to an end.*

Staring across his kitchen counter, he momentarily studied the piles of unopened mail on the family room coffee table and then the glass case holding his collection of Civil War-era knives. He rubbed his hand across his face, the lack of a full beard still bothersome after he had sported one for so long. It was temporarily replaced by a raggedy scruff that had not reached full fruition. *It had to go. But it will be back shortly.*

He made the call. "We have her," the Judge said confidently. "But she's on the move."

"She? Who is it?" William inquired.

"Her name is Madison Callum. She's a thirty-two-year-old college professor who lives in Savannah."

"Do we need to go to Savannah, then?"

"No. My people tracked her on Interstate 95, heading north, and she has already entered South Carolina."

"Do they know where she might be headed?"

"No, but we're going to find out. Get what you need. I'm going to head toward Richmond. I have a feeling she's heading in that direction. My men are close and will let me know when they can intercept her. You need to be ready."

The Judge felt a confidence he had yet to encounter on this journey. For the first time, this topic broached a level of authenticity and not just some fanciful hobby. He had always believed it existed, though generally hesitated to display full confidence, concerned he would feel the fool for attempting.

The day he first encountered William gave him the freedom to venture into this territory. This latest development now bolstered his beliefs that this fantasy could in fact be reality.

Chapter 32

Capitol View, Virginia

William had run the gamut of emotions since he first learned the legends of the treasure. Hope, frustration, joy, and sadness were all a part of his repertoire. Yet this was the first time he felt fear. The Judge, who had started as a benefactor, now looked more like a detractor.

No matter how hard he tried, he could not convince him of the true nature of the treasure. He could not see it was for revitalizing the nation, not wealth. He would read him passages from the journal that spoke of the hope this treasure would bring, but he never caught the inferences. It was so obvious to William, but no matter the effort, it never resonated with the Judge. His only desire was material wealth, the treasure's original intention he had apparently not figured out, and if he did, he must have felt it was unimportant.

He knew he was going to have to make sure the treasure was used in the appropriate manner. Now that things were put in motion, he needed to make plans and preparations. He could not allow the Judge to be reckless.

The problem lay in the fact that he still needed the Judge's resources. In addition, in formulating his plans, he had to make sure they were thorough in every detail. The Judge was a very intelligent and determined man who recognized changes in intentions and demeanor very quickly. *I have to pick his mind. I have to know his moves.*

William sat in contemplation. He knew the Judge's wishes in the short term—how could he make it an advantage? Once again, he began his ritualistic behavior. It was the methodical nature of doing things in precise measurements and actions that cleared his mind. Bathing and dressing with an almost-ceremonial approach, eating certain foods to induce energy and thought, and concentrating to increase his sensitivity to all stimuli gave him the resources leading to inspiration.

After several hours, William had reached his epiphany. His bags were packed, his thoughts clear. The deception was ready to be implemented, but most importantly, the purpose of the treasure would be realized.

Chapter 33

Charlottesville, Virginia—following morning

After checking out of their respective rooms at a small Charlottesville motel and grabbing some coffees, Des and Madison were eager to get started on the day. Pulling into the visitors center at Monticello, both were in high spirits. Neither had been to Thomas Jefferson's home, but both found him fascinating. To them, Jefferson, though brilliant, was a collection of contradictions. His writings, works, interest, social and emotional life had intrigued and confounded scholars for nearly two hundred years, and neither could escape their curiosity when it came to this historical icon.

He, like many legendary figures, had been memorialized in bronze and marble effigies throughout the country. These monuments honoring them had become havens for tourist, mainly focusing on their seminal accomplishments. The Lincoln Memorial prominently displays his greatest speech with words that had echoed through time. Washington had representations throughout the country. The bronze statue standing atop the steps of New York's Federal Hall, the needle-like structure reaching for the sky in the nation's capital, and even a state with his namesake were examples of how these men were set in the collective consciousness, not as flesh- and-blood human beings, but as stoic singular-minded individuals. While these central points of honoring the past served an important purpose, historians like Des and Madison also recognized they tended to deny a full picture of the human beings they were, with all their flaws as well as their admirable qualities. Jefferson was certainly one of the recipients of this homage treatment, which made the truth about his life all that more interesting.

Madison was especially intrigued by this genius who was one of the true paradoxes of the American identity. As she immersed herself in this world, these illogicalities became prominent in her mind. The man who penned perhaps the greatest document on liberty in human history was also one of the largest slave owners in Virginia. He was the individual who advocated personal responsibility and independence yet was constantly mired in financial problems, usually caused by his inability to control his spending habits. He was the Southerner who recognized slavery was something that needed to be eradicated but did not free his own children he had fathered with one of his slaves until after his death. He was the man who shunned the idea of a powerful central government but increased its strength a hundredfold with the largest land acquisition in the nation's history, the purchase of the Louisiana Territory. She had a reverence for him, as it was impossible not to admire Jefferson. At the same time, there was a part of her that recognized the irony in doing so.

They walked through the visitors' center, making their way to the tram station for the ride to take them up the hill to the residence. While waiting on the benches, they gazed upon the life-size bronze statue of the former owner of the property. Jefferson was every bit as distinguished looking as one would imagine a man of his reputation. Standing over six feet tall, very unusual for the day, he stood out among his peers, and even though this was just a modern representation of the man, they could feel the wisdom and power of his presence.

The tram arrived a few moments later. As it made its way to Monticello, the beauty of the grounds came into view. Majestic oak trees lined the road as manicured lawns full of rich greenness gave way to breathtaking views of the rustic brick structure capped with its gleaming white dome.

When the tram unloaded at the base of the grounds, Des and Madison located the dirt path that would bring them to Monticello's doorstep. Walking about a hundred yards, they made the turn, which emptied at the massive green lawn in front of the mansion. The trail did not run directly to the front door, instead curving, forcing the visitor to take a circuitous route. The two young historians were taken in by the beautiful flowers and massive trees encasing the area. Small signs posted every few yards indicated points of interest, while gardens and vineyards reminded them this was once a working plantation.

However, as they came within fifty yards of the entrance, they were struck by maybe the most sobering aspect of the property, a small sign indicating the burial site for slaves. The enchantment of the beautiful estate was suddenly dulled by the physical reminder that it was run on the blood, sweat, and tears of bought and sold human beings. The degradation of these people was demonstrated even in death, as most were buried without grave markers, lost to history.

Even though they were here to view the grave site, Des and Madison were not about to miss the opportunity to enter the residence. It was just as striking up close as it was in the distance.

The redbrick facade, interrupted by the rectangular windows trimmed in white paint, were distinctive enough. However, the white columns with their classical Greek architecture crested by the octagonal-shaped cupola made any visitor recognize this was no ordinary colonial home. Perhaps more than any of his contemporaries, Jefferson embodied the concept of the Renaissance man. Author, philosopher, scientist, farmer, philanthropist, statesman, and architect, Jefferson made sure in designing his home, it held the latest in the technology and modern comforts of the day.

The grand entrance hall, with its polished floors, glowed. The walls were covered in decorative items collected throughout his career in public life, including maps and nature samples presented to him by Lewis and Clark after their exploration of the Louisiana Territory. The room was crowned with the only working twenty-four-hour clock from that time period. Resting just above the main entryway, it operated on a pulley system with specially drilled holes in the floor to hold the massive chains that extended beyond the length of the room.

As they ventured into the pantry, another pulley system used to raise bottles of wine from the cellar was hidden in the panels of the fireplace, ensuring private conversations with visitors would not be disturbed by servants entering the room. Considering them to be eyesores, staircases were hidden and narrowed to not interrupt the architectural lines of the interior. Every detail was attended to, perfectly describing the individual who once roamed its halls.

They could have stayed there all day, but the desire to follow the clues had them heading toward the rear of the home. Exiting the mansion, they located the trail leading to the Jefferson burial site. It passed more gardens, where cabbage, carrots, and grapevines adorned the hill overlooking the valley. The trail became shaded and seemed quiet, as only a few people were moving in that direction. The path began to slope downward, and as it turned to the left, surrounded by a grove of trees and a decorative wrought iron fence, the cemetery came into view.

The site had been maintained by the Jefferson family and still served as the burial grounds for more contemporary members of the lineage. At its northern side, the large obelisk tombstone was the most unique, distinguishing it as the grave of the master of the house.

Madison pulled out the copy of the instructions and began to read. However, she suddenly felt awkward. There was a small collection of people wandering the cemetery, a husband and wife and their two young children and a group of three men. Realizing she was slipping into the same mind game trap Des had fallen into at the Foxy Loxy back in Savannah, she once again began to read, although a little bit more cautiously.

It begins with the author who in death ignores the office and overlooks the dome.

They stood directly in front of the tombstone, looking at the remarkable epitaph. It still was stunning that Jefferson had ignored the fact he was the third president of the nation he had helped found.

"I don't understand what this means when it said he overlooks the dome. The cemetery is below the mansion. How could he overlook it?" Madison asked.

"I don't believe that's the dome they were referring to," responded Des.

"What other dome is there?"

"Well, just north of here in the valley below is the University of Virginia," he said while typing on his smartphone. "And its most famous structure is also the symbol of the university." With this explanation, Des handed Madison his phone. On the screen was the logo for the University of Virginia, a rotunda dome originally designed by Jefferson.

Madison smiled, returned the phone to Des, and continued reading.

Stand at the base in the corner of his ordinance and look its opposite.

"I searched the word *ordinance* and cross-referenced it with Jefferson, and what came up was the Northwest Ordinance," she said, looking for confirmation from Des that she was going in the right direction.

The Northwest Ordinance struck a chord of irony in relation to this situation. Signed into law by President Washington in 1789, adding the Northwest Territory to lands already under the new federal government's control, it set a precedent with the acquisition of additional territory. Instead of expanding the size of the original thirteen colonies, it created new sovereign states. It also demonstrated the federal government would have influence over slavery, as it was prohibited in this newly acquired land. The irony lay in the fact that this ordinance, designed by Jefferson, was what many historians believed created the slippery slope leading to the Civil War, which, in turn, led to where Des and Madison now found themselves.

"If my thinking is correct, then that would mean we need to stand at the base of the tomb in the northwest corner and look in the opposite direction," Des stated as he started to move.

Madison stood staring southeast, hoping for some indication of what this would reveal. Though now she felt even more conspicuous, her paranoia returning. And though she convinced herself it was their weird movements that were attracting attention, she could have sworn the group of men circulating the cemetery were watching them.

Resting at the heart of his highest learning.

They scanned the grounds, taking their field of view a full 360 degrees. Nothing their eyes brought them gave any indication of what the cryptic clue meant.

"Do you see anything that makes sense?" asked Madison.

"Nothing at all."

Des thought there might be a symbol or some kind of object that would stand out. Yet it appeared barren of anything. No insignia, no set of words or collection of letters seemed connected to this clue in any way.

Madison stopped for a moment to gather her thoughts. She looked over at the young family still walking around the cemetery, reading the various graves. She could see the three men also exploring the area. One of them, a man in a black jacket and black slacks with matching jet-black hair, looked directly at her and smiled. Madison gave a polite smile back, wondering if he was flirting with her. It made her uncomfortable. Yet the thought this was all he was doing gave her some comfort, relieving her suspicion.

"Des, come over here." She motioned for him to join her. "What college did Thomas Jefferson go to? Obviously, I know it wasn't the University of Virginia."

"I think it was William and Mary."

"That's in Williamsburg, right?"

"Yeah, it is. Oh, wow! I see what you're getting at."

"William and Mary is southeast of here, the exact opposite of northwest. We're not looking for something here. They're giving us directions. It's a clever way to convey where to go. I keep forgetting these clues were written in the 1860s. I guess Google Maps was not available yet," she said with a slight giggle.

"You're right, for a person in the 1860s, there would have been no way for them to know which way Jefferson's tomb was laid out. I doubt there were any pictures available of it at that time. They would have to come here to see. I guess, with the rest of these clues, none of them would be relevant to this place. We'll have to find them in Williamsburg."

Madison saw the man in the black jacket looking at her again, but this time, she caught him glancing at Des as well. Nervously, she grabbed Des by the arm. "I think we better get going," she said, pulling him insistently.

Des immediately took notice of Madison's sudden change in demeanor, following her down the dirt trail leading to the paved road the tram utilized. Wondering what was going on, he caught her looking behind them, as if checking for someone in pursuit. He followed her example, looking back, though the trail was empty.

"Are you okay?" he asked.

"I got a bad feeling back there. Those men kept looking at us."

"Are you sure?"

"I don't know. Let's just get on the tram and get out of here."

They stood at the bottom of the trail, waiting for the tram to arrive, checking behind them every few moments. But the trail remained silent. Soon the tram arrived. They boarded, noticing they were the only ones on the vehicle.

"I'm sorry, I guess I'm just being overly cautious," she said embarrassedly.

"No, it's okay. I get nervous, too, sometimes."

The tram slowed down as it got ready for another pickup. It came to a stop, the doors opened, and the same three men at the cemetery boarded the vehicle. Visibly startled, Madison immediately bowed her head, trying to avoid making eye contact.

Des's reaction was different. His army training kicked in, and he instead studied the men, attempting to get a read on who they were. There was indeed something odd about these individuals. It was a relatively comfortable day, but he could see, looking at the men's wrist, they were wearing long-sleeved shirts underneath their jackets. He focused on the gentleman sitting directly his opposite. Des noticed the shirt was black, making anything of contrast stand out. Then he caught it and knew Madison's fear was justified.

The tram returned to the visitors' center. Des and Madison hurriedly exited the vehicle without saying a word. The men followed them off, keeping their distance, though leaving no question they were eyeing them.

The pair moved rapidly through the center. Leaving the complex, they made a mad dash for their car, Madison's anxiety growing as she recognized Des's concern.

Des hit the button on his key to unlock the car doors. "Let's get out of here!"

They jumped into the vehicle, and Des turned the ignition and proceeded toward the exit of the parking lot. As they pulled past the visitors' center, they saw the three men standing at the top of the stairs, watching them depart.

Chapter 34

Charlottesville, Virginia

"Who were those guys?" Madison asked, visibly shaken.

"I don't know, but they weren't amateurs."

"What do you mean?"

"Somebody is following us."

"What do you mean they weren't amateurs?"

"Somebody hired those men. They were wearing communication wires. I saw it underneath their sleeves. When I was in the Army, I knew guys in intelligence who wore those same devices."

"How did they know we were here?"

"I don't know."

Des drove about five minutes and then turned down an isolated street. Pulling to the side of the road, he tried to get his bearings on where they were.

"Do you think that someone knew at the foundation?" Madison asked.

"It's possible, but I don't know how. We were the only ones there when we found the original clues. Did you speak with anyone about it or tell anyone where we were going?"

"No, I knew better than to do that." She was irritated that Des would even consider that a possibility.

"I'm sorry, you're right," he said, embarrassed. Des placed his hand on her arm apologetically and then reached over to put the car back in drive.

It was the screeching sound of a skid that sent the first warning. A black SUV lurched in front of them, blocking their path. Des tried to throw the car in reverse, but another SUV jutted behind them. They were trapped.

Madison screamed as two men jumped out of the car in front with guns drawn. Des looked in the rearview mirror and saw the other man from their group approaching from the rear, armed as well.

"Get out!" yelled the dark-haired man, who first made eye contact with Madison at Jefferson's grave. Madison was shaking nearly uncontrollably.

"Keep your hands up and do what they say," Des said calmly.

The men pulled open the doors and yanked Madison and Des from the car. At once, they started searching them. Finding the paper Madison had copied the clues on in her back pocket, the man unfolded it, examining what he had discovered.

"I found that paper she was reading from!" he yelled.

"We'll call him and let him know," stated the dark-haired individual.

Des was trying to get a grasp on who they were and what they wanted. They were definitely ex-military or at least governmentally trained within some defense or security agency. Two of them looked to be in their late thirties or early forties; however, the obvious leader appeared to only be in his mid to late twenties. He had striking black hair and a thin, wiry frame, while the other two both had light-brown hair and more muscular builds.

The dark-haired man pulled Madison over next to Des. "Is this everything?" he asked, holding the paper in his hand. Neither moved or said a word. Madison was shivering so violently she couldn't even speak, let alone focus on his question.

"Don't make me ask you again," he said, moving the gun closer to her head.

"We don't know what you mean," pleaded Des.

"Don't lie to me! Don't you fucking lie to me!"

"That's everything we have."

Des knew Madison was not going to be able to last much longer in this situation. She was hyperventilating to the point she might pass out.

"I'll shoot her in her goddamn head if you don't give me everything you have!" he screamed while touching the tip of the barrel to Madison's temple.

The fear in Madison's face was nearly unbearable to witness as tears streaked down her cheeks.

"She doesn't know anything. I just brought her along with me. Look, you can take anything you want. Everything we have is in the car. Please, just relax, point the gun at me. She doesn't know anything."

The man paused as he and his co-conspirators calculated what they should do. With a nod, the two with the light-brown hair started to move toward Des's car to begin their search. An audible hum of an engine emanated from around the corner. Everyone looked in that direction.

A car drove by the adjacent road without the slightest hesitation at the scene unfolding just a few yards away. Des's heart sank, wishing someone had noticed and come to their aid. Dropping his head in disappointment, he searched for his next negotiation tactic. He closed his eyes to gain peace and reflected on his training to refocus.

The men, noticing the possible interruption and threat, walked over to their dark-haired leader. Once again, the impending hum of an engine approached. Des tried not letting it break his concentration. He couldn't afford to be distracted. Blocking out the sound, he was opening his mouth to give his next selling point. But the hum of the incoming car was becoming louder and louder, turning into a roar. He shot his head up in time to see another vehicle, a white pickup truck, heading directly at the unfolding scene, bearing down on where they were grouped.

Des leaped and tackled Madison, their captors throwing themselves to the ground as the truck slammed into the lead SUV. A cloud of dust flew upon the impact. Des, disoriented, turned to see a young man with sandy-blond hair get out of the vehicle and level a gun at the three men lying before him.

"Drop your weapons!" he yelled. The men, looking bewildered, at first did not comply. "I said, drop your guns, goddamn it!" he screamed.

The men let their guns tumble to the ground. Des picked up Madison off the dirty road, keeping an eye on this latest development. The young man returned Des's gaze, instantly conveying there was a new commander in charge.

"Okay, kick your guns over to me," the young man ordered. The disgruntled men complied.

Pulling out three sets of handcuffs from his back pocket, the blond kid threw it at the men. "You three, handcuff yourselves together and then to the bumper of my truck." He motioned with his gun for them to move in that direction. Des and Madison fell in line as well, moving with the others, not knowing what he had in mind until looking at him. He shook his head.

The three men did as instructed, the action effectively immobilizing all of them. Picking up their guns, the young man, his eyes never leaving his captives, threw the weapons into a grove of adjacent bushes. He then turned his attention to Des and Madison.

"Get in your car," he said, pointing his gun at them. "You drive. She needs to get in the back seat."

Des and Madison moved, unsure, to their vehicle. Still shaking and barely functioning, Madison complied and got into the back seat. Des got behind the wheel while the young man sat in the front passenger seat.

"Take us back to the highway," he demanded, pointing his gun at him.

Des started the ignition, turned the car around, and headed toward the highway onramp. They drove in complete silence for about two minutes, the young man still focusing on him. Madison, still visibly frightened, did not move.

The scene was becoming unbearable. Des couldn't take it. He was about to speak when the young man broke the silence.

"Are you two okay?" he asked, putting his gun down in his lap. "I'm sorry about what happened back there. I didn't mean to scare you."

Des and Madison were in shock, not knowing how to respond. After taking a second to process this unexpected situation, Des interjected. "What's going on? Who are you? Who were those men?"

"Slow down, it's okay. My name is William. Those men work for someone who's looking for the treasure like you. I worked with him, but we don't see eye to eye anymore. He's not going to share it with anyone. He's been tracking you. Let's stop somewhere so we can talk," he calmly replied.

"Where do you want us to stop?"

"Keep driving for a while and turn off your phones and wrap them in these," he said, pulling aluminum foil out of his jacket pocket. "Otherwise, they can track where we're going."

Des handed Madison his phone, so she could do what William instructed. With her trembling hands, it was a difficult task.

William, noticing her fear, tried to calm her. "Don't worry, I'm not going to hurt you."

"What do you want?" Des asked demandingly.

"I want to help. I couldn't let it happen. I had to protect you."

Chapter 35

Twenty miles northwest of Richmond, Virginia

Highway 64 is an offshoot of Interstate 95, crossing through various small towns and eventually traversing through Charlottesville. Its terrain is both flat and hilly and usually full of rich greenness, encompassing forest, and farms alike.

Patiently waiting for notification from his men, the Judge sat in his parked car, sipping the cheap coffee and gnawing on the stale pastry he purchased at a local doughnut shop. He could do without a lot of vices if need be, but coffee wasn't one of them.

Although the Judge could be an excitable man, he also had the uncanny ability to stay calm in tense situations. Maybe this was from spending years dealing with volatile attorneys, or it could be from experiencing the equally volatile women in his life. Regardless, he could always dissociate himself from an emotional response. This personality quirk worked well in the courtroom. However, it was disastrous in the rest of his relationships.

Wondering whether every detail had been covered, he stared out the car window, looking at the light mist that had gathered over the fields off in the distance. He had competent people in place to make sure things went as planned, and even contingencies in case they didn't. However, he continually evaluated and reevaluated any situation.

It had been about an hour when the high-pitched jingle of his phone broke the stillness. He recognized the number; it was the lead individual he had sent to find the woman.

"Did you locate her?" he asked in a monotone voice.

"Yes, but we have a situation we weren't expecting."

The Judge listened coolly to the details, biting his upper lip to control the flood of emotions. He listened carefully without interrupting, making sure he was able to fully understand the entire scenario.

"Read me what you got off the girl." The Judge copied down the instructions they had extracted onto his yellow legal pad, which he always had with him. "Are you sure that's everything?"

"Yes, word for word."

"Okay, and we should be able to track them again?"

"Yes, sir, that's in place."

"Very good. Let's stay focused. I'll call you soon."

The Judge felt his nerves on end as he ended the call. The other facet of his plan would have to be put into motion. The text was simple and to the point, just as he was instructed. *Sometimes I wonder who is working for whom,* he thought. *I wish I didn't need the son of a bitch.*

Trying to keep things in perspective, he remembered he still had access. The treasure was within reach. *Just use your resources and you will get there. Don't lose yourself in the stress. Just stay focused and it will all come together.*

Chapter 36

Location unknown

He was simply called Osiris, his true identity was a mystery to all. It was a name taken from the Egyptian god of knowledge and death, an all-seeing entity who was worshipped for his ability to pass on information to mere mortals. It fit him perfectly.

Even his actual existence was the privileged knowledge of only a few who could afford his services; the rest relied on myths and legends. Stories were abundant, with various intelligence agencies, at one time or another, claiming he had received his training through their branch. The tales were so prolific it was impossible to tell which was truth and which was fantasy. Some likened him to a real-life James Bond, while others stated his reality was based in as much fact as the unicorn. After twenty years of anonymity, the doubters outnumbered the believers, which was just how he liked it.

He began operating in the shadows of the government's intelligence apparatus, starting as a low-level analyst. But his talents would not be contained. Within a few years of his initiation into the business, he became the go-to man for collecting filth on foreign governments, corporate espionage, and bureaucratic sabotage. With the passing of time, his skills only sharpened.

As his legend grew, so did the demands. Handpicked for some of the most important and dangerous operations the agency ever tackled, he had a success rate that was enormous. Told he was saving the nation, he risked his life daily.

Yet while the missions became more difficult, their objectives became just as murky. Eventually, the only thing he could not decipher was which side he was actually serving. The passing years only brought a greater sense of disenchantment, while the bullshit he was fed by his government employer grew more difficult to swallow. What did not change was the pay. *I don't need this shit anymore. I'm not working for the side of good, I'm working for bureaucrats who serve their own political objectives. If I'm going to do that, I might as well get paid!* And just like that, he was gone.

He didn't look the part; the dashing secret-agent type, he was not. Of medium height, trim build, bald head, and a thick beard interspersed with gray, he appeared more like a museum docent than a highly trained and skilled infiltrator.

Yet those limited few who had access to him learned to never doubt his extraordinary ability. His skills were wide ranging, from research to reconnaissance to assassination, and the attention to detail and results he provided were worth every pretty penny he charged. And he didn't come cheap. Yet if you needed to collect information, if you needed to spy on someone you believed was beyond reproach, or if you wanted to eliminate an individual without a trace, no one could compare.

His lifestyle was of complete disconnection. His communication with others was curt, especially when it came to business. It was a fleeting existence, purposely designed for people to take little notice, allowing him to disappear like a specter, a vapor that dissipated and then was absorbed by the atmosphere surrounding it.

His calling card was word of mouth, and only those with the highest connections would be granted access. The Judge only managed to learn of him through a fluke. An FBI contact had caught wind of Osiris's services through a clandestine operation. With someone hurting for money, it took only a little palm greasing and a promise to never say where he obtained it to get the information.

Osiris's price was steep; a week's worth of work would easily surpass six figures, all paid in advance. But the job was guaranteed. Any failure to deliver on what was promised would result in a full refund. In seventeen years and hundreds of cases, he had never needed to make good on that policy.

Normally, he would not take a client like the Judge. It seemed fanciful. *A treasure hunt… really?* As was his practice, he researched. And though the Judge seemed potentially troublesome and difficult, the argument was surprisingly convincing. *What the hell, it's easy money. Who knows, maybe there will be a little extra fruit at the end of this labor?*

For now, the request was simple. Keep an eye on who the Judge was working with. If what his client was after was real, trust could not be extended to anyone, let alone those who might gain access through outside means. It was a game as old as the spy trade and meant to answer the same question the Romans put forth so long ago: *Quis custodiet ipsos custodes?* Who will guard the guards?

Chapter 37

Twenty miles north of Charlottesville, Virginia

There was an eerie calmness in the vehicle while the three of them reflected upon the horrific situation they had just experienced. Des did not know what to make of this young man, although he was feeling better that he no longer had a gun pointed at him. He wanted to grab it off William's lap but thought better of it. Whoever he was, he just saved both of them from a deadly situation. If he really wanted to harm them, he would have done so by now, and if he was here to help as he claimed, then it would be best to listen to him and find out about this other individual targeting them.

Des could see Madison in his rearview mirror still in a state of semishock. Something that was understandable, considering she just had a gun to her head. Beads of sweat dotted her face, which appeared nauseated.

"If we go somewhere, I want it to be a public place," Des demanded.

"That would be fine. Wherever you want to go."

They had been on the road for about an hour, and after taking several concerned looks behind them to see if they were being followed, they felt safe enough to pull off the highway after catching a billboard for a local burger joint. Pulling into the parking lot and noticing it was fairly crowded put Des a bit more at ease. If this young man had ill intentions, it was unlikely he would do anything in such a public setting.

After Des parked the car, William put his gun in the glove compartment and exited the vehicle. Upon seeing this, Des realized he might be a blessing. Des looked back at Madison to see if she had noticed what William had done with his weapon, but she did not react. Noticing her blank stare, Des opened her car door.

"Hey," he said, touching her arm. "It's okay, we're all right. He's not here to hurt us. I think he can help. Come on, I'll get you something cold to drink. You'll feel better, I promise."

Madison nodded, then slowly moved her left leg out of the car, and then her right. Taking Des's hand, she gradually stood up. William stood to the side, far enough away, to be respectful. He did not wish to make her feel any more uncomfortable than she already did.

"Are you okay?" Des asked.

She nodded again. Des started toward the door when he felt Madison's hand on his shoulder. He turned to face her, and before he could speak another word, she embraced him tightly, putting her head on his shoulder. Des wrapped his arms around her in a comforting hold, kissing her forehead while reassuring her she was safe.

"We're going to be fine, I promise," he said, smiling.

It helped her regain composure. Wiping a tear from her eye, she took a deep breath and managed a slight grin. "I'll be fine. Let's get something to drink."

The diner was the epitome of a local hangout. Most everyone there was on a first-name basis with the waitresses as well as one another. The owner of the establishment, a heavyset man with gray hair, who looked to be in his early sixties, filtered through the crowd, greeting his friends with a warm smile and kind words.

Within a few minutes, the three of them were seated at a small booth near the back of the room. Its red vinyl benches and darkstained wood walls created a little secure cocoon where they could discuss the situation privately.

Des and Madison sat directly across from William, making sure to keep him within sight at all times. Not wasting any time, Des started the conversation within moments of sitting down.

"I guess we should thank you for what you did getting us out of that situation. You mentioned we're being targeted by another individual, someone you used to work with. Who is he?"

"Well, we never worked together directly. We're not friends. We're more like business associates."

"Business associates?"

"This started out as a business venture, but it never really was for me." William, noticing Madison eyeing him suspiciously, wanted to ease her concerns. "Madison, I'm truly sorry about what happened to you back there. I'm sure it was horrible for you. I didn't mean to scare you, but I had to make sure those hired guns knew I was serious."

"How do you know my name?"

"We know a lot about you. Ms. Madison Callum," he recited. "Originally from just outside Nashville, currently living in Savannah, Georgia, working as a part-time professor at Savannah State, specializing in African American studies."

Madison was stunned, as if she had been violated in a very strange way.

"Whom I don't know much about is you," he said, looking directly at Des. "You see, we knew she had been looking for the treasure. We weren't expecting another person to be involved. How did you fall into this mess?"

"I'm kind of the one who started it. I found some information and shared it with her."

"Who is this other person you were working with?" asked Madison.

"I just know him as the Judge. Apparently, he's a pretty influential federal court judge who has contacts everywhere. He's a very powerful man who has an extreme interest in finding the lost Confederate treasure."

"How did you get involved in this? Have you always had an interest in the treasure?" Des inquired.

"Yes, but for different reasons than what you might think."

Madison and Des, looking confused, both took a long drink from their sodas the waitress had just placed on the table, wondering what their next question should be.

William attempted clarification. "I have a special connection to the treasure. My great-great-grandfather served under General Lee during the war. He was his personal courier. He left a journal that has been in my family for generations. In it, he tells how he was summoned to meet with Jefferson Davis to deliver instructions to a contact in Georgia. This was right before the capital had to be evacuated. He said it had extreme value. We've always believed he was involved in evacuating the treasure but didn't give any more details."

"What happened to him?" Madison asked.

"He was killed in Georgia in a minor skirmish with some of Sherman's troops."

"What happened to the instructions?" Des said, suddenly energized.

"Well, that's just it. They never found them on his body that we know of. For a very long time, I've been searching for it. I want to complete the journey for my family's legacy. However, it was expensive and frustrating, because I kept running into dead ends. And that was when I met the Judge."

"Had he been searching for it too?" asked Madison.

"Yes. We met at a Civil War reenactment, and he overheard me speaking about it with some other people. We talked for a while, and I told him about the journal and he told me about his passion for Civil War history and his beliefs that it still existed, which was different from most people I've talked to, who believe it is either long gone or just a myth. That was when we decided to pool our resources. He would provide the finances if I would provide him the clues from the journal to help locate it."

"How did you find me, then?"

"I set up a specialty program on my computer that looks specifically for what other people are searching for on their computers. It looks for key phrases or words that I input. Some of those key words matched with some of your searches. The Judge did the rest."

"What do you mean did the rest?" Madison asked, getting irritated.

"Like I said, the Judge has contacts everywhere. He has access to electronic surveillance, investigators, as well as hired guns. I knew he was interested in finding it, but I became concerned over the past couple of months because his attitude started to scare me. He talked about not being willing to share the treasure with anyone else, and I knew what that meant. I knew I had to intervene."

"What do we do now, go to the police?"

"No, you can't do that. He has access to people in law enforcement everywhere. He's a federal judge who can get the FBI on you at a moment's notice. The only thing that will happen is, you'll be captured, and I think after what you've seen today, you know what the result will be. Plus, what are you going to tell the police, that some unidentified men that you have no information on assaulted you over a lost Civil War treasure? Come on," he said, almost mockingly. "By the time you reported that information, we would all be dead before anything would ever happen to him, and that's even if they took you seriously in the first place. Even if I vouched for your story, the Judge is smart enough to disavow all knowledge, and he certainly wouldn't leave any trace between him and those men who came after you today."

"So you're telling me that he plans on killing us regardless of what we do?" Des asked nervously.

"Yes. He sees you as getting in the way."

"Well, what if we just stop looking and go back home?" Madison asked.

"That won't work either. He thinks you have more information. He knows where you live, and he has already shown his hand. He also knows that I'm with you now, giving you his secrets. He needs to get what you have and then eliminate you from the picture."

"He can have our information. We don't want the treasure that badly," Des said sternly.

"It doesn't matter what you want. He's going to do what he thinks is necessary. There's no way he's going to stop coming after you just because you give him what you have. He's paranoid. He'll get rid of you to make sure no one else ever has access to your information. He will not risk having to share this with anyone."

"Why did you tell us all this when you know it puts us in danger?" an angry Madison asked demandingly.

"You don't get it. It doesn't matter if I told you or not. Now that you're with me, he's going to assume I'm telling you. There was no way around it. The minute I intervened, that was going to be the result. I had to choose between getting you out of there with the possibility of surviving this or letting you get shot right then."

Madison was becoming visibly scared, as Des could see her starting to tremble again. Putting his hand gently on her arm to calm her, he took a deep breath.

"What do we do now? What's our next move?" Des asked.

"If we find it before he does and make it public, he'll have to stop. You'll take away any motivation for him to do otherwise."

"So you're saying we continue looking for the treasure?"

"Yes, we have to see this thing to the end."

Des dropped his head in despair. He could not believe this journey, which started out as an innocent treasure hunt, had now become a forced chase of something that, if he wasn't successful in obtaining, could mean his and Madison's death.

"And there's no other way?"

William looked down and shook his head. "I'm afraid not."

"I guess we're going to have to move forward, then, aren't we?" Des said exasperatedly.

"I'm sorry, this is not what I intended. I never wanted to get you involved like this."

Des nodded in resignation, while Madison's fear had returned to its prior levels. She grabbed Des's hand resting on the vinyl bench underneath the table and squeezed tightly.

"We'll be okay," he said underneath his breath. He wasn't sure he could keep his promise.

Chapter 38

Forty-five minutes later, the three anxious individuals exited the restaurant. Each of them looking physically and emotionally drained. But they did not have time to rest. The chase had commenced, and any hesitation would jeopardize their chances of survival.

As they got back into the car, a sense of urgency overtook them. William politely went to the back seat, surrendering the front to Madison.

"Did those men take anything from you before I got there?" William asked.

"Yes, they took the paper I copied down the clues on," Madison answered.

William sighed in frustration, knowing the Judge's men were going to relay the information to him. "What did the clues tell you?"

Both Madison and Des hesitated. They did not feel this young man with the innocent-looking blond locks was a threat, but their protective instincts made them reticent to giving out additional information to someone they hardly knew.

Seeing their hesitation, William knew he needed to gain their trust. "Des, could you please pull to the side of the road for a second?"

Des complied, wondering what this was about. Although he knew it was out of his reach, he could not help but keep his attention on the glove compartment, fearing its contents might be used against them again. Yet William gave no indication that was what he desired to do.

"Look, I understand why you don't trust me yet, and given what you've already been through, I get it. But if we're going to get through this, you're going to have to start trusting me. I don't know if you truly appreciate what we're up against. The Judge has tons of resources, he's smart, he understands history, and don't forget, he's still willing to kill you to get what he wants. I'm happy to give you everything I have, but I need you to share with me what you know so we can all avoid ending up in a grave," William pleaded.

He then reached into his jacket pocket. Madison, seeing the motion, let out a little gasp, believing he might possess another weapon. What he retrieved, however, was not another gun, but a tattered leather pocketbook appearing to be well over a hundred years old. Its brown covering, cracked and frayed, was like some of the items they had seen at their work at the foundation. He handed it to Madison, hoping this would engender trust.

"Is this what I think it is?" Madison asked, looking surprised.

"Yes. Now you have everything. That's my family's legacy."

She began delicately thumbing through the pages, being careful not to damage them. She studied the writing, which was obviously written in iron gall ink, its brown color giving away its age. She glanced up to see William staring at her intently, looking for any sign of belief in him.

"I need to know where we're going next, as I might be able to find something in the diary that can help us," William stated.

Madison sighed almost with embarrassment for not giving this individual any credit for saving them and continuing her unwarranted suspicion. "Williamsburg. Everything we found out at Monticello points to Williamsburg," she said.

"Well, we better get going, then. If they have the clues, they'll figure it out as well." Then he paused. "Wait, didn't you say that they took the clues off you?"

"Yes, but we have the originals," Madison answered.

"You should make some new copies," Des suggested.

"Can I see the originals?" asked William.

Madison looked at Des for confirmation. He gave her a reassuring nod. Reaching over, she retrieved Des's blue backpack in the back seat. Opening a pouch with Des's army unit insignia patch sewn onto it, she took out the manila folder holding the original instructions. Then she removed the wooden box they had dug up at the church. She handed William the first set of clues, hoping the contents would be meaningful.

William accepted it with an expression of gratitude. As he opened the folder, the look on his face could only be described as wonderment. He sat speechless for several moments, his eyes moving all over the paper.

"Where did you find this?" he finally asked.

"We were working on a historical preservation project. I was opening a small picture frame to scan a photo when that fell out of the back," Des explained.

"What made you think it was related to the treasure?"

"When you look at the top, it says, 'The instructions are simple,' but we realized when we examined it more closely, it really says, 'The instructions are Semple's.' I knew Semple was—"

"He was the contact who was supposed to evacuate the treasure out of Savannah," William filled in. "I'm sorry. I didn't mean to interrupt. I just can't believe I'm holding this." William's eyes started to tear up. It was a feeling of astonishment, like being reconnected with a missing piece of his soul after having lost all hope. "I have a feeling these were the instructions that my great-great-grandfather carried with him. It makes perfect sense that they would be found in Georgia, where he died. What are these stains?" he said, lightly brushing his fingertips across the paper.

"I think it might be blood," Madison replied.

William felt a chill go down his spine. He knew his great-great-grandfather had given his life for the cause. It had always been prevalent in his thoughts. However, he never saw it presented in such a visceral form. He could not think of a more fitting tribute.

"When we realized what the first sentence said, we understood what we possibly had in our possession. So we decided to follow the instructions. We were skeptical that we would find anything but wanted to give it a shot. We never thought it would turn into this," Des said regretfully.

William seemed lost in another world, not being able to stop looking at the wrinkled paper. His eyes were the size of saucers, straining to make sure he took in every inch of this historical treasure. The only way Des and Madison knew he was still listening was the monotone "Uh-huh" sounds he made in five-second intervals in response to Des's information.

"So where did you determine these clues pointed to?" William asked.

"South Carolina, Old Sheldon Church. And that was where we found this," she said, holding the wooden artifact, then opening the lid, revealing its felt-covered interior.

"May I?" William asked graciously.

"Of course."

Gently taking the box out of her hands, he admired the symbol emblazoned on its lid. "This is unbelievable," he said in amazement. He ran his finger over the small wooden chest, feeling the rough edges of its cracked and weathered wood. The movement of his finger was interrupted by the circular medallion on its top. "CSN," he whispered in a barely audible voice.

He reached into the interior, its softness caressing his fingertips. William knew something this well-thought-of could only hold the most precious of items.

Once his study of the box was complete, Madison handed him its contents. Viewing the red wax, he immediately recognized the mark of the president of the Confederacy. Carefully holding the paper, its crinkling sound filling the air of the now completely silent vehicle, he meditatively went over each line.

The emotions were indescribable. William felt a validation he had never experienced. All the years of searching, all the heartache of those belittling his belief that this existed had been wiped away.

"I assume these are the instructions that brought you to Monticello. But what makes you think we have to go to Williamsburg?"

"When we went to Jefferson's grave, it instructed us to look in the opposite direction of his ordinance. The only ordinance associated with Jefferson was the Northwest Ordinance, which would make sense, since that ordinance was directly related to the prohibition of slavery. The opposite of northwest would be southeast. Then it told us it 'rested in the heart of his highest learning.' Jefferson was educated at William and Mary in Williamsburg," explained Des.

"You two are smart. Des, you have far too much knowledge to be a novice. What's your background?"

"I'm a graduate student in history at the University of Georgia."

"That makes sense. We have to get to Williamsburg. The Judge is not as knowledgeable about historical references as you are, but I guarantee you, he'll figure it out. Like I said, he has resources. The only advantage we have is, he's paranoid about sharing too much with anyone, so it may take him a bit longer to decipher this information."

Des put his car back in drive, restarting the trek to Williamsburg. The joy of discovery had been washed away and replaced by the growing fear that they were not pursuing a treasure but rather their survival. And that which was never a factor before was their biggest factor now, time.

Chapter 39

Heading southeast on Highway 64, Virginia

The Judge grabbed his phone, making another call to try to see if he could get a bead on where these individuals were heading. It rang but was not immediately picked up, causing his stress level to jump two octaves. Finally, there was an answer.

"Yes, Judge."

"Do we know where they're headed? Because I already have an idea. But I wanted to double-check," the Judge inquired. "Okay, good, keep on it. We'll engage them there. We just need to make sure we get the information. There's no way I'm going to miss out on this, and they're not to have any part of it." He ended the call and continued to head toward his next destination.

He was able to slightly relax, yet it was short-lived. There was always an internal panic, a makeup in his personality that forbade him from ever enjoying the moment. He had always been self-pressed to succeed, and the fear of never accomplishing anything of significance haunted him constantly.

His life to this point had been, by all accounts, immensely successful. Though it never resonated with him. He could never take pleasure in the attributes others saw in him and his career. It was a source of constant torture. Living in a reality that could never meet his own expectations. Thus, he was unable to take satisfaction in what others considered a life well lived.

The drive to attain the treasure had wealth at its heart. But the Judge was not a monolithic creature. His motivation amounted to more than just the monetary value. This treasure represented a chance to drown the demons that had always haunted him. In finding it, he would reach a level of self-realization which would finally allow him to have some peace in his existence.

As a lover of history, he admired the visionaries whose names were etched upon the world consciousness. Washington, Franklin, Newton, Churchill, and Darwin were just some of the men he admired. His veneration for them was not just in their accomplishments or how they affected the world; it was in their effort to implement change. They left a legacy of greatness, a foundation for whoever followed to build upon. He always desired to be able to be thought of in those terms. The path he took to have those opinions formed of him was inconsequential.

However, nothing in his life had brought him close. In his opinion, he had failed in a plethora of missed opportunities or, even worse, failed recognition of what could bring him his confirmation of greatness. This was his last chance. If he faltered here, his existence could no longer be justified. He would just go on, a shell of the life that could have been lived.

He was dreamlike in his thoughts. The winding road served as a hypnotic elixir fueling his desire to reach the next destination. Failure would not be tolerated. This was it. They must not be allowed to share in his glory.

Chapter 40

Twenty miles southeast of Charlottesville, Virginia

The call ended as abruptly as it began. This was not unusual in conversations with the Judge and something that if you worked for him on previous assignments, you got used to very quickly. Chris Wells was accustomed to clients being edgy, short in verse, or jittery. It was the nature of the business. It never fazed him, for he always received his pay and, due to his connections, never seemed to be wanting for work.

Chris was one of those individuals who had a knack for being in the right place at the right time. There was nothing about his skill set, experience, or even intelligence that set him apart. But it did not seem to apply to his level of success.

His colleagues recognized him as lacking in many areas and having questionable ethics; thus, they were always bewildered that even after botched performances, he kept being rewarded with new assignments. Attaining plum jobs or advancements in positions was commonplace for Chris as he understood the key element in reaching his goals was not skill or performance but through the ability to figure out the right alliances and then exploit them. Nonetheless, the fact his colleagues did not see him as a talented purveyor of the craft was always a source of anger and embarrassment.

His first job in security was through a private agency, where he befriended an aging owner nearing retirement who came to see him as the son he never had. Using his ties with people working in the federal government, the owner made it his personal mission to make sure Chris was awarded jobs that would normally require a great deal more experience.

When Chris faltered, the owner acted as a safety net, catching him and using his influence to gain an even better position in the future. Often ignoring people who had served by his side for years, the owner, and now benefactor, would push his protégé for every desirable position, realizing there would be a payday in it for him as well.

Chris did not make it easy, committing massive mistakes that were often the results of his immaturity and, sometimes, his incompetence. Yet it made little difference. His mentor would explain them to his superiors as part of a learning curve, almost making it an endearing quality, which would, in turn, make them ignore his evident shortcomings.

After working in the security sector of the federal government for only about four years, Chris recognized there was more money to be made in private work bordering on the mercenary. With a striking look that included a thin but strong physique, jet-black hair, and an impressive-looking résumé if one did not delve too deeply into the reality, the young former government agent began farming himself off to top clients as a security and investigative expert. Through the help of his mentor, Chris was able to carve out a niche, garnering salaries a federal employee could only dream of while having the freedom to pick and choose his assignments.

He was first contacted by the Judge two years ago, after his benefactor had already established a relationship going back decades. The Judge wanted some investigative work done on a former defendant and now business partner, who he felt was being less than forthcoming in some of their financial dealings, costing the Judge a great deal of money.

Although the Judge never requested the use of violence or threats, it was not a discouraged practice and left Chris to his own professional judgment, or lack thereof, to do what was necessary to extract what he wanted. What was done to reach the desired result was not discussed, and the Judge, being a wise customer, would never question how it was attained. To him, the only concern was if the job was performed to his satisfaction. The fact his business partner was never heard from again was not taken into consideration, as long as an alibi was provided and no knowledge divulged.

This assignment, however, was quite different. It required travel over great distances and the people being targeted did not have any previous dealings with his client. He was now tracking them heading north, as the monitoring device placed on their vehicle was operating perfectly.

Initially, Chris thought this would be a fairly simple assignment. A young woman, part-time college professor who happened to stumble onto information needed by his client, hardly seemed to be a complicated target. This was unlike the typical seasoned person of interest that was routine in his previous hunting.

Yet this latest development was making the job much more complex, requiring Chris to delve deeper into his skill level. Unfortunately, for those who knew his level of expertise, that pool was a shallow one. This could force him to use methods a more qualified individual would only rely on as a last resort.

But for now, his instructions were simple, just trail them and then make contact with the Judge once they stopped. He needed to observe rather than react. Yet frustration was settling in. The Judge was excruciatingly elusive when asked for details. Chris did not receive any information on what was being sought or the reason for the varying locations of the assignment. Other cases included details for the collection of sensitive information, allowing for a better understanding on how to engage the target. In this circumstance, no guidance was specified, leading to a blind spot for Chris and his team.

Even though the chasm in information created a difficult wrinkle, he knew better than to request items not readily given from the client. For now, though, the targets were in range, and he had already provided an important piece of information, pleasing the Judge.

Everything is under control. I will provide my services effectively. Chris's own feelings of his professional conduct, at least in this case, were confirmed. The amount of money he was receiving would serve as a testament to his quality of work.

He had heard the naysayers, the ones who had maligned his advancement while he was with the company, and later the government. Even though he pretended not to be bothered by the whispers, it gnawed at him. He wanted them to believe he deserved his positions and they were not simply products of the coddled treatment of his mentor.

Chris checked his monitoring device again, making sure he was within effective range of the target. The best prey was one who thought they were not being pursued. They were always the most vulnerable. A feeling of security ultimately bred complacency, making mistakes inevitable.

Chris could not help fantasizing about what success in this case would mean. He would attain not only an incredible payday but also what he really desired, credibility. This job would be done perfectly.

My client will be satisfied.

Chapter 41

Forty miles northeast of Williamsburg, Virginia

Des, Madison, and William were relatively quiet, only breaking the silence with mundane questions or conversations rehashing the clues. Unfortunately, conversing about history only added to the stress. But as they went through this part of the country, it was hard not to reflect on the Civil War.

The Commonwealth of Virginia is home to more Civil War battlefields than any other state in the nation. It hardly seemed one could travel more than a few miles without spotting a historical landmark sign. Names echoing throughout the American landscape, Fredericksburg, Chancellorsville, and Bull Run were all a part of Virginia heritage, which also was home to the most famous army of the Confederacy.

William sat in the back seat, trying not to disturb his fellow passengers while thumbing through the journal. He had read this collection of verses countless times but was always searching for something new, an item, a clue, some indicator he might have overlooked. When he failed to find those, he always found inspiration.

Although they did not contain any clues, his favorite entries were the ones offering insight into his great-great-grandfather's mindset. The man whose name he had taken to honor his memory was no ordinary soldier. He was educated, well versed in philosophy, science, and the political events of the day. Unlike his contemporaries, his reactions to the crisis were meticulously thought-out and not based on the irrational emotions that were so indicative of the time. He did not see the people of the North as hated enemies, rather as misguided brethren who had lost their way. It was these calmly stated arguments that captured the present-day William's imagination. These writings meant more to him than the treasure itself, because they indicated what it was for and what those who protected it hoped to accomplish.

The passage when he anguished over the breakup of the Union displayed this sentiment best.

> *The Yankees have destroyed the nation. They have forgotten why this union was formed, to protect us against the tyranny we faced when we first separated from the British. I do not rejoice in this most recent separation; it does nothing but give me heartache. I fear we have lost something great and that this secession will never fully heal us.*

William felt his ancestor's remorse. He understood the most prevalent questions asked before the war were never truly answered. The problems that threatened and nearly destroyed the nation then were now tearing it apart from its foundation. It hurt William deeply. He did not wish to see his nation lose its way again, yet from every indication, it was faltering. He continued to read.

> *President Lincoln is so determined to free the slaves he is willing to sacrifice the nation. He has failed to see this is more than just about the freeing of a people; it's about a country remembering its roots and what its forefathers had fought for in the first place.*

William experienced a range of emotions, frustration, anger, sadness. It filled him with a sense of mission, a purpose that needed to be completed. He would help his new companions as their expertise would help him. However, he did not expect them to understand the meaning of the treasure. That concept seemed lost on everyone he had tried to enlighten. The reenactors did not understand; neither did the Judge. Why would they be any different?

William glanced at Madison, wondering if this educated individual could ever comprehend his calling. *How could she? She still envisions the treasure solely as material wealth. She does not see it for what it was meant to be.*

Madison didn't notice William's gaze. She sat quietly, intently copying the clues onto notebook paper to preserve the originals. Making sure every detail of the wording was perfect, she would stop to examine her work.

Des was lost in thought, trying to predict what dangers might await them. He had encountered violence before, but this was not war; it was a twisted contest. He was involved in a game he did not want to play and never intended to be a part of. He was trapped, facing an adversary whom he did not know, nor had he ever been in conflict with. He also felt responsible. Even though Madison was a willing participant in the initial search, she had her life interrupted in the most terrible of ways by his curiosity. If he had just walked away when that paper first fell from the frame, had he just scanned it as a part of the original preservation, things would be different. However, if there was one thing he learned during his service in the Army, it was that dwelling on past mistakes would not solve present problems. He glanced to his right, looking at her again, realizing he must do everything in his power to get her through this. *She must not suffer for my gaffe.*

"What are you thinking about?" she asked Des.

"Just thinking about how ridiculous this all is. I'm so sorry that I got you involved in this."

"It's not your fault. I chose to get involved. I'm as guilty as you are."

"I should have gone with my initial instinct and just scanned the letter and filed it like we were supposed to. If I had done that, we wouldn't be involved in this mess."

"Des, you can't blame yourself. How could you predict this would happen? Nobody could. It was supposed to be something fun. It just happened. It's nobody's fault."

Des appreciated Madison letting him off the hook, but he could not escape the feelings of guilt. He felt responsible. Madison's gesture was kind, yet it did not change the reality. She was not prepared to deal with individuals like this, and in all honesty, he did not know if he was either.

William witnessed the exchange, though he acted as if he did not take notice, keeping his head buried in the journal. His emotions were mixed. They provided him with vital information, but they were also in the way. He did not dislike these individuals but resented having to protect them. They were now a necessary evil as much as they were a hindrance. Hopefully, they would not be under his care much longer.

Chapter 42

Near Petersburg, Virginia

He detested the game. It was messy, complicated, and worst of all, indirect. To the Judge, it created problems that had not existed previously, yet he also could not deny its advantages.

Up to this point, everyone was in the dark, and he realized operating blindly was unproductive, to say the least. Yet now he had no choice. He thought he could acquire it relatively quickly. It was not meant to be.

Unexpected circumstances were always a possibility, so implementation of the other option had now become a necessity. Relying on one group of pros would not be enough, and he knew it.

Chris wouldn't like it. Using an outside party, someone who was not part of his team, would not be swallowed easily. But then again, Chris didn't have a choice. *Fuck him.*

The text came in. It was simple and innocuous: "Subject under observation." The Judge reacted with a scoffing laugh. *Who the hell does he think he is?*

He should have seen the signs. William's continued concern about losing information. His constant insistence that any source, whether attained or yet to be extracted, must be protected should have been a red flag. It was a notice that would not be placated. But he ignored it and now had this situation forced upon him.

Second-guessing served no purpose. Whether he liked it or not, the game had been changed. Thus, he had to go with the alternative.

When he was introduced to his other operative, he failed to see the irony. In this case, his appearance made perfect sense. He was engaged in a chase for a Civil War treasure with an associate who looked like he had been pulled from the pages of history. Round spectacles, a bald head, a bulbous nose, and a thick beard gave him the look of Confederate Army captain.

The Judge inhaled deeply. Maybe he was looking at this situation in the wrong light. He had not previously seen the advantages of ridding himself of a presence who was a constant source of annoyance and questionable value.

He would eventually deal with William. He would take care of the issue efficiently. But until that moment, his patience would be severely tested.

The Judge weighed his words carefully. He never fully trusted anybody. His response to the text was just as generic as the one he received: "I'll be in contact with a location."

Chapter 43

Twenty miles north of Williamsburg

"I just realized something. We need to get some information on where we're going if we're going to be able to make a quick and intelligent search," stated Des.

"You're right, but there's one problem: we cannot go onto my computer or on our phones, or they'll be able to track us," responded Madison. She then looked back at William with an idea. "Hey, when you tracked our searches, was it only on my computer?"

"Yes, you were the only one."

"Do you have your laptop handy?" she asked Des.

"Yeah, right back there," he said, pointing toward the back seat. "If we can find a coffee shop with Wi-Fi, we could make a quick search for info."

"I don't mean to be a pain, but if we do stop, we need to make sure that we're fast. Remember, they have the same clues we do, and they'll figure them out. We won't have time to sit there and do a full research project. We don't want them to arrive in Williamsburg before we do," William warned.

After about fifteen minutes, Des spotted a populated area off the highway, certainly one to have a local chain-type coffee house, which they located very quickly. Pulling into the parking lot, Des grabbed his laptop, and the three of them hustled into the shop.

When they opened the door, the rich smell of coffee grounds wafted around them. A varied collection of people were waiting in line for their chance to order their daily caffeine fix. Local housewives sharing gossip, young college students preparing for class, truck drivers trying to stay awake on a long haul, and construction workers on a break milled around, conversing or burying their heads in electronic devices.

Finding a place near the back of the shop, Des and William sat down at an awkwardly shaped table with uncomfortable wooden chairs and started searching on the computer, while Madison grabbed some beverages.

He opened his search engine and found the link to the University of William and Mary website. Combing through the page, he clicked on the "History" link, scouring the site, looking for prevalent information. As expected, the college today was much different physically than in the days of Jefferson or the Civil War. Most of the structures on campus did not even exist just fifty years ago, let alone one hundred and fifty.

"Any luck?" Madison asked, returning to the table with a tea and two coffees in hand.

"Well, I think we can limit ourselves to a few structures on campus because most of the buildings there now were not there during the times of Jefferson Davis," Des said before taking a sip. "That one clue said something about a rector."

"Yeah," she said, quickly reaching into her pocket and pulling out her copied instructions. "It says it's 'fixed in the home of the rector.'"

"Home of the rector… home of the rector," Des repeated. "A *rector* can be a lot of things. It could be a lecturer or a professor."

"Or a pastor or clergy," Madison added.

"Clergy! It must be a church. I wonder if the original college church is on the campus grounds."

Des clicked on the "Ministries" link on the web page. The first match he came across was of the Catholic ministries chapel. This he could immediately eliminate. First of all, Thomas Jefferson was not Catholic, and second, the chapel was not constructed until 1932. Des kept searching, looking for the most famous structures on campus. One kept appearing as the most prominent, the Wren Building. However, the Wren Building was not a church and did not match the criteria.

"Can you see what's inside or what's offered in the Wren Building?" Madison asked.

William sat silently, tea in hand, watching Des and Madison hover over the glowing screen. Colonial history was not his strong suit, and he felt out of place trying to contribute, as these two had a much more extensive background in the subject.

"Wait, what does that say?" Madison asked, pointing at the screen. "It has a chapel inside. That has to be it."

"There's no other chapel there that would have been around when Jefferson was alive," said an excited Des.

"I don't understand the next clue, though," she said, reading the paper again. "'Above the sound of God's calling lies the key at its anchor.'"

"I'm not sure about that one either."

"Guys, I don't want to be a pest, but we really need to try to figure this out on the road," William insisted. "Remember, we're not the only ones looking for this treasure." The young man was becoming antsy. He, more than anyone, understood the stakes. Time was running short. It had to be found within the framework he needed to work in. If it was not, the treasure would not reach its full potential.

Seeing the urgency in William's expression, Des and Madison realized he had a valid point. Nodding, Des folded up his laptop, and the three of them quickly exited the coffee shop. Getting into the car, Madison felt her heart rate increase as the brief respite ended. The chase was on again.

"I wish we could be doing this under better circumstances," she said.

"So do I, so do I," Des responded.

Chapter 44

Williamsburg, Virginia

As they exited off the highway onto Lafayette Street, Colonial Williamsburg was a short ways away. Madison started to gather her belongings, making sure she would have everything necessary for the search. Seeing William prepare, she felt the intensity of the situation increase a hundredfold. By the time they neared Francis Street, all their nerves were on edge.

Des started scanning the area, looking for any signs of the three men who had accosted them earlier. Thinking better of it, he made the decision to not leave his car in the visitors' center parking lot, as it would be the likeliest place to be spotted. Parking in one of the residential areas adjacent to the college, they would make the walk onto the campus via a less obvious route, keeping an ever-watchful eye on their surroundings.

Williamsburg, Virginia, is a fascinating collection of original and reconstructed structures that serves as a major tourist attraction while, at the same time, being a fully operating town where many of these same attractions still maintained their original purpose. The most significant of which was the College of William and Mary, the oldest public university in the nation.

The institution of higher learning was first established in 1693 and had educated some of the most prominent people in the nation's history, including presidents Thomas Jefferson, James Monroe, and John Tyler. A total of sixteen signers of the Declaration of Independence had once roamed its halls. It had been in continuous operation since its founding, having had only a few interruptions, with one halt in classes being the result of the British invasion during the Revolutionary War.

The three treasure hunters walked through the campus, noticing the students studying at benches and under the large oak trees all over the grounds. The college was breathtakingly beautiful, having much of the landscape appearing as if it had dropped off a postcard. The river running through the middle of the campus empties into Lake Matoaka and was crossed at various points by bridges that had a fairy-tale quality about them. Many of its quaint brick buildings were surrounded by wooded areas combining a mixture wispy trees and soft foliage, making it the perfect component to the serene atmosphere.

As they crossed over the Crim Dell Bridge, it was hard for them not to notice its beauty. Its yellowish wood grates highlighted by the brick-red post supporting the connection was the perfect accent to the scene.

They continued their trek, heading toward the main Williamsburg grounds, until they arrived upon the oldest and most prominent structure on campus, the Wren Building. This would be the starting point.

Resting at the heart of his highest learning.

Like most of the older structures on campus, the Wren Building was charming and utilitarian. It was made of red brick, with its most prominent edifice being the white tower protruding from its center. With a clock at its base and a weather vane cresting its pointed roof, the Wren Building hearkened to the colony's English roots. The back area was rectangular in design and surrounded by a courtyard on three sides, with a brick road leading to a back doorway. Walking around the building toward its front, they connected with another brick path heading to doors, which were mounted under an arched entry way.

Reviewing the encompassing structure, Des imagined a young Thomas Jefferson with his reddish hair and tall thin frame walking through this very courtyard on his way to study the great minds of the day. This was where the framer of the Declaration of Independence was introduced to the intellect of Locke and Voltaire. It was here that the seeds that would later explode into a revolution that would change the world were planted in his young mind.

Yet Des was nervous. Like many buildings of such advanced age, the Wren Building had undergone changes. Gutted by fire three times, including during the Civil War, when Union troops set it to flames, much of the structure no longer existed. In each case, however, the outer walls had been saved, keeping the original shape of the architecture intact. But with the interior having been rebuilt and remodeled several times, the possibility items would have been relocated within the building, altered, or removed altogether was a real concern.

"Madison, could you read that first clue again?" Des asked.

Madison took the folded notebook paper out of her pocket and recited the clue. "'Resting at the heart of his highest learning.'"

"Well, this is the heart of the William and Mary campus," he stated, trying to reconfirm in his own mind that they were at the right location.

Upon entering the building, they were greeted by warm wood floors, tannish in color, with rich grains running through each plank. The walls were adorned with oil paintings depicting important people in the college's history. A warm light entering through the square windows gave the reddish-stained benches a rich illumination. Elegant lighting from brass-fitted chandeliers helped brighten the white walls.

Looking for someone wandering its halls, Des spotted a young man with a backpack draped over his shoulder, head down, rifling through his phone. Des approached him, asking if he could be directed to the chapel. The student gladly obliged, pointing to one of the building's wings, informing him it would be just past a very large conference room.

The distinguishing juts on the Wren Building's north side made up part of its rectangular shape, and it was also the area of some its largest rooms. As they walked through the hall on their way to the chapel, they peered into the other accommodations lining its sides. The quarters displayed a simple elegance, attractive to the eye but plain in its setup. Passing a conference area highlighted by turquoise-green walls and a round table at its center covered with a matching tablecloth, they realized they had found their marker and made the final turn, heading in the direction of the chapel.

Entering through the doors of the religious edifice, they were struck by how small and intimate the chapel appeared. It had gray tile floors and oak pews on both sides of the room, only allowing for three rows of seating, and its slight size left few places to actually search. At the back of the chapel was a large rectangular wooden wall mounting with an arch at its crest.

Above the room was a decorative chandelier, and its walls were adorned with plaques honoring great minds such as James Madison and Sir Isaac Newton. The windows perched above the pews allowed for a pleasant light to cover any congregate.

Des wandered around the chapel, trying to figure out where to begin but was drawing a blank. There were no nooks or crevices in which to hide something, and even if there were, the chapel had obviously been rebuilt and remodeled since the times of the Civil War.

"Do you have any ideas?" he asked, looking for help.

"'Above the sound of God's calling lies the key at its anchor,'" said Madison, stating the next clue.

"God's calling… God's calling. Do you have any ideas, William?"

William shrugged his shoulders, feeling quite useless that he was not able to contribute anything meaningful.

Des kept repeating those same words, "God's calling… God's calling," but nothing came to mind. His eyes wandered over the ceiling, scanning the tops of the pews, checking the windowsills, yet still, there was nothing.

"You're forgetting the words that come before that," Madison stated. "You're forgetting that they say the *sound* of God's calling."

"The sound of God's calling… the sound… the sound…" Des paced the floor, finger raised to his chin, staring down at the gray tiles. "What is the sound of God's calling?" He paused momentarily. "Oh, you idiot, Desmond!" he said, whipping around and facing his two companions, arms outstretched, imploring William and Madison for the answer. "The sound of God's calling—it means being called to worship. What is used to call people to worship?"

Madison, who was raised in a religious household and spent many a Sunday in church, knew right away. "Church bells," she said, grinning.

"That may be correct, but there's one problem. This chapel doesn't have any church bells," William pointed out.

"Did it ever?" Madison wondered.

"William is right, it doesn't have any, and I doubt it ever did. Probably the only bell on this property would be the clock, and that's not used to call people to worship. Damn, that leaves us at a dead end."

"Well, if it never had one, then this couldn't have ever been the place. It has to be somewhere else," she pointed out.

"Well, I'm open to suggestions," stated Des.

"Do you think there's another church on campus?" William asked.

"There was nothing on the website mentioning anything else other than that Catholic church, and I think we can rule that out," said Des.

"I just had a thought. There probably wasn't much around here in terms of campus grounds at the time the clues were written, maybe just a few buildings and whatever was in the outlying community," said Madison.

"Yeah, that was probably the case. What are you getting at?" Des asked.

"The campus then was just part of Williamsburg as a whole. I think they may have been referring to the entire community of Williamsburg. Remember, this was a long time ago. The college probably served as the focal point of the town but it was still just one part of the town. All this tourist stuff wasn't here yet. They were probably speaking about the main church that serviced Williamsburg at that time."

William watched the interaction between the two. He suddenly realized the distinct advantage he now possessed. They were learned in history, and their education and keen abilities of reasoning were beyond his training and talents. If he were on this task alone, he would certainly falter. This was a race against time. The treasure had to be found soon; otherwise, its true potential would never be realized. He would have eventually deciphered the clues by himself, but the exorbitant amount of time it would have required would have left him without options.

The trio hurriedly left the chapel and began moving down the hallway toward the front door, where they exited the building. They moved rapidly in the direction of Colonial Williamsburg, making their way to the center of town on Duke of Gloucester Street. By this time, the street was crowded with tourists visiting the shops and stores lining both sides of the thoroughfare.

As they were ever aware they were not alone in this search, any new challenge added to the hunt was met with great concern. With the number of people wandering through the expanse, they became increasingly nervous, as they thought it would be difficult to spot anyone who might be observing or trying to approach them. Exploring this historical space was not going to be easy, as Williamsburg was as intricate in its design as was its history.

For many years, Jamestown served as the capital of Virginia, until the Statehouse Building, the center of the colony's political life, burned to the ground. At the urging of many of the representatives as well as a small group of students from the college, a new capital center was envisioned at Middle Plantation. After its approval as the capital site, the town changed its name to Williamsburg, in honor of the king. In keeping with the tradition of glorifying dignitaries of the mother country, the main thoroughfare was christened Duke of Gloucester Street in recognition of the son of Queen Anne.

Williamsburg soon became the center of Virginia culture, with its brick-paved streets and sidewalks, its distinctive architecture, as well as its three main sources of economic growth, the college, the courthouse, and a local lunatic asylum, which kept jobs at the ready and small businesses thriving.

However, by the end of the Civil War, much of the town fell into disrepair, mainly from neglect. It was later through the inspiration of an energetic preacher, W. A. R. Goodwin, and the philanthropy of the world's richest man that the town would see a revitalization, restoring it to its former glory and making it a tourist destination for hundreds of thousands of visitors a year.

Des attempted to take in as many details of the attraction, which was originally the vision of oil magnate John D. Rockefeller, as he could. It was made up of dozens of buildings that were either reconstructed from original colonial designs or refurbished from existing structures, the result of which was a beautiful collection of historical monuments offering insight into America's past. It provided a myriad of sights, sounds, and smells to assault the senses.

Realizing if he was going to find what they were looking for, he was going to have to be able to separate the originals from the replicas, Des looked for a place where he could research. "We need to find another area with Wi-Fi. I need to find other historic churches in this area."

Pushing in between them, William stepped out in front, stopping abruptly. "No, you don't."

Chapter 45

Williamsburg, Virginia

Thirty yards in front of them was something that met the criteria perfectly, Bruton Parish Church. The magnificent three-hundred-year-old structure, even though it had been restored, was an original building whose brick facade was the inspiration for most of the reconstructed ones surrounding the area. The church is the oldest continuously operating religious institution in the country.

Built in the early 1700s, it became the house of worship of some of the most prominent residents in the history of Williamsburg, including George Washington, Thomas Jefferson, Patrick Henry, and George Mason. Even though the church claimed continuous operation since 1715, records had its predecessor establishment, Middle Plantation Church, reaching as far back as 1658.

Des and Madison move toward the structure, with William in tow. It was surrounded by a thick chest-high brick wall that master craftsmen had used their artistry with to round at the top. As they moved within the wall, they viewed the courtyard surrounding the main building, which once served as the community cemetery. During the 1700s, most families buried their loved ones on their property. However, this created a burden on the pastor, who had to oversee the funerals, oftentimes forcing him to travel great distances to the site of the burial. After raising objections about these extended duties, families began to inter their loved ones on the church property.

The three moved slowly, making their way through the grounds while reading some of the tombstones scattered in imperfect patterns throughout the yard. Some of the grave markers were large and ornate, others were quite modest, and still others were so simple they did not even identify the name of the buried.

People who lived at the time of the revolution, Confederate soldiers, and prominent community members were just some of the people who had made this area their final resting place. Generals, governors, and even a Supreme Court justice who had signed the Constitution respected these grounds enough to wish for their remains to be buried in its green fields.

The church itself was one of the tallest buildings in old Williamsburg, topped by a white spire reaching for the heavens. Beautiful arch-shaped windows with lead-paned glass were simple but elegant in design. The brick making up the structure was faded and had a brownish red color, adding to its rustic charm. The pointed rooftop had two matching apexes on its side, accentuated by a round window resting at the center of the design. It was what any visitor would imagine as the ideal representation of the colonial era.

As they rounded the corner, something stopped Des in his tracks. Madison and William, not noticing his pause, kept moving in the direction of the church entrance. Becoming aware that Des was no longer with them, Madison spotted him out of the corner of her eye staring at a neatly kept grave marker about twenty feet away. It was made of polished granite and, unlike most of the graves in the cemetery, was situated in the brick walking path rather than the surrounding field.

"What is it, Des?" asked Madison as she approached him.

Des did not say anything at first, continuing to gaze at the tombstone. "Look who's buried here."

Madison moved her eyes onto the gravestone and was caught completely off guard. "Oh my god."

Directly in front of her was the final resting place of James Semple, the Confederate Navy officer who was the intended receiver of instructions they now had in their possession and started them on this odyssey. William walked in behind them and, taking notice, was every bit as stunned. It was if they all had come full circle.

For William, though, there was a special meaning. He was on a journey to fulfill the mission of his great-great-grandfather, and here in front of him was the man representing the completion of his ancestor's duties. It was a striking moment.

"This is getting unbelievably weird," Des said, shaking his head.

"Come on, Des, we need to keep moving," Madison said, gently pulling on his arm.

The three walked through the reddish-brown door, entering the main foyer of the church. The room was bright white, with tiles shaded in various tones of gray. An aisle at its center was enclosed by wooden benches on both sides painted white on their base and stained brown on their backs. The design of the room led one's eyes to the end of the church, where a large gold cross was mounted on the back wall, its color standing out perfectly against a blackish background.

They moved toward the cross, looking at each aisle as they passed. As they drew closer, they noticed small plaques on some of the rows of benches, recognizing the famous individuals who once sat in those sections. It was an intimate way to relate to those seminal figures of American history. Although many of these monumental personalities were quite cognizant of limiting the church's influence, they still were deeply religious and made efforts to connect to a higher power through traditional and nontraditional means.

"I don't see a way to access the bell at the top of the church," Des said. "Do you?"

Madison looked up but could only see the flat white ceiling and gold organ pipes hanging just above the cross. "No, I can't see one either. There must be another access point. I wonder if they even let anyone up there."

"I don't know. I think it's doubtful, with all the tourists that come through. It would be a problem letting that many people into such a confined space."

"Well, there has to be some way to get up there. But if they don't allow anyone from the public, how do we access it?"

Des thought for a moment, looking back at the entrance of the church. His eyes moved up the wall and above the doors, following its line, which ended near the front pew by the cross. Still searching, he focused on the doors on both sides of the pulpit.

"We need to get to the other side of this church. Let's go across the street," Des said, motioning for Madison and William to follow.

The three of them exited the building, walked through the cemetery, keeping a steady pace as they moved back onto Duke of Gloucester Street, and then turned west toward Henry Street. About a block away, there was a Barnes and Noble bookstore, which would be sure to have Wi-Fi.

They needed to get some information before attempting to access the bell. Des learned in the Army that no mission went well without meticulous planning. This was not merely walking into a deserted area like Old Sheldon Church; this needed a methodical, detailed strategy of operation. It was time to formulate one.

Chapter 46

Arriving at the visitors' parking lot of Colonial Williamsburg, the Judge anxiously anticipated tracking his adversaries. He was quite familiar with this attraction, having come here many times over the years both as a young boy and an adult.

Leaving the parking lot, he walked through the main entrance of the visitors' center. The doorway was decorated with a collection of flags representing the colonies and their transformation into the United States. The colorful grouping was a festive invitation into the attraction.

The center itself was a modern and slick operation featuring a wide brightly lit space, a wood panel ceiling, and a brick-color tile floor. It was filled with various amenities, including information kiosks and stores peddling in the typical touristy fair.

He waited patiently for his team to meet him, where they would then move into the main part of the attraction. After about fifteen minutes, a time spent standing next to a kiosk and habitually checking his watch, he finally saw Chris Wells come into sight.

The young man approached in a very businesslike manner, not even bothering to remove his sunglasses in the indoor facility. With one of his two team members at his side, they still looked the intimidating force for which the Judge had hoped.

"They parked over by the campus, but our man saw them head over toward the main part of town. He's keeping an eye on them now. Do you still want us to only observe?"

The Judge paused for a moment, always believing in a thoughtful approach to any question posed to him. He was feeling intense emotion, though he did not wish for it to color any of his decision-making. "Yes, for now just observe. I want to see what they're up to. These two seem to have some abilities, far more than William's."

"What should we do about William?"

"Leave him alone for now. Trust me, he'll prove to be useful to us before this thing is over."

"Sir, I don't typically ask this, but it would be helpful to know what exactly we're looking for them to do here. It will be difficult to know how to react to their actions if we don't know what's important."

The Judge fidgeted nervously. He understood he was handicapping the young man with the lack of information, but did not want to release too much. It was best not to mention a life-altering treasure to a hired gun.

Choosing his words carefully, the Judge responded, "We're looking for them to find more information, probably another item that can be written onto a piece of paper."

"That's it, nothing more?"

Although he was not completely sure, the Judge felt fairly confident the treasure was not here in Williamsburg. Everything he had studied to this point indicated a different location. In addition, Williamsburg was already occupied by Union troops for nearly two years by the time Richmond was evacuated by the Confederates. The College of William and Mary was even used as barracks for housing Union troops. There would have been no way to hide that amount of cargo with so many Northern soldiers present. If something was hidden here, it had to be small enough to be relatively undetectable.

"No, there's nothing more."

"Sir, I don't mean to harp on this, but—"

"Chris," the Judge interrupted. "I'm paying you a lot of money to follow my instructions. If I felt there was more information I could provide that would be effective in helping you attain what I want, then I'd give it to you."

"Yes, sir," Chris replied, feeling completely rebuffed.

"Call your man now and let me know where they are."

Chris walked a few feet away and dialed his associate in the field. Getting confirmation of their targets' whereabouts, he walked back over to the Judge. "They're at the Barnes and Noble bookstore about a half mile from here. They went there after leaving Bruton Parish Church."

"Okay, they haven't left, which means whatever it is that they're looking for must still be here," the Judge said excitedly. "Let's head that way."

Chris nodded and motioned for his team member to follow. The three of them headed to the exit, which emptied onto Duke of Gloucester Street. Moving onto the main avenue, the Judge, even now, could still appreciate the history of this place. Although harsh and oftentimes cold, he was not above sentimentality. With its festive appeal and rich tapestry of sights, it brought the veteran justice back to a simpler time when exploration of the past was a joy and not an obsession.

As they walked north, the rebuilt capital building came into sight. Its redbrick arches and round edifices capped with its spearlike, pointed roof gave it a fairy-tale quality. Like the college's Wren Building, its center was crowned with a white spire proudly flying a flag with the American representative red and white stripes covering three-fourths its space and a British Union Jack placed in its corner.

Hastening toward the Governor's Mansion, the three stopped for a moment by the entrance to the gates of its courtyard. The Tudor-style home had a prominent entrance with a glistening white gate guarding the impressive structure. The Judge stared at the front of the residence, contemplating his next action. His eyes swirled over the front of the mansion. Its fourteen front windows and white-accented woodwork created a spellbinding effect.

He inhaled deeply. He was not impetuous and hated nothing more than having to make up his mind on the fly. Yet this situation had thrown some wrenches into his well-thought-out plans. He always knew it was a possibility, though he abhorred it nonetheless. He never wanted to complicate the matter. However, he would resort to any action necessary to get what he wanted.

"If we have to," he said, looking right at Chris, "we'll need to take them. I'm not sure what they have come upon here, but if I feel it's necessary, we're going to have to move. I sense we're getting closer to the information I need to have."

"How far do you want us to take this?"

"Well, I believe in being thorough. I want to make sure I get everything. So they need to be in a condition to provide me that."

"Understood."

The three regained their momentum once again as they headed down the street. They had to be careful, as this would be challenging due to the fact the targets could now identify some of the people in their party.

With Bruton Parish Church just a few yards away, Chris signaled for them to move into a small eatery across the way. They would wait there until they heard from their accomplice, who was observing their targets at the bookstore.

The Judge tried to keep his composure but could not completely hide his nerves. He ordered some coffee and a pastry, hoping to replace the feeling with simple comforts. But his concentration was constantly broken. It was impossible to stay focused, fighting his lifelong battle to not project toward the future and instead live in the moment. He had to resist the urge to fantasize of what the acquirement of this goal would mean to his life. Sipping his coffee, he eyed the tourists as they passed by the front door of the eatery. *Be patient. Everything is in your control.*

Chapter 47

Across the street from Parish House, the administrative wing of Bruton Parish Church, the Barnes and Noble bookstore blended in well with the historic colonial town. The brick sidewalk surrounding the corner retailer negated the requirement of the visitor to transition their experience to the modern world.

Des, Madison, and William entered the store, ignoring the display cases greeting every visitor. The book enclave's warm interior had an inviting feel, ideal for concentrating on the matter at hand. Finding a table, Des got out his laptop and prepared to do his search.

"We have to find out more about that bell," Des said as he booted up his computer. "We have to find a way to get up there."

"What kind of info are you going to look for?" questioned Madison.

"I'm not sure yet. I'm just trying to get some ideas."

Des entered the key words "Bruton Parish Church Bell" into his search engine. Of the list of matches, most seemed useless, until he noticed an article about a bell cleaning. Clicking on the link, he came upon a story in a community paper, *The Daily Press*. It highlighted the efforts of local seminary students to clean the bell in preparation for the church's three hundredth anniversary. The article was short, just a few paragraphs, but it sent Des in motion.

"We might be able to do something with this," he stated.

"What do you have in mind?" asked William.

"Restoration projects usually have follow-up inspections to see how they're holding up. This cleaning only took place a year ago, so it would be good timing."

"What are you getting at?" Madison asked.

"It's not a very big area, and we only have to be up there for a few moments. So we should be able to be in and out of there quickly."

"Uh… Des, do you mind filling us in?"

"We need to pose as students who are doing a follow-up inspection of the bell to see if it needs any additional cleaning or restoration work. But there are a couple of problems," Des said as he looked through photos of the students working on the bell.

"What problems?" William asked.

"Well, first of all, I look too old to be a young seminary student, and second of all, that space is so cramped we'll never all be able to fit up there. It will have to be just one of us," he said, looking directly at Madison.

"Oh god, you want me to do it, don't you? I don't think I'm really qualified for that over William."

"Yes, for one main reason, you're prettier than both of us," Des said, smiling. "Women are much more disarming than men, and if the person in charge of the facilities is a man, then so much the better."

Madison ran her fingers down the side of her head by her temple, her brown skin becoming slightly lighter as the blood rushed out of her face. This was something she was not expecting, and up to this point, she had only worked in tandem with Des. She did not hide her anxiety, though knowing time was an issue, she still complied.

"Okay," she said hesitantly. "But where do I look?"

"It says that the 'key lies at its anchor.' I would look at the top of the bell, where it's fixed to the structure."

Madison sighed nervously. She knew what Des was planning made sense, yet that small truth did not ease her stress level.

William, recognizing her fear, smiled at Madison. "You'll be fine. The worst that could happen is they don't let you up there. But I really doubt they'll do that. Just go in there like that's where you belong. I mean… who would claim to be a seminary student to inspect an old bell if they were not one? What are you a threat to do, steal the bell?"

"He's right, Madison. Nothing bad will happen, I promise you. Also, I was looking on the church directory. The person in charge is a man, so you're already at an advantage," Des said, grinning.

"Okay, I guess we better get going," she answered hesitantly.

The trio exited the store, making their way back to the church. They walked silently. Des wanted to say some comforting words but thought it best just to allow her to concentrate on what she had to do. He was hoping she was not noticing his own stress level. Although he conveyed confidence the best he could, inside, his emotions were in tatters. He was not so concerned about whether she would be discovered as much as he was about her not finding what they needed. In his opinion, it was always most important to focus on the greatest threat, and that certainly was not coming from a person who worked at a church.

The tension among the small group increased as they got closer to their destination. Madison stared down at the brick sidewalk, becoming transfixed on the maze of patterns it created. Her breathing accelerated. Her heart was pounding. Trying to calm herself, she started to recite in her head what she needed to say and how she would present herself.

Arriving just outside the church, Des turned to Madison to give her some final suggestions. "Do you have your reading glasses with you?" Madison nodded, taking the glasses out of her bag. "Put them on. You'll look more studious. Also, unbutton another button on your shirt."

Madison looked at him curiously as to why he would request such a thing. Seeing her expression, he knew he had to give her a reason.

"Like I said, there are some advantages you have over William and me. You're prettier and you have breasts. Don't be afraid to use both of them."

Madison flashed Des a sarcastic look but complied. Deception needed the use of misdirection, and he knew there was nothing more distracting to a man than cleavage.

Taking another deep breath, Madison adjusted her glasses, teased her hair, and looked down at her chest. Grabbing her notepad, she stared at Des. "How do I look?"

"Beautiful," Des answered confidently. "You're going to do fine, I promise."

She took another deep breath. "Okay, here I go."

Turning assertively, she marched toward the church and entered the courtyard. Des and William stood, watching her make the short journey.

Giving each other a look as if to say "I hope she makes it," the two of them fidgeted, knowing how much was riding on her success.

"She'll be all right," Des said as much to comfort himself as it was to confirm his thoughts to William.

"I hope so. God, I hope so."

Chapter 48

Passing James Semple's grave, Madison entered the church but at first did not see anyone who appeared to be working. Looking in the direction of the pulpit, she noticed a tour guide speaking with some guests. The guide was motioning to the placards on the side of pews, probably explaining the importance of those who had once been in the church's congregation. Madison walked to the guide and waited for him to complete his explanation to his curious visitors.

"Hello, my name is Ella," Madison said, deciding to use her middle name rather than her first. "I'm with the college seminary. We did a restoration on the bell about a year ago. I'm here to do a follow-up inspection, if that would be okay."

"Oh, yes, I remember when the students were here last year. They spent a lot of time on that project."

"Whom do I speak with to get access to the bell? I don't need to be up there long, just a quick inspection."

"You need to speak with our facilities manager. He's in the back room. If you go through that door near the pulpit, turn left and then turn right. He should be in his office. His name is Hal."

"Thank you."

Madison was nervous, but so far, it seemed to be going well. She was just hoping Hal would be as accommodating as the guide. As she had been instructed, she passed through the white-painted door and turned left at the first opportunity and then made a quick right. She moved down the hallway until she saw an open door leading into a small room.

She peered inside, and there was a slightly pudgy man who looked to be in his late forties. He had thinning dark hair that receded to gray by his temples. He sat at an old wooden desk, hovering over some forms and filling out requisitions for various materials.

"Hello, are you Hal?" she asked, trying to put on the most pleasant and innocently alluring look she could.

"Yes, can I help you?"

"I was told that you're the person I needed to see. My name is Ella. I'm with the college seminary, the group who did the bell cleaning last year."

"Oh, yes, what can I do for you?"

"I'm here to do our follow-up inspection. We want to assess if there was any more cleaning or restoration that needed to be done. If so, we we're prepared to send another group in to do it."

"Well, I can tell you that your team did a great job. I don't think the bell really needs any more cleaning. In terms of restoration, I don't think that was originally what they were here to do, anyway."

Recognizing her mistake, Madison quickly corrected herself. "I'm sorry. I'm so used to saying *restoration*. I know we just did a cleaning. I've worked on a few of these projects myself at other locations, and we always did restorations along with the cleaning."

"I see. Well, you can tell your group leader that the bell is in great shape and to thank everyone who worked on the project."

Madison's heart sank. This was not going well, and she needed to figure out quickly how to convince him to let her into that space. "My group leader really wants me to check up there. He'll be quite upset if I don't."

"I assure you, it's fine. You can tell him that I confirmed it. Plus, I have a large tour group coming in later today that I have to prepare for, and I don't have time to take you up there."

Madison was feeling sick. This plan was going south fast. Hal did not seem to have any interest in the project, and she was running out of ideas on how to get access to the bell. In desperation, she resorted to what Des had suggested. Reaching into her pocket, she pulled out a piece of paper as if she were going to read from it and then dropped it onto the floor. Then shamelessly, she bent over, making sure the view of her now-revealing top was in direct line with Hal's eyesight. Looking up, she caught Hal taking her in.

"I'm sorry, I'm so clumsy. I took some notes from some of the people who did the cleaning. One of the things they pointed out," she said, staring at the paper, pretending it actually had instructions on it, "is that the mooring near the top of the bell needed checking. It showed signs of deterioration. This is important, because if it's deteriorating, the bell could literally fall off its hinges when it's rung. It could be just a matter of time. It could happen the next time it's rung or the fiftieth time it's rung. We would hate to see that happen."

Madison hoped this would strike a chord. The three hundredth anniversary of the church was soon approaching, and it would be embarrassing, not to mention destructive to the church itself, to have the bell come crashing down during the celebration. "Please, I'll only be a few minutes, I promise," she said with her sweetest seductive smile, making no attempt to adjust her blouse, which was now revealing more than it did when she had retrieved the paper.

Hal, enjoying this sight, started to soften his stance. He was finding it impossible to deny this young woman. "You promise to just be a few moments?" He sighed.

"Yes, I'll be really quick, I swear."

"Okay, follow me."

Hal led Madison through another room and then past the sanctuary until he arrived at the entrance at the base of the spire. It was made of brick, with an interior stairwell arriving at a wooden structure divided into two tiers. They ascended the stairwell, which narrowed as it climbed higher. The stairs finally tapered into a small set of rickety old flights where one could barely go single file.

At that point, Madison turned to Hal, trying to ensure she would be in the space alone. "I'll only be a few minutes. I know you're busy. If you need to do anything else, I can close up," she said, trying to encourage him to take the bait.

"I do have to get some things done for that group I have coming in. I'll be back in a few."

"Thank you so much," Madison said, standing on the stair above him and leaning over to touch his shoulder."

Hal blushed at the flirtation and then turned and proceeded down the stairwell. As soon as he was out of sight, she quickly began her inspection.

The top of the spire holding the bell was a maze of wooden beams smelling as old as it looked. The wood was not stained, reflecting the wear much like that of a wrinkled old man. Not having time to examine every inch of the spire's interior, she went straight to where the bell was housed.

Taking a few steps more, she could see the brass chime on her left. The Tarpley Bell, later renamed the Virginia Liberty Bell when it was rung in celebration of the signing of the Declaration of Independence, was first set into the church in 1769. Unlike so many relics of the past, the bell was still used, calling worshippers to this day.

For nearly one hundred and fifty years, the bell went untouched until it was cleaned and restored at the time of Theodore Roosevelt's presidency. This remained the only time it had been cleaned until last year, when students from the college volunteered their time to do it.

Madison examined the bell from the outside. She looked to see if there were any relevant markings on its outer shell but saw nothing of importance. She ducked her head underneath the bell, and though she found nothing relating to her search, she was astonished to see the two-hundred-year-old graffiti of past students who had marked their name inside its casing, forever preserving themselves for posterity.

The words kept repeating in her head. *Above the sound of God's calling lies the key at its anchor.* She had to get to the top, where the bell was fixed to the wooden beam. Looking for a location to raise herself, she placed her foot on one of the crossbeams, pulling herself up near the hinge. The wood creaked as she moved, making her nervous the old structure would give in and collapse. The beam was angled, making her unable to reach the hinge. She slid herself farther across, moving slowly as to not cause any undue stress to the relic wood supporting her.

The hinge came into view, but there was nothing descript about it and certainly nothing it could hide. *It must be above the bell.* She eyed the load-bearing girder, trying to see if there was something at the top, but could not glimpse its apex. She slid over, reaching her hand up and touching the surface. The powdery feel of accumulated dust met her fingers. She blindly moved her hand around and then over and across. She could feel nothing out of the ordinary, just weathered notches of old dried wood.

Out of desperation, she moved her hand over and away from the center of the hinge. Still nothing. *Has it been removed?* Pulling herself a little higher, she reached back to the only point she hadn't explored. Her fingers crawled over the beam as the piles of dust informed her that it had not been cleaned during the student project. Madison was becoming nearly despondent. *Did I miss something?*

It stopped. Her hand couldn't move, blocked by what felt like metal. Her breath halted. Running her index finger on the corner, she could tell it was not part of the surface. There was nothing here that needed to be supported or connected to something else. There was no reason for it to be there.

It felt like a small box, yet she still could not bring it into view. It was about two inches long, maybe two inches wide, and an inch deep. It was mounted onto the wood, and trying to pull on it gently did nothing to make it budge.

Worried her time was running out, she desperately yanked harder on the tin box. It started to wiggle, encouraging her to increase her force. With the extra effort, the box started to loosen from its perch. Madison began to wrench at it with all her might. Finally heaving with one last massive exertion, flinging with her entire body weight. It gave way, the action throwing her back as she lost her footing. She flew in the air, her back striking the hard floor near the stairwell, knocking the wind out of her, while sending a shooting pain down her spine.

"Ella, is that you?" a male voice called from down the stairs. "Is everything okay?" It was Hal, returning from his office.

Madison soon realized that whatever it was she had pulled off the beam was not in her possession. Looking frantically, she could not locate it. The footsteps became louder as she scoured the floor. It was a faint glint. Something reflecting the light pouring in from the arched window at the top of the spire. It was a small rusty tin box.

"Oh my goodness, Ella, are you okay?" Hal asked, rushing over, seeing her sprawled on the floor.

Madison reached back, acting like she was trying to prop herself up. Grabbing the box in her left hand, she shoved it into her waistband as Hal grabbed her free hand to pull her up.

"What happened?"

"Oh my goodness, I feel so stupid," she said, stumbling purposefully into Hal's arms to distract him further. "I was examining the hinge of the bell, and I stepped back to look on the other side and I hit that wood beam and fell back."

"It sounded like you fell pretty hard," he stated, wondering how such a loud thud could have been produced by what would be a relatively short fall.

Realizing her story needed more embellishment, she added to it. "When I fell back, I hit my back against that rail and then fell here. I'm so embarrassed. Please don't mention it to my professor," she begged, looking at him with sorrowful eyes.

A little bewildered but, at the same time, slightly enthralled with the attractive young woman, Hal considered his options. Not wanting to cause her any more embarrassment and wishing to keep himself on her good side, he looked at her with a wry smile. "It's okay, your secret is safe with me," he said, winking at her.

"Thank you so much. I really appreciate it. You're such a sweetheart."

He gave her time to compose herself, and then Madison and a blushing Hal proceeded to walk down the stairs. As they made their way to the bottom, Madison gave him a report on the condition of the bell, ensuring the visit appeared legitimate. Yet the whole time, she could feel the tin box rubbing against her waist with every step.

"Are you sure you're okay?" he asked, putting his hand on her shoulder. "Can I get you something cold to drink?" he asked, hoping to get the attractive young woman to engage in a little more conversation.

"Oh, thank you, you're so kind. I really have to get going to prepare my report for my professor. I'm fine, just feeling a little stupid."

"Well, I hope we can stay in touch. I really would like to work with you and your group in the future."

"Me too," she said, smiling. "I'm sure we'll be in touch."

She touched Hal on his shoulder one more time, thanking him, and then exited out of the spire and quickly moved through the courtyard and back onto main thoroughfare. As soon as she was free from his sight, she reached back and pulled the tin box out from her waistband.

Taking a few more steps, she felt the pain of her fall needle through her body, requiring a moment to gather herself. She rubbed the base of her spine and then achingly hurried over to where Des and William were waiting.

She was anxious to open the tin box but knew doing so in the middle of the street was probably not the best idea. Madison emerged from the area, looking for her companions. Spotting them caddy corner to the church, she moved toward them with a relieved expression on her face. Before Des could even get a word out of his mouth, she held up the tin box.

"Wow, that's awesome!" Des said. "Were they suspicious?"

"Well, he wasn't going to let me up there at first, but let's just say you know how men think very well."

Des and William laughed. Madison did as well, but it hurt, as with every movement of her chest, she could feel the pain rush through her body.

Des, noticing her grimace, became concerned. "Are you all right?"

"I took a pretty bad fall up there, but I'll be okay, just a little sore, that's all. We need to find a place to open this, someplace that's not so exposed."

"Let's head back to the college. We have to go that way, anyway. We can find some place to open it there."

Turning back onto Duke of Gloucester Street, the three made their way through the crowds of tourist. Smells and sounds filled the air of this living recreation of the American past. The aroma of hot chocolate, pastries, and a campfire from a Continental Army exhibition swirled around the ever-gathering throngs of people. Voices of excited children, tour guides speaking to their groups, and even the loud bangs from the firing of replica muskets added to an atmosphere that was both thrilling and fascinating.

Even though the scene would be distracting to almost anyone, the three hardly noticed. Their focus was solely on this new item they had attained, and nothing would pull their attention away from it.

"Is this how it felt when you found your first set of clues?" William asked as they continued their trek back to William and Mary. "The anticipation to know what's in that box is killing me. I want to stop and break it out right here."

"I completely understand. We felt the same way when we found the clues in South Carolina," Des replied.

"I hope it's what we wanted," William said excitedly.

Des smirked. "To be honest, the only thing that's coming to my mind now is 'be careful what you wish for.'"

Chapter 49

The three kept moving in the direction of the college until they could see the Wren Building. Passing the historic structure, Des remembered seeing a small grass field with some benches near one of the bridge crossings, a perfect place to examine this new item. There were many of these parklike settings positioned sporadically throughout the campus, adding to its tranquil beauty. Students routinely gathered in these places to study or hang out with friends. If they camped in one of these areas, it would not draw attention as something unusual.

As they made their way to their destination, Des spotted the beautiful bridge they had crossed when they initially headed to the Wren Building. Finding a bench, he directed the group to be seated.

Madison pulled the tin box out of her pocket. Turning it around and around, she could see there was nothing noteworthy about it. What must have been its original gloss had dulled with age, and no patterns or markings of any kind were displayed. It had no noticeable entry points, and the only interruption in its design were the two small holes extending out from its base where the nails secured it to wood.

Turning it over once again, Madison noticed some grooves in the bottom, appearing to be the side of a panel. Squinting to study the anomaly closer, she realized she had discovered a possible entry point. Wanting to make sure she did not damage the box or what was inside, she turned it once again to confirm there were no other details she had overlooked.

Running her fingers along the grooves, she made certain there needed to be only one action to open it. Glancing at Des, she looked for reassurance.

"Do you think you've figured it out?" he asked.

"I think so, but I'm scared to open it. What if there's nothing in there? Then we're in trouble."

"I can't imagine this would just happen to be there for no reason," William said. "Think about it. This has been so improbable up to this point, and yet you're still finding things where the clues have led you to be."

With William's encouragement, Madison pressed the box between both of her thumbs and index fingers, pulling on the separate halves. At first, it did not move, as rust and age made stubborn adversaries. With slightly more stress, though, Madison began to make the box part with its secrets. She gave another slight tug, and with that last energy, the panel withdrew. Instantly, a small metal object fell into her lap. She looked down and saw what had descended was an old-style skeleton key.

"A key lies at its anchor," Des said excitedly.

Madison picked it up, looking at it like it was a long-lost friend. She ran her index finger over its spines. It was definitely nineteenth-century technology. William marveled at the discovery as well, knowing this put him one step closer to realizing his destiny. However, he also understood his destiny had a timeline, and the end of that timeline was soon approaching.

"Is there anything other than that key?" asked Des.

Madison turned the box over and looked inside. There, wedged at the top, was a folded piece of parchment. Taking great care, she gently attempted to pry it from the crevice. It crinkled and cracked as it started to come loose, making her nervous she might destroy it. Des, noticing her anxiety, reached out his hand, and Madison gladly relented the responsibility, giving it to him.

Des took his pinky finger and slowly dislodged the paper. Then with great care, he placed it on a notebook pad he had removed from his backpack. Staring at it for a moment, he proceeded to carefully unfold the paper, stopping every few seconds to breathe or when he heard what he thought might be a tearing sound. William watched with great focus, only interrupting his attention to look up, making sure no one else was watching.

Des made his way to the last fold until it was completely open, exhaling with both thrill and relief. It was a new set of instructions, another step bringing them a little closer to ending this once-fantasy journey that had now turned into a nightmare.

The legacy of the father holds its place.

It lies in the northern shadow of the symbol of Darius's defeat.

The message is engraved in the sorrows of the nation.

The knowledge you seek turns its back to you.

The values you possess match the language of the empire.

It will lead to the entrance of the gateway of the second invasion.

At the precipice of the stairs' flight, buried two vara, lies the portal.

Travel through the tunnels to the stone with the mark of our leader.

Break through to find the treasure, thousands enCased in black sands of the fallen.

"God, every time we look at these things, they get more complex," an exasperated Des stated.

"There's another reference to Darius's defeat," Madison pointed out as she looked over his shoulder.

"Is that significant?" asked William.

"I'm not sure, but it's the second time they mentioned his name in the clues. It was also the thing I searched on my computer that eventually led to you finding us," she answered.

"Madison, this paper is in really bad shape. You should copy these instructions down on another piece of paper as soon as possible. I don't think it's going to hold up that long. It's in worse shape than the others," Des said.

Madison took the notepad from Des with the parchment on top of it and lightly moved it to her lap, being careful not to touch the original. She then took a piece of notebook paper and carefully began to copy the instructions. She moved very deliberately, making sure every word in the original made it onto her copy. She knew any mistake could cause a gap of information, misdirecting them in their quest.

After she finished the replication, she handed the original back to Des, then folded her copy and placed it in her front pocket. Des, not wanting to refold the paper because of its delicate condition, took the original and placed it in the manila folder with the first and second set of instructions. Seeing Madison had commandeered his backpack, he placed the folder inside the front of the navy-blue jacket he was wearing.

"Can I see the first two sets of instructions?" William asked Madison.

Madison gave him a curious look, then reached into her backpack and pulled out her copies and handed them to William. Laying them next to each other, he studied them for several minutes.

"What are you looking for?" she asked.

"I'm trying to see if there are any other matching words or similarities in phrases. I have pretty much memorized my great-great-grandfather's journal, and I wanted to see if there was anything in any of these instructions that rang a bell. Can I see the copy you just made too?"

He took the copy from Madison and placed it neatly next to the other two sets of instructions. She could see his eyes moving over the pages in a frenetic dance, displaying an unusual intensity. He then closed his eyes, reaching deep into his memory, searching for any match.

There were few similarities, yet there was one match that filled him with a sense of joy and power. It was the mention of the *tunnels* and *black sands of the fallen*. It confirmed that his understanding of the treasure was correct, beckoning him to complete his search. Trying to contain his excitement, William looked down at his watch. Seeing the date, May 23, his exuberance was quickly abated. He already knew the date; however, seeing it once more made his heart race. He was running out of time.

His exercise of constantly checking the details was how he trained himself. Evaluate and reevaluate. Always have backups for your backups. But there were no more backups. The quest needed to be completed soon, or the opportunity for it to be used as intended would be gone.

"Did you find anything of interest?" she asked.

"Unfortunately, no. There's nothing there that struck any chords," he answered quickly, hoping Madison did not notice a change in his disposition.

William handed the copies back to her and watched her fold them carefully and place them in the backpack. She then took the key, put it back inside the tin box, and stuck it in the backpack's outside pocket.

"What's on your mind?" Madison asked, seeing Des's perplexed look.

"Well, I was just thinking about the first clue of this new set. It doesn't give any reference point at all. When we figured out we had to go to Monticello, it was because it was referenced in the clues. Remember? It said that the number of arches represented the 'lineage of leadership.' It gave us a physical structure to help figure out who and where we needed to search. This set gives no such clue. It just hands us a very cryptic reference to a 'legacy of the father.' That could be anyone, anywhere."

"You're right. It seems pretty vague. We're definitely going to have to brainstorm on this one. But I don't think it would just be random. We have to place ourselves in the minds of those living at that time, what 'legacy of the father' may have meant to them."

"What now?" asked William.

"I'm not sure. We could head back to the car, but we don't know where we're going," Des answered.

"Well, why don't we start heading in that direction and we can talk about it on the way?" Madison suggested.

"I have to use the restroom. I'm going to see if there's one in that building," William said, pointing to a small brick structure located just on the other side of the park. William left while Madison and Des stayed by the bench.

"What do you think 'legacy of the father' meant to people back in 1864?" Madison questioned.

"There are a lot of things it could have meant. Southerners have always had a keen awareness of their ancestry. They often refer to their history for all sorts of things."

"Yes, but there has to be some relevance to the people that left these instructions. Legacy had to mean something that was important to them."

"Well, let's think here for a moment. The person who left these instructions was probably Jefferson Davis himself."

"How do you know that?"

"I'm assuming it would have to be, considering that the other item we found had the presidential seal on it. I don't think he would have written one part of the instructions and then left the rest to someone else."

"You have a good point. What was important to Jefferson Davis other than winning the war? Where was he born?"

"Kentucky."

"Isn't that amazing?" "What?"

"The two presidents involved on opposites sides of this conflict, Davis and Lincoln, were both born in the same state. It's incredible that they took such opposite stances, considering they were from the exact same place."

"One of those ironies of history, I guess. But where he was born, I don't think, is what they were getting at when they used the word *legacy*, but who knows?"

Madison inhaled deeply and moved her eyes around the park, taking in the sight of the beautiful oaks, their branches swaying gently in the light breeze blowing from east to west. She looked at the bridge crossing the brook whose waters moved silently past where they now sat. When she was young, her mother taught her how to concentrate whenever she was struggling in a subject at school. It was a meditative exercise: fixate on a point or image of peace and focus on what made it special. In the study of its peacefulness, the answer would present itself.

Madison strained to shut out the world, following her mother's advice, but still, no answer came. The stress of the imminent consequences of the situation impeded her abilities to concentrate. She dropped her head in frustration.

Looking at Des for assistance, she could see he was struggling as well. The expression on his face was of quiet frustration mixed with a look of desperation. She could hear him muttering under his breath as he implemented his own concentration techniques. *Maybe his will work.*

In the distance, she could see William returning from his restroom excursion. His walk was brisk, like he was in a hurry to get something to them. Madison was hoping that he had a revelation. Maybe something he had forgotten about in the diary suddenly invaded his consciousness, imparting some useful information to break them out of this stalemate.

Madison got off the bench in anticipation. William approached, raising his hand in acknowledgment. She lost sight of him as he turned behind a small grove of trees and bushes.

Expecting him to appear any moment, Madison turned to Des. "It seems like he has an idea."

"I hope so, because I'm out of them. Where is he?"

"He was there just a moment ago. He was heading around those bushes. Where could he have gone?"

Des rose to his feet, seeing if he could spot William, but did not lay sight on him. Madison scanned the area, but still, William was nowhere to be seen. Des started walking toward the grove, becoming more concerned with each step. Soon his walk had transformed into a jog, and then a sprint.

Des rounded the corner near the brush. Everything went fuzzy. The sensation of his face being buried in wet grass was all-consuming. Nothing else was clear. Muffled shouting, like he was in some kind of surrealistic dream, was the only other stimuli, while a gray haze clouded everything. Thoughts that had no relevance to anything he knew or understood flew through his mind. His body felt heavy, as if it were sunken in cement. None of his appendages responded to his wish to move.

He tried to regain his senses. His vision slowly returned, transitioning from blurry shapes resembling an ink blot test to definitive objects. He started to get a clearer view of his environment. A pair of black shoes was the first sight of any differentiation. His head was shooting with a piercing pain. The warm trickle of blood dripping down his forehead made him aware he had been struck. He tried to get up but once again was dealt another blow directly to his midsection. He gasped for breath, unable to focus.

It was pure panic. He could hear Madison scream and William struggling to fend off their attackers. The black pair of shoes was joined by another. Des managed to peer up and see the dark-haired man who had assaulted them earlier moving away. He spotted a faltering William desperately running in Madison's direction. Trying to stand up, he still could not find his balance and fell once again.

He furiously tried to right himself, finally managing to get to his feet. But the grogginess from the blow had not left him. Moving as quickly as he could toward the chaos, his rubbery legs fighting him with every stride, he found himself several yards back of the assaulters.

It was a horrifying image. He witnessed the terror of Madison, helplessly trying to stay out of their control. One of the men grabbed her by the hair. She let out a yelp as he yanked her behind the bench. William, now on his knees, was grabbed aggressively by his shirt and thrown in the same direction.

Screeching to a stop, a black SUV pulled up behind the bench. Des managed to get his legs into a run, yet still, they were out of range. Forced into the vehicle at gunpoint, a wailing Madison and defeated William became hostages, fueling Des's panic. He mustered what strength he had left and hurled himself toward the car, grasping for its door handle, but to no avail. It sped off, leaving him sprawled on the ground, watching helplessly as the vehicle disappeared from view. They were gone.

Chapter 50

Des lay prostrate on the grass. The world had gone totally silent. His body ached, and the pain in his head kept increasing. Blood ran down the tip of his nose as the wound continued to spew. He looked up at the bench—they had taken everything. Both his and Madison's backpacks were gone. Now, not only did they have his companions, but all their research, notes, and clues as well.

He slowly got up, his dizziness sending him stumbling. Holding his hand against his head in attempt to stop the bleeding, he tried to regain some semblance of focus. No longer was this just a search for treasure; it was a race to save his friends, especially Madison.

In the Army, he was taught to deal with a horrific situation by relying on his training and concentrating on the main objective. Des had a choice: he could panic and accomplish nothing, or he could figure out an avenue to get his friends out of this terrible situation. The only way to do that was to get to the treasure before the Judge.

Although his head was splitting, he gathered up enough strength to jog back to his car. While running, he sensed something bouncing inside his jacket. Reaching inside his coat, he felt the folder holding the original set of clues. *Thank God I still have these.* However, even though he still had the instructions, unlike before, he no longer had Madison to bounce ideas off. He was going to have to figure everything out on his own.

Des arrived back at his car, fumbling through his pockets to find his keys. It suddenly occurred to him that he still had no idea where he needed to go. He also realized he did not have a computer to conduct research. Knowing his first order of business was to determine his next destination, he decided to use his phone. He understood the risk, but it was one he was willing to take. Even if they were tracking him, the only thing they would see was he was still by the college.

Des took his phone out of the back seat of his car, unwrapped the foil, and called information for the nearest public library. There he could research more quickly than on his cell phone, not be tracked, and at the same time, have a library of information available to him, which would allow him to search off the grid.

While driving, he could hardly concentrate, having to remind himself to get back on task. His thoughts kept straying to a frightened Madison and the danger she was in. He knew, if the Judge got what he needed, her value would drop tremendously. Once she was of no use, she would become dead weight, to be discarded. The thought sent shivers down his spine.

As for William, Des held out little hope. If the Judge was as ruthless a character as he described, then he would not take to betrayal very well. His willingness to use violence to the extent he had demonstrated thus far only confirmed his worst fears. Hopefully, William was smart enough to convince the Judge that he still had information, giving him value, which would buy him enough time for Des to find the treasure first.

Come on, Des, stay focused. Think of the task at hand.

Des went back to work, repeating aloud, "The legacy of the father… the legacy of the father." Madison had made an excellent point. It had to mean something relevant to Jefferson Davis or a mid-nineteenth-century Southerner. *What were common Southern legacies?*

He began to recall stories his father had passed down to him. The Old South had hundreds of myths and legends. Tales of courage and greatness were abundant and were cultural anecdotes passed down for generations. He wondered whether it was something in this Southern lore that could give an indication of what the word *legacy* was referring to. Nothing immediately came to mind or even remotely approached the concept of a legacy that Jefferson Davis would have understood.

After a few minutes on the road, Des pulled into the parking lot of Williamsburg Regional Library. It was a rather modern building, certainly in stark contrast to the structures he had just encountered in Colonial Williamsburg. Entering through its main doors, Des knew the evidence of his beating would draw attention. He immediately tucked into the men's room to clean up his wounds.

In the mirror, Des appeared exactly as he felt, roughed up and exhausted. His face was covered with a mixture of dirt, sweat, and a streak of dried blood crusting on his forehead, nose, and chin. Splashing water on his face, he let the shock of the cold provide some soberness, waking and alerting him to the reality of what he now he faced.

Exiting the restroom, he passed through the central hallway and turned into the main part of the library. An inviting design, it had patrons of all ages, ranging from kids perusing Dr. Seuss books to mature women congregating around the romance novel section. Des was not interested in any of that. What he needed was a computer.

As he looked toward the back, past a counter displaying a local elementary school art project and just near decorative red tables with the yellow trim, he saw a line of computers available to the public. He planted himself in front of one.

When he pulled out the folder, it struck him. He remembered another distinct disadvantage he now suffered. Madison had the key. In the struggle at the college and the pummeling he received, he had forgotten that not only did they have access to the clues, but they also now possessed the only hard artifact necessary to the search. Des had no idea how he would solve that issue, but it was not something he could dwell on. The key would not be of service to anyone unless they actually found the location to use it. So this had to be his mandate.

Going onto the computer search engine, he typed in the key words "Southern legacies," "Southern mythologies," and "Southern myths." Up came matches dealing with everything from a jewelry mart to books discussing the impact of Southern music on popular culture. None of which applied to what he was searching for. He switched around his key words and added a few more, and Southern cooking recipes and a few articles concerning legends of monsters living in the Florida Everglades were what graced the screen.

Des massaged the back of his neck, attempting to relieve the growing tension. His head was still pounding from the deep cut, which throbbed with every movement. The pain constantly broke his concentration as the clue ran through his mind but was now interspersed with images of a frightened Madison being taken hostage. He rubbed his eyes, taking his focus away from the glare of the computer screen. Relying on concentration techniques he learned during his service, Des slowed his breathing and closed his eyes, trying to reach deep into his mental data banks.

But it didn't work. His focus was continually broken. The anger at his attackers was now redirected at himself, as he felt inadequate, not up to the challenge. Fighting a losing battle against these emotional interruptions, he got up and paced the floor.

Some nights, when he found himself in the midst of writer's block, walking or any kind of movement would loosen his mind, allowing him to see things from another angle. Yet as he traversed the library aisles, he was flailing at the clue with no progress.

Des looked at the clock hanging in the back of the library. It only reminded him of time running out. Staring at the rest of the walls, he noticed a poster by the kids' section displaying towering oak trees, the ones so common to the streets of Savannah's historical district. It was the type of presentation most people associated with a school setting, the ones showing nature's beauty, accompanied with some type of inspirational sentence below it.

Des became fixated on the picture of the weeping oaks with the Spanish moss descending from their branches. It transported him to the times he and his father walked hand in hand down the dreamlike streets of Savannah. Lost in a trancelike state, Des recalled some of the conversations they had had during those walks. One in particular stood out.

His father was an avid baseball fan and frequently took Des to see the Braves play in Atlanta. The sport was always a major topic of conversation whenever they were together. Although he could not explain it, his mind drifted to one specific conversation.

Des was playing Little League baseball at that time and was in the middle of a horrendous hitting slump. While walking the pathways of Savannah, the young Des was nearly in tears as he explained his frustration to his father. His dad responded not with words but by squeezing his hand so tightly it hurt. Seeing his son wince at the discomfort, he began to make his point.

"Did you feel that?" his father asked.

"Yes," the young Des answered.

"You know, when you hold someone's hand gently, it's a nice feeling. But when you squeeze too tight, it becomes unpleasant. Some people think that giving more of something is always a good thing, but really, it's not. It's kind of like hitting."

"I don't understand."

"In hitting, when we're having problems, we tend to press too much. But if you tense up and grip the bat harder, if you swing with every bit of your strength, you'll most likely miss the ball and your problems will continue. It's when you relax and just do what you have practiced, that's when you'll get your hits. Even Major Leaguers make the same mistake. The minute they start pressing, squeezing too tight, they stop getting their hits. Just relax and let things come to you instead of always chasing, and you'll see that it will get easier. Do you understand?"

The young Desmond nodded in agreement.

When he returned home, the very next game, he went three for four, including the game-winning hit. His father gave him a life lesson he repeated until his death. Whenever Des was stuck, whenever he seemed to be pressing too hard, his father would always refer to the hitting lesson.

Des calmed down, feeling his father's presence surrounding him. He tried to relax, breathing in deeply, remembering the wisdom of not to press when trying to deal with a problem.

Let it come to you. Don't force it.

Chapter 51

Virginia, ten miles north of Jamestown

The interior of the car was unnervingly quiet as it made its way down the highway. The only audible sound was the hum of the SUV's engine. Madison and William were huddled in the back seat between the two muscular men with the sandy-brown hair. They had no expressions on their faces, just a sternness that was accentuated by the large guns they had leveled at their captives.

Madison was terrified, not knowing what they were planning. The wiry man with the jet-black hair was at the wheel, while in the front passenger seat sat an older gentleman with graying hair and a scraggily beard. They had been in the vehicle for about thirty minutes, traveling north, although no one mentioned a word about where they were headed.

William, feeling the tension, broke the silence. "Judge, you have everything you need. Let her go. You don't need her anymore. You took everything we had."

The middle-aged man turned and faced his hostages. He sized them up but did not immediately speak. Madison glanced directly at him but then averted her eyes, not wishing to be addressed. He then looked at his underlings in a manner suggesting he approved of their current aggressive postures.

"William, how did you think that this was going to end? Did you really expect to be able to take advantage of me like that and I wouldn't respond?"

"Look, she didn't know what she was getting herself into when she started going after it. She's no longer a threat to you."

The Judge gave a slight laugh and looked at Madison. Her fear was palpable, and he recognized the advantage of that immediately.

Countless times in his courtroom he had witnessed the same expression from frightened defendants who were either about to be convicted or sentenced. It was the moment he relished the most. The sense of absolute power over another human being was intoxicating and something he always tried to find in his life away from that environment.

"William, you know me better than that. I will always be thorough. So stop wasting your breath."

"Where are you taking us?" Madison asked in a barely audible voice.

"Ms. Callum, we're going somewhere private where we can all sit down comfortably and chat. I must congratulate you on the progress you've made so far."

"There's nothing to talk about," she said defiantly. "You took all our information. William told you the truth. We didn't even know there was anyone else looking for it until today."

"I'm inclined to believe you. However, your friend is still on the hunt, I'm sure."

"I guarantee he's not looking for it."

"You know, Ms. Callum, I've spent the better part of the last twenty years examining whether or not people were being sincere with me. Oh, I get all kinds in my courtroom. You couldn't imagine some of the characters that have appeared before me. Most people think all the cases that come in front of my bench are different, and they may appear that way to the outsider, but to me, they all have one thing in common. And that's the defendant is always trying to make the best deal for himself. Because of that fact, I recognize they're always motivated by what's in their best interest and not in mine or the general public's, and in that time, I have come to one conclusion. I should always make my own decision on whether or not to show leniency. I rarely do, and I never do when it gets in the way of what I want."

It wasn't what he said as much as how he said it. His low, expressionless, almost-monotone voice made Madison's body run cold. This was not a man to be taken lightly. He was going to get what he wanted, and whether she was still breathing at the end of this journey was of no importance. In fact, it seemed he would find it rather a hindrance.

They traveled for approximately ten more minutes before exiting the highway and heading to a very remote rural area. Thick trees lined both sides of the road as pathways sprawled out into the distance. Madison noticed none of them had any signs indicating their names. They made one final turn onto a dirt trail, driving for a little over a half mile before coming upon a wood cabin that looked like something straight out of the 1800s.

They parked just a few yards from the front door, and the men, still with their guns drawn, pushed Madison and William out of the vehicle. Madison noticed the man with the jet-black hair staring at her with a sullen expression. Not saying anything, he motioned for them to enter the residence.

It was a stark interior, depressing to look at. The windows were covered with white pull-down plastic shades that had dulled with the collection of dust coating their sides. There were hardly any furnishings, just a set of old wooden chairs and a medium-size maple wood table in the center of what would be the family room. It had a stale odor, probably because none of the windows had been opened in months, if not years.

"Please sit down," the Judge said.

Madison and William cautiously took their seats, warily awaiting their next instruction. The Judge walked over to the table and took a chair just across from his two captives. The man with the jet-black hair sat next to him, while the other two stood behind William and Madison with weapons drawn.

The Judge reached over to the man sitting next to him and grabbed the notepad paper Madison had copied the instructions on. Studying them a few moments, analyzing the information, he only briefly lifted his eyes to view his captives' reactions and then went back to the papers once more.

"So where did you get these?" the Judge asked.

Madison and William did not speak, sitting in silence, not knowing if they should give the correct answer. Finally, William tried to address him. "Does it really matter where we got them? You have them now."

The Judge nodded at the man standing directly behind William. With that, his underling reached back and struck William in the face with such force it knocked him out of his chair. Madison jerked in her seat, making a slight yelp at the sight of the young man sprawled out on the cabin floor.

"William, we can do this all day. If you think I already have all the information, then you wouldn't be so concerned with telling me what you think I already know."

"We found the instructions at Bruton Parish Church," Madison said quickly, hoping to avoid a beating.

"Ms. Callum, I know where you found these instructions," he said, holding up the latest of her copies. "I want to know what started you on this search in the first place."

"We found a set of clues in Savannah inside an old picture frame. We just wanted to see where they would lead us."

"Where are the originals?"

"These are exact copies of them, you wouldn't—"

Before she could utter the next syllable, Madison was sent flying to the ground. A stinging sensation filled the side of her face as her body slammed into the wood floor. Her eyes welled up with tears, and a searing sensation of pain ran up her spine, reaggravating the injury to her back.

"Ms. Callum, as you can see, your answer, I felt, was counterproductive. I didn't ask you what these were," he said, holding up the papers. "I asked you where the originals are."

Madison sat up on the floor with her hand pressed to her face. A tear streamed down her cheek. William reached over with a helping hand, bringing her to her feet once more.

"Now, let me ask you again. Where are the originals?"

Madison didn't speak; instead, she looked down in despair. She did not wish to expose Des, whom she believed was now searching for her.

"Your friend has them, doesn't he?" The Judge got up and started to pace the floor, with his index finger gently touching the base of his mouth. He appeared to be deep in thought. Stopping momentarily, he looked directly at Madison, then resumed his activity.

Turning once more, he walked right toward her and then leaned over, his face only a few inches from hers. She instinctively shied away, expecting to be dealt another blow.

"You know, Ms. Callum, I already knew your friend had the originals. I just wanted to see what kind of tolerance you had. You're a tough young woman, but it's obvious your tolerance has its limits. I'm sure you're going to be useful to me, at least for a little while."

His inflection was chilling, and she knew his ruthlessness would only be limited to how much she could provide him. Given the fact he had most of her information already, it gave her pause.

The Judge looked at the man with the black hair and nodded. He, in turn, pointed to his two subordinates, who snagged their captives firmly by the arms and took them to a small room in the back of the house.

Shoving them into the tight space, they slammed the door behind them and locked it. The room was dingy and smelled worse than the front of the house. There were no furnishings, and the windows had been boarded shut. The only items there were a small light bulb dangling on a wire from the ceiling and a beat-up, filthy mattress laid out in the corner.

"Are you okay?" William asked.

"Yes, I'm okay," she answered, touching her cheek.

"They're going to keep on us until they get what they want."

"But I don't have anything else to give them. They have all the clues and the key."

"You need to think. Was there anything you left out? Anything you can remember that wasn't on you when they took us?"

"Nothing I can think of. I copied those instructions down to the letter."

"Well, keep thinking, because if the Judge doesn't believe we have anything to sell, then we're of no use to him, and that wouldn't be good."

Madison sat down on the floor and put her head in her hands. It was a feeling of complete despair. She tried remembering anything that seemed unusual or a piece of information she might have neglected to share, yet there were no images, no ideas coming to mind.

She was in a catch-22; if she couldn't recall anything, they would dispose of her. But if she did remember something and was forced to give it up, then after they extracted the information, she would be left to the same fate.

They remained locked in the small crusty room for over an hour, saying little. Occasionally, as the hardwood floor played havoc on their backs, they would stand up and pace, only to return to the floor a few moments later. Madison sat with her back against the wall, across from the disgusting mattress. The room didn't offer much in terms of mental stimulation. There was nothing on the walls, and every time she moved, it would kick up clouds of dust that would hang suspended in the air, illuminated by the light emanating from the single bulb.

She looked around for anything of interest. The closet doors were off their hinges and leaned awkwardly against the wall. On the floor of the closet was a broken picture frame containing a copy of the famous painting *Dogs Playing Poker*. It was slightly ripped on the front, and the backing lining the matting was falling out of its encasement.

She stared at the picture, not for any particular reason, but because it was the only object of color in the room. As she kept the frame in her sights, she noticed the old newspaper making up most of the backing spilling out of the frame. Walking over to the mangled decoration, she reached down and pulled out the tattered paper. It was torn and yellowed from age.

Opening it up, she read the date at the top of the paper, Tuesday, September 23, 1982. The section of the paper was the entertainment portion, and the lead story was about the death of country singer Jimmy Wakely.

Madison was not much of a country music fan but began to read the article anyway. Quickly losing interest, she looked to another article and noticed something about the way the paper was designed. The layout always started the story with a greatly enlarged first letter of the first word of the article. When she reexamined the story about Jimmy Wakely, she noticed it began, "Country music singer Jimmy Wakely passed away from heart failure yesterday at…"

The next article began the same way, and so did the next. It was an effective method used to draw attention to the story. By increasing the size of the lettering, it added an appearance of importance to the content that followed. Madison went from one article to the next, never reading the whole story but just the first few sentences.

She did not understand why this seemed so significant to her. She knew it was something important, though; otherwise, it would not be standing out in her mind to such an extent. Then she realized the connection.

"I think I might have something," she said, turning to William.

"Really, what is it?"

"I'm not quite sure, but I think I might have missed something when I copied down the instructions."

William got off the floor and started moving toward Madison when he was interrupted by the sound of the latch on the door being turned. Before he could take another step, the door flung open, the two muscular men charging through it. They grabbed William forcefully by the arms, while Madison remained pinned to the back wall, fearing what their next actions might be.

Being yanked toward the door, William struggled briefly before turning to Madison. "You keep thinking. Make sure you're right."

Madison nodded in confirmation. With a few final heaves, they pulled William out the door and thrust it shut. The familiar sound of turning latches sealed the realization that she was all alone.

Chapter 52

Williamsburg, Virginia

Des walked over to the library's history section, stepping down its aisles, touching the books as he passed. Titles flashed before him as he moved by; *Battles of the Civil War, Invasion at Normandy, The War of 1812* were all familiar to him, as they had been part of his academic curriculum. Another aisle covered the Constitution, and another the Senate. His walk was quickly turning into a tour of his high school social studies career.

He made another turn, creating an S pattern on his journey, taking in more volumes of America's past. Every topic seemed to be represented, politics, inventors, statesmen, presidents, and generals. Des proceeded to the section holding the biographies on the chief executives.

Running his fingers over the rough binders he read the names. "Madison, Jefferson, Lincoln, Washington…" *Washington… Washington… Washington… wait a minute, there's something here.*

The legacy of the father.

George Washington, often referred to as the father of the nation, was the perfect match for the clue. He was a man deeply admired throughout the country, but his close connection to the South in particular was undeniable.

A Virginia gentleman who extolled the virtues of old Southern culture, Washington was the ideal candidate to be used in this cryptic method by Jefferson Davis. He represented everything in which a Southerner of the time might identify. He was a revered leader of men who believed in a limited central government.

Ironically, Washington did speak of the eventual elimination of slavery, but somehow he did not seem as conflicted as some of his contemporaries, such as Thomas Jefferson. A slave owner since he was eleven, he acquired hundreds during his lifetime and found it to be a necessary institution. Though he sometimes spoke eloquently of its elimination, when he had opportunities to show his support for integrating slaves into the free world, he fell short, not releasing any of his slaves until after his death. Even during the Continental Army's darkest days, when a shortage of men was an everyday concern, Washington refused to endorse the arming of slaves to fight for American independence, possibly jeopardizing the cause altogether.

The legacy of the father holds its place.

Des's mind was flooding with thought. *Legacy… legacy* kept pumping through his brain. *That has to be the key to this.* Des closed his eyes again, trying to imagine what Madison would say in this situation. She seemed to have a way of interjecting the right idea when it was needed most. *God, I could use her now.*

He went back to the table and looked through the folder containing the original clues. He didn't know what else he was looking for but was hoping the stimulation of all the instructions together would bring something to the surface. He stared at the tattered pieces of parchment, reading each line again and again, hoping the ritualistic behavior would bring a revelation.

Legacy is the key, the legacy is the key. He eyed the first set of instructions. He reflected on the conversation he and Madison had at the Foxy Loxy and how they figured out its messages, which, at that time, seemed every bit as nondescript as the ones he was currently trying to decipher. He remembered the process leading to their comprehension. *We were looking too deeply. Maybe that's what I am doing here.*

Reading the first set of instructions again, Des utilized this method.

> *Burned in the first revolution, the mark is represented in the pillars of our faith in the home of the beginning of the second.*

They originally had looked at the four words *pillars of our faith* as a metaphor, believing the author would not be that literal. Influenced by current popular movie and book culture, they thought a clue would not be so mundane, that there had to be some hidden meaning. Yet they were not thinking like its author. Instead, they were placing themselves in a romanticized version of a treasure hunt rather than the very real military operation this must have been.

Des now believed the use of the word *legacy* could have been in the same style of literal context that was used previously. *What does* legacy *mean?* He returned to rubbing the back of his neck, trying in vain to relieve the building stress. Forgetting momentarily about the cut, he moved his fingers over his forehead, touching his wound while sending a sharp, needlelike pain through the center of his skull. Though instead of having a distracting effect, it focused him.

A legacy must be someone that has a direct relation. George Washington never had any children of his own. By the time he married Martha, she was already a young widower who had four children with her previous husband, Daniel Parke Custis. However, only two lived to adulthood. While Des knew Washington did not have any blood descendants, he could not imagine any other president matching the clue so well. Deciding this would be the best use of his limited time, he focused on studying how Washington's stepchildren might tie into this whole situation.

Des went back onto the computer, researching the first president's genealogy. As he perused the information, he took notice of the tragedies people experienced in those times. Even individuals with such tremendous financial means as the nation's first family could not escape this all-too-real part of colonial life.

Martha had experienced devastating loss during her lifetime, burying not only a husband but eventually three of her children as well. Des recognized how people today took for granted they would live relatively long lives. However, at the time of the revolution, death was common, and if not brought on by man, it was brought on by nature. The regularity of heartbreak was extraordinary.

Delving deeper into the lineage, he also learned of the death of Martha's son John during the war, leaving two young children, whom George and Martha informally adopted and both of whom took the Washington name. The intensity of trying to follow Washington's lineage was only matched by Des's fascination with the personality of this iconic figure.

There were so many facets to the nation's first leader and how situations could dictate different and oftentimes conflicting behaviors. While Washington was a determined and sometimes-brutal commander, he was a gentle and kindly father who was devoted to his adopted children and always attentive to their well-being.

Washington's own stepchildren did not seem to have any significance related to this Confederate wealth, but his adopted grandchildren did live accomplished and prominent lives. Nelly, his step-granddaughter, married a nephew of Washington and settled into one of Virginia's aristocratic planter-class families. She never moved far from Washington's home at Mt. Vernon, staying devoted to her grandfather and eventually being buried at his estate after her death.

Yet it was the grandson drawing most of Des's attention. Named after George and affectionately called Wash by his family, he became a famous orator and writer who campaigned for agricultural reforms. However, throughout a life of accomplishment, his most lasting achievement was the prominent monument he had built to honor his grandfather, Arlington House.

Constructed in the early 1800s near the banks of the Potomac River, just across from the nation's capital, Wash wished to memorialize his grandfather in a home that paid tribute to his heritage. Des stopped in his tracks. *This could mean something!*

Des remembered from his studies that Arlington House was used as Union headquarters during the war and acted as a staging ground for many of the North's incursions into Southern territory. It made sense, but at the same time, it didn't. Continuing to read, he learned it was Wash's daughter who married her second cousin and lived in the house until she was forced out at the beginning of the war. The name of that second cousin was Robert E. Lee.

The legacy of the father holds its place.

Yet this realization was troubling. Why would Jefferson Davis leave a clue sending the searcher into the heart of the very place he was trying to run from? It seemed not only foolhardy but quite improbable. Des was stunned. *Maybe I missed something. Maybe the word* legacy *meant something else.* However, no other possibilities came to mind. *It couldn't be.*

Des looked at the second instruction, hoping it would shed light on this mystery, providing another possibility.

It lies in the northern shadow of the symbol of Darius's defeat.

Madison had researched Darius. He was a Persian king during the time of antiquity who created a vast empire, the largest in history up to that time. He also fathered Xerxes, who became famous as the villain to the Western world when he challenged the three hundred Spartans at the battle of Thermopylae.

Des was perplexed how a twenty-five-hundred-year-old Persian king could possibly be related to a Civil War treasure. This was something he was not prepared for in any way. He never thought he would have to research the pre-Christian world to find out more about his own, though Des began to recognize there were some correlations.

The ancient Western world had always had direct connections to early America. The Greeks of the mythological age influenced new world culture with their ideas of democracy, which, in turn, had a tremendous impact on the forefathers of the nation and their concepts of representative government. But even armed with this knowledge, it seemed like such a long shot. Still, he continued to press forward.

Typing in the search words "Darius' defeat," he came across the Persian emperor's greatest embarrassment, his loss to the Greeks. Steeped in legend, Darius's debacle on the beaches of Greece haunted him for the remainder of his life and fostered a hatred of his Mediterranean rivals, one that was inherited by his son Xerxes. The victory defined Greek independence and saved Western culture. It was so significant that a runner was sent across the twenty-six miles of the Plains of Marathon to spread the news of the victory across the isthmus. Later, the most famous temple in human history was erected, the Parthenon, to celebrate their triumph. It was a monument, a symbol, the symbol of Darius's defeat.

Des quickly typed in "Parthenon" into his image search. Popping up were photographs of the magnificent ancient structure. Its mighty pillars and classic architecture set the model for buildings all over the world, especially in eighteenth- and early-nineteenth-century America. Des now knew he had not made a mistake. The image of the Parthenon confirmed that he was headed for Arlington. Its design had direct influence over the home overseeing what was now the National Cemetery of the United States. It was the Americanized version of the symbol of that Greek victory.

Although he couldn't comprehend why Jefferson Davis would send someone into the lion's den to preserve their greatest wealth, he could no longer deny this was what occurred. Maybe once he arrived, some sense could be made of this bewildering development. For now, he did not have time to ponder; he had to get to Arlington before the Judge. This race was just beginning, and there was no reward for second place.

Chapter 53

Twenty miles north of Williamsburg, Virginia

The room felt suffocating and cramped as Madison strained to hear what was happening beyond the door. She could not make out any voices, but what did meet her ears was horrifying. The sounds of thuds and grunts of a body being slammed against sizeable objects conjured up brutal images of a defenseless William being beaten into submission. Her powerlessness to be of any aid only added to the terror.

Trying to compose herself, she pulled away from the door. The only help she could provide was to figure out what it was she was missing. She grabbed the newspaper, studying the oversize letters at the beginning of each story. *Why is this so significant to me?*

She repeated the first sentence of the column about the death of the country music singer, hoping it would jog her memory. However, the noise of the beating kept breaking her concentration. *Come on, Madison, you got to figure this thing out.*

She began pacing the floor, studying the newspaper, continuing to repeat the sentences aloud, while trying to drown out the noise filtering in from the other side of the door. The sound of the violence was making her nauseated.

Gripping the yellowed newspaper, walking back and forth between the front of the closet and the door, she examined the interior of the room, gazing at the picture in the broken frame. The painting was familiar, as she had seen copies of it in dorm rooms and fraternity houses during her college days.

It was an iconic image that was the most famous of C. M. Coolidge's works. Madison scanned the image, mainly due to the fact it was the only stimulating material in the room. There it lay, a painting of canines gathered around a table, cards in their paws and cigars in their mouths. It was both humorous and creative.

But the image was not what was grabbing Madison's attention. Rather, it was the signature of the artist in the lower right-hand corner of the painting. She observed the large first letters of Coolidge's signature looming over his lowercase ones. She then looked at the newspaper again, seeing the same pattern. And as she reversed her attention between the paper and the painting, it finally hit her. She knew what she had left out.

Hearing the latches turning on the door once more, she turned and faced the portal, not knowing what to expect. A couple of more clicks, and it swung open. The two muscular men were holding up a slumped William and then, with a heave, hurled him to the floor, causing Madison to gasp.

They then turned and slammed the door, trapping them inside once again. She hustled over to the injured young man; his lip and nose were bleeding, and his face was covered in sweat. She tried to comfort him as he moaned in pain. His eyes were looking right through her as he tried to regain his senses.

"William, let me help you up." Madison reached underneath his arms, pulling him hard enough to where he was sitting upright. He was breathing heavily, like he had just finished sprinting. "Are you okay?"

He nodded in confirmation, but he sure didn't look it.

"What did they want from you?"

"Nothing… nothing at all. That's the Judge's way of exacting revenge," he said, coughing in between words. "Unfortunately, it's not over. The man is a goddamn sadist." William tried to speak some more but had to pause to catch his breath.

"Take your time."

"You said before I got pulled out of the room that you may have missed something. What was it?"

"I remembered something. I didn't think anything of it at that time, but I remembered that some letters in some of the words were larger than the others."

"Do you mean in the last set of clues?"

"No, in all of them. There were words where the letters were larger than the rest. Each set of clues had letters right in the middle of a sentence or even in the middle of a word that were bigger than the others. They were not at the beginning of sentences, and they weren't names, so there was no reason for them to be presented that way. But I didn't really think it was important, so I didn't make their appearance any larger when I copied the instructions down."

"Which words were they?"

"That's the problem, I can't remember. I've been trying to picture them in my head, but I can only remember maybe one or two of them. I would have to see the originals again."

"And Des has the originals, doesn't he?"

"Yes."

"Shit, that's going to be a problem. He's going to want to know," William said in despair.

"We may be able to use it as a way of getting out of this thing, or at least to buy us some time."

"Well, we're going to have to think of a plan quickly, because they've been able to track Des heading north."

"How?"

"I'm not sure. I guess he used his phone."

"Do you know where he might be headed?"

"I was hoping you would know."

"No, I don't. Damn it, this is so maddening. That first clue didn't make much sense. God, I wish I had Des here. He's the Civil War buff. He's so good at figuring this stuff out. You said he was heading north, right?"

"Yes, but that doesn't mean a whole lot. He could be going anywhere. Is there anything else you figured out about the clues? Because that might give us an idea of where he may be heading," he said, hoping for some enlightenment. William kept shifting around, like his discomfort was coming from more than just the beating. Madison also noticed how concerned he was about the time, looking at his watch repeatedly. Maybe it was his way of processing stress. We all have our little peccadillos we use to relieve pressure. This was probably his.

"I don't remember all the clues, but I do remember the first one, though. It said something about the 'legacy of the father holding its place,'" Madison said.

"Yeah, I remember reading that one too, but I don't know what 'legacy of the father' means. I'm sure the Judge is researching it now."

Madison tried to change her approach, attempting to look at the clues utilizing the same method Des would use. She reflected on their first search at Old Sheldon Church, remembering how they were able to figure out that it was Thomas Jefferson's home they needed to visit next. *I wonder if the next clue has to do with a president.* It seemed logical, given the fact they focused so much on Jefferson in the second set of clues. However, it was hard to match this latest set of instructions to any presidents. *Well, that's except if we...*

Before she could travel down any more paths of deductive reasoning, the horrifying sound of the door latch echoed throughout the small room. The door did not fly open this time, but creaked ajar, something that only added to the terror.

The man with the black hair walked in silently, with his gun drawn. "The Judge would like to see you now."

Chapter 54

Heading north toward Richmond, Virginia

Des understood there was little time to waste. He left the library knowing his destination but having no idea what he was looking for once he arrived. The third set of instructions seemed to be more cryptic and vague than the ones preceding them. Because it mentioned, "It lies in the northern shadow of the symbol of Darius's defeat," he figured it was a good bet it was at Arlington National Cemetery. Yet the next three clues were a complete mystery.

The message is engraved in the sorrows of the nation.
The knowledge you seek turns its back to you.
The values you possess match the language of the empire.

Des repeated the sentences to himself. Slowing down with each recollection, he was hoping the pace would reveal something. Frustratingly, no matter what technique he used, none of it made sense. One clue seemed to suggest an object that moved; otherwise, how could it "turn its back to you"? While the word *engraved* appeared to be pretty straightforward as something written.

The other question haunting him was what *empire* they were referring to and whose *language*. He did have some time to work on the problem, as it was about a 130-mile drive to Arlington.

But now, another obstacle was slowly creeping into the picture, daylight. He was running out of it. It was already late afternoon. The drive would take him well over two hours, and that was if he did not hit any traffic. There would be no way he would be able to access the cemetery today. He would have to wait until tomorrow, which was just as well, as he needed to do more research.

He was going to have to find a place to stay for the night. However, how was he going to do that without accessing his phone? Seeing no other alternatives, he pulled it out of the back seat, his wariness of William's warning grating on him.

His mind began wandering back to his companions, especially Madison. He could not help but feel responsible. It was his curiosity which led them on this quest, and because of that, two people were now in imminent danger.

Guilt nearly consumed him every moment, the determination to right the ship only increasing. *What if I just had scanned the first set of clues and filed it away like I was supposed to? We wouldn't be in this mess. Come on, concentrate, Des. Madison is depending on you.*

He sped along at a decent clip, the highway fairly clear, and it would only be a short time before he was driving through Richmond. As he got closer to the former Confederate capital, Des pondered what he considered to be the most perplexing mystery of this chase so far. *Why would Jefferson Davis send something so important into the nerve center of the Union? Wasn't the whole goal to keep the treasure out of Union hands?* Maybe it was a diversion of some kind, but it seemed rather unlikely. None of it made sense, and he knew this contradiction in historical sagacity would have to eventually be worked out.

For now, though, he was going to have to take care of more pressing matters, such as finding a motel room near Arlington. Even though this would most likely reveal his location, he would have to chance it. However, if he was going to do it, he thought it best to do so while still far enough away from Arlington that they would not be able to ascertain where he was headed. Pulling off the highway, Des unwrapped his phone, turned it on and entered a search for hotels in the Arlington area, trying to be as quick as possible. What it looked like and its amenities were unimportant. He only cared whether it had internet access and, hopefully, a complimentary computer on its grounds. Not wasting any time, he chose the first place coming up on his search, the Arlington Inn. He made the call.

"Hello, Arlington Inn, can I help you?" a polite voice answered.

"Yes, I would like to book a room for tonight. Do you have any available?"

"We're pretty booked up. We only have a couple of rooms left, and they're smoking rooms."

"That would be fine," Des answered, not caring, as long as it had a bed. If he had to deal with the unpleasant odor of cigarette residue, then so be it. He got out his credit card and gave the young woman his information. It seemed like it was taking an eternity as he was aching to finish the call. With every word he uttered, he could feel himself being observed. Trying to remain composed, Des finished the transaction and then turned off and re-wrapped his phone, effectively concealing his location once more.

He turned his car back onto the highway, reinitiating his trek toward Richmond. A little under an hour had gone by when the downtown area of the former Confederate capital came into view. From every indication, it was a modern city that would be difficult to differentiate from any other medium-size metropolis in the country. Large office buildings dotted the downtown area. Factory smokestacks could be seen outside the more recently built section, with industrial-style bridges crisscrossing the James River at various strategic locations.

Des tried to picture what this city, once the heart of the Confederacy, must have looked like in the mid-1800s and the chaos that ensued when it fell to Union forces in April of 1865. *It must have been so different back then.*

Although most people focused on its designation as the South's headquarters, Richmond was more than the political capital of the South. It also served as its military equipment supplier, as many munitions and armament factories were either in or surrounded the area. By the end of the Civil War, it had supplied the South with nearly 50 percent of all its artillery. Because of this, it was always an important target of Union forces. Ironically, even though its relative proximity to the North was quite close, it held out longer than many of the other major Southern cities. Robert E. Lee's brilliant defenses combined with the heroics of such infamous names as Jeb Stuart and Stonewall Jackson kept Richmond in Confederate hands for almost the entire duration of the war.

Still, the fact that it was only about one hundred miles away from Arlington was amazing. Due to its easy river access and ability to disseminate men, materials, and information to the rest of the Confederacy, it did make sense, but one would have to believe there had to be some trepidation among Southerners when designating it as the capital. Des could only imagine what Jefferson Davis's thoughts must have been when George McClellan landed such a sizable Union force on the Virginia peninsula.

Although thinking about history was usually something he enjoyed, in this sistuation it was more of a burden than a blessing. Wanting to find ways to calm his nerves but at the same time not wishing to break his concentration, Des looked for useful distractions. Turning on the radio, he hoped something melodic would help him focus. Yet as soon as he hit the button, he felt guilt. *How can I listen to music when Madison is suffering?* Almost as soon as powering it up, he pressed the button to shut it off. The sound of the car's engine and the passing traffic filled his ears, and Des tried to allow the trance of the never-ending road to put himself into a hypnotic state.

Seeing images and pieces of the words flash through his mind gave him an indication this technique was working, but it was also frustrating. While he could catch glimpses, the messages were muffled and fleeting. *Don't press. Let it come to you.*

He still had quite a ways to go. The late-afternoon sun was edging farther west, glaring into the driver's side window, forcing him to pull down the visor to minimize its blinding effect. The day was preparing for its final moments, but he knew the long night he had ahead of him. Even if he was able to figure out these clues, it was only part of the process. So many questions remained. How would he implement his search? If this led to another set of clues, would the Judge figure he had no need to keep Madison and William around? If he found the treasure first, what would be his next move? How could he convince the Judge to not harm his friends? It seemed overwhelming and hopeless. So many complications and so little time to solve them.

He was now just about thirty minutes outside Arlington. The sun, once pouring through his window, had now settled halfway beneath the horizon. A mixture of oranges and purples painted the sky, creating a surreal effect that was both beautiful and discomfiting.

But he was exhausted. This whole episode had covered just a little over two days, yet it seemed as if it had been going on for months. His eyes felt heavy, and his stomach burned with hunger. His energy level, once fueled by excitement, had dissipated into a state near emotional and physical collapse. There would be no time to rejuvenate, just enough maybe to grab a few moments of respite. He had no answers, but hopefully by this time tomorrow, he would have reason to celebrate a positive conclusion.

Chapter 55

William gave Madison a nod, then was moved out of the room, followed by her and then their captor. Walking down the short hallway to the small family room, she took notice of the knocked-over chairs, a sign of the episode William had experienced a few minutes prior.

"Well, Ms. Callum, your friend, it seems, is heading north. Where's he going?"

"I don't know," she answered, feeling a lump in her throat.

The Judge walked directly to her. "Ms. Callum, patience is not one of my virtues. It would be in your best interest not to lie to me."

"You know as much as I do. You have my copy of the last set of clues."

"Yes, that's true, but I think there's something more. What is it?" he screamed.

Madison flinched and fell back at the Judge's aggressive cry, bumping into the man who escorted them out of the room. Feeling his gun hitting her spine, she immediately lurched forward. "I don't know where he's going," she reiterated, her voice quivering. "I was trying to figure that out before you came and got us."

"We're leaving now. I'll give you back the clues, but if I don't get something in return, then you are of no use to me, and I don't keep excess baggage around." The Judge's tone was as serious as a heart attack. His eyes gave away the lethality of his nature.

How much should I reveal? She had to play her cards right. She needed to give enough to maintain her value but could not reveal too much, or he might figure her usefulness had dried up.

They were swiftly taken to the car, where they were once again shoved into the back seat. The men did not speak much, only sporadically about where their target was heading. The Judge took his place in the front passenger seat, holding a small device that had a screen showing a map. Although she could not make out what the map detailed, she did notice a small luminous light moving slowly across the display.

"He's still moving north," the Judge said. "I think he may be heading to Washington."

Madison couldn't believe Des would be so foolish as to leave his phone on. He was quite aware he could be tracked. As time passed by and the Judge was still able to follow Des's movements, she realized they must have another way of monitoring him, perhaps something they attached to his vehicle without his knowledge.

They continued to travel as she worked on recalling the enlarged letters but could only think of one. The rest were a blur, a mishmash of consonants and phrases not having any cohesiveness. William kept glancing down at his watch, displaying an increase in his nervous habit.

Dusk had given way to nighttime, and the highway was rather desolate, with only the occasional passing car to break the sound of the whisking wind. The encroaching blackness added to the desperate feeling of this whole predicament.

"Have you figured out anything else, Ms. Callum?" the Judge asked.

"No. Not yet."

"That's too bad."

The Judge motioned for them to pull off at the next exit. As they withdrew from the highway, Madison saw nothing of significance. Large grass and wooded fields encompassing uninhabited areas were all she could make out. Making another turn, the vehicle began bumping, shaking its occupants from side to side. It was obvious they had moved off a paved street and onto a dirt trail.

Do they have another hideout?

The powerful SUV didn't slow; instead, it plowed over the uneven road. There were no buildings or cabins, just wilderness, trees, and thick shrubs, which became increasingly dense. The only illumination was a little bit of moonlight and the intense beams of the headlights. The sound of a quick skid over the dirt and then a sudden jerk to a stop was the next sensation.

"Get out," said the man on Madison's right as he flung open the door and pulled her from the car. William was shoved in the same direction. The man with the black hair exited the driver's side, which was followed by the click of a pistol being cocked as they were shoved in front of the vehicle.

The Judge opened his door very slowly, walking with deliberateness. Approaching his two hostages, he placed his hand on William's shoulder. "Come with me, you two," he said, directing them farther away from the car in the direction of the woods. "I'm trying to see why I would keep both of you around, as neither one of you seems to be of much assistance. Tell me, Ms. Callum, am I correct in my assessment?"

Madison was petrified but tried to stand up for herself and William. "I think we—"

"We're valuable to you," William interjected. "We can both provide insight into the clues as well as my family's journal."

"William, I wasn't speaking to you, and quite frankly, I don't think you can offer me a goddamn thing," the Judge said sternly.

"He's right, we can help," Madison said.

"Really? Well, so far, he has been of little service, and I haven't been impressed with you either. You have to do much better than that, Ms. Callum."

"I think I've figured out some missing information from the clues," she stammered.

"I'm listening."

"When I copied down the clues from the originals, there were some letters… enlarged letters. They didn't seem to be important, so I didn't put them in my copies. They weren't names. They were just at random places, either at the beginning or in the middle of a word. They have to mean something."

"Which words were they?"

"I can't remember all of them, but I can remember some. I think if I have a little more time, I can figure it out."

The Judge paused for a moment and then, grabbing her arm, started walking back to the car. William stayed where he was and observed.

"Ms. Callum, how do I know you'll be able to figure these out, much less if they are important at all?"

Madison felt a sudden wave of confidence. Her survival instinct had kicked in. "I don't think you want to chance that. Remember, Des still has the originals, and he's better at figuring this stuff out than I am. I can help you. William and I can get the information you need."

He paced a little more, contemplating her offer. He looked back at William standing in the glow of the headlights, waiting to hear his response. Walking back and standing directly in front of her, he used the front of his shoe to carve a back-and-forth pattern in the soft dirt.

"You know, Ms. Callum, you do make a pretty convincing argument, although I have my doubts. However, I do agree with you about one thing. I think you can help me." The Judge smiled.

Feeling a reprieve, she turned to face William with a relieved expression. *We'll be okay.*

The Judge moved over to the man with the black hair and patted him on the shoulder. "You hear that? I think she's going to help us. I guess that makes our choice easy."

"You're right," the man responded.

Madison took one step toward the car when she saw the black-haired man turn quickly and point his gun at William. Her view switched to her helpless companion in time to see the expression on his face go from relief to disbelief, raising his hands in one last helpless gesture.

"No!" she shouted.

It was too late. The shot rang out, deafening her ears and overloading her senses. Blood spurted from William's chest as he fell backward, landing on the ground and twitching a few times before lying completely still.

She let out a bloodcurdling scream, the sight of the lifeless young man bringing the moment into terrifying focus. She fell to her knees, the reality too much of a burden, as she could no longer support her own weight.

"He could have helped us. Why did you do that?" she screamed, crying hysterically.

"Like I said, Ms. Callum, I hate carrying excess baggage," the Judge said calmly.

With that, he walked back to the car with a leisurely stroll, like he was traveling to a church picnic. The black-haired man moved behind Madison to make sure she would go straight to the vehicle.

"Shall we go, Ms. Callum?" the Judge said, standing beside his car door.

All the confidence, all the relief she had enjoyed a moment ago was gone. Sweat mixed with tears covered her face as she trembled. Slowly pulling herself up, she felt frozen to the ground, the horror still sinking in. The man standing behind her gave her a slight nudge, forcing her to move.

I'm not going to make it through this. I'm dead.

As she sat back against the hard leather seat, her guilt was all-consuming. How was it fair she had survived and William was gone?

The SUV backed up, kicking into the air a cloud of dust, which was picked up by the headlight beams, hovering for a second and then finally settling over William's body. Madison peered out the back window in an attempt to pay her final respects, catching only a glimpse of William's pale face. He was gone, and Des was miles away.

Chapter 56

Listening to the fading sound of the SUV's tires scraping across the trail, he caught the glare of the headlights receding off the brush above him, returning all to blackness. William then fixated on the tiny pinpoints of light created by the stars as they pierced their dark canopy.

Many times he had imagined what this moment would feel like, what the sensation would be when he felt the departure, the moving from one life to the next. Surprisingly, the pain was not as intense as he anticipated, and whatever discomfort he was experiencing was, in turn, soothed by being free of the burden.

As he felt himself melting into the earth, a tear escaped the corner of his eye, trickling down his temple. And before the last vestige was gone, one question entered his mind. Would the treasure ever see its intended use?

Chapter 57

Arlington, Virginia

Des pulled his car into the motel parking lot, feeling like he was on the verge of a breakdown. His body ached, and his head was splitting, mostly from the beating, with the remainder being a product of stress. As he grabbed his bag out of the trunk, his emotions were dragged farther down as he saw Madison's bag pressed next to his. *God only knows what she must be going through.*

Once he entered the main lobby, all he could think about was getting to his room and taking a hot shower. The guilt of having the luxury of bathing bothered him, considering Madison was in such a horrible situation. However, he also knew, the better he felt physically, the better he would be able to concentrate on the massive job he had in front of him.

Checking in with the desk clerk, he found out where the guest computer was located. He got his key and trekked up to the room, the small bag he carried feeling like it weighed a ton due to his ever-increasing fatigue. It was a quaint accommodation, typical in its few amenities, but clean and comfortable. Although they had tried covering up the smell with a flowery deodorizer, the strong hint of cigarette smoke was undeniable.

Not caring about anything else other than hitting the shower, Des threw his bag on the bed and entered the bathroom. He turned the shower knob, the welcome sound of running water was as soothing as a melody. Disrobing, he inhaled deeply as the steam surrounding him hung heavy in the air. As he stepped into the enclosure and let the hot water pour over his aching body, he could feel the tension begin to wash away.

Although it stung at first when the spray struck his wound, the relaxation it brought outweighed the pain. Des put his hand against the shower wall, leaning forward to let the warm fluid run down his neck and back. It felt like heaven, and it would be easy to get lost in the comfort. Still, he was not going to lose sight of his mission. He took a couple more deep breaths, gathered his thoughts, and ended his short respite.

After drying off, Des took the folder from his bag and laid the papers onto the bed. He decided the best way to figure out the clues was to focus on the ones he didn't need to be physically present in order to understand the purpose of. The first two, "The legacy of the father holds its place" and "It lies in the northern shadow of the symbol of Darius's defeat," he believed he had figured out.

The third and fourth clues, "The message is engraved in the sorrows of the nation" and "The knowledge you seek turns its back to you," would, on the surface, appear to require him to be present at a location to understand them. "Engraved" suggested a physical marker, while "Turning its back to you" indicated movement.

That left the next clue, "The values you possess match the language of the empire," which did not fall into either of the previous two categories. However, "The values you possess" seemed peculiar. Unlike the previous clues, it was suggesting that what he was looking for, he already had with him. Des's first reaction was to think of the only hard artifact they had collected, which was the key Madison pried from the beams of Bruton Parish Church. Unfortunately, she still had it, and a more horrifying thought was, so did the Judge.

Well, I can't analyze what I don't have. What now? Des paced the room with his hand on the back of his neck. Strain started to build again, and the fear of not having what he needed soon started heading toward panic. *Okay, calm down, Des.*

Changing his mode of thinking, he reflected on his education. Although this time, it was not the numerous history classes he was recalling; it was a course in psychology. While at the University of Georgia, he took a class covering the art of living in the moment or what psychologists commonly referred to as mindfulness. Mental health professionals found that people who projected toward the future were greatly susceptible to depression. This was because human nature usually caused one to focus on negative possibilities and adopt them as fact. This was done regardless of whether there was any evidence something bad would happen or not. Eventually, acceptance of those feelings on many issues or situations led to adopting harmful opinions even though they were often times not based in any reality. His professor captured this theory succinctly, writing on the board before every class, "What you feel is real but ain't necessarily true." Des wanted to make sure he was not falling into that trap. He didn't know what was happening with Madison, and as long as he kept assuming the worst, he would not be able to concentrate on solving the issues at hand.

Walking back to the bed, he looked at the papers. *What am I missing?* His eyes danced over the instructions, checking for every detail. He went back to the beginning, to the first set of instructions he found that fateful day.

> *Burned in the first revolution, the mark is represented in the pillars of our faith in the home of the beginning of the second.*
>
> *It lies shallow at the pinnacle of the single Roman Vestige, a half of Vara.*
>
> *The bows that lay at its entrance suggest lineage of leadership.*

He then looked at the second set they had dug up.

> *It begins with the author who in death ignores the office and overlooks the dome.*
>
> *Stand at the base in the corner of his ordinance and look its opposite.*
>
> *Resting at the heart of his highest learning, it is fixed in the home of the rector.*

Above the sound of God's calling lies the key at its anchor.

It will lead you to the symbol of Darius's defeat.

Wait a minute. What's with some of those letters that are larger than the rest? That doesn't look like an accident. Noticing this obvious aberration, he quickly drew his attention over to the last set of instructions.

The legacy of the father holds its place.

It lies in the northern shadow of the symbol of Darius's defeat.

The message is engraved in the sorrows of the nation. The knowledge you seek turns its back to you.

The values you possess match the language of the empire. It will lead to the entrance of the gateway of the second invasion.

At the precipice of the stairs' flight, buried two vara, lies the portal.

Travel through the tunnels to the stone with the mark of our leader.

Break through to find the treasure, thousands enCased in black sands of the fallen.

They had that same random placement of larger letters that were either at the beginning or even in the middle of some of the words, but only in some sentences. There was no question this meant something.

The values you possess match the language of the empire.

As he read the line over again, his mind was sent tumbling over the possibilities. *What are* values? *Values… values… values.* The word was on a loop. *Values have lots of meanings. They could mean morals. It could mean monetary wealth or wealth of knowledge.* While these seemed reasonable options, there was something amiss. He studied the sentence once more, paying close attention to the second part of the phrase, "Match the language of the empire." Recognizing this had nothing to do with morals or wealth, he went to the only other possibility, measurements. *Measurements are expressed in values, and values are expressed in numbers! These represent numbers!* Des was so excited he could hardly sit still. It all matched. The "language of the empire," the Roman Empire. *That's what it has to mean!*

Des went back to the first set of instructions, siphoning out the large letters he now believed were Roman numerals. There were two 1s in the first sentence, two 5s in the second sentence, and two 1s in the fourth sentence. The next set had a single 1 in the first sentence and a single 1 in the third sentence. Finally, the last set of instructions had three 1s in the seventh sentence and the Roman symbol for 100 in the last sentence.

Although he was overjoyed at the discovery, it was soon tempered by the realization that he still did not know how these numbers were to be applied. There was also one more element drawing his concern. He knew, having seen Madison's copies, that she did not include the Roman numeral markers. On the one hand, this was good news, because it gave him an advantage in finding the treasure over the Judge. Yet it was also bad news, because it hurt Madison's usefulness to her captor.

Des wanted to continue delving more into these issues, but he needed to get some nourishment if he was going to keep this pace. He hadn't eaten anything all day and was famished. Gathering up the papers and placing them in the folder, he grabbed his coat and headed out the door.

He wanted to stay close to the motel and figured he would just go to one of the local restaurants within a short walking distance. Remembering seeing a small café just down the street, he figured that was as good a place as any.

Entering the café, he felt a bit like a college freshman. It had been a while since he had pulled an all-nighter, all those late hours, nose buried in papers while clutching a cup of coffee.

He scanned the eatery, not really knowing why, but for some reason, he was feeling uneasy. He hadn't used his phone in a while; however, after the experience he went through today, being away from the confined space of his car and out in the open gave him pause. *You haven't used your phone since you were outside of Richmond. There's no way they could know where you are.*

Des continued to try to control the feelings of guilt as he rapidly consumed his food. Though he kept thinking of the lesson of his psychology class, the worry of how Madison and William were being treated was always there. Pushing hard against those feelings, he rushed through the clues. It was not helpful. *Des, slow down. The cemetery will not be open until tomorrow. Rushing your thinking is just going to hold you back.*

Realizing he could not do any more with the numbers, he decided to focus on one of the instructions he had skipped over. "The message is engraved in the sorrows of the nation." Des remembered visiting Arlington National Cemetery as a youth. He was only nine years old when his father brought him to the hallowed grounds. His recollections of that day were fuzzy. The images he was able to dig up from his memory had no cohesiveness and consisted of things like the Visitors' Center, Arlington House, and the flame at JFK's tomb. None of which, of course, with the exception of Arlington House, were there at the time these clues were written.

Des's knowledge of Arlington was basic at best. He did know some of the background of the house and its former well-known residents. He also knew when the grounds were converted from private ownership to a cemetery during the Civil War. But that was it.

Although he read the line many times, one word stuck out: *sorrow. What is the sorrow of a nation?* This could only mean one thing; the most painful suffering and deepest sadness of war was the loss of life. It was obvious to him that, whatever was *engraved* would be on a tombstone.

Like so many times during this search, the enthusiasm of discovery was tainted with the stress of an additional obstacle. In this case, there were literally thousands of tombstones at Arlington, and even if he eliminated the ones placed after the Civil War, it would take someone forever to sift through them all.

It also raised another question: What information was he supposed to look for in the first place? From what he could remember, the tombstones only had the name of the individual, maybe their rank, the year of death, and nothing else. What information could he possibly obtain from them without further guidance?

This was going to require more visual information. It was time to head back to the motel. Des left a few dollars on the table, grabbed his stuff, took one last swig of his coffee, and exited the café.

Chapter 58

*Heading north on Highway 95,
an hour south of Arlington, Virginia*

Chris stared at the darkened road in front of him. The young man felt edgy. He had followed the Judge's instructions to this point, and now that William was no longer with them, it was easier to maintain control. But already, this assignment had gone far beyond what he had anticipated.

Glancing over at the Judge, he became frustrated, even angry. He wanted to speak about his concerns, but the look on his employer's face being illuminated by the glare of the location monitor he was holding, was intimidating.

Chris looked in his rearview mirror, seeing his accomplices and the girl. They were stoic in their expressions. The girl's head was tilted slightly down and to the left. She was obviously frightened. With her having witnessed what had happened a short time ago, it was understandable.

Although working off the cuff was not his strong suit or his preference, the information he learned in bits and pieces had heightened his interest about this job. He had overheard his captives speaking about a treasure. Given what the Judge had asked him to do thus far, it meant whatever it was they were after was of considerable value. *There has to be a way to make this whole situation more worth my while. And why not? The Judge has required me to do so much more than what he originally stated. I deserve a piece of whatever this treasure is.*

Although he was no valedictorian, he was smart enough to realize the Judge was not just going to divide this wealth without a compelling reason. The question now was, How could he convince him this would be the best course of action? Chris was never known for his patience, yet in his government training, he learned that in situations such as this, the best opportunity would present itself to you rather than you looking to create it. *There will be a time during this process for me to make my move. Just be patient, Chris. You need to just be patient.*

"I found where he has settled in for the night. It looks like he's at the Arlington Inn," the Judge said.

"The only thing of interest in Arlington is the cemetery," Chris answered.

"Yes, you're right, but it could be that he's just stopping there."

"Judge, he doesn't know he's being tracked. So he's not trying to throw us off the scent. He could have stopped anywhere. He must have chosen that location for a reason."

"Well, we're only a short ways away. We'll find out soon."

Chris glanced again in his review mirror and saw Madison look up. She had been listening, appearing to want to interject something, but he could tell she was thinking better of it. He got that impression from her quite a bit.

The Judge had frightened this young woman to death, yet Chris felt he still had failed to get all her information. *I can get it out of her. I just need an opportunity.*

As he thought more about this new wrinkle of wealth, Chris became excited at the possibilities. For years, he had heard the whispers of people who doubted his abilities. They said he was a kept man and did not deserve or earn the success he attained. According to his many detractors, he was just a product of his mentor's knack for cashing in on favors. Sometimes these criticisms were not just muttered underneath the breath but took the form of blatant public detractions.

Although he tried to tune them out, these naysayers ate at him. If he could pull this off, he would establish himself, have his own identity, and their negativity would be quieted once and for all. For now, though, he had to concentrate on the matter at hand, getting to their target and obtaining those original instructions.

"What are your plans?" Chris asked.

"We need to get those instructions from her friend," the Judge replied.

"Yes, I understand that, but we can't just go barging into a motel without drawing a lot of unwanted attention."

"He has to leave sometime. Plus, we can get our other man on him as well."

Chris looked at the Judge with a nervous expression. He did not have a lot of confidence in the other person his employer was working with on this matter. His presence seemed ridiculous, even overkill. "Are you sure he's not going to fuck everything up? This doesn't really seem like his type of assignment."

"He'll be fine. He has all the details we need to get this thing done."

"I hope you're right. He makes me nervous."

"Chris, I'm always thorough."

Chris nodded but did not feel any better. He knew the Judge was detail-oriented, but at the same time, this operation did not seem as tight as it should be. There were a lot of holes needing to be filled, and he was not sure the Judge had enough dirt to top them all off.

They were only about a half hour outside Arlington as he continued to brief the Judge on ideas on how to apprehend their target. In the end, they felt that they would check if he was in his room and then, after inspecting the premises, make their determination.

Although they were not 100 percent sure he was going to the cemetery, their examination of the clues and the target's decision to stay in the area left them pretty confident in their assessment. This, in addition to having another man tailing him to make sure any additional information would be quickly obtained, made the subject, at least theoretically, completely under their control.

Chris did not believe this chase could continue much longer. It had to be coming to some kind of a conclusion soon. William's demeanor, as well as the statements he made, gave Chris the impression the treasure was near.

Wait for the opportunity. It will come. Chris would cooperate for now, but he would not be denied a true reward for his efforts. The Judge was going to give him a piece of this prize, and he will realize his goal of respect.

Chapter 59

Arlington, Virginia

Des made his way to the motel. The evening was cool, as it had lightly sprinkled earlier in the day, and his breath was clearly visible as he passed some of the streetlights lining the boulevard.

Although he was as nervous as ever, the shower, followed by the quick meal, had a rejuvenating effect. His mind was not as cluttered. Anxious to get started on his research, he entered the motel and hustled to the other side of the lobby to the office with complimentary computer access.

It was a small room with a table near its doorway and a small workstation in the corner. Placing the folder next to him on the desk, Des opened a search engine and immediately typed in "Arlington National Cemetery." As expected, a ton of matches appeared, everything from the history of the cemetery to features on Arlington House, to special ceremonies, including the president's traditional visits.

However, Des needed visual information. He had to see the cemetery in order to assess the next clue. Opening up the folder, he removed its contents, the papers' crinkling and cracking making him concerned they would not sustain much more handling.

He thought about copying down the clues on sturdier stock as Madison had before. Yet he was hesitant to rely on copies, cognizant he might leave out important information, just as she had.

Unlike before, where he had read each clue before getting started on solving the puzzle piece by piece, Des went straight to the instruction that baffled him at the diner.

The knowledge you seek turns its back to you.

He pulled up images of the cemetery, ones quite familiar to him. There were the photographs of the sea of white headstones contrasting sharply with the rich green grass carpeting of Arlington's fields. Images of Arlington House, with its majestic Greek facade and arched windows, also covered the screen.

Des examined them closely. Nothing jumped out at him. Everything looked like he remembered it on his visit with his father.

However, there was one item he had forgotten—not all the tombstones were gleaming white. The grave markers that had been placed in more recent times shone in the sunlight, yet the older stones erected in the cemetery's early days were not so striking. *It has to be in the older section of the cemetery.*

Des typed in "Civil War, Arlington Cemetery" into the search engine. His heart sank as the images appeared. There were thousands of Civil War-era headstones gracing the fields, and many of them had been replaced due to wear. He immediately realized, if the particular grave site he was searching for had been supplanted, there was a possibility the inscriptions were altered. If this was the case, the information he was looking for might be lost. *Don't get discouraged by the what-ifs. Stay on task, Des.*

Temporarily stymied by this possibility, he refocused his efforts on the other puzzle. *What is turning its back to me?* He went back to the pictures, staring at them intently. Nothing was of interest. *How am I going to find the right grave? This is impossible! It will take me forever to search through all these tombstones. There must be thousands of them.*

Dismayed by the overwhelming chore, he rubbed his eyes, feeling the growing frustration. He scanned the screen with no real thoughts in mind. How he wished his father was there to advise him. He always had a way of making sense of the most difficult of situations. It was his true talent. No matter the problem, he could calmly dissect it, placing it in its clearest light.

Scrolling through the plethora of information, he could hear his father's voice gently giving him direction.

Relax, Des. You're pressing. Remember what I told you. Just let it come and it will happen.

Des nodded as the voice was as tangible to him as it was when his father was alive. *Okay, Dad, I will. I promise.*

Retracing his steps, he went back to Arlington House. The images were eye-catching but did not seem helpful. There was one showing the house from its side, another glowing in the midafternoon sun, and still another was a sketch of the mansion done in the nineteenth century. It was all lovely but mundane, and basically useless.

He examined the luminescence of the structure while imagining Robert E. Lee riding his horse over its tree-covered paths, the shadows of the mighty oaks breaking up the sunlight on his journey.

Wait a minute. The shadows.

One of the photographs he remembered was taken during the late afternoon. He looked and looked for the image now monopolizing his thoughts. *Where is that picture?* Filtering through the dozens of images, he could not locate it.

Altering the search words, he finally captured what he was hunting for, a beautiful snapshot of Arlington House, backlit by the sun, its shadow cascading northward toward the tombstones gathered near its base.

It lies in the northern shadow of the symbol of Darius's defeat.

That had to be it! Des laughed at himself, wondering why he kept making the same mistake over and over. He was always looking for some hidden meaning in the clues instead of just looking at them literally. *God, Des, stop it! What do you think this is,* National Treasure?

Being a student of history, he loved all movies of that genre, *National Treasure, Raiders of the Lost Ark*, and even *The Goonies*. He had to remind himself what he was looking for was not some mythical reward hidden by pirates or some Dark Ages religious organization like the Templars. This was a real documented asset hidden during wartime. The intention was to keep it out of Union hands and to recover it later to continue the war effort. It was not left with the hopes some lucky individual would prove themselves worthy enough, like some knight on a quest out of the King Arthur legend.

Feeling better having narrowed the search down to at least a general area of the cemetery, he realized he still needed to focus on that nagging part of the clue, "The knowledge you seek turns its back to you." *Okay, Des, let's get into the literal part of this. What has backs?*

He started entering more key words into his query when he was interrupted by a voice filtering in from the lobby. It was strong and clear and terrifyingly familiar.

"Hi, I'm looking for a Mr. Desmond Cook. Could you tell me what room he is staying in?"

Des's heart leaped into his throat.

How did they find me?

Chapter 60

Arlington, Virginia

The interior of the car smelled of the Judge's cologne, a sweet aroma that when mixed with the scent of the coffee they had been drinking gave off a sickly smell, making Madison queasy. It had been over two hours since she had spoken. Still in shock over William's death, she decided it would be in her best interest not to engage in any kind of conversation unless a question was directed at her.

When they arrived at the motel, Madison felt intense fear. But she was torn between dread and hope. She wanted to see Des and, at the same time, desperately hoped they wouldn't locate him. If she was ever going to have a chance, her emotional need to be comforted would have to be placed on the back burner. She needed him to remain free, so he could find this great reward before the Judge could get his hands on it.

Perhaps the most frightened she had been thus far was watching Chris and his assistant disappear into the lobby. Her mind ran wild with terrible thoughts, praying Des would elude them. The sight of his car in the parking lot filled her with angst, almost obliterating any belief she could get out of this.

"Ms. Callum, are you hungry?" the Judge inquired.

"No," she said defiantly.

"We'll be getting something soon. I suggest you eat something anyway. We need you to be able to work at your best if you're going to be of any use to us."

"Why should I help you? All you're going to do is kill me when you don't need me anymore."

"I only do what I think is necessary. Don't assume you know what my actions will be. I'm sure they appear to you a certain way, but I assure you, what I did with William was absolutely necessary in order for me to get to my goal."

"Killing him in cold blood when you already had all his information? How was that helping you get to your goal?"

"William never saw this search the way I did. He served his purpose, but not having him with us is now serving mine. I have always believed in incentivizing people, Ms. Callum. As long as you prove to be useful and don't hinder me, then you will continue to have something to gain. But don't test me."

Chapter 61

Peering around the office door, he could see, standing at the front desk, the profile of the face of the dark-haired man and one of his accomplices. Pulling back quickly, Des frantically wondered what to do. The room was small and offered no cover whatsoever.

"I can check for you. Would you like me to call him down?" responded the desk clerk.

"Oh, thanks, no. That won't be necessary. We're old college buddies. Haven't seen each other in years. It's his birthday today, and we're going to take him out on the town tonight. I kind of wanted to surprise him, so if you could tell us the room number, that would be great."

"Hey, it smells like you have some coffee brewing. Can I grab a cup?" asked the accomplice.

"Of course. It's right over there by our computer office. Help yourself."

Des was in near panic mode. The coffeepot was located on a table right next to the entrance of the room. If he happened to walk in front of the door, he would be in plain sight, a sitting duck. He could hear the footsteps approach as he held his breath. *Don't make a sound.*

"Okay, let's see about getting that room number for you. It sounds like you have a fun night planned, certainly more exciting than my evening," the desk clerk said while typing into his computer.

Des could hear coffee pouring and then the pot being placed back on its holder as he stayed pressed against the wall, attempting to keep out of sight.

"Um… let me see here. Ah, yes, Mr. Cook is in 227. The elevator is down the hall and to your right."

"Thank you."

"Ah, shit," he heard the accomplice say. "I'm sorry."

Des could see a stream of black coffee leaking toward the computer office door. *Damn, he spilled.* The man's shoes came into view at the edge of doorway. Des recognized them immediately. The last time he saw them, he was facedown in the grass at William and Mary.

Convinced he would be discovered at any moment, he waited for the inevitable, body tightening, his fist clenching, waiting to throw a punch.

"Oh, don't worry about that. I'll take care of it. It happens sometimes," the desk clerk said.

"Thank you. I'm sorry about that."

The feet retreated from the doorway as the sound of footsteps quickly faded into the hallway. Finally exhaling, he now had to figure out his next course of action. Peeking around the office doorway, he could see it was clear but also knew he couldn't go out the front. There were only two men there, which meant most likely the Judge and the other accomplice were in the parking lot. *There has to be another way out of this building than just the front door.*

Trying to reassess his options, he was startled by the desk clerk perched on his hands and knees, cleaning up the spill. Jumping back with shock, he quickly recovered.

"Wow, I didn't see you there," Des said, looking out to the side and spotting an exit door at the end of the hallway.

"Sorry, sir. I'll be out of your way in just a second."

"No problem," Des responded, nervously looking down the hallway again, hoping the men would not return.

In this sudden predicament, his nerves almost caused him to forget the clues. Throwing the papers back into the folder, this time with little regard to preserving their condition, he went back to the door, where the clerk was still crouched on all fours, blocking the exit. He waited patiently. It was taking an eternity, and he was about ready to jump out of his skin as the clerk seemed to be purposely moving slower than erosion.

"Thanks for waiting, sir," the clerk said, standing back up.

Finally, Des thought as he gave the clerk a nod. Moving rapidly until he was out of sight of the lobby, he then opened up into a full sprint down the hallway in the direction of the side door of the building. He passed the elevator, which rang, signifying it had arrived at the ground floor.

Des did not slow down, practically diving for the handle as he heard the elevator gate open at the very moment the side door started closing slowly on its hinges behind him.

The glass was tinted, not allowing a person inside to see the exterior during the night. Des looked through the door just in time to see the two men turn down the hallway. The man with the jet-black hair then stopped, reacting to the sound of the door clicking shut. He turned, giving it a curious look.

Shit! Des stood still, praying to God his motionlessness and the tinted glass would cover his position. The young man approached the door while Des instinctively held his breath, remaining completely still, convinced momentarily he would be discovered.

Reaching for the door, the hired gun halted, placing his hand into his pocket to answer his phone. Des could see him speaking with an aggravated look on his face. He then turned and walked with urgency back down the hallway and into the lobby.

Letting go of his breath, Des felt like throwing up, and it took a few seconds for his heart to start beating again. Hyperventilating like he had just run a marathon, he walked to the edge of the building, peering around its corner.

As expected, he could see the black SUV parked right near the entryway. Within a few moments, the two men who had gone searching for him appeared, making their way back to the SUV. The man with the black hair walked over to the passenger side of the vehicle, clearly communicating with someone; however, Des could not see the individual.

When he moved away from the window, Des quickly slid behind the wall, his nerves still raw from the shock of encountering these men for the third time today. Taking a deep breath, he looked again, watching the man go back over to the driver's side and open the door. The light inside the car brought its interior into view. Des's heart started pounding in his chest. There in the back seat, clearly visible, was Madison.

Her head was tilted down, only allowing him to glimpse a small part of her face. The way she held herself filled him with sadness. She looked dejected and beaten. His first impulse was to run and yank her out of the car, but he had to control himself. He could not help her by acting irrationally. The only way to get her to safety was to find the treasure. The good news was, she was still alive.

Yet there was also something that disturbed him greatly—he did not see William. He remembered thinking how furious the Judge would be with the young man. When he abducted him at the college, the Judge might have been looking for revenge. *I hope he's okay.*

As if he didn't have enough, Des now faced another problem. He could not go back to his room as long as these men were camped at the motel. It was starting to get late, and he no longer had access to a computer or even a bed. It was not going to take them long to figure out he wasn't coming back, and by staying in Arlington, they would know his next stop.

Des waited a little while, planning his next move. His first order of business was to get away from this location to some place he could continue to research. The second item was to figure out when would be the most opportune time to visit the cemetery and conduct his search, hopefully avoiding coming in contact with these individuals again.

Des looked behind him, there was a wall, of which he had no idea what was on the other side. Figuring it was a better option to hop the obstacle than to go traipsing out in front of his pursuers' car, he catapulted up the five-foot-high barrier, pulling himself over.

Landing in a bushy thicket below, Des grunted as the branches burrowed into his side. Making sure to hold in the pain as not to alert the men, he dragged himself out of the bushes and looked for his next option. There was another similar barrier about ten yards away. Cascading over it as well, he landed in the parking lot of a strip mall.

He took off running as fast as he could while, at the same time, looking around for some place to hide. Though he knew he was not being chased, he felt exposed, as the large lot offered little cover.

Loping toward the street, he spotted a yellow cab and pursued it. The vehicle was stopped at the light near the intersection, and Des, urgently wanting to get to it before the light turned green, pushed as hard as he could.

Continuing his sprint, he was within a few yards when the light changed and the taxi began its gradual acceleration. Des reached out, desperately trying to gain the driver's attention.

He screamed at the cab, but it gave no sign of stopping. In one last distressed effort, he managed to tap the trunk with his hand. The brake lights quickly shone bright red as Des smashed his knee into the bumper when it came to a sudden halt.

"Hey, buddy, you're going to get killed trying to get a cab that way!" the driver yelled out the window.

Before he could pull away, Des opened the door and hurled himself into the back seat of the car. Trying to catch his breath, he could barely speak.

"Take it easy there, buddy. Where to?"

Des hadn't planned that far ahead. All he knew was he wanted to get away from the motel. He took a few more breaths while trying to come up with a location.

He blurted out the first thing that came to mind. "Library of Congress, please."

"You do know that it's closed at this hour, right?"

Des was grasping at straws, and he knew it. He had to think of something making sense. "I was hoping there may be some good twenty-four-hour restaurants around there. I'm really hungry. Do you know of any places around there that would be good?"

"I do know of one called The Diner. It has good food, and it's not too far from that area. Most stuff is pretty close in DC."

"That'll be fine."

The driver made a U-turn at the light and headed back in the direction of the motel. Des watched the black SUV, still parked in the lot, awaiting his return as he passed them. Pulling out of sight, he didn't know how to feel. He ached to help Madison yet knew that if he went with those instincts, they would both be doomed.

He was armed with almost nothing, just the original instructions buried in the folder inside his jacket. It was supposed to be a long night, though he never expected it to be this long.

Chapter 62

When Chris came back to the car less than ten minutes later, with no sign of Des to be found, she breathed a sigh of relief. *Thank God he's not here.*

Madison closed her eyes, trying to calm herself. However, the action of shutting them also brought another reality: she was exhausted. Leaning her head against the back of the seat, she could feel herself drifting off. The adrenaline that had been pumping through her veins had begun to wear off, and like a drug addict coming off a high, the crash was hard. The need to rest and the lack of nourishment were taking a heavy toll.

She had been fighting it for some time, trying to focus on the clues, yet the tension of the situation had left her ill prepared to work effectively. She was convinced the Judge was never going to free her, and so the motivation to continue trying had abated. The only thing she was hoping for was that Des would be successful and somehow get her out of their custody.

Her body was becoming heavy, making her feel like she was being absorbed into the seat. She could hardly function. The desire to fight the onset of a deep rest was no longer existent. With no more questions being directed to her and with her ability to be of any service to Des completely eradicated, she no longer fought it. She let herself go.

Chapter 63

Waiting for the return text always seemed like it took an eternity. But unfortunately, he could not control this individual. *Maybe Chris is right.*

Finally, it came. "Yes?"

"Are we still on?" the Judge sent back.

"You texted me to find that out? Really?"

"I don't think you understand the nature of the situation. I need him watched. I don't trust him."

"Maybe you should be more careful with whom you choose to associate."

"I'm beginning to think he has ulterior motives."

"Most do."

"I've noticed a change in his demeanor, and I don't like it."

"I'll keep an eye on him. He's going to be a little more difficult, given his background. People like him are harder to read."

"Well, I don't think for a man like you it would be a problem."

"Don't fucking patronize me. I'll get the job done."

What an asshole! The Judge knew Osiris's reputation. He was the best. But he hated having to deal with him. Unfortunately, the value of what he was chasing was far too great to risk. He had to put his ego aside.

Things were getting dicey. He could not afford any slipups. Everyone needed to be vetted. He already took care of one problem; he needed to avoid a potential new one.

"Everything okay, Judge?" Chris asked as his boss walked across the parking lot and heaved open the door.

"Everything's fine!" he said, eyeing his underling suspiciously.

Don't look at me, you son of a bitch! From now on, I keep things close to the vest.

Chapter 64

Washington, DC

Crossing over the bridge, Des was trancelike as he took in the night-lights dancing off the Potomac River. The famous body of water had shaped this area for hundreds of years, both figuratively and literally.

Forming at the borders between Washington, DC, and Maryland, as well as Virginia and West Virginia, it flows for over four hundred miles, eventually emptying into Chesapeake Bay. Named after the European spelling of its Native American name, it was so ingrained in the nation's history many called it America's River. Even George Washington himself was raised and spent most of his life on its banks, with his elegant home at Mount Vernon overlooking its beauty.

As the cab transported him across its edges, some of the architectural wonders of the city could be seen glowing in the bright lights washing over them. Washington, DC, is a treasure trove of historical and iconic structures, making it one of the most interesting cities in the world. Monuments and landmarks were interwoven into a metropolis designed to be functional as well as intimidating and humbling to foreign heads of states. Unlike so many other famous cities and national capitals, Washington, DC, is an evolving one, still adding to its landmarks and traditions, while other capitals survived off their legends and history.

The first edifice in view was the Jefferson Memorial. Looking much like what it was influenced by, Jefferson's design of the Rotunda at the University of Virginia, it had a splendor that was supposed to hearken to the former president's love of architecture and symmetry when it was first constructed in 1939. As the monument faded from view, images of what had occurred over the last twenty-four hours at some of the most significant locations of Jefferson's life flashed in bits and pieces in Des's mind.

Although he struggled not to think of it, the look of a horrified Madison being taken hostage and the picture of her sitting dejectedly in the back seat of that SUV tore at him. He was literally racked with guilt, clouding the process of trying to help her. *Don't go there, Des. Stay focused.*

Railing against those thoughts, Des changed his plans. He needed to get some rest and have computer access in order to be effective. Heading to another restaurant, while it was a convenient excuse to get the driver to move, was not serving him now.

"Hey, you know, on second thought, I'm really pretty tired. Is there, like, a good motel around here? Nothing fancy, just a clean place?"

"Yeah, I think there's a place not too far from here," the driver answered, looking mildly annoyed.

"That would be fine."

Des had been successful in cracking so many of the mysteries he had encountered thus far; however, how the Judge found him at such a nondescript place was one that continued to baffle him. It was reasonable to expect, since the Judge possessed the clues, that he would be capable of deducting that Arlington National Cemetery was the next location. *But how did they figure out what motel I was staying at?* The last time he had even touched his phone was just outside Richmond. Since then, he had been vigilant in his adherence to William's warning about staying off the device. *They must have tracked me using another method.*

Taking off his jacket, he searched its pockets and lining to see if there was anything that could be used for such a purpose. The only other items he carried, his wallet, his powered down tinfoil wrapped phone, and the folder, did not have anything that could be used to monitor him. *What other items did they have access to?*

Trying to recall the details of his encounter with the Judge's men, he recognized his mistake. He was only concentrating on their struggle at the college, not on their first encounter outside Monticello. The men accosted them while he and Madison were in his car. They had seen his vehicle. The man with the black hair had placed his hands upon it.

He must have inserted a tracking device on the car. Well, that's no longer a problem.

He was free for now, unfettered by their watchful eyes. But the Judge would be someone whom he would have to confront again. At least this time, he was not at such a disadvantage.

"We're only about five minutes away, sir."

Des nodded and then gazed at the city. The tip of the Capital Dome and the Washington Monument could be seen beyond some of the more modern office buildings in the foreground. His thoughts were swirling, though not cohesive.

"Are you going to any of the celebrations this weekend?" the driver asked.

"Celebrations?"

"Yeah, you know, for Memorial Day."

Des was so overwhelmed and consumed by the situation he had completely forgotten about the holiday. This was going to add to the level of difficulty for sure. Not only was the city going to be completely flooded with tourists, but one of the most visited sites would be Arlington National Cemetery. Spotting trouble was going to be nearly impossible as thousands would be expected to be there this weekend.

"I'm not sure. I just thought I would check out some of the activities happening at the Washington Monument."

"Well, sir, we're here."

The driver pulled into the parking lot, and Des paid his fare. He felt awkward. He was checking into a motel with no luggage, not even a toothbrush. He was hoping they would have one room available.

As he entered, he noticed an office with computer access, although the only thing that would excite him now would be a bed. To his relief, there was something available. Des eagerly took it and promptly marched up to his room. Opening the door, he placed the folder on the nightstand and fell onto the covers. Just a little rest would set him right. It took only moments before he would be at peace. But he knew it was only temporary.

Chapter 65

Heading north on Highway 66

The hard bump jolted Madison awake to a blurry and confused world. For a moment, she had no idea where she was or whom she was with. Seeing the cloth-covered ceiling of the vehicle, she blinked over and over to refocus her sight. As she moved her head, trying to get some idea of the location, the bright streetlights on the other side of the car window signified they were still in a metropolitan area.

Sitting next to her was one of the men while the Judge was at the wheel. Noticeably absent were Chris and one of his two accomplices. She looked at the clock display on the dash. The time read 1:37 a.m.

"Where are we?"

"Well, hello, there, Ms. Callum. Don't worry, just a little side trip I needed to take," the Judge answered.

Fifteen minutes later, she still could not get her bearings on their location. Scoping every window, she finally caught a glimpse of something familiar. There in the distance, the glowing white obelisk of the Washington Monument came into view. Even in this pressured environment, the stunning figure of the tallest stone structure in the world, gleaming against a deep-black night sky, was enough to shake Madison out of her semicomatose state. *Washington, DC. What are we doing here at this hour?*

Making a couple more turns, they pulled over, parking near an intersection. The Judge got out of the car and walked to a corner where a man was standing underneath a streetlight. Although it was not well lit, Madison could make out some of the individual's features. He was thin, wearing a long tan cover nearly trench-coat length. He looked bald, was wearing dark-rimmed glasses, and had a fairly long thick beard.

At first, the conversation seemed to be routine in nature. However, as the Judge continued to speak, he became visibly more animated, gesturing and pointing. The man put his hands up in a calming manner in an attempt to get the Judge to relax. Then as quickly as the Judge went into anger, he just as rapidly moved toward laughter, patting the man on the back. It was a strange altercation, to say the least.

The Judge returned to the car with a smile on his face, looking as at ease as Madison had seen him since they first met. "Well, we're in business. Even if we don't find your friend tonight, we'll locate him tomorrow, I'm certain."

Madison felt sick. She was hoping he was bluffing, but everything that had happened up to now gave no indication he was even capable of pulling that off. The Judge turned the car around and headed back toward the highway. Madison looked out the rear window to see the bearded man walking away, fading into the darkness.

"Where are we going?" she asked.

"Back to the motel where your friend is staying."

Madison hoped to God Des would not be there. The fact the Judge had not been notified that Des was in his men's custody gave her a little confidence, that at least for now he was still free.

In any case, there was nothing she could do. She felt useless, completely inept in aiding the cause of her own safety. Not used to relying on anybody, the fiercely independent woman had to fight those emotions and give in to her powerlessness. She closed her eyes and laid her head back against the seat. Letting herself drift off, she fell into a deep sleep, with her final thoughts being for the safety of Des.

Chapter 66

Washington, DC

Des awoke at a little after 7:00 a.m., disoriented and confused. Looking at the clock with its red digits aglow, he started regaining his senses and then remembered where he was and what he had to do.

The shades of his room were drawn, with the only light filtering in being from the small crevices near the edges. It was Sunday morning, and he had another long and trying day ahead of him.

Wanting to be sharp, Des decided to hop into the shower and bring himself to at least a semiconscious level. While he wanted to resist the temptation to start thinking about the clues before going through his morning routine, their ominous presence could not be resisted, and he succumbed to the job almost as soon as the water broke over his shoulders.

After getting out of the shower and wrapping himself in a towel, Des opened the only item he had brought with him, the folder, and started rifling through the clues once more. Still stuck on what "turns its back to you" meant, he thought of all the major items making up the cemetery. *I wonder if it will be obvious, or am I going to have to really search for this thing?*

Des considered the patterns of the clues thus far. While they seemed like a cipher on the surface, in reality, much of what they uncovered was sitting right in front of them.

The motel offered a complimentary continental breakfast. Hot coffee and a bagel sounded perfect. Having no fresh clothes, Des threw on what he had been wearing the previous night and marched downstairs with the folder in hand.

As he sat at the small table, sipping his coffee and reading the clues, he remembered what the driver had mentioned to him the previous night. It was Memorial Day weekend, and that meant another wrench could be thrown into the machinery. He now had to factor in several issues. Along with the challenge of finding the next item, there were going to be throngs of people marching through the cemetery grounds, possibly impeding him further. And this, of course, was not to mention he had individuals chasing him with evil intentions. Taking his last few bites and topping off his coffee, Des went over to the computer room near the hotel lobby.

The first thing he had to figure out was access. The hours of the cemetery were set pretty firmly, but this being a holiday weekend specifically catering to a location like Arlington, he knew there would be dozens of activities commemorating the occasion.

Diving back into the web, he located the schedule of events, and as expected, it was busy. There were ceremonies and activities with various organizations ranging from a motorcycle group to Japanese American Veterans, to associations of descendants of the Civil War who would be honoring the fallen. This, in addition to the traditional wreath-laying ceremonies at some of the more well-known grave sites, made for very full days.

While these memorials took place on Saturday and Sunday, the event taking place the following day was the one giving Des pause. The president would be speaking as well as laying a wreath at the Tomb of the Unknowns on Monday morning. While Des had today to find what he was looking for, he knew security would be heightened to a point where access might be denied to certain places while the Secret Service made its preparations. Having witnessed security details before while he was in the Army, he knew prepping the area prior to a VIP visit was a massive affair and didn't just happen on the day of the event. The president, being the most significant VIP in the world, always required an enormous security detail involving hundreds of agents who would swarm an event field like bees. If they saw anyone acting suspiciously, no matter the reason, that person would be detained, something Des could not afford. So his goal was to get to the area he needed to survey, retrieve his information, and get the hell out.

Des brought up images of the cemetery again. He had seen them many times, but its tranquil reverence for those who had served and given their lives for the nation still inspired him. All those souls, all those gleaming white headstones, it was still difficult to wrap his head around. Momentarily lost in thought, he shook himself to get back on task. That did not require much, only the thought of Madison.

He couldn't get the image of her trapped in the car out of his mind. *I can't let anything happen to her.* Yet while he stared at the computer screen, his thoughts of her began to change. They had somehow morphed into something different. While earlier he could only think of her terror and sorrow, visions of the special moments they had shared now crept in. He recalled her laugh, her gentle ribbing at his quirks, and especially the warmth of her embrace.

Previously despair had dominated. However, it was now replaced by anger. It burned inside him, and for the first time since this situation began, rage fueled his motivation. He would not let them succeed. He would do whatever was necessary to get her out of their grasp.

As he tried to figure out the best time to visit Arlington, he came to the conclusion that he was overthinking the problem. There were no opportune times. He could not predict what his pursuers would do, and trying to plan his visit on whether he might run into them was ridiculous.

Des grabbed his jacket and the folder and marched out the door. He was not going to approach this thing from the defensive anymore. Staring all day at a computer screen was not going to solve the problem. If he was going to get Madison back, he would have to move. He was going to Arlington.

Chapter 67

Arlington, Virginia

Madison was exhausted. Although she was allowed to sleep in a bed under guard at the motel, it was hardly restful. Her slumber was constantly interrupted by nightmares, and when the images of her dreams stunned her awake, she was not at all consoled by the reality of the barely visible sights confronting her in the dark room. When she awoke again that morning, it was to the picture of Chris sitting in a chair next to her with a gun on his lap.

"I had some stuff brought up for you to eat. Help yourself," he said.

Madison was groggy, but also famished. Sitting up, she looked at the food but immediately went for the coffee. "What time is it?" she asked while pouring herself a cup.

"It's almost eight thirty in the morning."

Madison took a sip. Although she was still not in the mood to consume anything, the act of eating was balancing nonetheless. "What are your plans for me today?" she asked defiantly.

"The Judge told me that he wants you to figure out what some of these clues mean," he said, displaying the copies of the instructions to her. "The computer is over there. You can get started as soon as you're done eating. Also, if you want to shower, I would do so now. You've got fifteen minutes. Here's your stuff. We got it out of your friend's car," he said, tossing her bag onto the bed.

"And you're going to stay in the room when I'm showering?"

"I'm afraid so. You can take everything into the bathroom, but leave the door ajar."

Madison gave him a look of disdain but was beyond caring at this point. Modesty was not something she could afford if she wanted to feel better. Taking a few more bites of toast and eggs and gulping down the remainder of her coffee, she went over to the bathroom and closed the door as much as she was allowed for some privacy.

While in the shower, she was thinking about the clues. Hers was an unusual quandary. She needed to get some information to the Judge but did not want to reveal everything, because it would endanger her and, just as importantly, it would endanger Des.

The shower felt wonderful, the hot water hitting her shoulders and especially her back, which still hurt from the fall she took at the church, loosened her muscles and allowed her to finally concentrate.

Getting out of the shower and drying off, she did her best to fix her hair and prep herself for the day. Looking in the mirror, she noticed her ragged appearance. The dark circles under her eyes and her furrowed brow displayed the evidence of the pandemonium her life was currently in.

She opened the bathroom door to the sight of Chris leaning against the wall with a wry smile on his face.

"Did you enjoy yourself?" she said mockingly, suggesting he had helped himself to a free exhibition.

"Don't flatter yourself. Standing outside a bathroom door is not my idea of an exciting morning. I've more important things to concern myself with now. I've hardly had any sleep in the last three days, which means that I'm not in a good mood. I want to go to my room as well, so I can get some rest. I'm trying to be patient. So I suggest before you piss me off any more, you get your ass in that chair, and get me some goddamn answers!"

Chris's tone frightened her. His expression was the same icy one he had before he killed William. Madison knew it would be better if she did not push him beyond what she had already. He had proven his willingness to use violence in the extreme, so this time, shying away from the snide remarks and just getting started on what he requested would be the most prudent decision.

Sitting down at the table, she hovered above her copies of the clues. She focused on what she had come across just prior to her and William being forced out of the cabin, and the analysis was begun anew.

She definitely remembered the word *pillars* in the first sentence in the first set clues had both of the *L*s enlarged. She also recalled there were two *V*s enlarged as well in the second sentence in the words *vestige* and *vara*. She vigorously jotted down the information.

In the second set of clues, she could recall images of just one item. In the sentence "Resting at the heart of his highest learning," the *L* in the word *learning* was signified.

The third set of clues was the most troublesome, as she had very little time to examine the originals before they were taken captive. She pressed into her memory, and while she recalled there were some enlarged Ls, she could not remember how many.

The other problem she was encountering, beyond not knowing what they meant, was the realization that she did not know if there was any significance tied to the fact that some enlarged letters were in the same sentence while other sentences contained none.

Madison pondered the possibilities, but it was frustrating. She and Des had made such a good team, as they were always able to reach the right conclusion. She needed someone to respond logically to her questions in a manner promoting thought. It was part of the process. However, even though she had people there to bounce ideas off, she did not want them to have access to information before she did. Her only sense of control in this situation was the ability to pace what information she gave up and what she withheld.

Having been relieved of the duty of figuring out the location of the next place to be visited, Madison tried to use that to her advantage. It seemed little more could be done with the "enlarged letter" question. She had to continue searching the rest of the instructions to see what additional information could be peeled away.

Moving on to the next sentence, she remembered discussing the instruction "It lies in the northern shadow of the symbol of Darius's defeat" with Des. While the other clues stimulated ideas and historical conversation, this one only caused anger. *If it weren't for the fact I searched this particular clue, I wouldn't be in this situation. Come on, Madison, that's not going to get you anywhere.*

Knowing where they were already gave her a head start on this item. The only structure vaguely resembling anything looking like the Parthenon was the House at Arlington. Its front facade was classical Greek and mimicked the iconic building. She had her first idea of where to look.

"Where's the Judge? I need to see him," she asked.

"What do you need him for?" Chris responded.

"I've figured out some information."

"You can tell me. I'll give it to him."

"I want you both here so nothing could be lost in the translation. I don't want to be accused of leaving anything out," she said in a challenging manner while, at the same time, trying to hide her fear.

Chris, to her surprise, gave in, taking out his phone and calling the Judge. "He'll be here in five minutes," he said disgustedly.

Madison looked down at her notes. She noticed another peculiarity. *They're not capitalized, just larger.* Examining the rows of information she had created, it was obvious it meant something.

I I V V

I

Those look like Roman numerals. They're numbers! Her heart raced. She could not remember all of them; still, she had enough to buy herself some time. Madison had no idea how to apply them, yet this moved her forward. She was no longer stagnant.

At that moment, a knock was heard at the door, and Chris let in the Judge. He walked in with an aura of arrogance. His clothing was that of a casual Friday office look, gray slacks and a light-blue polo shirt. Yet no matter how much he dressed down, he always seemed formal.

"Ms. Callum, I've been informed you have some information. I pray, for your sake, it's not something I already possess."

"I know what the symbol of Darius's defeat is. It's the—"

"Yes, yes, I already know that it's Arlington House. Please tell me that's not all you have for me."

Madison hesitated, hoping he would be more impressed with some of the other items she had come up with. "The letters I told you about that were larger than the others, they're Roman numerals. They represent numbers."

The Judge did not respond immediately; instead, he walked over to the table and poured himself a cup of coffee. He then casually strode over to where Madison was sitting and looked at the computer screen. Slowly sipping his coffee, he studied the young woman, sizing her up, trying to gauge how forthcoming she was being.

"So they represent numbers. Okay, to what?"

"I don't know."

"How many numbers are there?"

"So far, I've remembered a total of five Roman numerals."

"What about the rest? You're implying there are more."

"Yes, there are more. I'm going over the clues again. I think if I have a little more time, I can come up with them," she said with ever-increasing nerves.

"Now, you wouldn't be holding out on me, would you, Ms. Callum?"

The Judge bent over, placing his face just a few inches from her. He didn't say a word, just looked directly into her eyes. She felt his hot breath against her face, making her sick to her stomach. Madison wanted to look away but knew if she did, the Judge would not believe her. He then stood up, walked over to Chris, and placed his hand on his underling's shoulder, just as he had done prior to executing William. Madison's heart jumped into her throat. She looked at Chris, shaking her head in disbelief while mouthing the word *no*.

The next sound in the room was of a pistol being cocked. Everything started to spin. Her stomach was in knots. "What are you doing?" she said desperately.

Chris marched over to her, placing the gun against her forehead. Madison began panting as tears started welling up in her eyes. The tip of the barrel was pressed so hard against her skin she could feel it leaving an impression on her head.

"You don't have to do this. I'll get you the information you need. I promise… please."

The Judge stood behind his hired gun, smiling ever so slightly. With him not saying a word, the room fell nearly silent, with the only sound being the panting of their helpless victim.

"So you think you can remember those other letters?"

Madison was petrified but managed to mutter, "Yes."

She stared at the Judge, waiting for any response. He only watched, taking obvious pleasure in the trembling of his terrified captive. Waiting a few moments as the frightened woman sat in desperation, he gave a nod to Chris. Madison closed her eyes, waiting to hear the last sound to ever meet her ears, only to be shocked when the barrel was removed from her forehead. Slowly opening her eyes, the Judge was once more just inches from her face.

"I would suggest you get working on those clues and figure them out as quickly as possible. Otherwise, next time, I won't feel so lenient. You don't have much time. Better not waste it." He took one more sip of coffee and walked to the door. "We'll be leaving here in about two hours."

He proceeded to whisper something to Chris and then stepped out of the room. Madison let out a gasp, as if she had been holding her breath for eons. Putting her head in her hands, she tried to hold back the tears, but they ran down her face like a dripping faucet. She took a few moments and forced herself back to a state of composure. She grabbed the instructions to give off the appearance she was working. However, as she now felt her death was imminent, any level of concentration was impossible. There was little else she had left.

Chapter 68

Washington, DC

What a fucking cesspool. It served as his office for almost twenty years, and he hated it. People, when they think of the world of espionage, conjure up images of exotic foreign lands, expensive mansions, and beautiful women. *If they only knew.*

In reality, most espionage happens right in Washington, DC, and usually the spying involves entities who are supposed to be allies. One agency stealing from another, politicians who didn't trust a colleague, a lobbyist suspected of not being forthcoming, or someone simply wanting to be in the know is where much of the intelligence community's resources are allocated. *Fucking cockroaches!*

As Osiris continued his drive past the city's landmarks, he felt an oppressive weight around his neck. He tried to avoid his old stomping grounds at all costs. Unfortunately, this job had brought him back, making him even more irritable and impatient than his usual grouchy demeanor.

It could be the city, or maybe it was the constant changing demands of his client, that set him in such a mood. One day it was vetting, the next it was research, and today it was simply an observation. *Who the hell knows what the next day will bring?* As he prepared for his current assignment, he shook his head in disbelief at the subject under his surveillance. *I can't believe I'm being paid to do this,* he thought with equal parts disgust and humor. *This guy is so beneath me. Anyone could have pulled this off. But it's his money.*

Parking his car on the other side of the lot, he waited. It would be only moments before his subject would be there. Then it was a long day

of either sitting on his ass or tailing the subject like a lost puppy. In the
end, he would most likely inform his client of some very mundane news.
James Bond can go fuck himself.

275

Chapter 69

Arlington National Cemetery,
Arlington, Virginia

Pulling up to the entrance of Arlington National Cemetery, Des first noticed the black wrought iron gates marking its front access. Those were highlighted by gold-crested points and large gilded war office plaques displaying their insignia surrounded by a wreath that glimmered in the sun. The gates were a majestic reminder of the solemn subject matter they encompassed.

Des exited the cab and walked to the entrance as he took notice of the growing crowds attending the Memorial Day weekend rituals. Upon passing the initial access, he was greeted by a stone structure on his right, a geometrical monument gleaming of white cinder blocks and topped by a giant bald eagle sitting in a position of observance and vigilance, guarding the landmark.

The asphalt road was a long and winding one, leading to parking access in one direction and the visitors' center in the other. It had been years since Des had walked this path. He had few memories, and though he did know its dimensions, the sheer enormity of the grounds still took him aback.

As expected, the cemetery was flooded with people. Many came with flowers and small American flags to place at the grave sites. Uniformed military personnel as well as aging veterans wearing their regalia shuffled through the throngs on their way to the entrance. Vietnam and Korean War veterans groups, several with hats signifying their unit regiment, circulated in the crowds. There were World War II veterans, now in their late nineties, feeble with the ravages of age, being aided as they made their way to pay their respects. Des had immense admiration for these men, and while he felt a link with them, a camaraderie from being a veteran himself, the fact they felt the responsibility to come to this sanctified place so many years after their service ended made his respect for them so much more.

As he made his way down the road to a smaller path, he saw the visitors' center in the distance. Decorated in the same bravura as Arlington House, it displayed a Greek portico complete with columns guarding its entrance. The theme of the architecture of this place was well-thought-of during its construction, with the only difference being its crown. Instead of a triangular-shaped crest, the roof gave way to an archlike atrium with hundreds of glass panels, allowing the natural light to flood its halls.

Entering the glass doors, the visitor walked upon polished granite floors into a world that paid reverence to the past and those who had served the nation with the ultimate sacrifice. There were displays giving the history of Arlington. Elegant exhibits with pictures that had been burned into the American consciousness lining its walls. The photographs were both striking and beautiful and reminded the visitor of the country's greatness and, oftentimes, the tragedies required to maintain its existence. Arlington was a place to honor those sacrifices and remember its most heartbreaking losses.

Des went to the large display map outlining the details of the grounds. The streets crossing through Arlington had names that reverberated throughout American history. Roosevelt, Grant, Lincoln, and Sherman were just some of the iconic references.

Following the pathway, he located Arlington House positioned southwest of the visitors' center. He then followed the map north from the mansion to the oldest graves in the cemetery. *That's where I need to go.*

Des began his long trek in the direction of Arlington House. The crowds in the visitors' center were just the tip of the iceberg, as literally thousands of people were walking the beautifully manicured lawns whose rich green color was only interrupted by the simple white gravestones. Pictures could never do this place justice. The enormous number of military personnel buried in these fields was staggering. So many people, so many lives lost. Even with the duty he was here to perform, it was impossible not to be moved by the surroundings.

Passing more graves, he recognized some of the distinctive names. Ironically, these noteworthy individuals were known more for their contributions in areas other than the military realm. It was the expanse known as Section 5, and it contained many of the giants of the US Supreme Court. The first name instantly drawing his attention was Oliver Wendell Holmes.

Even though he was mainly recognized for his service to the court, Des was aware of his direct connection to the Civil War. Holmes was a decorated veteran of the conflict, wounded three times in battle. A man who once met President Lincoln and made significant contributions to the nation prior to his most famous service, he was appointed to the court by Theodore Roosevelt. Later, he produced some of the most important landmark decisions in United States legal history.

Des stopped for a second to scan the area, wanting to make sure he was not being followed. Although with the number of people gathered around the grave sites, it would be hard to spot anyone. But after what he had experienced over the last twenty-four hours, he felt his hypervigilance was justified.

Looking up the hill in the direction of the mansion, he saw evidence of the president's upcoming visit. Secret Service agents, with their recognizable black ties and suits, could be seen scouting the area for potential hazards. They were sprawled out over the various sections like a flock of pelicans hovering above a collection of fish in shallow water, walking the paths, examining every inch of trail the president would be accessing. They presented a professional and intimidating presence.

There were bomb-sniffing dogs, assigned lookouts, and snipers. Des also recognized the ground-penetrating radar machines from his military deployment days. They had brought those in, searching for buried threats, ensuring no stone was left unturned.

There was not much farther to go. The mansion could be seen in the background, and Des knew as he passed the John F. Kennedy tomb, with its eternal flame aglow, he was coming close to the search area.

The presence of the Secret Service only increased as he drew closer to Arlington House. Along with his many activities of the day, the president was scheduled to make a visit to the mansion before laying the traditional wreath at the Tomb of the Unknowns. With the added security, Des's own concern started to grow.

Turning around again, he cast an eye over the area, looking for any of the men he had encountered yesterday. There was an elderly World War II veteran wearing a khaki army cap saluting a gravestone. There was a young family with two small children walking around JFK's grave. Just in front of him, a trim thick-bearded man wearing dark-rimmed glasses held up by a bulbous nose, sporting a small cap to cover his bald head, was slowly moving past some tombs designated for Korean War dead. Still, there was no sign of his attackers.

Des studied the people for a moment, reassuring himself he was safe. But after a few seconds of examination, it was not the people catching his attention; it was the tombstones themselves. While he had noticed and even paid silent homage to the names appearing on the front, he had not detected that there were inscriptions on their backs.

Approaching one of the graves, he was surprised to find it was numbered. It wasn't just that gravestone, but every single one in the vicinity had a series of numbers, usually designated by a two-digit with a slight separation, followed by a three- or four-digit integer.

Everything started to flash before him. Words and sentences glowed in his imagination. Reaching out to the gravestone, he ran his fingers over the numbers, feeling the indentations. It was as if they were sending shocks through his body.

The message is engraved in the sorrows of the nation.

This is the message! The numbers are the key to this. They are on all the reverse sides of the tombstones!

The knowledge you seek turns its back to you.

Des pulled the clues out of the folder, looking for a correlation. He tried to quantify the Roman numerals with the engravings. The first set displayed *II* in the first sentence, the third sentence contained *VV*, the fourth sentence had an *I*, and the sixth sentence also had an *I*. He paused momentarily, working on the values of these Roman numerals. So far, he had 1, 1, 5, 5, 1, and 1. His excitement grew as he moved to the next set of numbers.

There were only two significant aberrations in any of the sentences, a single *I* in the first sentence and, again, another *I* in the third sentence. *So I have a 1 and another 1.* The final set displayed *III* in the seventh phrase and a *C* in the ninth. *I have three 1s and a 100.* Des felt flush as a wave of heat nearly overcame him. It was an odd combination of excitement, relief, anticipation, and dread.

He had an answer, yet it also added another question. *How are these numbers supposed to be utilized, as individuals or added together?* He needed the correct sequence, or he would never locate the right tombstone. The intensity of the moment grew with each passing second. His neck began to tighten. Even though he didn't notice himself performing the function, he had started to pace back and forth incessantly, a peculiar behavior, which, by the time he stopped, had attracted the attention of some bystanders, including a Secret Service agent. Noticing the unwanted interest, he tried to calm himself.

"Are you okay, sir?" asked the agent.

"Yes, I'm fine. I'm trying to find a specific grave for a history project I'm working on for my class, and I thought I found it, but I didn't."

"You picked a hell of day to try to find something. A lot of big crowds around, hard to get help."

"Yeah, I know, but what can I say? I procrastinated."

"Well, good luck."

Des nodded in appreciation and then let out a sigh of relief that he was not hauled in for questioning. The Secret Service was not known for its patience or understanding, and they could detain a person for as long as they wished if they felt something was suspicious or even slightly out of the ordinary.

As the agent continued down the path to assess the trail, Des noticed he had also garnered the attention of the bearded man who had been reading a tombstone just a few yards from where he stood. The man observed Des as if he recognized him but then went back to reading the grave marker. Des could not recall ever seeing this individual before, and while it made him uncomfortable, he tried not to pay much heed.

Stop creating drama where there is none.

Chapter 70

"Have you seen him?" the Judge texted.

Osiris squinted at his phone and then put it back in his coat pocket. Running his fingers through his thick beard, he decided not to respond. *I told the son of a bitch I would contact him when there was something to report.*

He was definitely more of a night person. Even though he knew if you were good, it did not matter whether you conducted your surveillance during the day or evening, he always felt more comfortable cloaked in a blanket of darkness. Operating in the shadows was always his preference.

So far, there was nothing to tell him anyway. *He'll get my damn report when I'm good and ready.*

This was the part of the job he liked the least. It was a facet completely defined by inaction. Breaking and entering, stealing vital information, violent tactics, and even research were preferred over observation. They included actual activity, where something could be quantified. Yet even though he knew it was an important part of his work, just watching gave him a sense of being unproductive. No movement, no physical evidence, an aspect completely devoid of anything but thought and opinion.

Thought and opinion… thought and opinion. He remembered how much he hated the analyst back at the agency. They never got their hands dirty. They never saw how dangerous the field could be. They sat behind a desk and then interpreted his work. *Assholes.* Who were they to make determinations? It was like evaluating a food without ever tasting it.

In his mind, the Judge was no better. Like all judges he had encountered, they set punishments, they decided on the consequences without ever having felt the degradation those decisions caused. And that was how they approached life. *Who the fuck died and made them God?*

He knew he would have to eventually get back to him. His reputation for accuracy depended on it. But first, he was going to revel in the small pleasure of making the prick wait.

Chapter 71

Des started moving in the direction north of Arlington House. Some of the oldest internments on the site were in that location. As he passed more grave markers, he looked back to examine the numbers inscribed on them. He soon realized the amount of numbers he had collected exceeded the number of digits engraved on the tombstones' reverse sides. *This can't be right.*

Des was now only a few yards from his destination. While there was no time clock on him, this numeric component to his search was creating a frantic feel. Arriving at his designated spot, he wasn't completely sure but was hoping he was in the right place.

The grave markers were not the iconic, polished white stones seen in most images of the cemetery. Rather, they were the traditional granite markers more common to the Civil War era. And as he stood before them, his confidence was still wavering on whether this was the correct spot. In an attempt to reassure himself, he turned to see the beautiful mansion behind him. It was so elegant—what an incredible structure! Though it was difficult to imagine, standing by these Civil War graves caused him to reflect on what this home had become after the commencement of the war. He envisioned Union soldiers standing on the porch and men on horseback bringing messages from battlefields to what was this most beautiful of military headquarters.

Des shook out of his dreamworld, forcing himself to concentrate. *There is no way that these numbers in these clues could be read individually. It would leave too many digits.* Des tried to reconfigure the numbers into a format equal to the number of digits displayed on the back of the tombstones. After the failure of trying to take them individually, he attempted to add the values in each sentence separately, hoping the new equation would give him the proper number of digits. Des walked behind a grave marker with the new calculations. Still, there were too many.

How do I condense this thing? Once more, he began to pace. However, this time, he caught the habit before it attracted attention. His stomach began to churn as he felt the pressing weight of time. It would only be a short while before the Judge figured out where they needed to go. He had to figure out how to resegment the digits.

He had already taken the numbers individually as well as attempted to add the values per sentence. Both failed to give the desired result. *What other way can I add these?* Des brushed his fingers through his hair, feeling the cut on his forehead once again. The pain from the sensitive wound mixed with the stress of the quickly closing time window. Des placed his hand on the tombstone, its weathered surface rough to the touch. *What's the next step? Come on, Des!*

He turned the sheets of the clues, examining the three pages carefully for something he might have overlooked. In doing so, he came to a conclusion. There was only one option left, and that was to add the values of each separate page. Counting in his head, he came up with 14, 2, and 103. Breathing in deeply, he prayed this was the correct approach. *It falls in the range. I don't know if this is right, but I'm out of ideas.* Writing the numbers on his palm, he commenced his search.

He moved up and down the rows of graves, skimming their backs, hoping to find the combination of numbers. There were hundreds of them, and after thirty minutes had passed and still no match, feelings of despair took hold. He needed to find this; he had to help Madison. He gazed up and noticed he was farther away from the mansion. *Maybe it was just a figurative statement when they said it was in the mansion's northern shadow.* Fatigue began to set in. He re-examined the section of graves. There were just a few areas he had not covered. Over by a lingering tree, he spotted some of the older-style tombs.

As he approached, a name came into view, "Private DW Baker, 61st NY Regt." He was killed in June of 1864. He read the next name, "Private H Baldwin, 112 NY Regt.," also killed in June of 1864. He read the next name, then the next, and then the next. He covered at least three dozen graves. They were all from New York and most of them killed in the summer of that year. *So much carnage, so much loss.* Over six hundred thousand people died in the War Between the States. It had been estimated that one in four men from the South who were of fighting age was either killed or suffered crippling injuries during the struggle. No other war in American history produced so much death and destruction or changed what the nation was more than the Civil War.

He slowly walked to the back of the tombs, rounding their sides until the digits came into view. A ray of hope presented itself. The first three digits of the grave were 142. Recognizing a possible match, he stared down at his palm, studying the black numbers, now partially smeared from perspiration. Continuing down the aisle, he saw the numbers 142 repeating, again and again. Some were followed by two numbers, and some by three. He read "142 88," "142 95," and then "142 101." They did not follow in exact numerical order, but he knew he must be close. *Come on, come on, it's got to be around here somewhere.*

Just like that, it appeared, number "142 103." He looked at his hand again, making sure he had not made a mistake. It was perfect.

He rushed around to the front, not knowing what to expect, but excited he could finally retrieve the information and get the hell out of there. The grave was badly weathered and partially cracked by the corner. It had definitely seen many years in the elements and most certainly had never been replaced. As he got ready to copy down the information, he felt a presence near him. He glanced to his left—there was nothing but open space. However, looking to his right, he saw him. The trim man with the beard whom he first noticed by the Supreme Court judges' tombs was trying very hard to look inconspicuous. But there was no question he was taking an interest in Des's actions.

First, there was a searing heat, followed by his hand, which vibrated in short intervals before keeping a constant rhythm. Who was this man, and what did he want? Not knowing his intentions, Des needed to be careful. *Don't give anything away.*

Des learned while in the Army, many times, the best way to deal with an enemy was not to engage but misdirect. With that thought in mind, he memorized what was on the tombstone and then slid over several yards, pretending to copy the information from another he now straddled. Trying to feign interest in the tomb in front of him, he wrote down what he recalled from the actual gravestone he came for, "William

H. H. Ross, Virginia, 1861 DE." He moved over again, putting on his best performance, mimicking the motion of collecting more information. Repeating this series two more times, he felt the deception was as complete as he could make it.

Having attained what he came for, he moved calmly off the slope and back onto the paved trail leading to the visitors' center. Peeking over his shoulder, he caught the bearded man hovering over the very tombs he pretended to copy the information from, while talking on the phone and pointing to the headstone.

It unnerved him, and once he was out of the line of sight of this mysterious person, his pace quickened almost to a jog. As he got closer to JFK's tomb, he had to rein himself in as more Secret Service agents were milling about. Running through the crowd would definitely mark him as a person of interest. *Slow down, Des, slow down.*

Moving through the growing throngs, he could hear Taps playing in the background, followed by gunshots, honoring another fallen soldier. The atmosphere, while at first inspiring, was now suffocating as the haunting trumpet played its somber tune.

Finally reaching the visitors' center, he was able to make his way to the tram that took passengers into the city. Arriving at the first stop, he hailed a cab to make his way back to the motel.

It was almost 10:00 a.m., and the nation's capital was stirring with life. As he passed Lady Bird Johnson Park and Constitution Gardens, the National Mall came into view. It was an impressive sight. The Capitol Dome was watching over the city, while the majestic spire of the Washington Monument performed its function of symbolizing the power the nation had become.

Des sat in the back of the cab, staring at the information he had gathered. There was nothing really descriptive about it, and the poor soul who was buried there did not ring a bell, as Des had never heard of him. Yet there was something off, something that did not quite add up. Yet he could not put his finger on it.

Laying his head against the seat backing, he thought about the tombstone, hoping he could figure out what was bothering him. Still, nothing jumped out. Arriving at his motel, he had resigned himself to the possibility he did not find the correct grave. *Maybe my calculations were off.* There was a very real chance he had made a mistake.

In the previous clues, the names and places were always prominent and well-known. This one did not fit the mold. It was not iconic, it was not dramatic, and it was certainly not a name on the tip of every schoolboy's tongue. It seemed to have no relevance whatsoever to what was occurring at that time.

His frustration grew as he became deflated. It had been such a whirlwind of a morning. Just a little over twenty minutes ago, he was feeling elation; now somberness had taken hold. Dejectedly, he exited the cab and walked into the motel lobby. As he passed the concierge's desk, he noticed the display case holding a menagerie of tourist brochures. Waiting for the elevator, his eyes were drawn to the color advertisements. There were brochures offering bus tours of the capital, outings to the Library of Congress and parks showcasing reenactments of Civil War battles. It was the last one that held his attention.

Emblazoned on the front of the pamphlet were pictures of the American and Confederate flags. He fixated on those symbols and then realized what was off about the tombstone. He couldn't understand why he failed to notice it before. *Des, you idiot!*

He did not make a mistake. It was so obvious. The elevator doors opened, and an elated Des got in. He knew he had the right tombstone.

Chapter 72

Washington, DC

Tapping his fingers on a table in the small café on the outskirts of the National Mall, the Judge waited for calls from his men. After taking a bite from his strawberry-jam-covered toast and sipping his coffee, he looked in the direction of the Lincoln Memorial, which he could glimpse beyond the man-made lake reflecting its image in the bright sunlight.

He had been anxious all morning. Although he was able to scare his captive sufficiently, the information she was providing was sporadic and incomplete. She was needed for now but was unsure how long that would last.

It was a disconcerting position to be in, as he had never before attempted to travel these uncharted waters. He had always been in control, always the man in charge. He ruled his courtroom with an iron fist and intimidated both defendants and attorneys alike. Yet in his attempts to grab the same power outside his chambers, he had failed to do so.

These two individuals, who seemed to have nothing more than adventure vested in their search, had turned into a great nuisance, and it was becoming much more challenging in emptying their reserves of usefulness to him. Thus, he was in the awkward position of needing people he felt were inferior and certainly not deserving of such a reward.

His thoughts wandered to his goal. How could anyone recognize what this treasure was worth to him? Yes, he wanted the wealth, but all his life he wanted notoriety as well. He was never blessed with physical prowess and was usually one of the last kids selected for any of the teams on the school playground. He remembered how much he hated them and questioned why no one, none of the cool kids, none of the pretty girls, recognized his other qualities. But most of all, he remembered the pain. It was the pain that became the driving force in his life. It was what pressed him through college and drove him through law school. It was what made him one of the most aggressive assistant US attorneys in the nation, using legal and illegal tactics to gain a conviction and, later, to push for the harshest of penalties at sentencing.

However, he knew this incessant drive had a damaging effect. It had hardened him, made him incapable of human connection, giving him an unrealistic idea of self-fulfillment. He had become a tortured soul searching for a ghost. He was forever in pursuit but no longer knew what it was he was chasing. *But this will fill the void, I know it.*

With a high-pitched jingle, his daze was broken. Seeing the name on the screen, he quickly answered the call.

"Tell me you got it," the Judge said firmly.

"I got a lot of information. I'm sure we can figure it out," he said, trying to sound reassuring.

"Well, what is it?"

"He copied down information from three tombstones. I'm going to have to analyze it."

"Goddamn it! That's going to take too much time. This guy knows what he's doing, I hope you're better at this than he is, because it seems like he has been one step ahead of us this whole time."

"Don't worry. We have your men on him now. He won't be able to make any moves without us knowing about it."

"Give me the information. I'll work on it, and we need to get the girl on it as well."

He hurriedly scribbled down the new clues on his yellow notepad. The Judge did not have a degree in history, but his attention to detail, which had served him so well in looking at case files, was also a bonus when it came to investigating the past.

"I'll meet you on the steps of Lincoln Memorial in twenty minutes. I have a feeling we need to go to the Library of Congress to look up some of this information. Make sure the girl gets the info as well. I want her working on this too. Maybe this new stuff will refresh her memory. If she can't help us, we'll have to get rid of her."

After finishing the call, the Judge didn't know what to think. His mind was bouncing back and forth between excitement, anger, and despair. He would have to keep his feelings in check. Under no circumstance could this be left up to chance. This was to be his reward, his success, his singular defining achievement.

Patience, patience, let him find it for you. His frustration quickly turned to confidence. There was no way he could lose this game. If he could not figure out all the details on his own, his opponent would do it for him.

Chapter 73

Des opened the door to his motel room and immediately retreated to the bathroom to splash cold water on his face. Grabbing a towel and patting himself dry, he still could not believe he had missed it. *I should have noticed that right away. Come on, Des, you got to be better than that.*

Looking at the folder again, "William H. H. Ross, Virginia, 1861 DE," he shook his head in disbelief that he had failed to recognize it immediately. The name still did not ring a bell, but the image of the Confederate flag on the brochure brought forth a glaring oversight that now gave him confidence he had discovered the right tombstone.

Whoever this individual was, he was from Virginia. Virginia had seceded from the Union to join the Confederacy. It made no sense that a Civil War veteran from the South would be buried among Union soldiers from New York. In addition, the first Civil War dead from the Confederacy were not interred at Arlington until long after the war had ended. This should have set off alarm bells right away. Nonetheless, he was aware of it now.

Yet beyond that striking disparity, the other engravings on the tombstone were not so obvious. In fact, they were only more mystifying. None of it struck a chord. There was also the confusing element of the etching "DE." While almost every tomb he had viewed listed the state and regiment in that order, he had no idea of what "DE" meant, and there was no regiment listed. Either this was the most stunning of unintentional aberrations or this anomaly was a purposeful attempt to communicate something.

Des hurried out the door and down the hallway to the elevator, his brain flooding with possibilities of what this paradox could mean. Rushing to the complimentary office, he was anxious to figure out the mystery of this individual.

He typed in the name "William H. H. Ross" into the search engine, and within a split second, a match on Wikipedia appeared. Ross was a prominent politician from Delaware who lived in the midnineteenth century and was active politically all the way up to the time of the Civil War. *DE—ah, yes, Delaware! But why would they list Virginia as well? Two states on one tombstone? That makes no sense.*

The information he dug up actually surprised him. For someone he had never heard of, this man had a great deal of prominent accomplishments, not least of which was the fact he had ten children. This, combined with his public service record, made him one of his state's most noteworthy residents of the time.

Delaware itself presented a fascinating case study of the internal state conflicts during the Civil War. Today, most view it as a Northern state. However, prior to the war, slavery was legal within its borders and a great many people who lived there were sympathetic to the Southern cause.

Yet while they practiced the institution, it also held a deep connection to the concept of Union. It was the first colony to ratify the Constitution and, according to its governor at the outbreak of the war, it would be the last to leave it. Though it decided to remain in the Union during the conflict, its delegates refused to ratify the Thirteenth Amendment abolishing slavery at its conclusion. Unbelievably, it took forty years after the completion of the war for its citizens to do so. Yet even though slavery had not been legally eliminated within the state at the end of the conflict, its slave owners voluntarily decided to free their slaves of their own volition, managing to quell any controversy.

But why does this gravestone claim him to be both a person loyal to the Union and loyal to the Confederacy? Continuing his investigation, he found Ross was active in an effort to get a north-south railroad connection beginning in his home state. He was heavily involved in local and regional government, serving in the state assembly as well as being elected its governor in 1851, becoming the youngest person in Delaware history to hold the office. However, many of his remaining plans were interrupted by political infighting and, later, the outbreak of the war. Still, this did not explain why this man was listed being from a Southern state when he was obviously not.

While Ross had a successful public career, his internal conflict on who rested on the side of right between the North and South reflected the same complexities as did his state. It turned out he was a strong supporter of Southern ideals and was very vocal about his opposition to Northern policies. He did feel great loyalty to the Union, but his backing of Southern interpretations of the Constitution raised the ire of his Northern brethren. So much, in fact, that he actually left the country at the onset of hostilities for fear there would be retribution. He attempted to return a little over a year after the outbreak of fighting but decided against it and remained outside the country until the end of the conflict.

The contradictions in Des's discoveries did not end with the state listings, with it becoming even more bewildering with the year of death given on the tombstone. *This makes no sense. It listed his date of death in 1861. He didn't die until years after that. What's going on? Maybe that was just another way of standing out.*

The questions were perplexing and, at the same time, reaffirming. Des realized, to modern day visitors, the grave would attract little attention. It would just be seen as another tombstone among the thousands maintaining Arlington as their final resting place. However, he was beginning to conclude these anomalies were meant to signify something unusual to a person from the midnineteenth century. To someone in the Civil War era, it would have stuck out like a sore thumb. He just had to put himself in the mind-set to decipher it.

Des added "history of Delaware during the Civil War" to his set of queries, hoping it would give more of an explanation to these incongruities. He already knew a good deal of its past and was quite aware it remained in the Union at the time of secession. Although he still could not place why Ross was listed from Virginia.

While history tended to reflect on the great political and regional divisions it created, oftentimes it paid little heed to how people were torn intellectually and emotionally by the plethora of issues surrounding its cause. Today, so much is seen in terms of black-and-white, both figuratively and literally. But then, it was so much more complex. Gray matter always filtered in, and often people found themselves sympathizing with issues on both sides at the same time.

In the end, however, once people did choose sides, the effects could be catastrophic. Families were ripped apart by differing opinions, citizens who were proud of their nation were now having to deal with the aftermath of what they felt was a great failed experiment. Wounds inflicted on faraway battlefields were many times matched by the deep injuries wreaked in the homes of differing viewpoints. It was a period when Americans lived in uncertainty of their future as a whole.

Today, most see America as a bedrock nation; despite its problems, it is widely considered to be destined to endure because of its solid foundation. However, at the onset of the Civil War, the United States had yet to hit its hundredth birthday, and to many, it was still in the trial-run phase of its development. Whether it would work or not was often called into question, and with the outbreak of war, confidence in its survival was waning.

Delaware, though not a border state, suffered from much of the same anxiety of those territories that were on the cusp of Southern boundaries. Des was fascinated by the extent of its inter-state conflict. Realizing this could be a possible key, he examined more of its active role in the war, particularly of its citizenry.

The majority of Delaware's fighting men served in Union blue. Although, it was the other side that stopped him in his tracks. Those from the state who served in gray typically joined regiments from Maryland and Virginia. This theme kept repeating itself over and over. With the exception of their excursion into South Carolina, this entire search was connected to Virginia. From Monticello to Williamsburg to Arlington, there was some reason this venture was staying in this particular state. Now, another reference to the Commonwealth of Virginia was added to the mix. This could not be a coincidence. Wherever this treasure was, it had a definite connection to this piece of earth.

Des feverishly scribbled on the small notepad he had taken from his room. While the computer was an excellent tool and certainly added the element of speed to this search, it still could not take the place of writing information down side by side. Somehow, the act of putting things on paper reinforced ideas and stimulated thought in a way that simply tapping on a keyboard could not. As he cross-referenced his findings on the state with his research on Ross, it seemed clear. This was the right grave marker, but how it applied to the set of clues, he had yet to figure out.

Reading more on his bio, he noticed there was one last piece of information that was the most stunning. William H. H. Ross was not buried in Arlington. His final resting place was in St. Luke's Church in Sussex County, Delaware. *What the hell! If that's not Ross in that grave, then who is?*

Des was more confused than ever. Originally, he was hoping the tombstone would bring this whole situation into focus, but instead it was murkier than ever. He had a grave marker that not only listed false information about the deceased but also apparently did not contain the remains of the individual who was supposed to be buried there. *This is crazy. I have more questions than I do answers.*

It will lead to the entrance of the gateway of the second invasion.

At the precipice of the stairs' flight, buried two vara, lies the portal.

Staring at the next two clues, longing for a glimmer of hope, he was at a loss. There was no continuity, no piece of the puzzle seeming to fit. He recognized it was speaking of a location, and like the clues they found leading them to Old Sheldon Church, this, too, referenced something buried. But there were no other indications of where he should look. No markers, no monuments, and no famous locations for him to search. It was as if he had hit a brick wall. The only physical structure identified was stairs, but it wasn't as if stairs in themselves were some unusual item uncommon to the period. It did mention a portal, but what design the portal came in was impossible to say, and even if he were to figure out its makeup, he still did not know where to begin to look for it.

I don't have time for this bullshit! Time is running out!

Des slammed his hand on the table in frustration, knocking his papers to the floor.

With the raucous, the concierge poked his head into the door. "Is everything okay, sir?"

"Ah… ah, yes, sorry about that. I knocked my papers to the floor and smacked the hell out of my arm against the table when I reached down to pick them up," Des said, trying to diffuse the employee's concern.

"Okay… well, um… be careful."

"Will do. That hurt. I won't make that mistake again," Des said, smiling.

He was beside himself. For the first time since this search began, anger was getting the better of him. He was tired of working on these problems alone and certainly tired of being chased while doing it. He knew he could no longer think clearly in his current state of mind. He had to get away from there for a few moments to collect his thoughts.

Grabbing his belongings, he walked out of the small office into the motel lobby. The afternoon sun was flooding in through the sliding glass doors, reflecting off the white tile flooring. Taking a few strides toward the door, he stopped just steps before the exit. He felt a wave of fear grasp him. *What if they're out there, waiting for me?*

Des turned around and walked back until he was directly in front of the brochure rack. It was only about thirty minutes prior that this display had stimulated his mind and gave him the inspiration for the direction to take his research. *Who was this Ross, and why was he so important to clues that were in Virginia?*

He was at a dead end. There were no other instructions to give any insight or even the slightest reference of where to look for these stairs and portal. Without any additional information, it left little to go on. The pent-up frustration was getting ready to boil to the surface, and he knew, if he did not find an outlet for it soon, he would not be able to contain himself. It was time to do what was best for his concentration and ignore his fear. *If I continue like this, I won't be worth a damn to anyone.*

Walking always helped him process things. Whenever he found himself stagnating in his studies, he would always take a walk. The movement loosened his head, allowing him to come up with a solution. He had to go through the process. He tucked the folder back into his jacket and walked out the door.

Chapter 74

Washington, DC

Madison was hovering over the clues, making notes and hoping she could provide the Judge with some information to stay alive. Although she had remembered some more of the enlarged letters, she could not recall them all.

Chris sat silently across from her, with an expression that frightened her to the core. Occasionally, he would stand up and walk over, peering over her shoulder to check on her progress, and then sit down again.

With the incomplete information, Madison was trying to hide her panic. It was only a short-time-ago that she had a gun pressed to her forehead, with the only thing saving her being her ability to convince the Judge she had something to offer.

Chris continued to sit, quietly sipping his coffee, waiting to hear back from the Judge and hoping for good news. *If he succeeds, I succeed. I will have my piece of this thing.* Even though his exterior didn't show it, as it was part of his training not to display emotion, he was becoming agitated. It was quite obvious to him this young woman served no purpose. Keeping her around was just slowing the whole process and adding unnecessary complications. Their energy should be focused on their other adversary, who seemed to be the one with most of the answers. *She's only getting in the way. God, I wish I could go back to my room and get some sleep. Maybe I can figure some things out on my own.*

In addition, by not terminating this situation, they were risking drawing attention every time they moved her, and they couldn't stay in this motel room indefinitely. She needed to prove her worth. However, in her state of mind, Chris could not imagine her being able to work effectively. Her eyes were red and filled with tears. Her hand trembled as she took down notes, and the expression on her face revealed she was not finding anything of significance.

Hopefully, the Judge was going to require only a few more actions before they could eradicate this impediment. Yet for now, he would continue to stay his post.

A loud jingle broke the silence, causing Madison to jerk like a bolt of electricity had passed through her body. Stopping everything, she watched Chris as he took the call. He showed no affect and gave one-word answers to whatever questions were being presented to him, so there was no indication of urgency.

Then his demeanor changed as he stood up. Anytime her captors moved, it caused Madison to lose concentration, making no attempt to continue her work until they had returned to less aggressive stances.

"Yes, let me get a notepad," Chris said, motioning to Madison to hand him the pad of paper on the table next to her. As he began to write, she tried to gauge the context. Although she could not make out everything, it was apparent by the names and dates that the information had come off tombstones.

"Okay, what do you want me to do with her, then?" he said, looking directly at Madison.

A lump developed in her throat. Perspiration formed on the back of her neck. Watching Chris finish the call, she waited for his orders, not noticing she was holding her breath in terrified anticipation.

Chris held out the instructions he had copied down. Feeling a sense of relief and finally exhaling, she knew they still felt she had value, buying her a little more time.

"What are these from?" she asked.

"They picked these off some tombstones at Arlington National Cemetery. They were the same ones your friend was seen copying from. We want to know why these are important. The Judge wants you to stop what you're doing and work on these alone. He needs results from you very soon."

Taking the paper with her still trembling hand, she read the information. Her heart took a dive. Nothing on there made sense. She did not recognize the names, and other than all the soldiers being from New York, there were no other distinct patterns.

Going onto the laptop they provided her, she began her research anew. The despair only increased as the results of her first attempt began to appear. There was nothing significant about these names. There were no references, no Wikipedia pages, not even blurbs on abstract historical websites. She went into library archives and even visited the national grave registry. Other than the same basic information on the paper, no other relevant items surfaced. *This is impossible. There's nothing here.*

Realizing the names were not going to open any doors, she went to the next available information, the regiments they served in. However, even though she understood getting data on these units would probably be fairly simple, the amount provided would most likely be extensive, if not overwhelming. Sifting through all of it would not only take a great deal of time, but it would also be nearly impossible to separate the wheat from the chaff.

Try as she might to focus, feelings of desperation began to pour in. Her thoughts drifted to Des and how much she wished he were there. At times, during this ordeal, she felt abandoned, even though logically she knew that wasn't true. Yet this fruitless search was leaving her full of anguish. The only comforting development was, she had learned Des was at Arlington. He had not given up. He was still out there searching, making every effort to retrieve her from this nightmare.

Enveloped by thoughts of him, she reflected on their embrace, the warmth of his body, and the serenity she experienced when he was near. His smile, intellect, and self-effacing humor had left an indelible mark. It was a dream, a fantasy destined to never turn to reality. She fought the hopelessness.

He hasn't forgotten me. Please, I need you.

Chapter 75

The Library of Congress is one of the great public accomplishments of the United States. It is the largest archive of books in the world, with its only rival being the British Library in London. Established in 1800, it is also the oldest cultural federal institution in the nation. Originally, it was housed in the Capitol Building, but after the British burned it to the ground during the War of 1812, its three thousand books were lost, as well as the structure that housed them.

America's founding fathers were greatly influenced by the Enlightenment, and literature always played a part in the formation of their political ideas. Benjamin Franklin, Alexander Hamilton, and James Madison were insatiable readers, and having a repository of knowledge was an extremely attractive idea, perhaps to no one more than Thomas Jefferson.

After the destruction of the first library, having it rebuilt became a top priority. In effort to replenish the book supply, Jefferson agreed to sell his own personal collection to restock its shelves. This worked out well for both parties. The Library of Congress received one of the most extensive book collections on the continent, and Thomas Jefferson could pay some of his creditors the enormous debts he had amassed over the years.

The current library is housed in four buildings, of which three are located in Washington, DC, on Capitol Hill, and includes some of the most impressive structures in the world. It attracts researchers and tourists from practically every nation on earth.

The Judge quickly ascended the steps of the main branch with his informant by his side. The building, which was constructed in the first half of the nineteenth century, is a monstrous edifice. Its rectangular shape hearkened to classical Greek monuments, yet it also had elements of the 1800s European style. It displays a geometrically attractive and powerful facade stretching nearly the full length of the manicured lawn at its base. Decorative railing combined with columns running down its second story level. Taking a page out of Thomas Jefferson's architectural playbook, it was capped by a dual dome with a golden flame crowning its pinnacle. Ironically, it would look right at home in London during the same era, having been influenced by the very nation that burned the original one to the ground.

Entering the main building, they made their way toward the Grand Hall. Bypassing the beautiful marble staircases leading to its second level and the gorgeously decorated ceiling laced with stained glass and gold leaf painting, they trekked to their destination.

The Judge normally would visit all the historical sites offered by such a location; this time, he ignored the precious displays, which included a rough draft of the Declaration of Independence and an original Guttenberg Bible. Instead, they marched straight into the famous oval setting.

Although it was just one part of a campus housing over thirty-five million books, not to mention countless other documents and artifacts, the domed hall is its most famous area. Featured in films such as *All the President's Men*, it showcases the magnificent grandeur of the landmark.

The tile floors with their intricate patterns and decorative seals invited the visitor. Rich brown oak tables were aligned in a circular configuration for people to peruse the various materials. Roman marble arches encapsulated the room with bronze statues of American greats standing guard on the second level, and all this was covered by the breathtaking dome.

Pictures simply could not do it justice. It was a mix of beautiful colors featuring depictions of various people next to signs of the culture they represented. They, in turn, were surrounded by geometric shapes reaching up to the heavens and were detailed in hypnotic blues and glimmering gold.

The Judge took notice of none of it. Finding a table near the south side of the room, he grabbed the papers from his informant and began his own research. His bearded associate leaned back and watched, knowing well enough not to intervene.

The passing minutes soon turned into large chunks of time. The informant now joined the search in silence. But nothing seemed to have any connection to anything they were looking for. Seeing the frustration in the middle-aged man's face, he held off on any conversation.

Feeling the vibration of his cell phone, the Judge checked for a text message. Their subject had just left the motel. Responding to the alert, he told them to keep him in sight and await further instructions.

No matches, no light bulbs turned on as the Judge's anger continued to grow. He studied the information over and over, the collection of words and names he found useless.

He was seething. "Are you sure these are the correct ones?" the Judge whispered angrily.

"Yes, I was standing just a few yards from him when he wrote them down. Everything's there, word for word."

"Well, I've come up with nothing. Either he screwed up or you did."

"I didn't screw up," he retorted loud enough for people to look up. Realizing he was causing a small disturbance, he quieted himself. "I did exactly what you asked me to do. Those are the tombstones he was in front of. Maybe he didn't have the right ones, but I didn't miss a damn thing!"

The Judge could see the certainty in the man's face. The magistrate briefly went back to his research. However, his patience was running thin, and the fact his adversary was on the move was racking his nerves. *What does he know that I don't?*

As he flipped through page after page of books and pamphlets, he felt himself falling behind. His concentration broken by images of his opponent wandering the streets of Washington, finding more clues and perhaps even the treasure itself—it all flashed in his head.

Standing up abruptly, he paced the floor, rubbing the back of his neck. *This is pointless.* "This is not the right information. He has it. I know it. We have to stop playing this fucking game. It's time to pick him up."

This would ratchet things up to another level. "If you think so, then you better do it before he gets any farther."

The Judge took out his phone and typed his message. "It's time, get him." He then slowly put it back in his pocket.

He never wanted it to be this difficult, but the situation called for him to take more drastic measures. One thing he promised himself and William at the very beginning: he would let nothing get in the way of his success. William learned that lesson. The Judge was a lot of things, yet when it came to business, he never welched on a guarantee. This was his ultimate prize, and he certainly would not break the streak now.

No more cat-and-mouse games. No more trying to analyze clues from afar. He always preferred a direct approach. In the end, it was always more effective.

"I will notify you when we get close. Keep your phone near," the Judge said.

"I understand."

The two parted, knowing the most difficult stretch of this journey was still ahead.

Chapter 76

Washington, DC

Des had been walking for about forty-five minutes, breathing in deeply, trying to refresh his mind as well as his approach to this whole situation. The small motel office had been confining to the point of stifling, and his search had slowed to where he was merely treading water. Leaving it was imperative to his success. So now he found himself aimlessly wandering the streets of Washington, DC.

Repeating the name to himself over and over, "William Ross, William Ross, William H. H. Ross," he appeared to be on the wrong side of sanity to the many passersby. But it was part of the process. He needed to hear the name in order for it to activate thought.

Turning down Independence Avenue, he walked in the direction of the Lincoln Memorial and the Potomac River. Just this morning, he was on the other side of that body of water, wandering through the solemn reminders of the sacrifices America had endured. It seemed such an ironic twist of fate that one of the most peaceful places in the country would be the scene of the most stressful time in his life.

He moved north in the direction of Constitution Gardens, hoping the wandering would allow him to relax enough to come up with the answers. Beautiful trees lined the man-made lake, which was situated between the bookends of the Washington Monument and the Lincoln Memorial. Geese gathered at its banks as people milled through the grounds, taking pictures and pointing to the attractions. It was as tranquil as it was impressive.

Seeing children holding hands with their parents brought back memories of his own past when he toured this same area with his father.

As he recalled asking his dad about Lincoln, one of his father's favorite topics, Des felt himself drifting away. *Come on, Des, don't lose it now.*

He reached the pathway leading around the gardens and continued his journey to the Lincoln Memorial. Passing a wastebasket, he took notice of a brochure on the ground. The cover read, "Attractions of Virginia from Arlington to the Shenandoah Valley." Picking it up, he saw it was your typical tourism pamphlet. Decorated with pictures of well-known places with small write-ups surrounded by advertisements of businesses who wanted visitors to patronize their establishments, it was what would commonly be found at distributors throughout the city.

As he thumbed through its pages, a menagerie of colors met his eyes. Photographs of colonial soldiers, beautiful images of Bruton Parish Church, and depictions of Civil War weaponry were cleverly laid out in a pleasing array that would attract any lover of history.

Des fumbled through it, hoping these images would trigger an idea. Unfortunately, it did not. He was beginning to lose hope as feelings of inadequacy filtered in. This challenge was seemingly beyond his abilities.

As he continued to look through the pamphlet, he came across its center section, a full pullout map of the state of Virginia. It was a well-detailed listing of all the major attractions and sights. His eyes wandered over the map, with his concentration resting on the red dots highlighting the touristy areas.

Des turned left, moving away from the gardens, figuring he should return to the motel. As he strode, he moved his eyes back and forth from the map to the pathway, making sure he would not run into anyone. Quite naturally, Des's eyes were drawn to his current location on the map.

Covering Constitution Gardens, he examined the details from across the Potomac to Arlington. He could not understand why, but his eyes were attracted to the river and not the land. He studied the blue expanse, moving north to south, and then back again. *Why is this significant?* He didn't have an answer, but one clue kept repeating in his mind.

It will lead to the entrance of the gateway of the second invasion.

He had stumbled onto something, though he was not sure what it was. Stopping abruptly, he repeated the clue.

It will lead to the entrance of the gateway of the second invasion.

Lifting his face from the brochure, he looked in the direction of the river, eyes peering across the landscape, imagining how it appeared in times of the war.

It will lead to the entrance of the gateway of the second invasion.

Come on, Des, what invasion? The Confederates invaded near this area at Bull Run, but that doesn't make sense. That's still a ways from here. Bull Run is more inland, so why am I so fixated on the river? Second invasion, second invasion… oh my god, that's it!

To this day, there had only been two times in American history that the continental United States had been invaded by a foreign power. The first occurred during the American Revolution by the British, the second, ironically, was by the same foreign power in 1812. In both invasions, the Potomac River was used as an artery by the British to gain control over its former colonies. Whatever he was looking for, it bordered the Potomac.

As he walked back to the motel, his pace increased. He moved away from landmarks and noticed the greater foot traffic as the city prepared for the Memorial Day festivities. Vendors selling flags, hats, and various other trinkets crowded the sidewalks. The smell of a plethora of culinary delights mixed in the air as food trucks prepared themselves for a very profitable weekend.

Des passed one after another, the shiny vehicles reflecting the image of the crowds in their chrome-plated sides. He knew he did not have time to stop for food, but the aroma of the delicacies wafting from these mobile diners made his mouth water.

Des moved faster, his walk turning into a full-blown jog. His eagerness to return to the motel was nearly overtaking him. Coming across a pastry truck a few minutes away from his destination, he noticed the enticing pictures of the treats it offered just above the vehicle's reflective plated sides. But what he saw below it caused him to halt like he had run into an invisible wall.

At first, he thought he was imagining things, yet upon second glance, he knew it was no mirage. There in the gloss of the truck's chrome, he caught the reflection, and it would be only seconds before he would be forced to make a decision.

Chapter 77

Washington, DC

Sitting in the motel parking lot and sipping coffee, Osiris was back to reconnaissance. The Judge would text him every hour. He would delay in answering. *What the fuck does he want from me? There's nothing to report.* Yet in a strange way, he empathized. *If I had that much on the line, I guess I would be paranoid too.*

The Judge had noticed aberrations. When they appeared, they were not glaring. Though as time went on, they could no longer be ignored. A changing demeanor was always the first clue. Being hesitant to do something when before it was met with enthusiasm. Willingness to serve was replaced by doubts. And maybe the ultimate sign, an abundance of questioning when their expertise lay elsewhere.

But it was also difficult to see why there would be a need for concern. His skills, at least from Osiris's viewpoint, were not well developed. He wasn't stupid but, at the same time, seemed disorganized, and there was a definite lack of focus. Given his background and from the information he had gathered of his past, there was nothing to indicate he would be able to pull off anything of consequence.

Nonetheless, the Judge was uneasy. Ever since they left the isolated cabin with their hostages, he saw a difference. He would inquire about things in which before he displayed little interest. He pried too much and would often profess ways of operating that were beyond his responsibilities, beyond his original duties description. He needed to be watched.

The client wants me to observe. Osiris's reputation was built on always getting the job done. He had succeeded in situations where anyone else would have failed, and certainly situations far more complex than this one. And he had never had a dissatisfied client. So he would study and report. However, somehow he knew his service would not end so simply.

Chapter 78

Des could not comprehend it. It was unbelievable to the point his mind was not able to process his senses. *It can't be.* But it was undeniable.

There, reflected brilliantly in the chrome of this diner on wheels, were the Judge's men, tracking him like predators. His head felt light and his mind was sent racing.

Don't tip them off, Des. Stay calm. He looked for a way to appear nonchalant, pretending not to notice his pursuers. He sauntered up to the vehicle counter and casually ordered a large coffee. As he waited to be served, Des thought about his next move. *Keep them away from the motel.*

After receiving his drink, Des crossed the street and headed back in the direction of the National Mall. Trying his best to display a look of inattention, he slowed his pace to give the impression he did not feel threatened. Of course, nothing could be further from the truth. His heart was pounding. His breathing quickened to near panting levels. Walking at a steady pace, fighting the desire to look back, he could not settle on a course of action.

Shock waves were going through his body. Torrents of fear and hatred washed over him, nearly choking on his own breath. His mouth became dry, feeling like it had been stuffed with cotton balls. Des glanced over the street signs. He had no destination in mind but knew he had to keep moving.

Two minutes… three minutes… four. The charade could not remain in its current state. He had to know how close they were. It would be unwise to keep going at the status quo. *I will not let them put me in that position again!*

As he approached the National Mall, he decided to stop, pretending to look at the brochure he had found. Knowing the longer he waited, the more at a disadvantage he would be, he turned slightly to assess his situation. One was upon him before he could complete his movement, rushing toward him, hand in pocket, getting ready to draw his weapon.

Reacting more out of instinct than thought, Des hurled his scalding coffee into the face of his attacker. The man screamed in pain as his partner rushed to aid him. Des took off sprinting down the street.

He could hear the injured man yell, "Don't worry about me, get him!"

Rounding the corner, he could see the men in pursuit. Deciding the National Mall was too open of a space, he swerved, changing his direction, heading for West Potomac Park. Crossing the street near the World War II Memorial, in the panic of the chase, Des threw himself into oncoming traffic.

As he put out his hands to take the brunt of the impact, a car came to a screeching halt, hurling him to the ground, slamming his body onto the hard asphalt.

He rolled on the street, the pain intense but negated by the adrenaline rush. Seeing the men approaching the intersection, Des pulled himself up and continued his sprint to the park. As he drew closer to the greens, the Martin Luther King Memorial came into view. The large white stone sculpture sat near the entrance of the park on the outskirts of the National Mall, where Dr. King gave his famous "I Have a Dream" speech. Des remembered seeing a grove nearby.

As he hit the edges of West Potomac Park, he desperately scanned for an area to give him cover. The men were only about seventy-five yards away.

Seeing a grove of trees, he ran into its thickest part. The men tailed him, realizing if they did not catch their target soon, they would have to discontinue the chase. As Des entered the grove, a ricochet of tree bark struck him in the face. He knew exactly what that meant. *Jesus! They're shooting!*

Des moved deeper into the roughage, heading for a large tree with branches dropping nearly to the ground. The smell of wet grass and rotting leaves encircled him as he heard the voices of his pursuers drawing closer. Trying to slow down his breathing in order to squelch any noise, he could hear the footsteps heading his direction. Twigs broke under the weight of each of their steps.

Des's nerves were on end. He strained to catch a glimpse. Perspiration welled up on his forehead, dripping down the tip of his nose.

"Do you see him?"

"No, but he has to be in here. We would have seen him come out."

Des tensed so tightly it felt like his appendages would snap off. They were only a few yards away. It would only be moments before he was discovered. Stepping back, he bumped against a branch, causing it to buckle and crack. It might as well have been on an amplifier. Instantly, he saw one of the men turn his head. *Shit!*

"I heard something over here."

Des quietly picked up a rock near his foot. He waited for his attacker. The muscular man approached, gun tightly gripped. Des could see him through the leaves. Creeping through the shaded knoll, the beams of sunlight breaking through the canopy of tree branches, pinpointing their location. Des squeezed the stone so hard its sharp edges broke his skin. Warm blood trickled down his palm. Two more steps forward and he would no longer have cover. Des cocked his arm back, getting ready to strike.

"Anything yet?" asked a voice in the distance.

"No, I'm going to look over here."

Noticing the man turn his head to answer his partner, Des took advantage of the momentary lapse in his attention. He heaved the stone as far as he could to the other side of the wooded grove.

"Hey, did you hear that? Come over here."

The muscular man hustled in the direction of the raucous. As Des watched him gradually move out of sight, he saw his opportunity and ran the other direction. He sprinted as fast as he could, branches and shrubs striking his body as he made his way to daylight. He could hear the men in the distance cry out. More pieces of debris sprayed his face as another bullet struck the foliage a few inches from him.

Heading for Independence Avenue, he had opened up over a hundred yards. He turned around to survey his predicament. They emerged, gave chase for a few feet, and then gradually came to a stop. He had evaded them.

Seeing a cab slowing down at an intersection, Des was able to get the driver's attention. Hyperventilating, he opened the back door and dived into the back seat, giving one last glance to make sure he had reached safety.

"Where to?" the driver asked.

Des hadn't given any thought to where he wanted to go; he just knew he wanted to be as far away from this place as possible. The city was not familiar to him, and other than the landmarks and memorials, he did not have any other places in mind. However, he did understand going to historical places of interest would probably not be the best idea at this point, as they might be the most obvious places to find him. There was, however, another option. Being a football fan, he blurted out the only location coming to mind. "Can you take me to RFK Stadium?"

"Will do."

Des let out an audible sigh of relief as he lay back against the seat with his eyes fixated on roof of the vehicle. He put his forearm against his head as the beads of perspiration dripped down the sides of his face.

This cat-and-mouse game was becoming intolerable. He still hadn't figured out this clue, and they were obviously losing patience with their current position. He couldn't keep this pace much longer. It also dawned on him that even if he were able to figure out this latest conundrum, he had no plan in place to get Madison back.

As he pondered these questions, he came to two conclusions, one comforting, the other horrifying. The fact they were still chasing him meant his deception at Arlington had worked. Yet it also meant Madison might not be of any more use to them. This made her disposable. The thought made his stomach churn. *God, I hope I'm wrong.*

Chapter 79

Washington, DC

Entering the motel room and slamming his hand on the desk caused Madison to nearly jump out of her seat. He had just received news her friend had eluded his men, and without any new leads to go on, he was dead in the water.

"I don't know what the hell I'm paying you guys for," he said, looking directly at Chris. "How in the hell does he get away?"

"Judge, this guy is not as simple a target as you think, and when you gave us the order, he was out in public. Grabbing a guy off the street in DC on Memorial Day weekend isn't exactly an easy job," Chris said in rebuttal.

"I don't want to hear any of your goddamn excuses! Now we have a real problem. We have no clues, no new ideas, and no way to get ahold of him! All we have is a bunch of incomplete notes and this bitch, and she's fucking worthless," he said, pointing directly at Madison.

Madison put her head down, trying to hide. She knew the Judge's patience had run out.

Chris tried to calm him. "Judge, we still have something he wants. He wants her. Let's not lose our heads here. We're still on the same team."

"You sure about that?" he said, staring his underling down.

Chris met his glare but did not say a word. He wasn't going to take the bait by addressing the slight.

"So," the Judge continued, "we have to figure out another way. We have no more leads. The information we got from Arlington led nowhere. It was obviously the wrong set of tombstones."

"Well, if we had the wrong one, so did he. Didn't you tell me the information came from the same ones he had copied?"

"Yes, but I have a feeling he deceived us somehow."

"Well, why don't we go back to Arlington and get the right one?"

"Do you know how many thousands of possibilities there are out there? Even if we eventually found the right one, it will take us forever, and I'm not going to risk him getting to my goal before we do."

"He has to materialize soon. He's certainly after it."

"Yes, I'm sure he is. But that still does not solve the problem. We have no idea where he is or what he has discovered, and I'm sure he's smart enough not to return to his motel."

Chris got up and started pacing the floor. The young man walked to the window, pulling its shades slightly apart. He looked at the beautiful blue sky. It was going to be a perfect Memorial Day weekend.

"You know, Judge, I still think we have the advantage."

"How do you figure that?"

"We still have her as a bargaining chip. He's not going to want to risk her."

"But he doesn't know if she's alive or not."

"But he believes she is, or he would have abandoned his search a long time ago. Don't you get it? It doesn't matter if she's alive or not. It's what he believes. As long as he still thinks he can get her out of our control, he's still within our grasp."

Madison was horrified at the statement. The way Chris was speaking, she was not a person, just an object to be bartered. If he could speak this callously, he would have no problem ridding himself of what he considered to be an unnecessary nuisance.

"So what are you suggesting?" the Judge asked.

"I'm suggesting we be patient. We don't need to go after him. He'll come to us."

The Judge nodded in agreement. He should have seen this possibility. Chris, though he harbored doubts about him, for once, was right. They were still in a position of advantage. They still had a bargaining chip. Des had yet to acquire one.

"Okay, Chris, I'm going to trust you on this one. But you need to ensure me that I'll be the only one to have access to what lies at the end of this. I'm not going to allow them to have a piece of it. I've come too far and spent too much money to let this slip away."

"Trust me, Judge, he'll reach out to us, and I promise you, they won't take anything that is rightfully yours."

Madison tried to hide it, but tears started to form again, dripping onto the desk. It didn't make any difference whether Des found the treasure or not. They would not be allowed to live under any circumstances. Faith was drying up, and for the first time, she wished Des would give up the search. There was no hope for her, but maybe he could escape this nightmare.

Chapter 80

How far are we from RFK Stadium?" Des asked.

"Less than five minutes."

It was getting a little cool outside, and having no reason to go directly to the stadium, Des started to look for other alternatives. Noticing a Starbucks as they turned onto Brookland Avenue, he decided it would be a better location. "You can drop me off here."

Des exited the cab and made his way into the popular chain coffee shop. He needed to get back into the frame of thinking he was prior to being chased by the Judge's men. He felt he was on the cusp of something important yet wasn't quite sure what it was.

Quickly grabbing a cup of coffee, still craving the drink since he threw his last cup in the face of his attacker, he looked for a place to sit. He walked to the back of the room and found a small table where he could study the map.

Before being interrupted, he had fixated on the Potomac. It was the "gateway to the second invasion" the British used during the War of 1812, resulting in the burning of a good part of the nation's capital.

However, the Potomac was a very long river, over four hundred miles from its northern tip to its southern access. The British utilized the river to launch attacks throughout its former colonies. Although Des felt whatever it was he was looking for was most likely close to its borders, the extensive distance it covered presented a problem.

Its northern tip extended into Maryland, parts of West Virginia, and nearly touched Pennsylvania. Heading south, it passed through Washington, DC, past Richmond, and eventually emptied into the Chesapeake Bay and then the Atlantic. While Des could eliminate some of these points because the British did not attack in certain areas, it still cut a wide swath, making the list of possible locations an extensive one.

Des decided he was going to stick with the immediate general area. Following the river, he trailed its banks. It was quite amazing how integral this water artery was to the development and defense of the nation. There were so many towns, so many locations ideal for trading, farming, and security. This river also bypassed some of the most significant landmarks that had become a part of American folklore and actually shaped the borders of some states.

Yet as he perused the chart, nothing seemed to fit. For a moment, he contemplated the fact the Potomac passed right by Washington's home at Mount Vernon. Yet as ideal and sarcastically typical a place it might be to keep something significant, he had to resist the urge to fall into the blockbuster movie pattern of a treasure hunt. Though Washington was one of the South's favorite sons and represented many of the ideals the Confederacy held dear, Mount Vernon could not serve any useful purpose in hiding something, and it was too far away from the general location he had settled on.

Des took another gulp of coffee and rubbed his eyes. He had not had a really good night's sleep in several days, and the fatigue and stress were hindering his ability to concentrate. *God, Des, what's wrong with you? This is no harder than the other clues, and you figured them out.*

Running his index finger all the way up to Washington, DC, he saw nothing on the map worthy of any more scrutiny. On the right was West Potomac Park, followed by the most famous of Washington's landmarks, memorials, and institutions. The center of the river held the occasional island, while the left bank's most telling area was Arlington. While he knew most of the significant places in Washington, DC, he was less familiar with the areas on the west side of the Potomac.

Investigating further, he started searching the area surrounding the cemetery. It seemed as if everything had a name followed by the word *heights*. There was Arlington Heights, Foxcroft Heights, and Radnor Heights. They moved in a semicircular pattern around the edges of the Arlington burial grounds.

Along with the National Cemetery, the immediate area also had a large active military presence. Aside from the Pentagon, there were other installations, and although not major in size, they still played an important role. Des saw on its western edge one could access the cemetery through Fort Myer, which, of course, true to the area, also had a Fort Myer Heights. However, moving just north of Arlington and a little past Fort Myer, there was a part of the county he had passed over several times without paying much heed. This time, though, he paused to ponder a name, Rosslyn.

Immediately, he wondered whether this place had any affiliation with William Ross, the name he got off the tombstone. In actuality, he was not holding out much hope. Other than the tombstone, he was not aware of any other connection William Ross had with Virginia. Then again, he did not know much about the man to begin with.

Damn, I don't have a computer to look anything up. Des jumped up in an action, making him appear like he was sitting on a spring. He surveyed the room because, if he knew one thing about this chain, it was that if there was a Starbucks coffee shop, a laptop computer couldn't be far off. Sure enough, there were three of them. Picking the person from the group he felt had the most inviting face, he decided to approach an attractive woman who looked to be in her early forties, near the area where customers picked up their sugar and cream.

"Hi! I was wondering if I could bother you for just a moment. I'm in kind of a bind. I need to find out some information really quickly, and my cell phone battery went dead. I'm such an idiot. I thought I plugged it in. I was wondering if I may be able to use your computer for just a second."

"Oh, I hate it when that happens. I make that same mistake all the time," she answered flirtatiously. "Sure you can," she said, leaning back, allowing Des access to her computer.

"Thank you so much. It's so kind of you. I promise I'll just be a second."

He sat down, quickly typing in "Rosslyn, Arlington, VA," which soon led to him to the Wikipedia page. Scrolling down to where it said *history*, he was only a few sentences in when he discovered that Rosslyn did indeed have a connection to William Ross. The section was named after his family, who owned a farm on the current day site. Des's heart practically jumped out of his chest.

Noticing his jubilation, the woman became inquisitive. "You seem excited. Did you find what you were looking for?"

"I think so. I just need to check one more thing."

"I see you typed in a search for Rosslyn. You know, I'm pretty familiar with that area. I grew up not too far from there," she said, trying to strike up a more extensive conversation.

"Really? So you know all the important places there?"

"Pretty much so. What is it that you're looking for?"

Des had to tread carefully. One reason was, he did not want to clue this woman in on his situation, and two, he didn't know what he was really looking for in the first place.

"Are there, like, any historical landmarks there? You know, like monuments or historical homes?"

The woman leaned back in her seat, eyes pointing up and to the left, accessing her brain to see if she could come up with some answers. "I don't recall any major things. Most of it is pretty modern. About the only thing there that's historical at all would be the park."

"The park?" he said with his ears perked up.

"Yeah, Belvedere Park. I think it's on the land of the original farm in the area."

"That might work."

Des typed in a search for Belvedere Park, and some matches appeared. Most were just listings as part of the parks and recreation department. Seeing the dead end, he used the same words in an image search. The first pictures appearing were mainly of condominium projects and apartments, but there was one picture that was completely different from the rest. It looked like two wooden blocks covered in dirt and surrounded by ivy. Intrigued, he clicked to enlarge the image, but it provided little detail. However, it did give a link transporting him to a news page that had an entire article on the recently refurbished Belvedere Park.

Des quickly perused it. Within two paragraphs, the name William Henry Ross appeared. *This is it!* As exciting as that discovery was, it paled in comparison to what he read next. The article praised the renovators for preserving the historic steps. Des laughed out loud.

At the precipice of the stairs' flight, buried two vara, lies the portal.

"Are you okay?" she asked.

"I'm great. I'm sorry, you must think I'm a nut. I just found what I needed."

"I'm glad."

"Thank you so much. I really appreciate it."

"You're welcome. I come here a lot, practically every morning. If you happen to be here in the a.m., make sure you borrow my computer again," she said with a wink.

"Absolutely, I will."

Des finally knew where the next step in this journey was taking him. He was confident, given the fact that every time a clue led him to a new location, he found what he needed. He had little doubt this new discovery would provide him the same result. Now all he needed was a plan to get Madison back, but to that question, he hadn't a clue.

Chapter 81

The thrill of the discovery was quickly doused by the knowledge Madison was still not safe. This, in addition to his fear she was no longer capable of providing them anything useful, made the time table to get her back all that much shorter. Eluding the Judge's men had both positive and negative components. It did give him more time to find the location, but the time he gained for himself was now being subtracted from Madison's time to live.

As he walked outside for some fresh air, he realized finding the treasure was meaningless. For all intents and purposes, its value had completely diminished. He remembered how William advocated for getting to it before the Judge as being the only way to stop this madness. Yet the situation had changed, and the only card he had left to play was access to the goal.

Des believed it was coming to an end. Everything the instructions displayed indicated that to be the case. However, the luxury of time was not a commodity he possessed, and not knowing exactly how much further he had to go to attain it was something he could not chance. He had to figure out a plan to barter the access.

As he had done previously, Des relied on his Army training. Before he could establish contact with the Judge, he needed to know intimately the lay of the land. Only then could he formulate some type of plan to get Madison back. He had to go to Belvedere Park.

Hailing another cab, Des headed to the location, which was situated just north of Arlington National Cemetery. He was in a daze-like state, lost in thought, emotions bouncing from excitement to fear. As he made his way past Capitol Hill with its distinctive dome, he had difficulty concentrating, instead, falling into a pattern of thinking his military trainers always warned him about. He was focusing on what he didn't have rather than what he did.

In difficult situations, it's usually easier to fixate on the disadvantages rather than the benefits you possess. It's human nature, and in looking at the situation, it would be easy to recognize everything he had going against him. For starters, he was by himself, was unarmed, and had no surveillance of his adversaries. Those three simple facts alone would be enough to make anyone distraught.

But focusing on the negative was not going to be productive and would inhibit his ability to see possibilities. Des had to constantly snap himself out of that negative mind-set, or else, he would not be successful.

As the vehicle progressed along Independence Avenue, the Washington Monument appeared. He had already seen it several times since arriving in the city. Although he used it more as a marker, a point of reference, rather than focusing on the man it honored. Previously, whenever Des found himself in a predicament, it was his habit to look for inspiration.

Many people he knew growing up in the South would lean on faith, hoping for divine intervention to help them out of their troubles. While Des was raised in a religious household, he instead looked at the lessons of history to draw his strength.

As the shiny white obelisk got closer, he began to reflect on the difficult times George Washington faced during the harrowing days of the nation's founding. Today, most see Washington as the truest representation of leadership. He was the father of the nation whose stoic single-mindedness left little doubt, either by him or his contemporaries, that he was destined to lead a group of ragtag colonies to freedom. To the modern-day American, he was and always had been the epitome of the flawless, self-confident guiding light. Of course, historians know differently.

While Washington was selected to be the head of the Continental Army at its inception, his decision-making was called into question on several occasions, with many suggesting he was not competent enough for such a task. In the early days of the revolution, he knew far more failure than he did success, enough, in fact, for some to call for his removal. Until his famous crossing of the Delaware and subsequent attack on the Hessian fort at Trenton, New Jersey, the Continental Congress was becoming nervous of an imminent defeat.

Prior to that victory, the general experienced some of his darkest days. Low on men, supplies, and ammunition, Washington himself had great doubts he could hold off the world's greatest superpower much longer and was probably thinking of the dreadful consequences awaiting him following the failed attempt at independence.

Although Des was not fighting for the independence of a nation, he could certainly empathize with what Washington's feelings must have been going into a fight with such wide disparities in resources. But as the former general did, he was going to have to find a way to overcome these obstacles.

Passing West Potomac Park, where just a few hours earlier he escaped capture, he was nearly overcome by feelings of foreboding. While he knew he was not being tracked, it did not ease his uncertainty. They had managed to find him two times already since arriving in Washington when it hardly seemed possible. So while facts led him to deduce this would not happen again, he still felt like he was being watched.

The cab made its way across Arlington Memorial Bridge, where parts of the cemetery could be seen in the distance. To the north of him was Theodore Roosevelt Island, a small outcropping of land lying in the middle of the Potomac between Virginia and the nation's capital.

After crossing the river, they turned north onto George Washington Memorial Parkway to make the short jaunt to Rosslyn. Passing the Marine Corps War Memorial with its famous statue of those brave men raising the flag on Iwo Jima, Des saw the first sign for Rosslyn. *Well, Mr. Ross, I hope you can help me now.*

"We're almost there. You said to take you to Belvedere Park, right?"

"Yes, that's right. Do you know it well?"

"Not really. There's not a whole lot there. It's not that big of a place. It's nice, though, has a great rose garden."

The cab pulled onto North Sixteenth Road, where a green expanse presented itself. Des took a deep breath, getting himself into planning mode.

"Here we are," said the cabdriver. "Hope you have a great day."

As Des exited the vehicle, he was thinking the same thing. However, his definition of a great day was far different from what the cabdriver imagined. If he and Madison simply survived, it would constitute that characterization.

325

Chapter 82

Rosslyn Heights, Virginia

The Rosslyn sector of Arlington is a contemporary town, with a population slightly under ten thousand and all the modern amenities one would expect to find in any American suburb. The area is home to families, military personnel, as well as government and corporate employees and reflects a comfortable lifestyle that would be the model to any middle-class citizen.

In looking at its current state, one would never be able to picture its rough beginnings. Getting its name from the Ross family farm, the largest in the area, it originally was the site of a ferry landing for those who were making the journey back and forth to Georgetown during the colonial period. It later became the connection point of the Aqueduct Bridge, which was completed in the 1840s, becoming a major lifeline to the Chesapeake and Ohio Canal.

However, after the end of the Civil War, the town fell largely into disrepair, as their main business turned from farming to gambling halls, saloons, and brothels situated at the base of the bridge. It was not until the end of the nineteenth century, with the advent of the electric trolley, that the town's fortunes started to turn.

Belvedere Park looked like most parks in an urban setting. Yet beyond its modern tennis courts, ball fields, and picnic areas, the recreational spot also held a unique historical place in the community. William Ross had purchased this large swath of land that he, his wife, and their numerous children occupied during the 1830s and 1840s. Like most places of the past, the original structures had been erased from the landscape. None of the major buildings of the Ross estate still existed, and if one did not know about the history, one would mistake the only item from the period to survive, the stairs, as being nothing at all. That was what Des was looking for, a small projection of steps that if he was not searching for it, he would easily pass right by. The flight supposedly led to a plateau that Mr. Ross would use to overlook the Potomac River.

At the precipice of the stairs' flight, buried two vara, lies the portal.

Des's concern, like he had with many of the places these clues led to, was if the location existed or was even accessible. Making his way past the tennis courts and through a large grass expanse, he kept his eyes open for any sign of what was left of the steps. After passing the scenic flower garden, Des located what he was looking for, and his initial reaction was one of utter disappointment.

What he found were the remains of a couple of steps so deteriorated and incomplete they might as well have been ruins from ancient Rome. It seemed to have no beginning and no end, leaving little indication of where this portal might be. *Is this all that's left?*

Des's confidence sunk. *If I don't find the top of this thing, I'm screwed.* Looking around, he hoped where he was currently standing was its base. But the problem lay in the fact that no other stairs were visible. Even if they existed at all, they were hidden under a collection of brush and dirt, or they might have been removed altogether.

Turning around to make sure he was not being watched, Des started plowing through the foliage, pushing aside branches and twigs, looking for any sign of additional steps. Climbing higher and higher, he found some evidence of the flight, but they were sparse and incomplete, leaving him to guess where the next one might be. He kept climbing until he could no longer ascend.

Reaching a point of a possible apex, he stopped. There was nothing there, no steps, no brackets displaying any structure, only dirt and ivy. Rummaging through the leafy plants, he was at a loss. *Where is its precipice?*

As he dug deeper in the line of the steps' path, the only thing appearing was more dirt and mud. *Maybe they're lower?* However, he eliminated this idea, recounting the words of the clue. Continuing to claw at the earth, he scanned the grounds. He was becoming despondent, knowing if he had nothing to sell, there would be no way to get Madison back.

He burrowed frantically as the stress of that thought began to take hold, the smell of decaying plants and dirt filling his nostrils. His hands were caked with mud as sweat dripped down his brow.

Finally, his hand hit something. Pushing his fingers farther into the soft earth, he felt the obstruction. He moved his fingertips over it; the surface felt rough to the touch. Pulling more at the ground, he tried to open up a window to see. Peering into the hole, he viewed what appeared to be a shale-like stone. He instantly recognized it.

Des jumped off his hands and knees and started running down the hill, almost falling as the gravity of the slope pulled him toward the bottom. He needed to see the stairs at the base. Arriving there, he stared intently, and to his relief, it looked exactly like it. He bent down and slid his fingers over the surface. It was the confirmation he needed. He had found its precipice.

Chapter 83

Washington, DC

The tension in the room was increasing with every passing moment, with the Judge displaying a side of himself Chris had yet to see. The middle-aged man had not taken a seat since he received the report that Des managed to escape his men. Pacing the floor, only stopping to periodically rub his eyes or glower over the clues, he was beside himself.

This was a position he was not accustomed to. He was now waiting and depending on the competency of another individual in which he had no association or even prior knowledge of before this undertaking. With the growing anxiety, his anger began to boil over, and every time he looked at Madison, his rage only amplified.

Movement always eased tension for the Judge. In his courtroom, whenever situations became overwhelming, he always took a stroll, using the time to reflect and decompress. Now there was no such outlet. He was stuck in this motel prison, suffocating on the fact he no longer was the only overseer of the details of this operation.

It was late afternoon, and the glow of the sun was changing from bright white to varying colors of orange as the day began to come to a close. The Judge stared out the window in a display, which would make one think he was expecting his adversary to come walking into the motel lobby. Obviously, he knew better. He was going to have to wait for the call he knew would eventually come.

"Have we decided what we're going to do with her?" Chris inquired.

"I've been thinking about it," the Judge responded.

"She doesn't serve a purpose anymore."

Madison listened in terror. They were speaking of her almost in the past tense. Her hopes had dwindled to the point she had accepted her fate. She was not going to get through this. If the Judge did not hesitate to kill his former business partner, he would not think twice about eliminating her.

It was impossible for her to comprehend. It was only a few days ago that she was in beautiful Savannah, living in one of the true jewels of American cities, getting ready to embark on the adventure of a lifetime. It had now deteriorated into the crevices of a dark motel room, surrounded by strangers whose only intention was to find the best way to dispose of her.

Madison moved her eyes over the scene, taking in the bleak picture. It had become a stifling space. There was Chris with his foreboding black hair, the two muscular men who never said a word, making their silence all that more petrifying, and the Judge, who held her life in his hands. All of them were crowded into this meager space.

The Judge finally sat down, glaring at Madison but not saying anything. It felt like his eyes were burning right through her. The thoughts entering her mind were merely a collection of wishes that they would make her ending quick.

"What's he like?"

"What… I don't understand," Madison answered perplexedly.

"What's your friend like? Is he a details person? What's his background?"

"I don't know if I would say he's a details person, but he knows a lot about history."

"What does he do for a living?" "He's a student."

"Student? Isn't he a little old to be a college student? Why such the late start?"

"He spent six years in the Army."

"He what?" the Judge said, jumping out of his seat. "The Army? What did he do in the Army?"

"I don't know. He doesn't like to talk about it much."

"Goddamn it!" the Judge yelled, slamming his hand down on the desk. "You hear that, Chris? The guy we're after has military training."

"Relax, Judge. I don't know how that's going to help him here," Chris said in an effort to calm him.

"Am I the only one here that finds that significant? Where did he serve?"

"I… I don't know? I think Afghanistan."

"What did he do there?" he screamed as he moved closer to her.

"What… I don't…"

Before she could get the next syllable out of her mouth, a crushing sensation moved across her face as she felt herself slam into the desk and then the floor. The room was spinning around her as everything went blurry. She could not get her bearings for a few moments. Eventually, an image came into focus of the terrifying man with the slightly graying hair and intense stare, standing above her. He was panting like he had been sprinting laps around the motel. Madison did not know how to react as the intense pain from the blow resonated throughout her body. The Judge just glared as the room went dead silent while everyone awaited his next move. Dreading what might happen next, she was relieved when the silence was broken by one of his usually mute men.

"Judge."

"What is it?" he answered angrily.

"Our target has turned on his phone. We know where he is."

The Judge realized he only had a short window of time to make contact. It was now or never, and staying in a motel room, terrorizing his captive, was going to take time he didn't have. "Get her into the car," he ordered. "We need to get out of here."

Chris grabbed Madison by the arm and pulled her off the floor. Within moments, they had moved her out of the motel and to the waiting vehicle. They operated with military precision as they forced her into the car.

"Let's keep him in sight," the Judge said. "I didn't want to stay there and not be mobile."

Madison was squished between Chris on her left and another of his accomplices on her right. As always, she held still, not wishing to draw any attention to herself, hoping by some miracle she would be allowed to live.

After they pulled out of the parking lot, Chris soon became restless in his seat. "Is it time, Judge?"

His boss did not say a word, instead pausing and then pulling his phone out to send a text, passing on the information that they were on the move and it was time to prepare.

"Judge?" Chris said again to get his attention.

The Judge gave an affirmative nod.

It wasn't intensely painful, but the sting in her neck caught her by surprise. She looked stunned at Chris as he sat there with the hypodermic needle suspended in his hand. The effects were nearly immediate. Her breathing slowed. She could feel the life draining from her. Making one last effort, she struck him by instinct. But her hands felt numb. Her coordination was gone. Then the realization her time had run out began to settle in. She couldn't cry, but the sadness was more intense than any she had ever known. There was so much promise. *It's not fair.*

As her vision dimmed and her limbs went limp, her last thoughts were of Des. *I hope he will be okay. Please forgive me.* Her chest felt heavy as everything faded to black. She would succumb. It was over.

Chapter 84

Washington, DC

It was a clash between the nineteenth and twenty-first centuries. A stark contrast, to say the least. As he stared at the photograph, he ran his fingers through his thick beard, squeezing and pulling on it in an attempt to shape it to a matching contour.

His modern clothing, as hard as he tried, did not seem to coincide with his face. It was something he had known for some time but had long ago accepted it as a consequence of making such a decision about his appearance.

When he first chose this direction for his life, he thought it would be excruciatingly difficult. Being able to completely separate oneself from the world, on the surface, appeared a nearly impossible task. Yet it was actually easier than anticipated, and he not once regretted his conclusion.

He had been waiting to receive the text, and when it came in, there was a sense of relief. He would finally be able to do what he had trained to do. No more waiting, no more research, and no more status updates.

The location was nearby. It would only be a few minutes. Gathering his tools, he packed them into his backpack with the knowledge this was coming to an end.

Chapter 85

Rosslyn, Virginia

Des stood patiently in the strip mall parking lot. He had turned on his phone knowing he would soon be tracked by the Judge. It was a tricky game. He wanted to leave his phone on long enough for them to contact him, but not for such an extended amount of time that it would give them the opportunity to find him before he could implement his plan.

He decided it would be best to remain close to Belvedere Park. Though there was a risk to this strategy, as Rosslyn was not a big place, which might allow them to figure out his general location even after the phone was shut off.

Several minutes had passed, and still he had not received a call. It was disconcerting. He knew he was being tracked. *Why haven't they contacted me yet?* It was obvious they needed him, or else, they wouldn't have tried that stunt this morning. *So why haven't they made any effort to reach me now that they had my voluntary access?*

Des became uneasy. If he didn't do something, he was going lose what little control he still possessed. Walking across the parking lot, he stared at his phone, wishing he could peer through it to see what the Judge was doing on the other end.

Despair began to dissipate as rage swelled within him. He had been living in fear for the past couple of days, running away from pursuers as they held his friend captive. No longer was he going to be a participant in this ridiculous contest under their conditions.

Pulling out the brochure that led him here, he studied the map again to see where he might wait this out. Fingering through the pages, he stopped momentarily to peruse some photos. One in particular garnered most of his attention, a photo of a statue of General Stonewall Jackson.

Thomas Jackson was one of the most legendary figures of the Civil War. A quirky man who was fervently religious and possessed a plethora of mental conditions that would provide any psychologist a field day of diagnoses, he was an intriguing figure. Yet while displaying all those quirks, he was also quite possibly the most brilliant tactician of the war. His specialty was using small forces to attack Union troops while creating the illusion he had a much bigger army under his control. His constant use of misdirection kept Northern commanders on their heels.

Des came to the conclusion he needed to do the same to his enemy. He could never allow the Judge to get comfortable. At that moment, hoping to enrage his adversary, he shut off his phone and re-wrapped it. Men like the Judge would often let their desire for a goal outweigh their deductive-reasoning capabilities. Des was going to play off this hunch. He would show the Judge they needed him more than he needed them. It was a dangerous ploy, but he had to demonstrate he was no longer going to play the victim role in this scenario. He also wanted to convey the idea of mobility. He did not want to give them any impression he was staying in a specific location for a reason.

After shutting off his phone, he made his way to the bus stop. He would go a few blocks farther away from Belvedere Park. The next time he turned it on, he would appear to have magically transported to a new location.

Exiting the bus, Des continued to fight the urge to power up his phone. He had to avoid thinking of Madison, as much as it pained him to do so. *I know men like him. He'll call when I am ready to hear from him.*

Chapter 86

"What do you mean you lost the signal?" the Judge yelled.

"He must have shut off his phone," Chris responded.

"Damn it! That's just great. He probably figured out something and doesn't want to share it. He probably doesn't even give a shit about the girl."

"I don't think we should jump to any conclusions, Judge."

"Well, he knows we can track him."

"That's my point. I think he's sending us a message."

"And what would that be?"

"That he's not going to let us have complete control. He knows we need something he has, and he's showing us that he knows that."

"Well, how in the hell are we supposed to get ahold of him now?"

"Don't worry. He'll turn on his phone again when he's ready."

The Judge's phone rang. Looking at who it was, he rolled his eyes. *Why does he have to call me now?* "Yes, what is it?"

As the conversation continued, Chris noticed the Judge was becoming even more irritated. He had a pretty good idea of whom he was talking to but dared not say anything, as he knew he would only become agitated beyond his current state.

"I'll let you know. Just be ready," the Judge said emphatically. He finished the call and struck the dashboard. He did not need any more pressure and yet felt it was being piled on unnecessarily. *He's just going to have to wait until I give him the go-ahead.* The text would come when their target was in position.

Chapter 87

*F*ucking amateur. Glaring at his phone resting on the front seat of the car, Osiris was in no mood to be put on hold. Yet that was exactly how he felt, put on hold. There was nothing else he could do but be patient. The Judge had a very specific plan. He said he would make contact when he was ready to have him join in.

Yes, he was being paid his standard astronomical rate. However, that in itself was not enough. Osiris hated assignments that he felt were beneath him, beneath his skill set. Being made to wait on a novice fell into such a category.

Unfortunately, once he received payment, it was professional ethic, something that trumped all his other personal codes. The client was the boss. His job, as much as he might despise it, was to do his bidding. *You're the fucking idiot who took the assignment.* So while as obstinate as he might be, as long as he accepted the money, he was obligated to follow through on the client's wishes.

Maybe in the end it will all be worth it. It was a hopeful thought. One that kept him motivated. If it was real, he might be able to convince the Judge to cut him a piece of the pie or, at the very least, give him a very lucrative role.

So he would wait. When it was time to involve himself, the Judge would give him the go-ahead. He had to keep his distance. Although he had not been seen in his current state, the threat of recognition was one he was always cognizant of, even with someone who he held in such low esteem.

If everything went well and the Judge was able to acquire this great reward, it would all be worth it.

It fucking better be.

Chapter 88

Des arrived in front of a condominium project just a few blocks away from the park. In his mind, he pictured the Judge frustrated and frantic. It almost caused him to crack a smile, even in this most desperate of situations.

He had decided upon a plan of meeting them in darkness. There was no way he was going to be able to pull this off in broad daylight. Knowing the Judge would not want to be seen in those conditions as well brought him to the conclusion that an early-morning operation would be best.

As time passed, he carefully went over the details in his mind. But after he had done that again and again, it was becoming counterproductive. He needed to move forward. He needed to implement it. Sometimes you realize there is nothing left to organize. You have to just do it or it no longer holds value.

He inhaled deeply, closed his eyes, and pressed the button, turning on his cell phone. He was fairly confident he would hear from the Judge in a matter of moments. Des had proven his willingness to wait it out; however, this did not keep his anxiety from rising considerably.

He stared at the screen, its light glowing more brightly with each moment as the sun started to set. Car headlights were becoming more pronounced, and the fact he could no longer see the faces of the people behind the wheel of their vehicles made him more insecure.

The oncoming night was bringing feelings of fear, and Des was just about ready to turn off his cell phone as he believed they were tracking him rather than wishing to establish contact. As he placed his finger on the button to shut it down, his phone rang. The number appearing was Madison's.

Excitedly, he answered, "Madison, are you okay?"

"Hello, Des," a gravelly voice responded.

Des clenched his fist. *Damn it, Des, that was stupid!* By answering in such a manner, he gave away the fact he cared, possibly showing his hand that he would be willing to do anything to get her back. He gathered himself. "I think I have what you need, Judge."

"I have to give you credit. You've done a very good job so far of keeping away from my men. However, your friends have not fared as well."

"Where are they?"

"Madison is here, but I'm afraid William is no longer with us."

Des bowed his head down and gritted his teeth. He feared when the Judge captured William, the penalty for his disloyalty would be high. The Judge's words confirmed this was what took place. "I want to speak to Madison."

"I'm sorry, that's not going to happen right now. You had to know this was going to be the consequences of your actions. It actually surprises me. Someone obviously as bright as you are did not even take into account there would be other interested parties. How could you be so arrogant?"

"Look, we had no idea there was anyone else searching for it. We were just following clues we happened to find. If we had known this was going to happen, we would have never started," Des said, frustrated.

"Well, there's a way out of this. I want those instructions."

Des felt a surge in confidence. The Judge admitted his need. Yes, he was playing rough, but there was now a glimmer of hope. "I know that in order for you to get what you want, you need what I have. But I'm telling you right now, if you do not release Madison to me and leave us alone, I'll destroy the instructions and you'll never find it."

The Judge fumed on the other end of the line. "I think you're forgetting, I've already disposed of one. I have no problem getting rid of the other."

Des had to fight mightily against his instinct. If he showed he was giving in to threats, then this operation would fail. Gathering himself and biting his lip, he prepared himself to respond. "No, you won't. I know men like you. You've probably fantasized about this treasure your whole life. You're not going to walk away from it now. You're going to do what I say."

"You're not in control here. I am," he said, the ire in his voice becoming more evident.

"Let's not bullshit each other. I have what you need. We both know that. Here's your choice. Either I get Madison back unharmed and you get the treasure, or you refuse and I destroy the clues and you'll never have it. Who knows, maybe I'll come back for it on my own. I know what it's worth."

"You son of a bitch! I will—"

"I don't have time for this shit! Here's the deal. I'll turn on my phone again in the next several hours. Meet me at that location and we'll make the trade."

"Listen, I don't need—"

Des ended the call and turned off his phone. He didn't want to give the Judge a chance to negotiate or attempt to intimidate. A threat does not do any good unless someone is there to hear it. As long as he controlled the dialogue, the Judge would not be able to make any more demands and would have to do what he was told.

Let's just hope he's as greedy as I think he is.

Chapter 89

The Judge gripped the phone so hard one could hear it start to crack as its plastic casing nearly gave way to the force. Chris did not say a word, seeing a rage in his employer he had never witnessed before.

"I can't wait until I get ahold of this guy. I'm going to rip his heart out of his goddamn chest!" Never before had anyone spoken to him in that manner. He gave the orders. He decided what was going to be done. He was always the one in charge. This could not be allowed to happen. "He's up to something. The son of a bitch is up to something."

"What did he say?" Chris inquired.

"He said he would turn on his phone in a few hours and to meet him at the location we track. I hate this!"

"Does he know about her?"

"I don't think so."

"What he doesn't know can be used to our advantage."

"I just don't want him to go to the police, or anyone else, for that matter."

"Look, he's not going to risk it, and we have enough men to cover whatever it is he's planning. We'll handle it."

"Maybe we shouldn't have injected her," the Judge said doubtfully.

"She hadn't provided us with anything useful in hours. She had no idea where her friend was, and she didn't have any idea where he might be going. She was useless. If we hadn't, she would have just continued to get in the way and slow us down."

"I guess you're right, and anyway, it doesn't do us any good to second-guess ourselves now. What's done is done. Did you bring the shovels?"

"Yes, they're in the trunk."

The night dragged on for what seemed like an eternity. Even though they discussed these latest developments, the last few hours were relatively quiet, with only short exchanges intermittently breaking the silence.

Although he tried to fight the urge, the Judge could not help but project to what his life would be like after discovering the treasure. Prior to this night, he was always able to keep from making such a mistake. But now, the conclusion of this journey was so close he gave in to the temptation.

He did recognize the fallacy in doing so, but the stress of dealing with this troublesome individual and his own interpretation of the clues had him coming to the determination that this ordeal was almost over. Although this frustrating development had impeded his original, well-laid-out plans, not for a moment did he believe he would not be successful. He knew if push came to shove, he was always willing to take things to the next level in order to reach his goal. He would do what others would not.

Chris, too, was deep in thought. There were so many opportunities that would open up to him if he could bring this assignment to a positive conclusion. He would have his validation. No longer would he be the young buck who was spoon-fed positions he did not deserve. He would not have to tolerate his colleagues whispering under their breath that he did not have the talent or the brains to justify the advancements he had been given. All those issues were in his consciousness, but they were not the only prospects on his mind.

Since they had taken William and Madison to the cabin and learned of what the Judge was pursuing, Chris had been considering the possibility he might attain a small piece of the treasure for himself. He would not dare bring up the idea to the Judge, as he knew it would serve no purpose other than to enrage him. He had to wait for the ideal moment. There would come a time when a situation would arrive. A crisis would surface that would force the Judge's hand.

While outwardly, Chris displayed concern and attentiveness, secretly, he was pleased his boss was experiencing difficulties. Though not expected, this wrench thrown into the machinery of the Judge's plans was giving Chris hope that this crisis might be appearing soon. He did not know exactly when an opening might appear but knew he would recognize it when it did. When the Judge had few options, he would take the opportunity and make it happen.

However, as the realization of a find for the ages drew closer, the Judge's feeling of it being taken from him only increased. Paranoia washed over him. His underling, once completely under his control, took on a deceitful and betraying appearance in the darkened vehicle. *I know what you want, you backstabbing son of a bitch! Don't think I don't! But don't worry, I know how to deal with you.*

He was ready to implement his insurance plan. It was a simple text: "It's time." There was a sense of relief that briefly caused the Judge to crack a slight smile. Soon, this would all play out.

Chapter 90

Rosslyn Heights

Sitting in the park, Des rubbed his hands together in an effort to stay warm. He had made the rounds, gathering items he would need for this evening, although it did not amount to a whole lot. His plan was relatively simple. He had to make them believe he was serious enough to destroy the clues.

Earlier, he purchased a butane lighter, a large bowl, some cotton rags, and lighter fluid at a local thrift store. Finally, he bought the most realistic-looking paintball pistol he could find at a local sporting goods shop, hoping the darkness would be enough to disguise the fact the gun, while maybe being able to cause a welt, was relatively harmless.

It was nearly five thirty in the morning, and the roads surrounding the park were completely silent. No cars or pedestrians, nothing to see but the flickering lights of the city shimmering off the Potomac River. Later today, this park would be full of activity, packed with Memorial Day revelers, playing baseball, barbecuing hot dogs, and enjoying the typical holiday fair.

Des carefully picked the moment to turn on his phone, wanting to allow enough time to get Madison back but not wishing to give his adversaries too much time before daybreak, so they would not get to feel comfortable. The big problem was the location of the stairs. They were hidden by a thick grouping of trees and bushes, covering very well, any attempt at excavation, possibly bolstering the Judge's confidence he could dig without being discovered. He also knew he could not reveal the burrowing point until the last moment.

Waiting for the time to initiate this scenario was painfully slow. He always hated dragging things out. He looked from his hideout and checked his watch once more. The moment had arrived. He exhaled, watching his breath dissipate in the lights. It did nothing to calm him.

"Oh, screw it!" He reached down with purpose and pressed the button. His phone came alive. He was now visible. It would only be a matter of minutes before they were here. This was it.

Anxiously looking back and forth, Des stayed in an area that he would not be readily discovered, a small crevice of bushes and trees. He left the phone in the grass near the street, hoping it would divert their attention long enough for him to get control of the situation. He was alone, with only the sound of his breathing to accompany him.

It appeared as two beams of light streaming across the street as the black SUV made the turn onto the thoroughfare running the park's length. It pulled up slowly, displaying the caution Des expected.

Not realizing he was doing it, Des held his breath until the car had pulled to a complete stop. Several minutes passed. To his surprise, no one had exited the car. *What are they doing?* Over five minutes had passed, then ten, and still no movement. He wanted to stand up to get their attention but knew if he did, whatever leverage he had would be gone.

I can't show my hand first.

Chapter 91

The resonances were muffled, and the vision blurry. At first, the smell of coffee was the only thing discernable. Clicking sounds as if something was being fitted to another object filled what felt to be a very cramped space. *What is this?* Movement seemed impossible, like something was constricting the limbs, and even the rotation of the head was labored. It felt like paralysis, yet textures underneath the fingers and temperatures could still be sensed. A waft of coldness hit the face as the opening of some type of portal was audible. Movement on the right side vibrated a cushioned seat enough to where a noticeable leaning was taking place. But the effort to correct the imbalance did not seem to take effect even though the thought was definitely present. A force pressed against the arm created a sense of equilibrium.

"Did you see anything?" a voice said.

"I found the phone in the grass just a few yards from here," another deep voice responded.

"He's here. He's playing a game with us. Send one of them to search the area."

Sounds were becoming clearer, and the voices recognizable. Soon the sight became focused. The dark interior of a car was becoming defined.

She still couldn't move very well but was beginning to recall the predicament she was in. Her throat was dry, and the stiffness in her muscles felt like she had been coiled in one position for years. *I thought I was dead.*

Madison looked to her right to see Chris screwing a silencer onto the tip of his gun. The man on her left was doing the same. She peered toward the front of the vehicle and saw the dark eyes of the Judge glaring at her.

"Let's get her outside."

Chris grabbed her arm as the man sitting on the other side of her exited the SUV to begin his search. As he pulled her out of the car, the pressure Chris exerted was firm, to the point of being painful. The cold air, while uncomfortable, had a sobering effect. Madison, though still not in complete control of her body, had regained her faculties of the mind.

Being held up by Chris and one of his accomplices, she could see the other member of Chris's team exploring the park, examining the baseball fields, tennis courts, and even looking over the expanse of the rose garden. She could tell he was not having any luck, and for a brief moment, she breathed a sigh of relief. *He's okay.*

The muscular man began rummaging through the bushes. Des could hear him as his pursuer seemed to break every low-lying branch and twig in his vicinity. He could barely make out his face in the dismal light provided by the street lamps but believed it to be the one who nearly caught him at West Potomac Park.

Des glanced down to the car. It was difficult to see, but he could make out the silhouettes of three people. It was hard to ascertain who they were as the shapes were pressed together, until one moved slightly to the right. It was at that moment he caught a glimpse of curly hair and instantly recognized it was Madison.

A feeling of reprieve as well as fury enveloped him. He wanted to rush down the hill and throw himself at the individuals who held her captive, yet fought the desire, remaining focused on the one who was currently tracking him.

He was now only a few feet away, and Des was relishing his new role as the hunter rather than the prey. He anticipated his arrival as the crunching noises of his foe's misplaced approach became louder and louder. *Come on, come on, just a few inches more, you son of a bitch.*

Des did not move a muscle as his target was falling for his trap. Then, a cocking of a pistol sounded as it pressed against the back of his rival's head.

"Give me your gun," Des said.

The man, stunned at first, knew he had no choice. Turning slowly, he allowed the gun to dangle helplessly from his index finger. Des grabbed the weapon. "If you make a sound, I'll blow a hole in the back of your skull. Do you understand me?"

He nodded in affirmation. Des studied the weapon he had just attained. He had not held one of this high a quality since he was in the service.

"Hold this," Des said, handing his captive a large bowl filled with rags reeking of lighter fluid.

"What do you want me to do with this?"

"Just hold it for now and shut the hell up until I tell you to speak. Now, I want you to walk down slowly toward where your boss is."

Des inched down the hill with his captive in front of him, being careful to use his hostage to obstruct any line of sight.

"He wasn't up there? What the hell are you carrying?" the Judge said, watching his man descend from the rise.

As soon as he spoke, he saw that his subordinate was not alone. The adversary he had been chasing had a gun pointed at his employee.

"Take this and light the rags in the bowl," Des demanded as he handed the butane lighter to the Judge's man.

He complied, grabbing the lighter, touching it to the rags, which burst into flames. The orange glow of the fire lit up the area and matched the deep-orange color seen above the Potomac River as the sun started to break over the horizon. The Judge just watched, wondering how he should approach this latest development.

Des looked intently at the unfolding scene. The men standing to the sides of Madison had their guns pointed at him while he used his captive as a shield.

The Judge studied his adversary. "Hello, Des. How are you this morning?"

"I want to make this as quick and painless as possible," Des replied, ignoring the Judge's sarcastic greeting.

"Okay, what do you have in mind?"

"I know all you care about is the treasure. It was never that important to me. Here's the deal. You let her go, and I'll let you have this." Des held up the folder with the original instructions in his free hand. "Without these, you'll never find it. You send her this way with me, and I'll leave these here on the ground for you."

"What if I don't accept your offer?"

"Then I'll throw them into this fire and no one will ever get them or the treasure."

"I see."

The Judge stood quietly, refraining from giving an answer. He needed what Des had but also understood he could not appear desperate. Yet the desire for the treasure was becoming overwhelming, and he was not, under any circumstances, going to allow it to slip away.

"What's it going to be, Judge?"

The Judge turned to his men and then back to Des. He gave a single nod, and they released Madison. She did not immediately go to her friend, still a bit woozy from the injection. Chris reached out, slightly pushing her in the general direction of where Des stood. Madison walked hesitantly, ever weary this might be some kind of trick.

"Madison, are you okay?" She nodded. "Stand behind me."

She tucked in behind Des, staying as close to him as she could without interfering with his ability to be mobile. The sun was getting brighter in the sky as the dawn was in full swing. She appeared tired and ragged, but it was good to feel her so close.

"Okay, place the folder on the ground right next to the bowl," Des said to his hostage. The accomplice slowly knelt down and did what he was told. The flames were burning brightly, and Madison could feel its heat on her legs. Des's eyes moved slowly over his enemies. First examining Chris, and then back to the Judge, making sure none of them made any unpredictable moves.

"Okay, start moving back slowly with me," Des said.

His hostage nodded. Des reached back, placing his hand on Madison's waist, gently moving her in the direction he wanted. He could feel her trembling as they took one step back, and then another.

At first, he was hoping the clicking noise was a twig or branch Madison had bumped into. But he knew it wasn't the case. He had spent enough time in the service to recognize the unmistakable sound of a pistol being cocked. Madison froze. Des closed his eyes, knowing his plan had gone terribly awry.

Chapter 92

"**D**rop the gun," the voice growled.

Des could not let it end this way. The Judge would show no mercy. Trying to buy time, he did not react. Des then slowly loosened his grip.

"Drop the gun, I said," the raspy voice demanded.

Des gradually bent down, making sure he did not show any threatening gestures. *This can't continue. Quick, do something! Take what they need! Make yourself valuable!* His heart was pounding. His breathing accelerated. He had not reached such a heightened state since his days in Afghanistan.

Des placed the gun gently on the ground. Directly in front of him, the bowl was still ablaze, with the precious instructions lying at its base. *I have no choice. You have to make yourself valuable!*

He saw the Judge and his men move toward them. They had an aura of confidence, exuding victory. *I have to act now!* Des lurched forward, knocking the bowl over onto the folder. The dry paper lit up like a torch, the ball of flame consuming the precious wealth of knowledge.

The Judge looked in horror. "No! Quick, put it out! Put it out!"

Diving the few feet forward, Chris removed his jacket, trying to suffocate the flames. But it was too late. Once the fire was squelched, he removed his coat to reveal nothing but charred ash.

The Judge's rage was all-consuming. He grabbed the gun from his muscular accomplice and leveled it at Des. Hearing the cocking trigger, Des prepared to take the full brunt of his anger.

"Stop," the voice said from behind. "If you shoot him, we don't know where to look. He's the only one who can lead us to it."

The Judge gritted his teeth. His finger increasing pressure on the trigger. The middle-aged man's body was shaking with rage. His face was bloodred. Sweat poured onto his forehead and upper lip. Des was not sure the Judge could maintain his composure much longer.

"Come on, Judge, we can still find it. Just stay with me," the voice said.

Des glanced behind him to see who was speaking. There, barely visible in the faint orange of the morning, was the silhouette of the bearded man he saw at the cemetery. His long coat, small cap, and dark-rimmed glasses gave the appearance of a kindly uncle, not a vicious killer. Yet appearances in this case could be deceiving, as the wicked weapon he was holding certainly interrupted any picture of serenity.

The Judge, still trembling with anger, stood over Des like some conquering hero. He then looked at the pile of ash that once held the clues to his glory.

Gathering himself, he turned back toward his adversary. "That was a stupid thing to do, Des."

"Maybe, but without the instructions, you're going to need us." "You're correct in one way, I might need you. But I don't need her," he said, pointing his gun at Madison.

She stiffened like she was encased in cement. Images of the helpless William taking that bullet to the chest and his lifeless body lying in the dust of the trail flashed in her mind. Des knew acting desperate would only confirm the Judge's belief.

He responded in a very calm and calculated manner. "You'll need her too. She holds information you don't know about, information that even I don't have. If you shoot either one of us, you will not find what you're after," Des said, staring directly into the Judge's eyes.

"You're lying. We got all we could from her. She's useless… dead weight."

"Do you really want to take that chance? It would be an awful shame for you to get this far just to lose it now. You see, Judge, if you get rid of her, then I will not have the final piece of the puzzle that was in the original clues. Then we're both dead weight to you."

Seething, the Judge took two steps back. Turning around to face the street, he watched as the city gradually came to life. The Potomac was a deep, rich blue, providing the perfect accent to the white structures covering the landscape in the background. Des glanced at Madison, who was displaying a blank look on her face. She had no idea what he was talking about, but his expression indicated to her she had better play along.

"All right, I agree. I have nothing to lose by keeping you both around a little longer," the Judge replied, turning around. "Where do we go now?"

Des stood up, grabbing Madison's hand and squeezing it tightly, trying to reassure her everything would be okay. Her palm was sweaty and cold. Her face displayed the fatigue the last few days had created. He could only imagine the hell she had been through.

"We need to dig," Des said.

"I thought we would," the Judge responded.

"The digging won't be the end of it. There's still a ways to go."

The Judge nodded.

Des gazed in the direction of the stairs. "I hope you brought shovels. I'll show you where it is."

It was going to be a busy morning. Des had bought some more time. However, he still had to lay the groundwork to get them out of this. Hopefully, an opportunity would present itself. Who knew what the digging would bring.

Chapter 93

Des led them to the base of the stairs at the bottom of the grove. Lining himself up with the shale-covered steps he had originally spotted earlier, he marched up the hill through the bushes to the location where he found the lone piece of rock resembling those at the bottom of the rise.

"This is where we need to dig," he said, pointing to the location.

One of the Judge's men arrived with some shovels he had retrieved from the SUV. Madison, noticing them earlier, assumed they were there to bury her body. Handing the car keys to the Judge, he awaited his instructions.

The Judge eyed Des with suspicion but understood he had to follow his lead. "How far down do we have to dig?"

"About five feet. A vara is about two and half feet. It says two vara," Des replied.

"What are we looking for?"

"Some type of entrance either made of wood or metal."

The men dug in rhythm as Chris kept an eye on their captives. The slim man with the beard stood back several feet in the shadows. He did not say a word, only occasionally lifting his head, his back turned toward them, looking at the sky and murmuring to himself.

The earth was quickly relenting, as the spring rains had kept the ground moist and soft. The only difficult impediment they were encountering was the occasional thick tree root, causing the men to hack away until it gave in. The park was now fully lit, as the sun had risen above the river. It was about seven fifteen in the morning, and it would only be a short while before family and friends would begin to flood in to celebrate the holiday weekend.

Des and Madison stood next to each other quietly, waiting to see what the results would be of this latest search. She had fully regained her faculties as well as her coordination, as the effects of whatever it was they injected into her had seemed to wear off.

"Are you sure this is the right spot?" she whispered.

"I hope so. I don't have any other ideas. According to what I figured, this is the only place that it could be," Des answered.

Madison took a deep breath. Even though they were nowhere close to being out of danger, having him here gave her some peace. "Thank you for coming back for me," she said, squeezing his hand tightly.

About thirty minutes had passed, and still nothing. Des was beginning to lose hope as the Judge glared back at him. He was giving off the energy of a man who was obsessed, a recreation of Captain Ahab from *Moby Dick*, forever chasing his white whale. He began to pace while looking out toward the park, cognizant that eventually, someone might see them. A jogger passed through the grass field adjacent to the bottom of the stairs' flight, causing the magistrate to implore his men to dig faster.

Angry that he had been misled, he prepared to assault his captives when he was interrupted by a loud ping. Everyone turned and stared down at the hole. Even the bearded man momentarily broke his trance.

"We hit something," said one of the men.

"Quickly, get the rest of the dirt off," the Judge replied.

The men dug around the metal shell, trying to see if they could locate an access point. The surface appeared old and rusted. Obviously, it had been sitting down there for over a hundred years. The men were on their hands and knees, removing earth as fast as they could. Soon a thin bar was uncovered. Although it was not clear, it looked as if it crossed the length of the metal obstruction. Rivets in the surface also became visible as the men cleared away more dirt. It took about ten more minutes before they had completely exposed the portal. It was certainly of mid-nineteenth-century origin. The thin bar, indeed, went the length of the entire metal casing. It was fixed to a metal crank that was attached to a handle.

"Can you move that handle?" the Judge asked.

The muscular man pulled on the bar, but years of age, muck, and paralyzing rust did not give way to the force. His accomplice joined in, yet it only moved an inch. Moving in a coordinated action, the men pulled and pulled, rocking back and forth. The Judge was beginning to panic as he saw the first cars arrive in the parking lot below them.

Finally, the handle began to give way to their movement. It creaked loudly as the latch holding it down strained to keep its secret. The men continued to exert their power, then suddenly, both of them fell back as it released. The Judge almost jumped into the hole with them, his excitement nearly getting the better of him. Then one of the men turned the latch as another set of clicking sounds signified it was now ready to be accessed.

As they yanked hard on its handle, the portal opened a couple of inches. Needing to clear more dirt off its hinges, they shoveled the excess earth away from its moorings. Removing the final obstruction, they pulled in unison, until with one last giant heave, it was thrown open.

It was pitch-black inside, with the morning light only providing enough illumination to expose a narrow stairway leading farther down into the earth. The second to last clue immediately appeared in Des's mind.

Travel through the tunnels to the stone with the mark of our leader.

This journey was coming to an end. One way or another, he was going to have to find a way out. There were no more clues left to follow.

Chapter 94

Take them down there," the Judge ordered, pointing at Madison and Des. He handed his men flashlights, and they fixed their beams on the dank opening of this awkward space. Carefully climbing into the hole, they made their way through the piles of soft dirt lying at its edges, stepping through the portal onto the stairway. The Judge and his bearded accomplice followed them into the dark crevice. Chris was last to go.

The smell was what one would expect from such an old hidden passage. Musty with the aroma of mold and rotten eggs, the putrid atmosphere was unpleasant, to say the least. The stairs were slippery, as they were caked with wet mud. Des held Madison's hand as they stepped cautiously into its depths.

It was difficult to make out objects or significant points, but the flashlights cut through the blackness well enough to reveal a floor about fifteen feet down. As they made their way to the bottom of the stairwell, the beam of light they grazed upon the bottom caught a glint of something shiny. Walking over to the object, they found three kerosene lanterns, obviously left for whoever might have been meant to come down there. Chris walked over and picked up one of the antiques. Sniffing it, he could still smell that it was full of kerosene. He took the lighter Des had used to incinerate the original set of clues and lit the lanterns, providing them with much-needed light.

The Judge walked slowly behind the group, gun drawn, bewilderedly gawking into the dark void. The tunnel was roughly ten feet wide and about seven feet tall. There were no distinguishing markers of any kind. Its ceiling was a mixture of dirt and rock, its surface only interrupted by wooden supports every few yards. It had been meticulously carved by individuals who must have had a background in construction or mining.

The passage looked to be quite long, as neither the bright beams of the flashlights nor the extra glow of the lanterns could locate the end of it.

Des and Madison looked all around them, but the walls were barren; no hooks or new passageways broke the succinct pattern other than the framing put in place to hold the structure solid.

The Judge marveled at the tunnel but was uncertain of how far they needed to travel. "Where do we go?"

"We keep going down the tunnel until we find the mark," Madison responded.

"What mark?"

"The mark of the leader."

"What is that?"

"It's hard to describe. I'll have to show it to you," she said, cognizant of trying to keep the Judge's belief that she still held important information.

They kept heading south, and as the journey continued, it became evident to Des they were heading in the direction of Arlington National Cemetery. *How can this be? Why would they place the treasure right under the feet of Union headquarters?* He was as perplexed as he was fascinated. Amazed this tunnel even existed in the first place, his logical mind was in conflict with what his senses were providing him.

In some ways, it did make sense. This would be the ideal location to dig such a tunnel. The land was privately owned by a known Southern sympathizer who had fled the country during the war. Its access to the Potomac would have easily allowed for supplies to be delivered, and its relative proximity to slave holders in Delaware as well as other Southern supporters in the Washington, DC, area, would have made this a place where activity such as this would be possible. Des thought about the last clue.

*Break through to find the treasure, thousands en*C*ased in black sands of the fallen.*

What encases the fallen? Could it be coffins? Could the treasure be in coffins? Yet this did not explain why they would hide the treasure in the heart of the Union. The thought obviously occurred to the Judge as well, his frustrated expression giving his feelings away. He appeared in a state of disbelief that this was even a possibility. He looked like a man who had discovered he had been tricked in a poker game.

"I don't understand. This makes no sense," the Judge said, looking at his captives. "Why would they do this? I may not be as educated in history as you two, but I know hiding a Confederate treasure in the middle of a Union stronghold would be a bad idea. They would have most likely taken it farther south."

"You're right, it doesn't make sense on the surface, but it makes perfect sense if you look at it another way."

The Judge shook his head in disagreement. It went against everything he knew about the legend. "It's a well-known fact that James Semple was the man given the responsibility to hide the treasure going through Savannah."

"Yes, but Semple denied to his dying day that he ever got access to it, and other than a few unproven rumors about the silver being hidden in Danville, it was never shown the treasure ever made it south of Richmond," Des stated.

The Judge stopped in his tracks. "This better not be some kind of ploy," he said, pointing a gun in their direction. "I'm getting damn tired of chasing dead ends."

"Look, Judge, the park we used to access this tunnel was originally on the family farm of a very prominent Southern sympathizer by the name of William Ross. He had the motivation, the ability, and the location to help the Confederacy. Think about it. What better place to hide the treasure than the last place anyone in the North would look for it, right under Union headquarters?"

The Judge paused. He then turned to Chris, looking for assistance, but knew the young man had little knowledge of this time period to be of any help. "Well, one good thing about this space, if you fuck with me, no one will ever find you down here," he said menacingly. He then motioned for the bearded man to follow him. He trailed, though remaining in the shadows. "Chris, I want you and your men to stay here. That way, if these two try to get past us, you guys can make sure they don't get far."

Chris gave the Judge an affirmative nod, remaining in that part of the tunnel. The bearded man continued to tail, forcing their captives south. They had already gone over a quarter mile, but the passageway kept going, with no end in sight. The bearded man remained silent, his darkened shadow of a figure displaying an ominous appearance.

Des thought it strange the Judge would make Chris and his men stay back. It was something that did not seem to be a prudent move. They had yet to see another way out of this tunnel, and the best way to keep track of your captives was to keep them close and well guarded. The Judge must have been sensing something.

Madison peered into the blackness, frustrated that the flashlight and kerosene lantern could not provide more clarity. She tried to examine every inch of the tunnel, searching for the stone engraved with the "mark." The Judge had his beam pointed to the ground. It was only a few more steps when they were presented a new clue that the journey was coming to a completion. The floors went from dirt to stone paving.

Des saw stones covering the walls as well. "Hold up the lantern," he asked Madison. As she lifted her arm, the antique illuminated their surroundings. There in the golden light, the tunnel had come to an end.

The space was wider than the rest of the tunnel and had the look of a medieval dungeon. There were water stains on some of the rocks, probably from the inability of the tunnel to completely shield itself from the spring rains and winter snow melts. At the base of the wall was a small mound of dirt running up to the edge of a deep crevice that turned the corner and ran along the rest of its foundation. This channel, which was most likely used for drainage, had to be more than a few feet deep, as one could not see the bottom of it.

The Judge, looking befuddled, turned to his captives. "Where are we?"

"Right under Arlington National Cemetery, most likely," answered Des.

"I still don't get this. Why would they create such an elaborate place to hide the treasure? It would have taken months to dig this tunnel. Wouldn't it have been easier just to have hidden it somewhere closer?"

"Maybe, but they had their reasons."

"I just don't see how they could have done this without anyone noticing."

"It had already been done in some places in Washington, DC, prior to this."

"What do you mean?"

"During the War of 1812, the British had dug many tunnels under Washington, DC. Some were discovered around the DuPont Circle area by construction workers in the 1920s. Up until that time, no one even knew they existed. They were able to build those tunnels right next to the Capitol Building without being spotted. So it is possible. Who knows, this tunnel could have been started at that time and just continued during the Civil War. I thought 'gateway to the second invasion' meant the Potomac River, but it could have meant this tunnel. Think about it, Arlington National Cemetery didn't exist, but I'm sure the British would have shed no tears destroying the home built to honor the man who defeated them in the revolution."

The Judge was stunned. As much as he wanted to deny such a structure could have existed or been built under the noses of Union forces, what his adversary was saying made sense. It was a revelation, but also unnerving. His knowledge of history was being far surpassed by his captive, leaving him edgy and feeling vulnerable. They could not share in the wealth, but he could not dispose of them either until he had extracted every bit of useful information.

Madison began searching the walls, looking for the stone carrying the mark of the leader. Clamoring over its east side, she looked everywhere, yet drew a blank. Not having any success, she moved to the back wall. It was intricately fitted with the same type of shale stones that covered the steps in the park. The craftsmanship was competent, but at times crude. This was not some decorative tomb made to display the grandeur of a cause; it was a utilitarian tunnel meant to serve a singular purpose.

"So where's the mark?" the Judge asked, quickly growing impatient.

"That's what I'm looking for now," Madison replied.

Examining the wall, she started from the bottom, working her way up. The low light making it difficult to differentiate shapes as she mistook patterns in the rock for something significant that turned out to be nothing of importance.

Des examined the west side while the Judge and his bearded companion in the shadows stood guard. Des tried to move slowly, realizing he was running out of time to find an opportunity for Madison and him to get out of this mess. There were no other apparent ways out of this tunnel, and even if, by some miracle, they were able to escape the Judge and his accomplice, they would still have the extra obstacle of getting past his men who were waiting at the other end.

As Madison scoured the wall, she noticed something on one of the stones near the middle of the corner that looked like blood. Reaching out to touch it, she thought it appeared out of place. Smooth to the touch, it was definitely not part of the rock surface.

"Shine the light over here," she ordered.

The Judge pointed the flashlight in her direction. The red color of a raised blotch became more prominent.

"What is that?" she said quietly to herself.

Touching the anomaly, she noticed more red blotches directly above it. She got her fingernail underneath the aberration and broke off a piece. It had almost a silky feel, and as she rubbed it between her thumb and forefinger, it increased in viscosity.

"This is wax," she stated.

The Judge watched carefully, hoping she had discovered something of significance. "What is it for?"

"I don't know," she responded.

Following the trail of red splotches, she made her way three quarters up the wall when she hit a large half-dollar-size object. Although the Judge had not held up the light to show what she had found, she immediately knew what it was. There in front of her was the same wax symbol they found on the letter attained at Old Sheldon Church, an engraving of George Washington on horseback, the seal of the president of the Confederacy.

"Des, come here. Do you think this is it?"

Des moved next to her while the Judge and his companion kept an ever-watchful eye on their activity. Madison pointed to the seal.

Des's eyes widened as soon as he saw it. "That has to be it," he said.

Touching the surface of the wax embossing, he noticed the stone it was placed on was protruding a little farther out than the others.

"What is it?" Madison asked.

"I'm not sure."

"Did you find the mark?" an impatient and quickly angering Judge inquired.

Ignoring the Judge's question, Des moved his hand over the surface of the curious stone. He felt the wax seal and noticed the etching of the insignia under his fingertips. As he moved his hand south to north over the surface, he tried to gauge what the stone was pressed up against to cause it to bulge out from the rest of the wall. When his finger touched the protruding rock, he froze. Wondering if his eyes were playing tricks on him, he repeated the action. Once again, the stone moved.

"Move back," he said to Madison.

"Wait, what are you…," the Judge stammered.

Before their captor could get another word out of his mouth, Des pulled the stone with his full force. It slid from its spot. At once, stones from the back wall fell in unison, crashing to the floor in a pile. One hundred and fifty years of dust kicked into the air as the captors, for a moment, lost track of their captives.

The flashlights appeared like lasers mimicking science fiction films as they moved up and down, piercing the swirling muck, looking for their targets. The dust was chokingly thick, obliterating any line of sight.

Finally, a beam skewered the area where Des and Madison had been standing, and although it tracked Madison and Des crouching against the east wall, it could not cut through the dust to see clearly what they had uncovered.

The bearded man squinted, desperately trying to see what they had unveiled. Des saw his darkened figure standing at attention. As the dust settled, they were in stunned silence. It had to be there.

Chapter 95

Chris leaned against the tunnel wall, nervously waiting for any news. His two employees were sitting on the floor opposite him, looking as if they could not believe what they were doing there. He had been on several assignments with these men, but this one definitely qualified as the strangest.

Most of their jobs together had consisted of providing security for a VIP, investigating and intimidating business rivals, and the occasional exciting sabotage mission. However, nothing had prepared them for this.

While the money was outstanding, there was still a sense of disbelief that this was what they were doing to earn it. Chris was not educated in history. In fact, many of the government training classes he took to qualify him for various positions, he had failed. However, his mentor, using his influence, pulled enough strings to get him passing grades. His lack of foresight and interest in the educational aspect of his job often caused him to miss important details. Instead, he focused solely on monetary potential.

Yet Chris was experienced enough to notice this new development. The Judge inexplicably had separated himself from him and his men, something that was neither operationally smart or safe and certainly something the Judge recognized as such. The only reason he could fathom that his employer would do such a thing was to keep him away from that which he did not want him to be a part of.

For the past two days, he fantasized and strategized about ways to get part of the treasure for himself. He had been repeating the mantra to wait for an opportunity to present itself. But not seeing any prior to this time and now separated from the access, Chris allowed his mind to deviate from sound operational planning.

As he stared at his men sitting up against the wall, their inactivity only fueled his fear that he had been left out. He began hearing the antagonizing voices of those who had criticized his lack of skills, experience, and intelligence, gnawing at him. He had to prove them wrong. They had to see the true competent and strikingly skillful man he was.

As each moment passed, the voices got louder and louder to the point where he could feel himself mouthing words of defiance back at his detractors. He started to tap his finger against the barrel of his gun, a nervous habit picked up during his early work in security. The situation was becoming intolerable. Chris took three steps in the direction he last saw the Judge and then turned back, still unsure of himself.

Damn it! He has found it. I'm losing out again! He rubbed his forehead as the strain of not knowing consumed him. Motioning for his men to join him, he began moving farther down the hallway. He would be calculated in his actions but needed greater proximity to the Judge. *He might try to exclude me, but I will be damned if I am left out of this one!*

Chapter 96

Washington, DC

It took him mere seconds to break into the motel room. Not a complicated job and certainly the easiest he had tackled in a long time. It was so quick, in fact, even if people had witnessed it, they would have believed he had the key.

Inside, it was surprisingly clean and organized, especially for a young bachelor. One would expect to see dirty laundry strewn throughout along with various other forms of clutter. But it showed almost no signs of habitation.

Maybe he's gay. It was a logical deduction. A young male this clean oftentimes was accompanied with the assumption of homosexuality. All gave off a level of sterility more in tune with a military barracks. However, in a way, it was logical. His background, training, attention to detail, and overall mannerisms would probably lend to this type of behavior.

As he moved through the room, he swiveled his head 180 degrees and then headed to the bathroom. It was just as immaculate. Seeing nothing of interest, he proceeded with the last part of the search.

The space was dark, and even turning on the light did little to bring any brightness to the space. The books on the table were what he expected. Along with the texts, he eyed a notepad with a funny sketch that made little sense but did not appear threatening. It was an odd and rough image in pencil of a tube leading to a greater opening underneath an indiscernible surface. But it was also disconcerting, and even to a person unaware of the subject's interest, it would seem odd. Yet for the current occupant, it also made perfect sense.

He opened up the laptop sitting adjacent to the books. Taking out his scanner, he connected it and began efficiently filtering through its contents. Lines of code and entries streamed in front of him. All it contained were historical references, not a music or porn website to be found. *Definitely gay.*

As line after line passed, he noticed a strange pattern. None of it was what he expected. There were hardly any references to the value of the treasure. No mention of any of the "trigger" words provided. "James Semple," "Savannah," "Jefferson Davis," even "Confederate treasure" were noticeably absent.

In its place were a few spotty searches and one prevalent one, "The Battle of the Crater." He clicked on the link, which took him to a description of the military engagement.

It was a clash that turned into one of the Civil War's great stalemates. The two armies had fought to a draw and then embedded themselves in trenches, hoping against hope that their adversary would surrender. It did not happen, as neither side could dislodge the other. In an act of desperation, the Union commander decided to use a tactic that, while innovative, would ultimately lead to catastrophe for his forces. He dug.

As he read, the scrolling became labored, as if the information had a weight to it, one that he could not bear. Then there was the brilliant illustration. A tunnel over a half mile long underneath the battlefield, which was followed by the horrific aftermath. It jolted him to a realization.

Jumping up from the table, he stared at the artwork on the computer screen, then examined the rough sketch on the notebook paper next to it. It was nearly identical. The devastating destruction pierced his vision. It hit him with such a visceral shock that he nearly buckled at the knees.

The man who had established his reputation on calm, cold efficiency, for the first time in his career, felt panic. It was a feeling brought on by the knowledge of a massive mistake, *his* mistake.

Osiris grabbed his phone and feverishly typed in two words: "Get out!" A few seconds later, an automated response came in: "Message failed." His client was out of reach.

Chapter 97

The cloud of dust blocking the view of the back wall gradually settled to the ground, and what first appeared as a nebulous gray object now showed a definitive structure. The stones that came crashing to the ground moments ago had given away their secret. There, just inches away from a crouching Madison and Des, was a large iron door.

It had the look of something one might see on a navy ship, with large rivets running down its west side and a bulky iron handle protruding opposite its hinges. It appeared ominous and powerful, certainly something appropriately installed to guard a cache of enormous treasure.

The Judge's eyes had a manic look reminiscent of the crazed Humphrey Bogart in the movie *Treasure of Sierra Madre*. He crept cautiously to the portal, almost in disbelief in what he was viewing.

He placed his hand against its cold exterior, while Des and Madison watched in fear, wondering what his next move might be. They both understood this had to be the journey's end, and by the look in the Judge's eyes, he felt the same way.

"This is it," the Judge said, turning to his accomplice, who was still cloaked in darkness. His companion nodded in agreement.

The Judge ran his finger down to the door handle. Below it, he saw the locking mechanism. It was an old-style latch, definitely from the mid-1800s. Pulling the skeleton key he had taken from Madison out of his pocket, he carefully inserted it into the keyhole and turned. The sliding sound of a bolt releasing from its casing was confirmation this journey was about to be finalized.

"There are no more clues," he said, turning to his captives. "Behind this door is the end of my journey."

Des recognized the irrevocability in the Judge's voice. He had made the determination they were of no more use to him. Des backed up, grabbing Madison's hand, knowing a decision was going to have to be made. However, no action, no plan came to mind. He was at a loss of what to do.

"We don't know that," Des pleaded.

The Judge, standing next to the door, was soon joined by his bearded companion, who tucked in behind him. His expression did not change. There was going to be no changing of his mind. He had already come to his conclusion. He was not going to be convinced otherwise.

"I'm sorry, Des, and I'm sorry to you as well, Madison, but this is where our partnership ends."

Des looked around him, trying to find some escape route. He glanced at the Judge's companion, hoping he would intervene. Yet his only reaction was to calmly reach into his pocket.

The Judge raised his gun as Des pushed Madison behind him, trying to protect her the only way he could. She was shivering violently, as he could feel her vibrations against his body.

"Judge," his companion interjected.

"What is it?"

The bearded man reached out with an index card in his hand and gave it to him.

"What's this?"

"I took it from the professor. It confirms my beliefs. It's the treasure's true value."

The Judge stared at the card, and within seconds, his eyes bulged with the look of shock and betrayal. A gasp exited his lungs, as if his soul had been ripped from his body. "It can't be… no, this can't be right… there has to…"

A sickening thud filled the cavern. Des's body jolted with the anticipation of what he thought would follow. It was not a gunshot. Neither he nor Madison had been hurt.

The Judge spasmed, mimicking a man being electrocuted. Des jumped back, accidentally shoving Madison into the wall. She yelped in pain. The Judge lurched forward, collapsing onto his face. There was no attempt to break his fall.

As they watched in terror, a horrifying image was on display. There lay the middle-aged man. A large Civil War-era knife protruding from his back. Des was stunned. Madison heaved, nauseated by the scene.

"He never understood what it was for," the bearded man said. "I know, Des, you haven't figured it out either. It surprises me. You seemed to understand."

"Who are you?"

He removed his cap, revealing a shaved head. Rubbing his hand over its surface now rough with stubble, he looked relieved to no longer carry the hidden burden. Then he took off his glasses and tore away his beard along with a large prosthetic nose.

Des and Madison were shocked beyond their abilities to express it in words.

"But I saw—"

"Me get killed. Yeah, I know," he said, interrupting Madison with a devilish grin. "The Judge figured the more threatened you felt, the easier it would be to get information out of you. If you knew he was willing to kill, that's the greatest threat of all."

The young man was disturbing to look at, not from his appearance, but from his mannerism. He was calm, not at all displaying the intense emotions of a person who had just stabbed someone in the back. This was an individual who had made his plans, and they were functioning perfectly. The fact a human life had been extinguished did not have any effect on him at all. His look was one of serenity, a man truly at peace with himself, even as he was pointing a gun at his captives.

"Look, William, we don't want any part of the treasure. You can have it. You can have all the gold. Take it," Des said.

"You still don't get it, do you? For someone who seemed so in tune with the clues, you never figured out the most obvious one," William responded, almost with sadness.

"I don't understand what you mean. All the clues, they all led to the treasure. There's nothing else."

"Think about it, Des! What started this whole thing? Why did they move the capital? What was the South after? Do you really think the only thing the South wanted to do was to protect their wealth?" William's expression changed from one of peace to one of frustration. Des had a blank look, not comprehending the young man.

"You'll never get it. You're no different from the rest. You're still looking at this as if it were about money. I'm disappointed in you, Des. I expected more from you. Just remember, 'Find the treasure, thousands encased in black sands of the fallen.'"

Des watched as William momentarily looked down at the Judge. The young man's eyes narrowed, preparing himself for his next slaughter. Des's mind unexpectedly fixated on the clue William quoted back to him. *Black sands of the fallen, black sands of the fallen* appeared over and over, like flash bulbs at a media event. *Encased in the black sands of the fallen... black sands... black sands... coffins... black sands encased in coffins!*

"Oh my god!" Des exclaimed.

William smiled, recognizing Des's epiphany. "Congratulations, Des, you got it. I'm just sorry you won't be here to see it."

William cocked his pistol and raised it. Des braced for the impact while Madison tucked in closer behind him. It was a contraction. A movement resembling a seizure. The Judge's body jerked and flailed. A death throe. William, startled by the movement, fell back. Protective instinct took over. As he discharged his weapon, blood was sent flying as the projectile connected with his former partner's flesh. The reflex knocked him off-balance, sending him cascading backward.

Seeing his opportunity, Des charged. As he tackled the off-balanced William, another loud shot echoed in the chamber. A searing pain in his left shoulder caused Des to shriek as the bullet tore through him. Madison screamed in horror as the momentum of Des's weight struck with full force on his adversary's torso, throwing him into a direct impact with the stone wall.

William's gun flew out of his grasp at the massive blow. His body slammed against the wall while smashing his head against the shale covering. The gun bounced off the stone floor and then slid into the deep crevice at the base of the wall.

Madison ran toward Des, seeing he had been wounded. William, dazed from the assault, panicked. As he sprung up, realizing he no longer had his weapon, his focus immediately switched to obtaining the treasure. He grabbed the flashlight, flung open the iron door, and disappeared into the blackness.

Seeing the blood soaking through the back of Des's jacket, Madison knew the seriousness of the injury. The bullet had ripped through the area just below his left shoulder, causing him to bleed profusely. Des's eyes fixated on the ceiling as he turned a ghostly white. He was gasping, as if he had been punched in the stomach, straining to catch his breath.

"Oh my god! Des! Please no! Des, be okay, please be okay," she said, sobbing. Pulling off his jacket, she tried to stop the bleeding by applying pressure to the wound. The compression made him groan, while causing Madison to shudder. Blood seeped through her fingers as he continued to hemorrhage. She was nearly hysterical.

At first, it was difficult to tell the source. Then they could make out the faint sound of approaching footsteps.

"It's the Judge's men… Quick, put on… my jacket and lie face-down," Des demanded as he coughed, struggling to keep himself coherent. Still shaking, Madison was not understanding why Des was requesting this when all she could focus on was how badly he had been hurt.

"They have to think we're dead. Do it," he said fervently.

Madison regrouped, throwing on his blood-soaked jacket and lying facedown, being as still as possible. The echo of the footsteps grew louder as Chris and his men continued running toward the sound of the gunshots.

When they reached the area where the violent scene had just played out, there was confusion. But rapidly, the picture became clear as Chris saw the Judge with the protruding knife and gunshot wound. Then he examined the lifeless bodies of Des and Madison.

A heat raced through him, anger exuding from every pore. "That son of a bitch! He was setting us up the whole time."

Chris hovered over Madison's body as she did everything in her power to show no animation. He remained above her for what seemed like an eternity. She could hear the air exiting his lungs and out through his nostrils. His knuckles cracked as he clenched his fist.

Chris was tense beyond anything he had ever experienced. Squeezing his gun handle with power he never knew he possessed, he struggled to think about his next course of action. Then the intensity relented when he came to a moment of clarity. The opportunity he had been waiting for had presented itself. *This is it! This is my chance. This is my time. I can have a piece of the treasure. I can have it all!*

"Come on, let's go after him," Chris ordered his men.

As the sound of footsteps dissipated down the portal, Madison felt safe enough to attend to Des. She slid over, hoping he had enough strength to get out of the tunnel. Running her fingers down the side of his face, she couldn't fathom Des not making it.

"Sweetheart, we have to get you out of here. We have to get you help. Can you get up? We got to get you to a hospital," she implored.

"No, we have to stop it. The treasure… it's not what you think."

Chapter 98

Madison did not comprehend what Des meant, wondering whether the shock of the wound and the loss of blood had affected his perception of reality.

"It's not what you think. We have to stop it… it will be a disaster," he gasped.

"Sweetie, what are you talking about? You're hurt. We don't need the treasure. Let William have it," she begged.

"This has nothing to do with that… you don't understand. There is no treasure," he responded, sounding like he was about to cough up a lung.

"Of course, there is. What were William and the Judge going after? You're not making sense. Please, let me take you to the hospital."

"I screwed up. I thought the clues meant the treasure would be buried under Arlington. I missed… I missed the most important clue. There's no gold buried there."

"What do you mean? Sweetie, you're not thinking clearly. The clues said the treasure was buried in coffins," she stammered.

"The coffins are filled with something, but not treasure. The coffins aren't buried in black sands, they're filled with them! Black sands! The coffins are filled with gunpowder! Thousands of them filled with gunpowder! 'Thousands encased in black sands of the fallen.'"

"So it's—"

"Yes, a bomb! One gigantic bomb! It's Memorial Day. The president will be at Arlington. William is going to kill the president and God knows how many others!"

"Oh my god!"

"Help me up. We got to stop it before he sets it off."

Madison struggled to lift Des to his feet. He groaned as the pain of the wound being pulled almost caused him to lose consciousness.

"Grab the car keys out of the Judge's pocket."

Madison, still disgusted at the sight of the Judge's mangled body, tried her best to ignore the gruesome scene. Rifling through his coat pockets, she found the keys.

Des leaned against the wall, trying to gather up what little strength he had to make the journey back down the tunnel.

"Here, put your arm around my shoulder," she said.

Everything hurt. Every movement, each slight flexing of a muscle, sent scorching sensations throughout his body. The blood had soaked through his shirt, dripping down his side onto his pants.

"It all makes sense now," Des said.

"What makes sense?"

"Arlington was the Union headquarters, and Lincoln would visit it often. They would not only kill the president but also destroy the operation center of the entire Union. They could also exact revenge for the Dahlgren affair and devastate Union command."

Madison listened intently, hoping in explaining, he was distracting himself from the pain. Yet she could not come to grips with everything he said. It was beyond her ability to believe it.

Madison turned to her injured friend. Blood was everywhere, and she knew he could not keep moving much longer. Taking a few more steps, Des fell to the ground and screeched in pain.

"Des, oh my god! Let me go and get help."

"No, we've got to stop it. Don't you understand? God knows how many people will die if we don't."

"Des, this doesn't make sense. I don't understand. Why would William want to kill the president?"

"He's completing the mission his great-great-grandfather didn't. It was his job to see this thing to the end, and he was killed before it was done. He could never deliver the message. William sees it as his responsibility now."

Madison picked him up again as the duo continued to make their way down the tunnel. Des's breathing became even more labored, and his pace had slowed. The energy was slowly draining from his body. Madison struggled to keep him on his feet. His body weight was quickly becoming too much for her to carry.

As they made their way to the entrance, his feet began to slide rather than pace. Des no longer had the ability to maintain his normal gait. Madison became more concerned he was not going to make it, but she could not accept losing him now.

Even though she was beginning to believe Des could be right about William, her desire to save him was overriding her will to stop the young man's bombing attempt. Instead, she kept trying to think of ways to convince Des to go straight to the hospital. He was having none of it.

"Won't the Secret Service protect the president? They'll keep him safe."

"There's no way to protect him from this. The threat… the threat is hidden," he said, laboring to get the words out. "Even the radar they use to detect things underground would only see coffins, which is what they would expect to see at a cemetery. They have no idea… what's coming." He stopped again, falling against the wall. He was having trouble seeing, and Madison's voice was becoming more difficult to hear. There was not much more time before he would pass out from the loss of blood. The only thing he could focus on was the glimmer of light coming from the tunnel's entrance.

Holding out his arm as a request for Madison to help him keep moving, she begrudgingly put it around her shoulder, weeping as they moved toward the entrance. Reaching the stairs, Des used all his might to climb the flight and reach the light coming from Belvedere Park. As they ascended to its apex, Des fell to his knees.

"We've got to get to the car," he said.

The park was now filled with people, most just north of the rise they had used to access the tunnel. Madison became concerned that if she carried a blood-soaked Des across the field, it would incite panic, but she had little choice. She concluded the jacket she was wearing was not as stained as Des's shirt and its dark color would hide the blood better.

"Put this on," she said, helping him.

"Close the door. We don't want the Judge's men following us or anyone else going down there."

Madison struggled to move the iron door. It was so heavy that she could barely lift it but managed to heave it shut. The slamming portal caused a loud bang, echoing throughout the park. Pulling its latch shut, she went back to Des to get him down the hill and to the Judge's SUV.

"Stay with me, Des."

Madison used her waning strength to pull her devastated friend to his feet. Letting gravity guide her down to the vehicle, she moved as quickly as possible, acting as if they were a couple on a date,

To her surprise, few people even noticed, as they were engulfed in the pleasures of the holiday weekend. The only person paying any heed was a little boy kicking a ball by a tree.

"Is he okay?" he questioned.

"Oh, yes, he's fine, honey." Madison gave Des a kiss on the lips, hoping the public display of affection would give the little boy fear of catching cooties.

He just smiled with a quirky expression. "Ewe!"

"You'll like it someday, honey, I promise."

Finally reaching the curb where the car was parked, Madison exhaled. Pressing the automatic lock, she could see Des's eyes starting to roll back in his head. "Stay with me, sweetheart. Please stay with me."

Opening the door for him, Des nearly fell into the car. He hardly had enough strength to even sit upright. Madison ran around the vehicle, got into the driver's seat, and started the car.

"Des, you have to go to the hospital. You've lost a lot of blood. You need help."

"No, take me to… take me to Arlington."

"Damn it, Des! What do you expect to do there?"

"I'll let you know… just…"

"Des, Des!" Madison screamed, noticing him slipping away.

"Just get me there!"

Smashing down on the gas, Madison peeled from the curb. It was just a short ways to Arlington. She had no idea what Des had in mind but knew if she was going to be able to get him help, she needed to first do what he asked.

As they sped through the streets of Rosslyn, swerving through traffic, and running red lights, the revelation of what William was planning was still not sinking in. Des was barely conscious; how he expected to stop a bombing in his condition didn't even seem remotely possible. But she was going to have to trust his judgment.

As they drew closer to Fort Myer on the outskirts of the cemetery, Madison was going to have to go more cautiously, as the increased presence of security was all around due to the president's visit.

"What time is it?" Des asked weakly.

"It's almost nine o'clock. Why?"

"The ceremony for the president starts at nine. I saw it on the website yesterday."

"Des, I don't understand what you want me to do."

Looking out the window, he could see the growing police presence everywhere. He was running out of time. He had to do something now.

"Park the car as close to the entrance as you can."

"What? Why?"

"Just do it," he said, wincing in pain.

Madison saw a shopping mall just on the other side of Fort Meyer. Pulling into the lot, she took the nearest parking spot she could find. She could only imagine what Des wanted her to do next.

Chapter 99

William had gone a little over a hundred yards, pointing his flashlight in all directions, looking for the access to the explosive treasure. Sweating profusely, he was exuberant about the final phase of this journey, which had taken over a hundred and fifty years to complete.

It was about completing the mission. It had always been about completing the mission. How it had eluded not just others' grasp but their understanding of its nature was beyond him. *It was so obvious.* It shouldn't have been a surprise, and it certainly did not come as such to William.

Maybe better than anyone, he knew what would protect his knowledge of the treasure's intended use would not be his ability to misdirect or cover its secret but basic human greed. People see what they want to see. Why people have one definition of wealth was something he simply could not comprehend. They had always viewed it as a chase of precious metals, a modern-day treasure hunt. Any enthusiasm in the pursuit always manifested itself in a childlike joy of living out one's Indiana Jones fantasy. They never saw its true value or how it was meant to be utilized.

Today, more than ever, the ideals driving this project needed to be put into motion. The Civil War was not just about the elimination of slavery, although if one took a history class, they would hardly be able to distinguish that truth. Every historian, every movie, and nearly every book dealing with the cause of the war always cited that institution as the major factor of the rift between North and South. While William acknowledged it played a central role, he never understood why no one focused on the South's relevant arguments to preserve it. Those arguments far surpassed the boundaries of the slavery conversation.

The voices speaking out against the North's incursion into the Southern economy often talked about the federal government's relentless pursuit of power. Taking the decision-making process out of the hands of the state, out of the hands of the people, and placing it in a centralized body hundreds and sometimes thousands of miles away went against everything the forefathers imagined. The erosion of individual liberty and the right to determine one's destiny had been a part of the American lexicon since its inception. It was the reason the colonies separated from their European brethren. They were controlled, forced to submit to the will of another. Slavery was really just the central cover hiding the underlying attack.

The battle was still going on. The federal government had only increased its efforts. The Civil War might have ended a morally corrupt practice, but it also emboldened those who wished to take true liberty away. They no longer were using the military as their instrument of force, but a pen that, with every stroke, brushed away freedom.

William understood their game. He recognized their efforts to use the media not as a tool to dispense information but rather as a method to distract the populace from the very chipping away of their own lives. He knew his actions would be seen as villainous, the act of a crazed terrorist. That was okay. *Eventually, they will appreciate my sacrifice.* They would come to an understanding that not all relics of the past should sit in a museum for those to stare at through glass in judgment of the object's morality. Some items of history could only be comprehended and appreciated once their final intent was realized.

Lines of information ran through his head. The books he had pored over, the archives he had accessed, and the countless hours he spent reading and rereading his ancestor's diary had now finally given him his reward. All his efforts had culminated to this. He was only moments away from completing his great-great-grandfather's mission, minutes away from changing history, changing the direction of the destructive path the nation was traversing.

The tunnel had returned to a dirt floor, like the original access point. He did not know exactly what to expect yet, at the same time, had a strong notion of what he was looking for. He needed to find the ignition point, a place where he could initiate the mechanism.

As his flashlight lit the walls, he found the end of the tunnel. It was nondescript, a flat dirt wall supported by wood beam buttresses. There was nothing displaying a point of ignition, though he was not dismayed. He knew it would be obvious once it came into view.

Pointing the beam to the side walls, he noticed it spider-webbed into a series of smaller tunnels moving upward, angling toward the surface. It made perfect sense. The tunnels were created as a way of aligning the coffins in channels to create a series of explosions. They were placed just a few feet down from the Arlington grounds, close enough to the surface, to cause the greatest amount of damage.

These new tunnels did not branch out far from the main corridor. William, turning to his left, ran the light over the walls, looking for anything standing out from the ordinary. It was evident to him that these passageways were not utilized to the same degree as the main hall. The floors were of a much cruder nature. They were obviously dug only to be used for the placement of or access to the coffins. Scanning up and down in a south-to-north motion, he stopped for a second as dried footprints appeared. They looked to have been there for years, causing William to feel a connection to his fellow warriors of the past.

Going underneath a small arch, he entered the next lesser hall. It was even more cramped than the other. It had no ignition point, but it did provide additional light, as William came across another kerosene lantern left by the original builders.

He glanced at his watch. It was almost nine in the morning. The timing could not have been more perfect. Soon, the president would be marching out from the mansion to greet dignitaries and veterans on his way to laying the traditional wreath at the Tomb of the Unknowns. William could only imagine the grandeur of the scene being played out just a few feet above his head. It only fueled his excitement and confirmed his motivation.

The glow of the lantern expanded his vision, quickening his search. He darted from space to space, examining the surroundings for a sign. Yet no success. The thought of not finding it began to enter his mind.

He was broken from his concentration. Jerking at the sounds coming from the corridor, William spun on his axis. It sounded like more than one voice. It was Chris and his men.

He hated Chris. His lack of vision and the reticence toward learning history made him a despicable character. The Judge, while at times irritating, at least had an appreciation for what was happening during the Civil War era. Yes, he was driven by greed and what he thought the treasure was, but he had studied the past and recognized its relevance. His only error was that he had given in to his human nature. He romanticized what the goal was, not seeing its reality.

Chris saw nothing but his own reputation. He served no one but himself, a hired gun without loyalty or a cause. He did not connect with anyone beyond somebody who could fuel his need to supplement his own self-importance. When it came to the world around him, he was negligent at best, and lazy at worst. He could not see that greatness was earned through sacrifice, not self-promotion. To William, he was the most detestable of human beings, cognizant enough of the problems surrounding him but too indolent to make any effort to change them.

Driven by the oncoming interruption, William hustled his search as the voices resonated louder down the hallway. He had to find it before they could stop him. Racing from one tunnel to the next, he had yet to locate it. No sign appeared.

Then another sound could be heard in soft tones. It was not the echo of human voices but of music. William could catch it faintly trickling down into the cramped, dark hallways. Looking at his watch once more, he noticed it was 9:05. The ceremony had begun. *It has to be leaking in from the surface. Follow the music to the access.* William sprinted toward the cascading notes.

"I see a light!" Chris screamed.

William turned, but the only thing staring back at him was blackness.

"He's got to be down there," one of his men responded.

William, for the first time, began to panic. *I can't let it end now. It can't finish this way. I have to find it!*

He listened, trying to trace the direction of the music. It sounded as if it was just behind him, though he couldn't see any more channels. Putting down the lantern, he desperately focused the flashlight beam in the direction he heard the melody. Then he saw it. There in the corner of the back wall was a tunnel less than four feet high. In his frantic search, he must have overlooked it.

Dropping to the floor, William got onto his hands and knees and dived into the dark crevice. With only the glow of his flashlight to guide him, he crawled down the shaft, knowing this was his best chance. Feelings of claustrophobia crept into his consciousness. He despised enclosed spaces, but under no circumstance was he going to allow it to keep him from completing his mission. *It doesn't matter. I won't have to feel this way much longer.*

The music got louder and louder. William's heart jumped into his throat, knowing how close he was to the end of the journey. Shining his light down the shaft, he gasped at what he saw. There, just a few feet from him, was a long ropelike strand hanging from the ceiling. Lunging for it, he grasped the twine, displaying the awe of a man who had just discovered the secrets of the universe.

The voices of Chris and his men desperately searching for their target filtered into the tunnel, but they were passing by it, moving in a back-and-forth motion without slowing. They would never find him.

William calmly crawled underneath the rope and crossed his legs. So intently was he concentrating on this undertaking he no longer could hear the voices or the music. Everything had fallen silent. Taking out a small pocketknife, he jabbed it into the earth directly above his head. A chunk of dirt fell. There, appearing to the right side of his face, was an outcropping of wood. It looked like it belonged to a larger structure. A grin from ear to ear spread across his face, and serenity filled his body. It was exactly as he expected. As he pried the knife into a split in the timber, a powdery black substance trickled down in a thin line. William stuck his hand into the black stream. He sat there as a man getting ready to drink from the well of life. It did not possess the luminosity of gold, but to him, it could not have been more beautiful.

He was savoring the moment, the last minute he would ever experience. It was time. No reason to delay. It had waited for over a hundred and fifty years for someone to allow it to do its work. He would make it pause no longer. It had been a patient soldier. Now it needed to be relieved.

The voices in the hallway increased in volume, yet now they soothed William, knowing his sacrifice wouldn't be one taken alone. Closing his eyes, he breathed in deeply. Thoughts of his lineage and their struggles flowed through him. *I'm going to join all of you soon. I hope you find me worthy of your sacrifice. All my love and respect to each of you.*

William felt himself relax. A tranquility washed over him like he had never experienced. As he crossed his arms over his chest, the grin stretching from ear to ear had settled into an expression of peaceful joy. He had found his purpose. Now all there was left to do was perform his duty.

Chapter 100

Madison sat, awaiting instructions from a nearly incoherent Des. His seat was covered in blood, and she was beginning to believe her friend would not survive.

They had parked in a strip mall on the outskirts of Fort Myer, on the opposite side of the cemetery's main entrance. Des had wanted to venture closer to the visitors' gate, but the police presence due to the president's visit became so thick it made it impossible.

"Des, how much longer do you think you can go like this? You can't be this way. Please, just let me take you to the hospital," she said in a quivering voice.

"Just take me outside."

"This is crazy! The coffins are underground. How will a bomb going off six feet below the earth hurt anyone?"

"Madison, there are hundreds, maybe thousands of coffins filled with gunpowder down there. They can each hold... hold about a hundred and fifty pounds of it. Add that up, it will be... it will be a massive... explosion," Des responded, nearly catatonic.

Knowing she could not convince him to get care before he was able to implement his plan, and stunned by this new information, Madison relented. "What do you want me to do?"

"You see that crowd... gathering near the entrance to Fort Myer?"

Madison nodded. "Yes. What about them?"

"I want you to take me over there and scream... scream as loud as you can, yelling my friend has been... shot... over and over again, until the police come to you."

"What's that going to do?" she asked.

"The Secret Service will implement its protocol as soon as a gunman... is reported in the area. They..."

Des was beginning to slip out of consciousness. He was not in pain but started to give way to the condition of shock. He could hardly keep his eyes open, and when his pupils were visible, they were partially rolled back in his head. Madison had to do something. They were out of time.

She grabbed Des and shook him slightly, the pain from the light jolt stunning him awake. Madison ran to the passenger side of the vehicle, hurled the door open, and pulled Des out of the car. He was barely responding to her efforts to stand him up, and his body weight was almost completely dependent on her ability to support it.

"Come on, Des, you got to work with me. Come on now, sweetie."

Seeing the crowds filing into Fort Myer, she tried to pull Des in their direction, but it was no use. His feet were practically dragging, and no matter how much she tried, she was not able to revive him. He was simply too heavy for her to continue. The performance would have to take place there.

Laying him down as gently as she could, Madison turned and gave the most bloodcurdling scream she knew how. "Oh my god, he's been shot, he's been shot! Somebody please help, he's been shot!"

Instantly, people took notice. Many started running toward where she was standing.

"Please get someone, he's hurt badly!"

A police officer who had been directing traffic about fifty yards away was sprinting in her direction. By this time, a crowd had gathered.

"What happened, miss?"

Madison had deduced what Des wanted her to do, and she did her best to embellish. The stress of the situation aided her in that she did not have to act. She simply had to be as she felt, horrified and worried.

"A man shot my boyfriend! Please get him help. Help me, please."

"Who was it?" the police officer asked.

"I don't know. He just screamed at us for no reason and ran toward the cemetery," a hysterical Madison replied.

"He ran toward the cemetery," he responded with a look of disbelief.

"Yes, I saw him running that way," she said, pointing. "He yelled something about the president. Please, he's hurt badly. You got to help him."

The officer, stunned at the news, did the very thing Des had expected. He radioed in that a gunman was on the loose, heading in the direction of Arlington National Cemetery.

"We copy that. We're notifying the Secret Service now. They need to secure the president," a voice on the officer's radio confirmed.

The plan was simple, but brilliant. His idea had initiated the process of protecting the president. He knew what he was doing.

"Miss, we're getting an ambulance. Just stay with him and sit tight."

The police radio crackled to life again. "The president is secure. He has been put back in the—"

A thunderous bang followed by an ungodly roar swept over them. The sound was unlike anything she had ever experienced. Her eardrums burst. The pressure hit the chest and the head. The shock wave was tremendous. Debris was sent hurtling in all directions, knocking people to the ground. Car windows shattered. The police officer was slammed forward, crashing into Madison as they were thrown in a heap onto the street. Screams echoed. A plume of white smoke like a thousand cannons had been fired at once rose above Arlington. Sirens and car alarms went off throughout the city as police cars already present were sent speeding in the direction of the national landmark.

Pulling himself off Madison, the police officer raced to his vehicle near the Fort Myer entrance. Then another series of explosions, louder than the first, dispensed their deadly rage. Once again, the percussion tossed Madison backward like a plastic bag being blown in the wind. Landing next to Des, she threw herself over his body to shield him from the rubble falling to the earth. Branches off trees and pieces of stone rained from the sky, striking the ground just inches from her. It was literally a tornado of wreckage.

Madison stood up slowly, in shock at the force and viciousness of the attack. It was pandemonium. People were running in all directions, and the sound of children crying was audible everywhere. Papers and lighter material that had been expelled into the atmosphere continued to hover above the landmark, an eerie and macabre scene reminiscent of so many tragedies.

It was hard for Madison to not dissociate from the reality. *Sweet Jesus, Des was right.* Madison stared into the distance, still in a haze. Her eyes were glazed as blood trickled from her nose and ears. Even though she had been a witness, it was nearly impossible for her to comprehend that nineteenth-century technology could display such power.

As the smoke started to drift north and she partially regained her senses, Madison couldn't begin to imagine the devastation left in its wake. "God help them," she whispered.

Snapping herself back to the here and now, she returned to tend to Des. The force of the detonations had shaken his body, tearing his wound even more, causing him to bleed heavily again. Madison had no more tears left. All she could do was try to save him, but with the extent of his injury and the amount of blood he had lost, it could be an effort made too late. *Come on, come on, where's that damn ambulance?*

Appearing down the street, a white transport made its way through the crowds, blurting its horn to implore them to move. Madison jumped up and down, waving her hands in the air, trying to gain the driver's attention. Its headlights flashed in response, letting her know he was on the way.

Leaning back down over Des, brushing his hair off his pale face, she kissed his forehead, begging him to stay with her. "Come on, Des. You're going to make it, I promise. Come on now. They're here. Everything is going to be all right."

The ambulance pulled in next to them. Two blue-uniformed EMTs jumped out of the vehicle. They immediately removed Madison from Des's side and started treating him. Although one asked her some questions, she was in a dreamlike state, simply answering out of instinct more than of thoughtful reply. Before she could comprehend what was going on, she found herself in the back of the ambulance, staring down at Des on a gurney.

As she looked out the back window of the vehicle, witnessing the ugliness of the events on the other side of the glass, terror filled her. She would have never envisioned this being the end of their journey, which had started only four days earlier. It had been a horrific experience. She had so many hopes when it began. Madison had only one hope left, that she would not be the only survivor.

Chapter 101

Washington, DC

The strong scent of Pine Sol filled the air, and a bright light streamed into the vision, creating the need to squint to avoid the glare. Closing the eyes brought darkness and peace, but the effort to fight the grogginess outweighed the desire to rest. As the head was turned, the view of an odd machine with unrecognizable dials and various lights confused and bewildered the senses, distorting the location.

A television broadcast blared in the background, describing the tragedy and miracles that happened at Arlington. The explosion had ripped up over six acres of land, sending debris hundreds, and in some cases, thousands, of yards away. There was loss of life, and many were injured. Yet no one seemed to comprehend how someone managed to cause so much death and destruction. The only thing determined was that the explosion was created by an antiquated type of gunpowder not used since the late 1800s.

Soon, the figure of a woman blocking the light appeared before him. It was followed by the warm and soothing sounds of a familiar voice.

"Hey, you. How are you feeling?"

"Hi, are you okay?" a muzzy Des responded.

Madison was struck by Des's first question. After all they had been through, even after getting shot and nearly passing away, his first concern was for her.

"I'm fine, sweetheart. You've been out for two days. You had me so worried. They thought you might have lost too much blood."

"Two days. How could I be out for… where am I?"

"You're at George Washington Hospital."

"How apropos," he said, raising his eyebrows.

"You were right, you know."

"Right about what?"

"About William. That was his intention. That was always his desire."

Des looked at the TV. The pictures were terrifying. Large gaping holes in the earth where once beautiful green expanse had lain flickered on the screen. The thick grass carpet bedding for those distinguished headstones was completely torn apart. In its place were demolished tracts of land with pieces of splintered caskets and tombstones strewn across a huge swath.

Madison noticed the aggrieved look on Des's face. She could see the desecration of this beautiful and hallowed landmark pained him deeply.

"How many?"

Madison took a deep breath before revealing the news. She knew how he would react. "Thirty-seven dead, about twice that wounded."

Des winced. "I should have figured it out earlier. How could I have been so stupid?"

"You did everything you could," she interjected. "I'm just glad you're all right. I thought I had lost…" As she trembled, tears streamed down her face. A mixture of joy, relief, and sadness swirled inside her. Though maybe the feeling most prevalent was guilt. She had grown so close to him. The only thing she cared about was that he was safe. She knew it was selfish but could not help how she felt.

"Hey, hey, it's okay. I'm okay," he said.

Des reached up, placing his hand on her cheek. She leaned into the gesture, allowing him to cradle her face. Gently she took his hand and kissed his palm, the wetness of her tears soaking his fingers.

Nothing else mattered. She was here. They would forever be bonded by the experience. The warmth of her skin comforted him. The pure joy of having more time together brightened his spirits.

He was at peace. He closed his eyes and let himself indulge in the happiness. It took only a few moments before his body completely released its tension. Waves of tranquility washed over him, allowing the return to sleep.

Epilogue

A plain-looking cashier's check from a bank in Switzerland left no clues to who was its source. Even to the individual who ordered it to be cut, it appeared just as great a mystery, as in all the years he had provided his services, not once had he needed to back up his guarantee. Yet even for one who was trained in espionage and assassination, there was still a level of professional pride.

Unfortunately, the client was no longer around to receive his refund. It irked him. Not from the fact his client had perished, but from his failure to successfully complete his task. The large amount of money received for those services would now only serve as a reminder of his miscalculation.

As he sealed the envelope and repeatedly ran his fingers through his beard, there was a sense of frustration. His record had a blemish, and he hated it. Although he did take some satisfaction in honoring his guarantee, not stooping to the level of prying money from a dead man's hand.

Three days later, a homeless shelter in Washington, DC, run by the Little Sisters of the Poor, received the largest single donation in their history. And though they tried, no one ever learned the identity of the donor.